SAMURAI SUSHI

A FIELD GUIDE TO IDENTIFYING AND APPRECIATING
THE WORLD'S MOST UNIQUE WRAPS, ROLLS, AND SASHIMI

Bobby Suetsugu

becker&mayer! BOOKS

ISBN: 1-932855-03-3

Printed in China

Design: Kasey Clark
Editorial: Conor Risch
Image Research: Shayna Ian
Production Coordination: Leah Finger
Project Management: Sheila Kamuda

10 9 8 7 6 5 4 3 2 1

Photographs by Keith Megay

Illustrations courtesy NOAA Fisheries

becker&mayer! Books
11010 Northup Way
Bellevue, Washington 98004

www.beckermayer.com

I dedicate this book to my mother, Betty Etsuko Suetsugu

Contents

Introduction

The Making of a "Sushiman"

In December 1959, I was born in Seattle to parents who had both immigrated to America from Japan. I grew up much like any other American boy, but parts of my life were uniquely Japanese. One aspect of my heritage in particular would change my life.

I began practicing the Japanese sport of judo at the age of five and continued it for the next ten years. When I was fifteen, after my first year of high school, my judo instructor, Mr. Yukia Ninomiya, presented me with the opportunity to go to Japan for the summer to learn about sumo wrestling. I took this chance and spent the next ten years of my life there training and competing as a sumo wrestler.

The experience of being a sumo wrestler in Japan was incredible. It is said in Japan that sumo wrestlers are godly figures who bring good luck, health, and fortune to those who are near them. I was treated like a king.

At twenty-five I began speaking with my stable master about the next life, about what I was going to do after sumo—like any professional sport, a career in sumo can only last so long. He suggested sushi, and helped me find a position as an apprentice in the *sushi-ya* (sushi shop) of one of our sponsors.

I trained for one year under master chef Yoshio Takasaki, and he taught me almost everything I know about sushi. I was then given the opportunity to go to Hokkaido and begin working as a sushi chef for two brothers who owned a restaurant there.

I spent two years working in Hokkaido, practicing what I had learned and continuing my education. Every day the brothers had me cutting fish. The most important ability for a sushi chef is using a knife, and after two years cutting fish nearly every day, my knife skills were excellent. The knife became part of my hand.

While I was in Hokkaido I decided that I wanted to return to the United States. I took an opportunity to go back to Tokyo to spend another year there working and completing my training.

On returning to America in 1989, I worked in two New York City sushi restaurants, and later returned to Seattle, where I opened my own place: Sushiman.

One of the most rewarding things about owning a *sushi-ya* is introducing something special to my customers.

As the pace of the world increases, we're losing the love that comes from food—the act of eating and sharing with family and friends. It has become increasingly hard for us to sit down and share a meal with the people close to us.

Because sushi is a new experience for many people, I get to share my knowledge with my customers, and in doing so I am able to help them explore their tastes and introduce things to them. And if their experience in my restaurant is a good one, they want to learn more about sushi, about the food that is part of my Japanese heritage, and they may also include their family and friends in the experience.

I view this book as an extension of the hospitality and love I try always to share with my customers. My goal is to provide people who are curious about sushi with a base of knowledge that will help them explore and appreciate this cuisine to the fullest. As you read this guide to the many varieties and incarnations of sushi, I hope you find a great deal of useful information that will make you excited to visit your local *sushi-ya* and explore the many flavors of sushi.

The Origins of Sushi

In its beginning stages, sushi was nothing like the sushi we know now. The history of sushi dates back more than two thousand years, originally developed from a method of preserving fish that was introduced to the Japanese by the Chinese. In this preservation method, the *sakana* (fish) was salted and then placed on top of a layer of cooked rice in a container. Another layer of rice was spread on top of the fish, another layer of fish added on top of that, and so on until the container was full. Then a lid would be placed on top of the container, and a large stone would be set atop the lid to hold it down. The combination of salt and fermenting rice, which produced lactic acid, drew the moisture out of the fish and prevented it from spoiling.

With time, this preparation method—the forebear of sushi—spread through all of Japan. Different areas had their own styles of fermenting fish, of using salt and rice in different time increments to produce various tastes and textures. Some places fermented their fish for more than a year before they enjoyed it at the dinner table.

Japan is split between two regions, Kanto (east) and Kansai (west). The Kansai region was for many centuries the political and cultural center of Japan. The Kansai style of sushi (from the cities of Kyoto and Osaka) began the trend of serving rice with pickled fish as a topping. *Saba-zushi* or *bo-zushi* is said to have originated in Kyoto more than one thousand years ago. In this preparation rice is compacted with pickled mackerel on top and wrapped in bamboo leaves. Also from the Kansai style came *bara-zushi,* in which rice, fish, and many other ingredients are mixed together in a bowl; *oshi-zushi* (pressed sushi), also called *hako-zushi* (boxed sushi), in which a rectangular mold is used to compact rice and fish together; and *maki-mono,* which are the rolls that are one of the most popular and identifiable forms of sushi today.

When the capital of Japan shifted from Kyoto to Tokyo during the Edo period (1603-1876), the Kansai style of sushi gave way to Kanto-style sushi, or Edomae sushi, as it is often referred to now. Edo means Tokyo, and *Edomae* means "in front of Tokyo," referring to the waters of Tokyo Bay. In those days Tokyo Bay was rich in seafood, and fishermen gathered beautiful fish out of the sea and sold them to sushi chefs who then prepared the fish for Tokyo's citizens.

The *Edomae* style was the first to use a variety of fresh fish served on top of rice, which eventually developed into the hand-formed sushi, or *nigiri* sushi, that is commonly seen in today's *sushi-ya.*

Konnichi Wa: Welcome to the Sushi Experience

The Basic Ingredients and Preparations

The following brief introduction to the ingredients and preparations essential to sushi will acclimate you to the world of sushi and provide a foundation for learning more about sushi in the pages to come.

INGREDIENTS

SHARI (SUSHI RICE)

Japanese sushi rice is the main building block of sushi. *Kome* (uncooked white rice) is cooked and then mixed with the sushi chef's own recipe of vinegar, sugar, and salt.

SU (RICE VINEGAR)

Rice vinegar, sugar, and salt are added to *gohan* (cooked rice) to flavor it and to preserve it.

NORI (DRIED SEAWEED)

Half sheets or whole sheets of dried seaweed are used in creating *maki-mono* (rolled sushi), and will sometimes be used for *nigiri-zushi* (hand-formed sushi)—as a small belt to hold the topping onto the rice—or as a garnish in preparation of other sushi dishes.

Wasabi (Japanese Horseradish)

Japanese horseradish grows naturally in the flowing, fresh water of Japan's rivers. It has a nice, sweet and spicy flavor when it's freshly grated, but fresh wasabi is very difficult to find outside of Japan. Most wasabi comes to restaurants as powder, and water is mixed into it to create the paste that is used for sushi.

Shōyu (Soy Sauce)

Soy sauce is an essential part of the sushi experience. It is brewed from a mixture of fermented soybeans, salt, and wheat. Some *sushi-ya* in Japan create their own soy sauce, sometimes cooking it with sake (rice wine) to produce tamari (sushi soy). But there is a wide variety of premade soy sauce available, so most restaurants purchase theirs instead of brewing it themselves.

Gari (pickled ginger)

The Japanese are fond of pickled vegetables, and pickled ginger is one of the most popular due to its role in sushi. While *gari* is said to aid digestion, its main purpose in sushi is to cleanse the palate and prepare the mouth to enjoy a new flavor.

Refer to pages 16-17 for a photo of these ingredients.

KOME (SHORT-GRAINED RICE)
SHARI (SUSHI RICE)
GARI (PICKLED GINGER)
WASABI (JAPANESE HORSERADISH)

SU (RICE VINEGAR)
SHŌYU SASHI
(SOY SAUCE CONTAINER)
SHŌYU (SOY SAUCE)
NORI (DRIED SEAWEED)

The Essential Preparations

Although there are many ways to prepare sushi, these are the three most commonly seen presentations.

Maki-Mono (Rolled Sushi)

Rolled sushi uses *shari,* nori, and wasabi as a framework for presenting the ingredients that give each roll its identity. *Hoso-maki* (thin roll) is the most basic form of *maki-mono*, with one or two ingredients in the middle surrounded by rice and wrapped in a half-sheet of seaweed with a hint of wasabi. *Futo-maki* (large roll) uses many ingredients, and *ura-maki* (inside-out roll) is presented with the rice on the outside. *Maki-mono* is made with a great variety of traditional and local ingredients, and sushi chefs all over the world enjoy being creative and developing their own signature rolls and styles.

Nigiri-Zushi (Hand-Formed Sushi)

Although *nigiri-zushi* looks very simple—a topping on a ball of rice—the technique requires a great deal of practice to perfect. To create it, sushi chefs use both hands, and in one fluid motion they form the rice, then add a bit of wasabi to the underside of the fish and place it on top of the rice.

Sashimi (Sliced Raw Fish or Other Seafood)

This ancient style of serving carefully sliced raw fish is popular in Japan as a light appetizer, although you will find that many restaurants offer sashimi as a full meal. Sashimi allows one to enjoy and appreciate the flavor of the fish on its own, and can be an excellent sushi option for people on low-carbohydrate diets.

The Main Ingredient: Fresh Seafood

Sushi, in all its forms, has always been about enjoying fish and other food from the sea. In the following sections, you will learn about the many different types of seafood that are used to create delicious and healthy sushi.

Samurai Sushi

How to Use This Guide

Information about each item featured in this book is separated into the following easy-to-understand categories:

Origin: Pertinent background information on each item, such as specific portions of fish used for sushi or ingredients for *maki-mono* (rolls) unique to Japanese cuisine, is covered in this section. Special preparations used for an item are also covered here.

Ingredients: Listed in this section of many of the entries are the various ingredients used to create the specific item.

Distinguishing Characteristics: This section, along with the photo, makes it easy to identify different pieces of nigiri, sushi, sashimi, and rolls.

Presentation: Items in this book are served as sashimi or *nigiri-zushi* unless otherwise specified in this section of the entry. Certain items, such as *kani* (crab) or *maki-mono,* are presented uniquely or served a number of different ways. The text under this heading covers how these items are generally served.

Taste & Texture: The flavors and textures that characterize each item are outlined in this section, making it easy to find items that match your taste.

AVAILABILITY: Not all the items covered in this book are available at every sushi restaurant (conversely, not every item available at every sushi restaurant is covered in this book). Information about where, when, and how frequently you can expect to find an item is covered in this section.

PRICE: Prices are relative to the overall cost of specific restaurants. This simple pricing scale helps identify the likely relative price of each item:

$—inexpensive

$$—moderately priced

$$$—expensive

$$$$—very expensive

! **ADDITIONAL INFO:** Interesting facts relating to each item are presented in this section of each entry.

KANJI: The name of each item is displayed in Japanese calligraphy (kanji) in the top right corner of each photo page.

Captions on the photo pages point out colors and patterns to look for in each item, as well as its ingredients.

The Japanese name for each item appears at the top of the page (and its English translation is listed in parentheses).

Types of Maguro (Tuna)

Identifying the Different Cuts of Sushi's Most Popular Fish

Today, tuna is the most popular and most enjoyed sushi item in the world. There are many different kinds of tuna used for sushi:

Mebachi Maguro (Bigeye Tuna)
Hon Maguro, Kuro Maguro (Bluefin Tuna)
Minami Maguro (Southern Tuna)
Kihada Maguro (Yellowfin Tuna)
Bincho, Binnaga (Albacore Tuna)
Kajiki Maguro (Swordfish)

Some of these names will change depending on where the fish come from. For example, *hon maguro* might be called *kuro* if it is from the waters of the Pacific Ocean, and *minami maguro* if it is from the Atlantic. Throughout the years I was training in Japan, I was told that a *sushi-ya* without tuna is not a *sushi-ya.* Tuna is that important to sushi. Ask the chef what kind of tuna they use and where it comes from.

鮪

Otoro (Very Fatty Tuna Meat)

Origin: This is the richest part of the tuna. The *otoro* can only be cut from bigger fish (more than two hundred pounds), like *mebachi, kuro, hon,* and *minami maguro*. *Otoro* is taken from the section of the fish just below the head and gills, which is richest in oils and fats.

Distinguishing Characteristics: *Otoro* is bright pink and shiny in color. The patterns of fat within the meat are white and different from cut to cut. The fat may be in diagonal lines or appear in patterns like snowflakes in the meat. Lean tuna meat is normally red, so the fats and oils give it its pink color.

Taste & Texture: The sweetness that comes from the flavor of *otoro* and the mixture of the sushi rice together is absolutely delicious. And served on its own as sashimi, it is just as good, as the meat alone gives nice sweet and smoky flavors. At the beginning *otoro* is meaty, and as you bite into it and release the oils, it appears to melt in your mouth.

Availability: *Otoro* is a rare find, because tuna with this type of meat are rare. Look for it in the wintertime when colder waters will result in more fat and oils in the fish.

Price: $$$$

Additional Info: Usually only true sushi connoisseurs know to ask for *otoro*. *Shimofuri*, or "falling frost," is the name often used to describe the marbled fat in *otoro*.

大トロ

FAT CREATES WHITE MARBLING

SHINY FROM OILS

SHARI

BRIGHT PINK COLORING

Chefs will often add extra wasabi to otoro nigiri because the fish's oils and fats counteract the spice.

Toro (Fatty Tuna Meat)

ORIGIN: Like *otoro,* the *toro* piece is cut from bigger tunas, like *kuro, hon,* or *minami maguro. Toro* is slightly less rich, but also has a good deal of fat and oils. It is cut from the belly area of a tuna just below the *otoro.* But if the fat content of a fish is low and no *otoro* exists, the *toro* cut will start just below the head and gills.

DISTINGUISHING CHARACTERISTICS: *Toro* is a darker pink than *otoro* because it has slightly less fat. Like *otoro,* the fat can appear both in lines and marbled throughout the meat.

TASTE & TEXTURE: *Toro* has a nice, sweet taste when combined with the sushi rice, and also tastes sweet on its own as sashimi. *Toro* has a stronger tuna flavor than *otoro* and is a bit more solid because of slightly less fat and oil content, but it still melts in your mouth as you're chewing and releases the oils.

AVAILABILITY: *Toro* is generally available, because tuna with the fat content needed to produce it are found frequently. Still, there may be times when it is scarce.

PRICE: $$$$

ADDITIONAL INFO: In Japan *toro* plays a major part in sushi—almost everyone loves it. *Toro* is becoming popular in the rest of the world too.

FAT APPEARS IN
LINES AND MARBLED
THROUGHOUT THE MEAT

SHARI

DARKER PINK COLOR
THAN OTORO

Sushi restaurants usually only have toro *or* otoro. *Seldomly are both available at once.*

Bincho (Albacore Tuna)

ORIGIN: At between five and ten pounds, *bincho* are much smaller than the other types of *maguro* used for sushi. Whereas larger tuna, such as *hon* or *mebachi maguro* are often caught individually due to their large size, *bincho* are netted in large numbers off the coast of areas such as Alaska.

DISTINGUISHING CHARACTERISTICS: *Bincho* has a light pink or beige color. The outside of a piece of albacore sushi is often white because the chef has lightly seared the meat.

TASTE & TEXTURE: In sharp contrast to the thickness of red meat tuna, *bincho* meat is very soft. The tuna flavor is also less strong than that of other *maguro.* A chef might sear the outside of this to add a smoky flavor, as well as to give more texture to the meat.

AVAILABILITY: *Bincho* will be available at most sushi restaurants.

PRICE: $$

ADDITIONAL INFO: Even though the color of *bincho* is so different from the larger red meat tunas, all tuna turns white when it is cooked. Also, you may have noticed that a lot of the canned tuna available in supermarkets is albacore.

ビンナガ鮪

DAIKON AND SCALLION GARNISH

LIGHT PINK MEAT

SHARI

SLIGHTLY COOKED EDGES

Ask for ponzu *sauce on the side of your* bincho. *It compliments the daikon and scallion garnish.*

Chu-Toro (Medium Toro, Half Toro)

Origin: This cut of fish comes from the area between the lean meat on the sides of the tuna and the *toro* section. *Chu-toro* is usually found in bigger tunas, but sometimes when a smaller fish such as *kihada maguro* gets big it may have *chu-toro* meat. *Chu-toro* can also come from the sides of the fish or even sometimes the back of the fish near the skin if the fat content is high enough.

Distinguishing Characteristics: The color of *chu-toro* depends on the type of fish and the cut. It may appear to have color gradations from red to pink, or it may have a lighter red color throughout.

Taste & Texture: C*hu-toro* combines the delicate sweetness of lean tuna and a rich *toro* aftertaste. It also features the solid, meaty texture of lean tuna and the melt-in-your-mouth sensation of *toro*.

Availability: This is available at most sushi restaurants.

Price: $$$

Additional Info: The most popular and most widely used cut of tuna with oil and fat is *chu-toro*, mainly because of its availability. Some people prefer *chu-toro* because it's not as rich as *toro*, but most settle for *chu-toro* when the richer pieces are not available.

中トロ

Only high-end sushi restaurants will have all three types of toro at the same time.

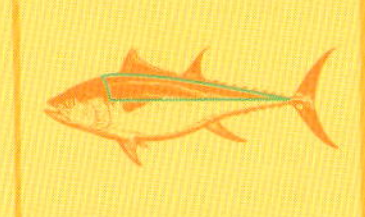

Akami Maguro (Red Meat Tuna)

ORIGIN: All the meat on a lean tuna is used for *akami*, but generally true *akami* is cut from the back and sides of the tuna where there is little or no fat or oil content in the meat. The types of tuna used for *akami* change throughout the year. Sometimes the tuna come from the Pacific Ocean and other times from the Atlantic. *Kihada maguro* is generally the fish that *sushi-ya* will use for *akami*. This is the tuna called "ahi" in Hawaii. But don't ask for ahi, because you might get *aji* (horse mackerel).

DISTINGUISHING CHARACTERISTICS: Fresh *akami* is generally bright red, although it may also be a lighter red depending on what kind of tuna is used. *Mebachi akami* is ruby red, for example, and *kihada akami* is a duller red.

TASTE & TEXTURE: *Akami* has a bold flavor like that found in canned tuna, but of course it tastes much more fresh, and much lighter because it has no fat or oils. The texture is firm and meaty, almost like that of a steak.

AVAILABILITY: Red meat tuna is the most popular item in the sushi world. You will find it year-round at any sushi restaurant.

PRICE: $$

ADDITIONAL INFO: Sometimes you will find *kajiki maguro* (swordfish) used as *akami*. This would be a treat to get a chance to try. *Kajiki* is not available often, but when it is, it's really good.

Akami *is a good introduction to raw fish because its texture resembles red meat.*

Types of Shiromi (White Meat Fish) The Healthiest Group of Fish Used for Sushi—Including Yellowtail, Bass, and Snapper

There are many fish in the *shiromi* group that are used for sushi. *Shiromi* are known for being low in fat and light-tasting—like *madai, hirame,* and *suzuki,* which are excellent as sushi and good for sashimi as well. The yellowtail family is in the white meat group also, even though they are richer in oils.

Usuzukuri (thinly sliced) is a wonderful way of enjoying *shiromi.* Cut almost paper-thin and served on a plate with chopped scallion and grated hot radish, this dish is served with a Japanese vinaigrette sauce called *ponzu.*

In the early days of *Edomae* sushi, *shiromi* were caught in many different parts of Japan. Now fish used for *shiromi* come from all parts of the world, and many are available year-round.

白身

Hamachi, Buri, Inada (Yellowtail)

Origin: Although yellowtail is commonly referred to as *hamachi,* the name will often change with the maturity of the fish. *Buri* weigh more than ten pounds, *hamachi* are generally eight to ten pounds, and *inada* are less than eight pounds. *Hamachi* are caught all over, but Japanese *hamachi* is generally considered the best.

Distinguishing Characteristics: The meat from the belly, where the fish is rich in oil and fat, is white, and the leaner meat on the back part of the fish is tan to light pink.

Taste & Texture: Yellowtail is meaty, light, and sweet. The richest part, the belly part, of the *buri* (the mature yellowtail) is called *buri-toro* because, like *toro,* it melts in one's mouth.

Availability: Yellowtail is best in the wintertime, when it is rich in fat. Because it is very popular throughout the world, most every *sushi-ya* will have it year-round.

Price: $$

Additional Info: This fish is in a group called *shusei-uo,* believed to bring good luck and success. Because hamachi is enjoyed at different stages of its life cycle, it is said that eating it will help you live a long life. *Buri* teriyaki is very popular in Japan. The collar part (*hamachi-no-kama*) is a delicacy, too. Some places might have this grilled with salt. If you get a chance, try it—you'll like it.

LIGHTER MEAT INDICATES MORE OIL AND FAT

LEAN MEAT IS DARKER PINK

SHARI

Negi hama-maki *(see page 150) is the most popular way to have* hamachi.

Kanpachi (Amberjack)

ORIGIN: *Kanpachi* is a type of yellowtail, grouped with the family because it shares the characteristic yellow tallow line that runs from head to tail. These fish are caught offshore in open water and weigh up to forty pounds.

DISTINGUISHING CHARACTERISTICS: *Kanpachi* sushi looks like *hamachi,* but the meat has a deeper tan color, similar to human skin, and might even appear golden in color.

TASTE & TEXTURE: *Kanpachi* has a buttery flavor and texture that distinguish it from other yellowtail.

AVAILABILITY: *Kanpachi* is best in the summer. A very popular fish in Japan, it is not well known to the rest of the sushi world. It is starting to be more available in North America, so you may see more of it.

PRICE: $$$

ADDITIONAL INFO: The buttery flavor and texture that make this fish desired are most evident in young *kanpachi.*

PINK COLOR INDICATES LEANER MEAT

TAN OR "SKIN" COLOR

CAN APPEAR GOLDEN

SILVER COLORING ON MEAT CLOSE TO THE SKIN

SHARI

Cuts of kanpachi *from near the skin are richer in oils and have more flavor.*

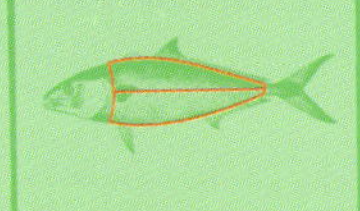

Shima Aji *(Yellow Jack)*

Origin: This fish from the yellowtail family is shorter and stockier than *hamachi.* There are *zengo* (the heavy scales near the tail portion of the fish) on both sides of the fish, and a yellow line that runs across both sides and *zengo*. It is probably from these heavy scales, which are also found on *aji* (horse mackerel), that this fish got its name.

Distinguishing Characteristics: The meat of *shima aji* is white to golden in color. Like its fellow yellowtail, *kanpachi,* the meat is a deeper tan color than that of *hamachi* and other members of the yellowtail family.

Taste & Texture: Like most white fish, *shima aji* is light and not too fishy in flavor, with a slight sweetness. The texture is meaty and a little chewier than yellowtail.

Availability: This fish, best to eat in the summer, is often not available—even in Japan. There seem to be more *shima aji* coming in from Hawaii now, so perhaps you'll have a chance to try it.

Price: $$$

Additional Info: *Shima aji* is considered a top-of-the-line sushi item in Japan.

縞鯵

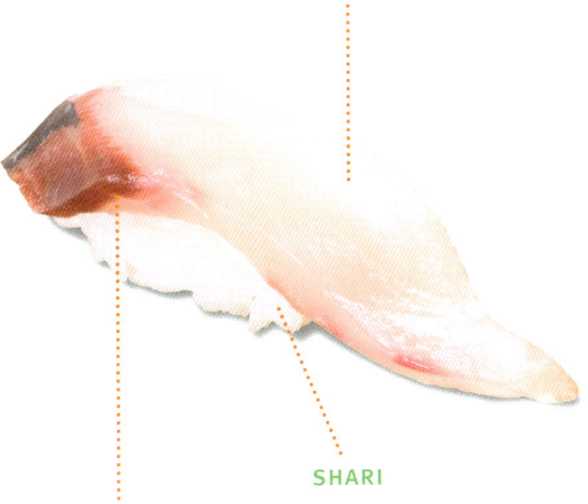

This is regarded as the best fish within the yellowtail family, because it is most flavorful.

Madai (Red Sea Bream, Red Snapper)

Origin: *Madai,* a type of *tai* (sea bream, also called snapper), often come from New Zealand. They live in rocky coastal waters and swim through strong currents, which keeps them lean and meaty. The best fish are around fifteen to twenty pounds, but usually these are caught at six to ten pounds. Strong and bold-looking, the red color of the fish brings out the beauty it has to show.

Distinguishing Characteristics: *Madai* meat is white and has red stripes on the side of the filet closest to the skin.

Taste & Texture: The taste is light, with a subtle and elegant sweetness to it that you will not find in all white meat fish. As with most white meat fish, the fat content is low, and because of this, the texture is thicker and meatier.

Availability: *Madai* is best in the winter to spring months. In the *shiromi* group, *madai* is one of the most popular fish used for sushi in Japan.

Price: $$

Additional Info: Also known as "the king of fish," *madai* has a signature role within Japanese culture. *Madai* are presented or shown in many celebrations and events, and even in festivals and religious rituals. For example, at the end of a sumo wrestling tournament, the winner will often hold up a whole, fresh *madai* as a symbol of victory.

真鯛

RED STRIPING ON MEAT CLOSE TO THE SKIN

WHITE MEAT

SHARI

Baby madai, *called* kodai *or* kasugo, *are pickled and served whole as sushi.*

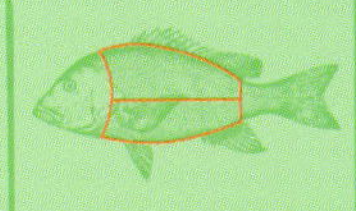

Hirame (Sole or Flounder)

ORIGIN: *Hirame* is a flatfish, with eyes on the top left side of its body. The underside is white, and the top is grayish brown with black dots. *Hirame* are generally three to four pounds.

DISTINGUISHING CHARACTERISTICS: *Hirame* is a pale white color, sometimes almost translucent in appearance.

TASTE & TEXTURE: Because *hirame* is low in fat and high in protein, the taste is light and has a pleasant, clean aftertaste with very little fishiness. Although the meat seems very thick, it is not tough and is very easy to chew.

AVAILABILITY: This fish is best enjoyed in the winter to spring months because its size is optimal during this period, and it has a bit of fat in it from the cold waters of winter. *Hirame* was once the favorite fish in Japan for *nigiri-zushi,* and it is gaining in popularity in the rest of the sushi world. But it can be difficult to find in a restaurant because it is often only available frozen, and chefs use only fresh *hirame* for sushi.

PRICE: $$

ADDITIONAL INFO: *Hirame* is very well regarded among Japanese women, because it is said that eating this fish benefits and beautifies one's skin.

鮃

Hirame *is unique because it yields four filets, whereas most other fish only have two.*

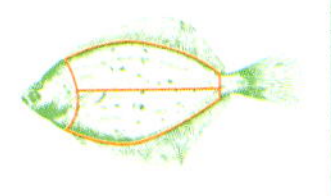

Suzuki (Sea Bass)

Origin: *Suzuki* is plentiful in the coastal waters of Japan, and many types of sea bass are fished all over the world. Like *hamachi*, the name of this fish changes as it grows, but only *suzuki* is used for sushi. It's called *koppa* at its youngest; *seigo* when it is six to ten inches; *fukko* at ten to fifteen inches; and then *suzuki* at the final stage of its growth of up to three feet.

Distinguishing Characteristics: The meat is grayish-white with patterns of gray lines throughout.

Taste & Texture: The flavor is on the light side, very subtle with a sweet aftertaste. It can taste like *kanpachi*, *shima aji,* or *hiramasa,* because like them it is a summer fish and is therefore less rich in fats and oils. *Suzuki* is very tender—easy to bite into and chew.

Availability: This fish is best enjoyed in the summer months, when it is most mature. Within the last couple of years, *suzuki* has become more popular and is widely available, although there may be some places that do not offer it.

Price: $$

Additional Info: *Suzuki* is in the *shusei-uo* category with *hamachi,* believed to bring good fortune and success because it is a fish eaten at different stages of its life cycle. It's rich in vitamin D and calcium, and is said to be good for bone development.

GRAYISH-WHITE MEAT

HINTS OF GRAY

SHARI

Suzuki-no-arai *is a dish made by shocking the meat in ice water and then serving it with* ponzu *sauce.*

Karei (Halibut, Lemon Sole, a Type of Flounder)

ORIGIN: *Karei* is the general Japanese term for a flatfish whose eyes are on the right side of its head. Generally halibut or lemon sole are served as *karei.*

DISTINGUISHING CHARACTERISTICS: This fish is related to *hirame*, so the meat looks very similar—pale white or translucent.

TASTE & TEXTURE: The taste of *karei* is like *hirame,* a soft and delicate flavor that is light because Karei is low in fat. There is a gentle firmness to the meat.

AVAILABILITY: Generally you will only see this fish a few times a year as sushi, because only the freshest *karei* are used, usually as a substitute for *hirame.*

PRICE: $$

ADDITIONAL INFO: *Karei,* a common fish in Japan, is enjoyed in many different ways. You might see it served grilled with salt or deep-fried. There are approximately six hundred kinds of flatfish known to us these days. The way to tell *hirame* and *karei* apart is easy: *hirame* has its eyes on the left, *karei* on the right. In Japan, *hidari* means "left," so it's easy to remember which side *hirame's* eyes are on.

鰈

Karei *and other light-tasting fish are often served with* shiso *to enhance the flavor.*

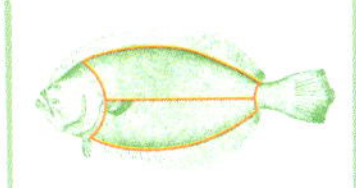

Hiramasa (Amberjack, Kingfish)

ORIGIN: *Hiramasa* is a yellowtail relative fished exclusively in the waters of Japan. Its characteristics are very close to those of *kanpachi,* with thicker tallow lines on both sides of the fish that run from head to tail.

DISTINGUISHING CHARACTERISTICS: To the untrained eye, *hiramasa* meat is nearly impossible to distinguish from *hamachi.* It can even be hard for experts to tell the difference between the two based simply on the appearance of the meat. Most chefs are only able to tell the difference between them by looking at the exterior of the whole fish.

TASTE & TEXTURE: Only experts will be able to tell the difference in taste between *hiramasa* and *hamachi*—they are both light and sweet-tasting. The meaty texture of *hiramasa* is nearly identical to that of *hamachi.*

AVAILABILITY: *Hiramasa* is only available in the summer months. It is a top-of-the-line sushi item in Japan, but it is not well-known in the rest of the world, so it will be difficult to find. Keep an eye out for it, and try it if you see it.

PRICE: $$$

ADDITIONAL INFO: This is one of the fish in the yellowtail family that is considered a delicacy. There are other fish, such as *kanpachi* and *shima aji,* within the same category that have similar tastes and textures, and are well regarded because they are only seasonally available.

平政

DARK MEAT JUST UNDER SKIN

LIGHT PINK MEAT

SHARI

During the season when it is available, hiramasa *will often be served as* hamachi.

Types of Hikari-Mono (Shiny Fish) Small Fish That Are Pickled for Sushi

Hikari-mono are smaller fish with silvery skin that shines in the water. In sushi, these fish are pickled and preserved so that they can be enjoyed even beyond the normal availability of the fish.

Most *hikari-mono* go through a pickling process that has been used for many years. As we know, some of the first sushi was pickled. To prepare *hikari-mono,* the chef adds salt to a fresh filet. The amount of salt used and the length of time it is left on the fillet depends on the type of fish and its fat content. After a certain length of time, the salt is washed off, and the fish is marinated in vinegar. The acids in the vinegar cook the meat.

The quality of the *hikari-mono* is a good indicator of a chef's skill. It takes a lot of talent to perfect the balance between the salt and vinegar.

光り物

Shime Saba (Pickled Mackerel)

ORIGIN: *Shime saba* are generally around two pounds. There are many different types of mackerel caught all over the world. We get ours from Norway.

DISTINGUISHING CHARACTERISTICS: The *uchikawa* is silvery blue with darker lines through it. The meat is usually white, but *saba* may have some dark meat in the middle.

TASTE & TEXTURE: *Shime saba* is very fishy. Although it is not as salty, the strength of its flavor is similar to anchovies. It has a nice, gentle, meaty feeling, and due to the level of oils and fat, it will give the effect of melting a bit in one's mouth.

AVAILABILITY: Fall to winter is usually the best time to eat *saba*. As they mature and the waters become colder, they start to get fat. *Saba* is available at most any *sushi-ya*.

PRICE: $

ADDITIONAL INFO: *Saba* has histidine, an amino acid, and is rich in omega oils, which is said to help your mind as you get older, protecting against Alzheimer's and other diseases afflicting the aged.

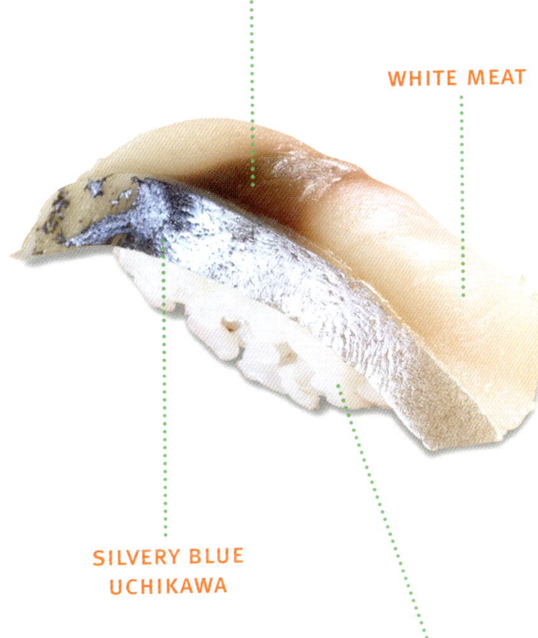

Most hikari-mono *are served with the* uchikawa *(the skin beneath the skin) showing.*

Kohada (*Gizzard Shad*)

ORIGIN: This small, spineless, silvery fish is part of the herring family. *Kohada* is another fish whose name changes as it matures. It will be called *konoshiro* or *shinko* at a young age, *kohada* at a slightly older age, and *nakatsumi* at a mature age. *Kohada* is a very small fish, usually not much more than a few inches long.

DISTINGUISHING CHARACTERISTICS: *Kohada* meat is white with a pinkish hint. The silver coloring and black spots of the under skin make it appear that the meat has not been skinned. But don't worry—the outer skin has been removed.

TASTE & TEXTURE: With its strong fishy flavor, *Kohada* tastes very similar to *shime saba.* It is marinated in vinegar for a long period of time to soften the tiny bones in the meat. *Kohada* has a nice, meaty texture and is not very rich in oils.

AVAILABILITY: *Kohada* is only available as sushi in the winter, when this fish is at the right age. *Kohada* has been around a long time in Japan, and it's starting to appear outside of Japan more often.

PRICE: $

ADDITIONAL INFO: In Japan, when you ask for *hikari-mono* they will usually give you *kohada.*

小鰭

Ginger and scallion are added to mellow the very fishy flavor of kohada.

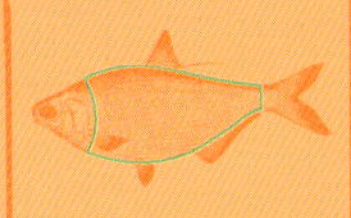

Aji (Horse Mackerel)

Origin: The most popular types of *aji* are *ma-aji, ki-aji,* and *kuro-aji*—the Japanese name changes depending on the waters where they are caught, but in English this is simply "horse mackerel." *Aji* are fished all over the world, but restaurants usually receive their *aji* from Japan, Hawaii, Australia, or New Zealand.

Distinguishing Characteristics: The meat of *aji* is a light tan. The *uchikawa* has a shiny silver color.

Taste & Texture: Like *saba, aji* has a fishy flavor, but it is much more mellow than *saba* because it is salted and marinated in vinegar for a shorter period of time. If you like tuna or yellowtail, you should try *aji.*

Availability: *Aji* is a basic sushi item in Japan, but it is now becoming more available outside of Japan, and will probably continue to gain popularity.

Price: $$

Additional Info: A very popular dish in Japan using *aji* is called *aji-no tataki.* In this presentation the meat is chopped or cut into small pieces and arranged with ginger and scallion. Onion and miso can be added to enhance the flavor. An artful chef might use the *aji* skeleton as a serving dish.

SHISO, GINGER, AND SCALLIONS FOR DECORATION

SHARI

LIGHT TAN MEAT

Shiso, ginger *and* scallions *are often added to a piece of* aji *purely to enhance the appearance.*

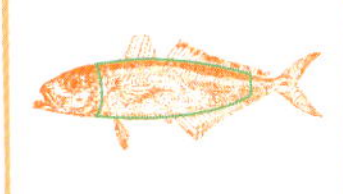

Types of Ebi (Shrimp, Prawns)

Common Types of Shrimp and Prawns Used for Sushi

There are more than a thousand different types of shrimp and prawns in the waters of our planet. *Kuruma* (wheel) shrimp, the signature *ebi* of sushi, was the first to be used for *nigiri* in *Edomae* sushi. Black tiger prawns are the ones most used for sushi these days.

Usually *ebi* is served as a cooked item, but there are shrimp and prawns that are served raw, such as *ama-ebi, botan-ebi,* and *odori* (live *kuruma*). To prepare *ebi,* the head is removed and the tail is skewered on bamboo to prevent it from curling, then boiled, peeled, and butterflied.

Today, *ebi* is one of the most popular sushi items around the world, often the first thing a sushi beginner would try.

蝦

Ebi (Black Tiger Shrimp)

Origin: *Ebi* is the universal Japanese term for shrimp or prawns, but the most common type of prawn served as *ebi* all over the world is the black tiger shrimp, which gets its name from the dark color of its shell and the dark gray stripes on its back that resemble a tiger's stripes.

Distinguishing Characteristics: Even though the shells of these shrimp are dark in color, *ebi* has white meat with red- or orange-colored stripes.

Taste & Texture: The taste and texture of cooked shrimp are familiar to most people. Ebi have a light flavor with a sweet aftertaste, and are solid and meaty.

Availability: As one of the most popular sushi items, *ebi* will always be available.

Price: $$

Additional Info: Black tiger is the most widely used sushi shrimp, but *kuruma ebi* (wheel shrimp) were the first shrimp to be served as sushi in Japan. They are not often found on menus outside of Japan, and one particular preparation of *kuruma ebi* is very rarely offered anywhere but in Japan. When *kuruma ebi* is served "alive," it is called *odori ebi* or "dancing shrimp," because the meat moves as if it is dancing. When you order *odori,* the chef first shows you the whole live shrimp, then tears off the head. The tail is then shelled, and the tail meat is butterflied and served *nigiri* style. The meat is still moving as you eat it.

蝦

ORANGE STRIPES
(MAY ALSO APPEAR RED)

WHITE MEAT

BUTTERFLIED

SHARI

When forming ebi nigiri *a chef tries to make the whole piece look like a large shrimp tail.*

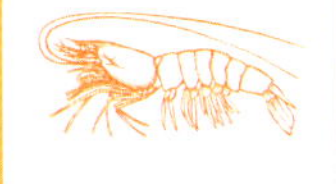

Botan Ebi (Spot Prawns)
Ama Ebi (Sweet Shrimp)

ORIGIN: *Botan ebi* is the largest of the shrimps used for *ama ebi,* sometimes growing as big as a small lobster. Usually this is served one whole shrimp to one piece of sushi. Spot prawns used in North America come from the Pacific Northwest and Alaska. In Japan, spot prawns come from the Hokkaido area.

DISTINGUISHING CHARACTERISTICS: The raw meat is light gray to white, with a red outer layer.

TASTE & TEXTURE: *Botan ebi* is very sweet, like its *ama ebi* counterparts, and is meaty and a bit slimy.

AVAILABILITY: Spot prawns are very popular in Japan and can be found in most any *sushi-ya.* People in the rest of the world tend not to enjoy raw shrimp as much, so many places do not offer these on the menu. Again, it never hurts to ask the chef at your local restaurant.

PRICE: $$$

ADDITIONAL INFO: In Japan, *botan ebi* is considered to be a high-class or high-society type of sushi because it is larger in size than the other shrimp that are served as *ama ebi.*

牡丹蝦

BUTTERFLIED THROUGH THE BACK

RED-AND-PINK OUTER LAYER

WHITE MEAT

SHARI

MORE INTRICATE FAN TAIL

Another smaller shrimp served as ama ebi *is* aka ebi, *or red shrimp.*

Shakko (Mantis Shrimp)

Origin: Mantis shrimp is not really a shrimp, but is part of the largest class of crustaceans on the planet, the *Stomatopods*. This shrimp looks more like an insect than a shrimp—kind of scary. It is served cooked.

Distinguishing Characteristics: *Shakko* has a purple to gray color, even when it's cooked.

Taste & Texture: Even though *shakko* looks different, the taste is just like any shrimp. It's served with *nitsume* (eel sauce) over it. *Shakko* is a *nimono neta* (a cooked item), so the texture has a meatiness to it like shrimp and crab.

Availability: In Japan, *shakko* is a well-known sushi item, but elsewhere it is new enough that most people are not yet familiar with it. *Shakko* from the waters of Tokyo Bay are very popular, and especially *shakko* that come from a fishing harbor in Tsurumi-ku of Yokohama. They are best in the summer months, before spawning, when they are rich with eggs.

Price: $$$

Additional Info: *Shakko* means "garage" in Japan. *Sha* is "car," and *ko* means "place." When you're at a sushi bar ask for "garage" and you will get *shakko*, and you'll also get a laugh out of the chef.

蝦蛄

PURPLE TO GRAY IN COLOR

BRUSHED WITH NITSUME

SHARI

DIFFERENT TAIL THAN OTHER SHRIMP

People who like shakko *prefer* komochi shakko, *which is mantis shrimp fertile with eggs.*

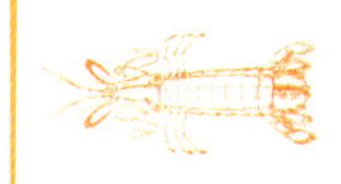

Types of Kai (Shellfish)

Shellfish Used for Sushi, Including Abalone, Scallops, and Razor Clams

There are two types of shellfish: the bivalves, which have a top and bottom shell; and the single-valve clams, which have only one shell, like a snail.

Around the waters of Japan, there are more than five hundred kinds of shellfish. The Japanese eat about half of the different kinds. For sushi, there are some thirty kinds of shellfish available in the markets. *Kai* were first used during the Edo period, but were served cooked because this allowed chefs to sell these for a longer period of time after the body was removed from the shell. Now that we have refrigerated food infrastructures, *kai* are available raw for sushi.

貝

Akagai (Red Clam, Ark Shell)

Origin: The ark shell is considered the superior shellfish item for sushi. Its shell is ribbed and it is generally about three inches across, from its hinge to the opposite side of the shell. *Akagai* live in the brackish water near the mouths of rivers.

Distinguishing Characteristics: The meat is usually red and can appear orange as well. There are three parts to *akagai* used for sushi: the body, the threadlike filaments (*himo*) that connect the body to the shell, and the adductor muscle (*hashira*). The latter two are considered more desirable by connoisseurs. Chefs add cuts to the body to tenderize it and for show.

Taste & Texture: The taste of *akagai* is like the scent of the ocean with a sweet clam flavor. The body is meatier and chewier than the *himo* and *hashira*, which are crunchy.

Availability: Winter to spring is the best time for this clam. *Akagai* is a very well known and popular clam in Japan, but it is rarely available at sushi restaurants elsewhere.

Price: $$

Additional Info: The bright red color of *akagai* is due to the presence of hemoglobin in its bloodstream. This is rare, and contributes to the mystique of this highly regarded clam.

赤貝

Chefs cut different patterns in the meat to enhance the appearance of many pieces of sushi.

Awabi (Abalone)

ORIGIN: *Awabi* has only a top shell. While it moves like a snail, it does not look like one—at a glance *awabi* resemble a rock or piece of coral. Most of the *awabi* that is eaten and used for sushi today comes from four major parts of the world. A*wabi* that come from the waters of Japan during the summer are said to be the best. *Awabi* also come from Australia, South Africa, and the west coast of North America.

DISTINGUISHING CHARACTERISTICS: *Awabi* meat is tan with dark edges.

TASTE & TEXTURE: *Awabi* has a very fresh ocean flavor that emerges with each bite. It is the chewiest clam used for sushi. The meat is very tough, especially the dark meat on the edges.

AVAILABILITY: *Awabi,* a protected species, are commercially cultured in Japan and elsewhere. Abalone is a popular sushi item in Japan and around Asia. The tough texture shows freshness, and this is what is liked there. Outside Japan, chewy items such as *tako* (octopus, see page 110) or *ika* (squid, see page 106) are less popular overall, simply because people's tastes are different.

PRICE: $$$$

ADDITIONAL INFO: Adding to their mystique as a valuable shellfish, *awabi* have mother-of-pearl, used often in making watches and jewelry, lining their shells.

SMALL CUTS TENDERIZE AND DECORATE THE MEAT

TAN MEAT

SHARI

DARKER EDGES

Mushi awabi, *or steamed abalone, is a very popular sushi item in Japan.*

Hokkigai (Surf Clam), Ubagai

Origin: This shell is on the brown side, hard and thick. These are larger clams, with thicker shells, that flourish in cold waters. Normally these clams are three to four inches across, but can grow as big as six inches or more.

Distinguishing Characteristics: The meat is white to tan, with reddish-purple tips. The *himo* are also served as a sushi item.

Taste & Texture: This clam has a very pleasant and mellow ocean flavor with a nice sweetness that emerges as you chew it. This would be a good clam to try as an introduction to *kai.* The meat of this clam can be tough. I like to put little cuts in the meat to tenderize it, which helps one to enjoy this clam a lot more.

Availability: *Hokkigai* are best in the winter to spring months when they are larger, and are widely available and used as sushi all over the world.

Price: $$

Additional Info: *Ubagai* is the formal name for this clam in Japan, but it is known as *hokkigai* all over the world.

北寄貝

WHITE OR TAN MEAT

CUTS TENDERIZE AND ORNAMENT THE MEAT

REDDISH-PURPLE TIP

SHARI

If a clam is very fresh the chef's cuts in the meat will expand and open up.

Hotategai (*Scallop*)

Origin: Scallops are bivalves, with a flat bottom shell and a larger, rounded top shell. Usually when you see scallops in a restaurant or market they are fairly small, but these can grow as big as your hand.

Distinguishing Characteristics: The color is off-white to beige when it is served raw. When cooked in a sweet soy sauce, it will be light brown in color.

Taste & Texture: Most people know that scallops taste sweet and light when cooked. Raw, they taste a bit fishier and even sweeter. Often these are served with *nitsume*. *Hotategai* is served raw more often now since it is available fresh. As you bite into the raw *hotategai* sushi, the meat is soft but firm. If you get it cooked, it's a bit more firm and meaty.

Availability: This is a very common item both in Japan and in North America. You will find *hotategai* at most sushi restaurants.

Price: $$

Additional Info: *Hotategai* is thought of as a *nimono neta* (a cooked item) in the Tokyo area, because these are native to Hokkaido and Tohoku, and traditionally were not available fresh to sushi restaurants. But in the areas where these come from they have always been served raw.

帆立貝

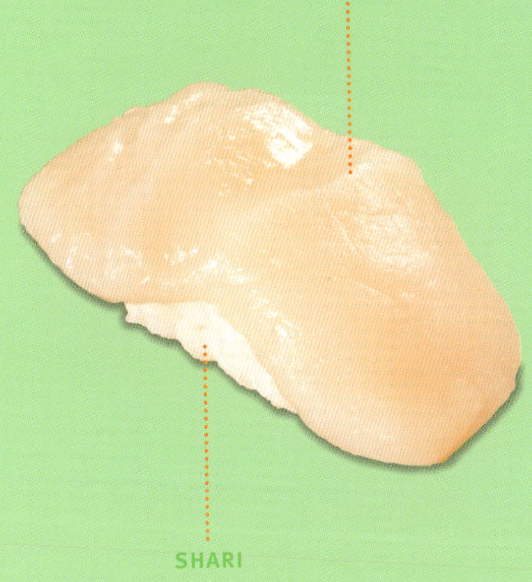

Like ebi, hotategai *are served butterflied and spread out across the ball of rice.*

Mirugai (Geoduck, Horse Neck Clam, Giant Clam)

Origin: *Mirugai* are among the biggest clams used for sushi, sometimes growing to a couple of feet in length. There are two parts to *mirugai* used for sushi: the body and the neck, or "siphon." The neck sticks out from the shell and acts as a siphon, ingesting water and nutrients. A lot of geoduck comes from the Pacific Northwest, and much of it is exported to Japan. Hokkaido has its own *mirugai,* which are a bit shorter than those found in North America.

Distinguishing Characteristics: *Mirugai* is light brown to white in color.

Taste & Texture: The taste is like the ocean and is sweet. Chefs often put cuts in the meat of the clam to tenderize it, so that when you eat it, it's crunchy not chewy.

Availability: *Mirugai* is best from February to June, but is available year-round in *sushi-ya* all over the world.

Price: $$$

Additional Info: In Japan, geoduck imported from the United States is called *shiroi mirugai,* or "white *mirugai.*" Some people say that *mirugai* is an aphrodisiac.

海松貝

CUTS TENDERIZE THE MEAT

NORI BELT

SHARI

LIGHT BROWN COLOR

Geoduck are usually alive until the chef cuts them. The fresher these are, the crunchier the meat.

Tairagai (Razor Clam)

ORIGIN: The shape of the *tairagai* is different from that of other clams. It looks like a fan. Inside there is a big adductor muscle, which is the main part of this triangular-shaped clam, and only the muscle is served.

DISTINGUISHING CHARACTERISTICS: The color is white to tan, and it looks exactly the same as a scallop.

TASTE & TEXTURE: These have a pleasant oceanic flavor with a hint of sweetness. Although *tairagai* look like scallops, their texture is firmer.

AVAILABILITY: In Japan, *tairagai* are found in the waters that separate Hokkaido from the main island. Although they are caught in both fall and spring months, fall is the best time to enjoy this clam because it is meatier and sweeter. This is commonly served in Japan and is becoming more widely available elsewhere.

PRICE: $$

ADDITIONAL INFO: *Tairagai* is nearly indistinguishable in appearance from *hotategai.* Unless the chef told you that you were eating *tairagai,* you might not notice the difference, although *tairagai* has a stronger flavor and slightly tougher meat than *hotategai.*

平貝

BEIGE TO OFF-WHITE MEAT

SHARI

INDISTINGUISHABLE FROM HOTATEGAI

Two or three pieces of sushi can be made from one tairagai *because they are larger clams.*

Torigai (Cockle)

ORIGIN: The *torigai* has one of the most beautiful shells of the clams used for sushi. They are generally about four inches across. The body of the clam is shaped like a foot. Although there are many different types of cockle found all over the world, it is mainly caught for sushi in the waters north of Kyushu, the large island located at the southwest end of the main island of Japan.

DISTINGUISHING CHARACTERISTICS: The color of *torigai* can be black, brown, or white. When you order *torigai* you may notice that it appears to have a tail sticking up into the air. This is actually the "neck" of the clam.

TASTE & TEXTURE: *Torigai* has a fresh ocean flavor and is sweet. It is not as chewy as many other clams.

AVAILABILITY: *Torigai* is available in the winter to spring months when they are harvested in Japan. It is generally only available frozen to restaurants outside Japan. We may start to see these brought in fresh to North America if they become a more popular item.

PRICE: $$

ADDITIONAL INFO: Generally the meat of the *torigai* is very thin, so the thicker and meatier the particular cockle, the more value it has. *Torigai* is very stiff when it is fresh, so the chef will often form the *nigiri* with the neck of the clam sticking up to display its freshness.

COLOR CAN BE WHITE, BROWN, OR EVEN BLACK

SHARI

FOOT-SHAPED BODY

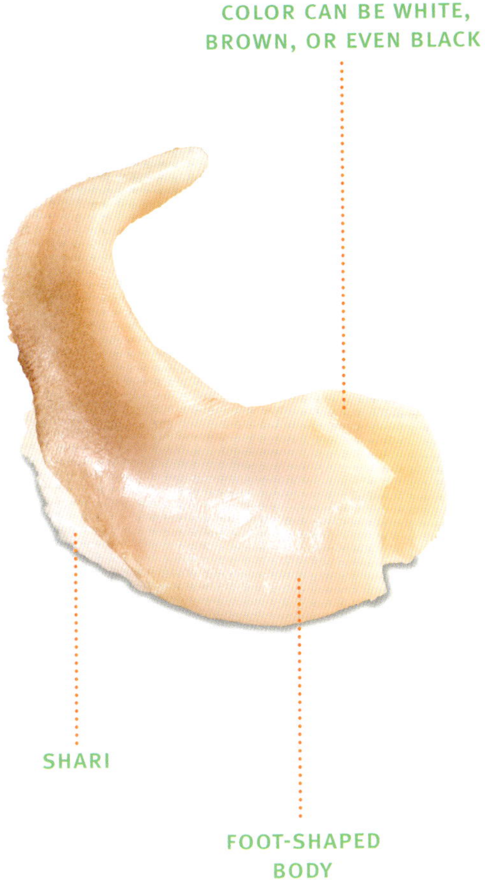

You can gauge the freshness of torigai *by how straight the neck stands up.*

Types of Kani (Crab)
Including King, Snow, Blue, and Dungeness Crab

There are many kinds of *kani* used in the world of sushi today, although it is a relatively new sushi item. In Japan, *kani* is an ingredient frequently used in hot pots (*nabe*), cooked with vegetables, or served as a *sunomono* (salad with a vinaigrette sauce).

At a *sushi-ya* you are likely to see crab served a number of ways: as an ingredient in California rolls, spider rolls, and even as *nigiri-zushi* or sashimi.

Each area of the world seems to have access to a different type of *kani,* and these regional supplies make using crab for sushi even more interesting. If you like crab, be open to eating what is native to the area where you're eating, because what you find might be really good and only available there.

蟹

Matsubagani, Zuwai Gani (Snow Crab)

Origin: This crab has long, skinny legs and looks like a spider. The name will differ across Japan, but it is the same crab and will always be called "snow crab" in North America. Around Japan, they are caught from the Japan Sea up to Hokkaido. In North America, snow crab come from Alaska and Russia's Bering Sea.

Distinguishing Characteristics: The meat is white with red coloring on the portions that were closest to the shell.

Presentation: Snow crab is served as *nigiri,* sashimi, or as part of a roll.

Taste & Texture: The snow crab is sweet, fresh and delicious, and it has nice, firm meat.

Availability: *Matsubagani* are best in the winter months when they are more mature. This is the most widely used type of crab in sushi. If a *sushi-ya* has crab, it will probably be snow crab. You should be able to order this at most any sushi restaurant.

Price: $$

Additional Info: In Japan, *matsubagani* are a very popular ingredient in *nabe,* where seafood, vegetables, and other items are mixed together as in a stew, and families or groups of friends share and eat from the same pot.

ずわい蟹

WHITE MEAT

PINKISH OR RED
COLORING ON OUTSIDE

NORI BELT

SHARI

Matsubagani *have skinny legs, so it usually takes two or three legs to make one piece of* nigiri-zushi.

Taraba Gani (*King Crab*)

Origin: *Taraba gani* is called the king of crabs because with legs spread they can reach a width of up to five feet. These are mostly harvested in northern areas such as Alaska, Russia, and Hokkaido. The top of the shell is bright red to orange and the bottom is white. Generally only the legs and claws are used for sushi.

Distinguishing Characteristics: The meat is primarily white but will also have a red color like its shell, similar to that found on shrimp.

Presentation: *Taraba gani* is one of the crabs used for *nigiri-zushi,* and it will usually be presented with a *nori* belt to hold it on the rice. It is very popular as sashimi as well. You can also ask the chef to serve this crab as part of a roll.

Taste & Texture: King is among the most delicious crabs, with an incredible natural sweetness. The legs and claws have a very pleasant meaty texture.

Availability: Although this is available all over Japan, it can be difficult to get anywhere but in North America on the west coast because it is expensive.

Price: $$$$

Additional Info: Studies say that king crabs can live more than thirty years, and male crabs weighing more than twenty pounds have been caught.

NORI BELT HOLDS
DELICATE MEAT TOGETHER

WHITE MEAT

SHARI

RED OUTER
COLORING

King crab are so large that often only a slice out of the thigh or claw will make a piece of sushi.

Soft-Shell Crab, Blue Crab

Origin: There is no Japanese name for blue or soft-shell crab, because it is native to the waters of the east coast of the United States.

Distinguishing Characteristics: Soft-shell crab is always served coated and fried with a bit of flour or cornstarch, so it is both dark and golden brown.

Presentation: Although some *sushi-ya* might serve a blue crab appetizer with a whole fried blue crab and *ponzu* sauce, this will most always be served as a part of the spider roll (see page 146).

Taste & Texture: The sweetness you normally taste in crabmeat is very subtle in soft-shell crab. The texture is very crunchy.

Availability: Soft-shell crab is a U. S. product, popular on the east coast. Most *sushi-ya* in the United States serve spider rolls, so you will be able to get this nearly everywhere. Since this crab is native to the U. S., it is considered a delicacy in Japan and can be hard to find outside of the U. S.

Price: $$$

Additional Info: Once the blue crab sheds its shell, crabbers have only four hours to get it out of the water before the new shell begins to harden. The blue crab gets its name from the blue coloring on the legs and claws of the male.

青蟹

COATED AND FRIED BROWN IN FLOUR AND CORNSTARCH

NORI BELT

SHARI

These smaller crabs are fried whole, and often half of the crab will be served as one piece of sushi.

Dungeness Crab

Origin: This sushi item has no Japanese name because it is native to the waters of the Pacific Northwest. The body of this crab is fat, its legs proportionally shorter than other crabs, and its shell is a brownish red.

Distinguishing Characteristics: As a sushi item, Dungeness crab is served cooked, so the meat is white with some red coloring.

Presentation: Dungeness crab is served as *nigiri*, sashimi, or as a roll. Some people may ask for a California roll (see page 138) with Dungeness crab, or this may be served as a simple Dungeness crab roll.

Taste & Texture: Dungeness crab has an appealing sweetness, and the crab flavor is very nice and strong. Like most other crab meat, it is meaty but light.

Availability: You will probably find this served only on the Pacific Coast of the United States and Canada.

Price: $$$

Additional Info: This crab got its name from Old Town Dungeness on the Olympic Peninsula of Washington. Interestingly, Dungeness and all other crabs are cannibalistic, although they eat a wide variety of sealife.

ダンジネス蟹

The shoulder meat and certain parts of the body of these and other crabs are often used for rolls.

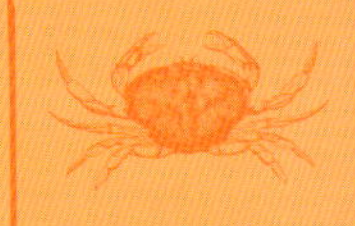

94

Additional Sushi Items

Other Favorites Such as Salmon and Eel

In the following pages are some other items that are being used as sushi today but do not fit into any particular category. Items such as *ika, tako,* and *anago* are long-time favorites, while *katsuo, sake,* and *ankimo* are relatively new to sushi.

他の魚

Katsuo (Bonito)

ORIGIN: *Katsuo* is a red meat fish that is related to tuna and mackerel, and generally weighs between five and twenty pounds. In Japan, *katsuo* comes from the waters off an island called Shikoku, but much of the *katsuo* served in North America comes from Hawaii.

DISTINGUISHING CHARACTERISTICS: The meat of the bonito is red. When serving this, chefs will leave the skin on, which is silvery or dark blue, and salt and grill it, turning it brown. This preparation is called *yaki-shimo*.

TASTE & TEXTURE: Bonito tastes much like tuna. It can be rich in oil and fats like *toro,* or lean and meaty like *akami.* In the springtime, *katsuo* has less oil, so the taste is much like *akami* tuna. This fish gets richer in fats and oils in the fall months, and some say it is superior to tuna.

AVAILABILITY: *Katsuo* is said to be best in the spring and fall. They are a very popular item in Japan, native to the waters of the Pacific Ocean. Bonito is often available at sushi restaurants on the west coast of North America, but may be difficult to find on the east coast.

PRICE: $$

ADDITIONAL INFO: *Katsuo-dashi,* a bonito-based soup, is eaten daily by many Japanese people. *Katsuo-no-tataki* is also a very popular dish in which cooked bonito is served with chopped scallion, grated ginger, chopped garlic, and *ponzu* sauce.

A fishy-tasting yellowtail relative, katsuo *is often served with ginger and scallion to reduce the fishiness.*

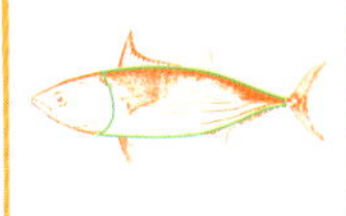

Anago (Sea Eel, Conger Eel)

Origin: *Anago* are long and skinny, like a snake, and can grow up to ten feet in length, although the younger and smaller *anago* are preferable for sushi. They like to bury themselves in the sands or hide in the rocks of Japanese coastal waters.

Distinguishing Characteristics: *Anago* is served cooked with *nitsume* (eel sauce) brushed over it. The color of this sushi can be white or light brown, but is usually dark brown because of the sauce.

Taste & Texture: The taste is not rich, but mellow and sweet. The texture is soft and delicate, almost melting in one's mouth.

Availability: *Anago* is available at sushi restaurants all year, but is best during the summer. In the early days of sushi, *anago* caught in Tokyo Bay were used as a *nimono neta* (cooked item) for *Edomae* sushi. Now, they are cultured in different parts of Asia and come in from China and Korea.

Price: $$

Additional Info: *Nitsume* is a very popular ingredient in Japanese cuisine, and many sushi chefs make their own. When a sushi chef receives a delivery of *anago*, he boils a number of them whole in a pot. To make *nitsume,* he then removes the *anago,* adds his recipe of soy sauce and sugar to the stock, and reduces the broth until it is thick and sticky.

穴子

WHITE MEAT

WARM NITSUME

SHARI

SKIN-SIDE DOWN

Chefs serve the meat below the bellybutton facing up, and the meat above the bellybutton facing down.

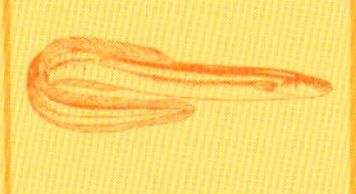

Ankimo (Monkfish Liver)

ORIGIN: *Ankimo* is a very unique sushi item because the meat of the fish from which it is taken is not used for sushi. Once the liver is removed, monkfish are served steamed or boiled. In Japan, the meat of the fish is usually used for a *nabe* (hot pot).

DISTINGUISHING CHARACTERISTICS: Tan, orange, or gray in color, the shape of *ankimo* will differ with the size of the fish from which the liver is taken. It is generally served as a *gunkan-maki*, or "battleship sushi."

TASTE & TEXTURE: *Ankimo* has the flavor and creaminess of fish pâté.

AVAILABILITY: *Ankimo*, very popular in Japan, is widely available, but elsewhere it does not carry the same status and you are less likely to encounter it. Monkfish is readily available from fish suppliers, so if you don't see *ankimo* on the menu at your favorite *sushi-ya*, it doesn't hurt to ask the chef.

PRICE: $$$

ADDITIONAL INFO: Some people call monkfish meat the poor man's lobster, but its liver is a delicacy and it is sometimes used for foie gras. In Japan, *ankimo* is believed to give you stamina because it is so rich in oils.

鮟肝

SHISO LEAF
FOR DECORATION

DAIKON AND SCALLION
ACCENT THE FLAVOR

TAN
COLORING

ORANGE
COLORING

Gunkan-maki *are created by wrapping a* shari *base in* nori *with the ingredients on top.*

Unagi (Freshwater Eel)

Origin: The Shizuoka prefecture of Japan is popular for producing green tea and is home to Mount Fuji, but it's also known for *unagi*, particularly that from Hamanako. China and Korea also export cultivated *unagi*.

Distinguishing Characteristics: *Unagi* meat is a darker shade of brown than *anago,* and the skin is black to dark gray.

Taste & Texture: *Unagi* has a somewhat plain taste, like that of chicken but with a little bit of fishiness. The flavor is often described as "nutty." *Nigiri unagi* is served warm with *nitsume* over it, adding a barbecue flavor. *Unagi* is popular for the richness of its oils. It has a meaty texture but is nice and soft.

Availability: *Unagi* is the most popular and widely eaten eel in North America. It is available in most sushi restaurants.

Price: $$

Additional Info: In Japan, a popular way of having *unagi* is *kabayaki* (barbecue style). The Japanese believe eating freshwater eel gives one strength and stamina. November first is Japan's national *unagi* day. If you have never had sushi, this is one of the things to try.

鰻

The Japanese eat unagi *to counteract the effects of* natsu-bate *(heat exhaustion).*

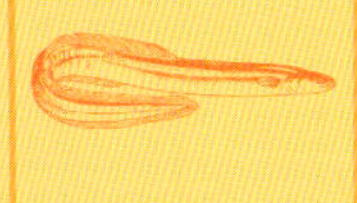

Sake (Salmon)

Origin: *Sake* are cold-water fish that swim in the open ocean and spawn in the fresh water of rivers. In Japan, *sake* are caught in the northern waters of Tohoku, in the northeastern part of the main island, and Hokkaido. The two main types of *sake* are Pacific and Atlantic, and while they are caught in the wild, the trend is toward farming these fish for food.

Distinguishing Characteristics: *Sake* meat is recognizable by its bright orange color and the white stripes created by the fat. The brighter the meat, the fresher it is.

Taste & Texture: Salmon has a very unique, pleasant fish taste. Its texture is soft and mild, and almost melting, depending on the cut and the amounts of fat and oil.

Availability: *Sake* are said to be best in the fall months, but are so popular that they are cultured and are always available at most sushi restaurants.

Price: $$

Additional Info: Some of the best-tasting salmon is caught once a year on Alaska's Copper River when the fish are spawning. Copper River salmon are sold in the Pacific Northwest and sometimes make it to markets on the east coast of the U. S. and Canada. The taste experience of this fish is indescribably delicious.

鮭

Those who like sake will often request pieces cut from the belly because they are rich in oils.

Ika (Squid, Cuttlefish)

Origin: There are more than 450 kinds of *ika* all over the world, and the name varies depending on the size and shape of the squid. The whole squid—legs, body, ears (the fins on the head), and sometimes even the guts—is used for sushi, but mainly the body is used.

Distinguishing Characteristics: Usually, *ika* is served raw. The color is white and appears translucent. When you get it as a *nimono* item, the skin of the *ika* becomes red and the meat a more solid white, and it is served with *nitsume*.

Taste & Texture: *Ika* tastes plain with a hint of sweetness, and it is chewy and a bit slimy. When it's cooked, it's less slimy but still chewy.

Availability: Although *ika* is not as popular outside of Japan as a sushi item, it is widely available year-round because there are so many different types of *ika* caught all over the world. Chances are your local *sushi-ya* serves *ika*.

Price: $$

Additional Info: *Ika* has a big role in the history of sushi. In the old days, *ika* was one of the main *nimono* items served as *Edomae,* or *nigiri,* sushi. Now that *ika* comes in from all over the world and is available year-round, it is almost always served raw.

CUTS TENDERIZE AND ORNAMENT THE MEAT

SHARI

SHISO ADDS A BIT OF COLOR AND FLAVOR

Chefs cut ika meat so that it is crunchy instead of chewy.

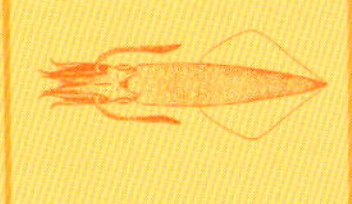

Uni (Sea Urchin), *Bafun Uni* (Green Urchin), *Murasaki Uni* (Purple Urchin)

Origin: *Uni* are found all over the world, but those from cold waters are the best. In Japan, the best *uni* is from Hokkaido. *Uni* are unique because only the ovary is used for sushi. To get to the ovary, the chef cracks open the shell, revealing a tangerine-like body. Then, he or she scoops out the ovary.

Distinguishing Characteristics: *Uni* may be different in color—yellow, green, purple, brown, or orange—depending on where they came from and their degree of maturity. Their shape resembles a tongue.

Taste & Texture: *Uni* tastes like the ocean, with a kind of sweet and salty flavor and a creamy texture.

Availability: *Uni* is a standard sushi item and is available most of the year. Nearly every sushi restaurant serves it.

Price: $$$$

Additional Info: Tsukiji, the big fish market in Tokyo, carries *uni* from all over the world. It's all available in one big room they call the *uni* room. Much like raw oysters in America, *uni* is a delicacy in Japan. Because the part one eats is the ovary, people in Japan regard *uni* as a giver of energy and stamina.

海胆

You may get more than one uni per piece of gunkan-maki. *This piece was made from two* uni.

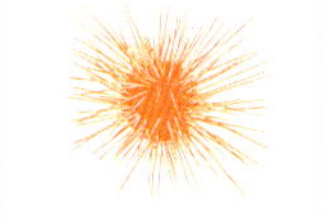

Tako (Octopus)

ORIGIN: Everyone presumably knows what an octopus looks like: a large head with eight legs. When alive, *tako* will change colors—from red to brown and sometimes even green—to adapt to their environment and camouflage themselves from predators. *Tako* is generally served steamed or boiled, but you might see it raw. *Tako* legs used for sushi can be as long as five feet, and generally these are shipped to restaurants already cooked and packaged. Only the legs are served as sushi.

DISTINGUISHING CHARACTERISTICS: *Tako* meat is white with red coloring on the skin when it is cooked. Depending on the cut, you may also see the *kyu ban* (tentacles).

TASTE & TEXTURE: *Tako* has a slightly oceanic flavor, with a subtle sweetness that comes out as you eat it. It is on the chewy side, but can be very tender, depending on the cut and the section of the leg. Make sure it's very fresh if you're having it raw.

AVAILABILITY: Like *ika, tako* is available in sushi restaurants almost everywhere.

PRICE: $$

ADDITIONAL INFO: *Tako* is called the "devil fish" and it's not very popular around the world, maybe because it has eight legs and resembles a spider. In Asia, *tako* is a delicacy enjoyed in many different ways.

RED COLORING FROM SKIN

NORI BELT

WHITE MEAT

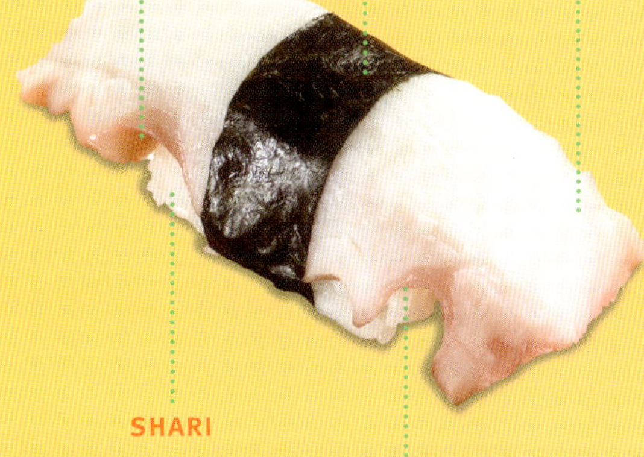

SHARI

"U" SHAPE FROM CIRCULAR TENTACLES

Tako is generally served cooked, but if you do have it raw, the meat should be moving when you eat it.

Inari-Zushi
(Tofu Pouches Filled with Rice)

ORIGIN: To make these, a chef deep-fries a tofu pouch, cooks it in soy sauce, and fills it with rice. *Inari-zushi* is a long-time favorite in Japan. It is a common food made at home and it is traditionally shared with others as a gesture of goodwill.

DISTINGUISHING CHARACTERISTICS: These are little brown pouches stuffed with rice. The size may vary depending on who makes them.

TASTE & TEXTURE: The taste of *inari-zushi* is a mixture of flavors. First, there is the sweet soy sauce with the taste of the deep-fried tofu, then the vinegar-seasoned sushi rice. All of this together creates the harmony of *inari-zushi*. It is very soft and mild in one's mouth.

AVAILABILITY: This should be available everywhere. If you don't see it on the menu, just ask for it, because any sushi chef will know of it.

PRICE: $

ADDITIONAL INFO: Oinari-san is the name of a Japanese god for which there are many shrines in Japan. Small statues of foxes protect these shrines, and it is said the favorite food of the foxes is *abura-age*—the deep-fried tofu pouches. The name *inari-zushi* is taken from Oinari-san and the practice of leaving food at the shrine as an offering to bring one good luck and safe passage.

Inari-zushi *is an excellent way to introduce children to sushi because it is sweet.*

Tamago (*Eggs and Fish Roe*) *Different Types of Eggs and Their Role in Sushi*

Tamago—sushi omelet—is one of the basic items in sushi and is used in literally every sushi restaurant in the world. Fish eggs, or roe, are also used in every sushi restaurant in some form or another. In Japan, roe is very popular, and a wide variety, from various fish, are available. Elsewhere in the sushi world, roe is less popular, but those who enjoy sushi usually experiment with and come to enjoy eating roe just as the Japanese do. Once you are ready for the full sushi experience, make sure you include roe as part of your adventuring.

玉子

Ikura (Salmon Roe)

Origin: Most of the *ikura* used for sushi in North America comes from Alaska, and sometimes from Canada. Much of it is exported to Japan.

Distinguishing Characteristics: These eggs are reddish-orange in color and very shiny, like little red jewels.

Presentation: These will most often be served as *gunkan-maki*, or "battleship sushi," in which the rice is wrapped with seaweed and topped with *ikura*.

Taste & Texture: The taste of *ikura* is salty. They are very soft and burst easily in the mouth. Because they are oily, they taste and feel very creamy.

Availability: Even though salmon spawn only once a year or less, their eggs are salted and frozen by a number of suppliers, so they are available year-round in most sushi restaurants.

Price: $$$

Additional Info: *Ikura* taken at the beginning of the salmon's spawning season are considered to be the best because the skin of the eggs is thin and that makes them gentle. Eggs taken at the end of the season have a thicker skin that may linger in the mouth. In Japan, *ikura* are popular among all age groups from the elderly to the very young, even babies.

イクラ

Ikura are often used as an additional ingredient because they add creaminess to any item.

Tamago (Sushi Omelet)

ORIGIN: *Tamago* is made using the same chicken eggs that are used commonly throughout the world. To prepare it, a chef will take a number of eggs and mix them with *dashi* (fish-based soup), salt, sugar, and a bit of sake, and cook them into a loaf.

DISTINGUISHING CHARACTERISTICS: *Tamago* is always yellow, and you will see it cut into rectangular pieces.

PRESENTATION: The most common way you will see *tamago* served is *nigiri*-style on top of rice with a nori belt. You may also see it used as an edible decoration for a larger dish, in rolls such as *futo-maki* (see page 152), used as a garnish, or served sashimi-style.

TASTE & TEXTURE: *Tamago* is a sweet, custardlike omelet. Every chef has his own recipe, so the flavors will differ slightly from place to place.

AVAILABILITY: This is a standard sushi item that is served everywhere.

PRICE: $

ADDITIONAL INFO: *Tamago* was traditionally made in the *atsu-yaki* style, in which ground shrimp is mixed into the egg to add thickness and richer taste. In Japan, it is said that trying *tamago* is a way of testing the chef's skill.

玉子

COOKED WITH SALT, SUGAR, SAKE, AND DASHI

NORI BELT

SHARI

This standard item is available to sushi restaurants pre-made, but true sushi chefs always make their own.

Tobbiko, Tobiuo-Noko

(Flying Fish Roe)

Origin: The *tobiuo* (flying fish) is not used for sushi itself, because the flavor is bland and lacks the richness of other sushi items. In Japan, flying fish are usually dried and cooked over an open flame. *Tobbiko,* however, are taken from the fish and prepared for sale to restaurants in half-pound boxes.

Distinguishing Characteristics: These are tiny eggs that look like caviar, but are red to orange in color. Green *wasabi tobbiko* is also produced by seafood sellers.

Presentation: Like *ikura,* these will be served in the *gunkan-maki* style, sometimes with a quail egg on top. They are also used in various rolls to add color.

Taste & Texture: *Tobbiko* are salty and crunchy. They burst in your mouth as you chew them. *Wasabi tobbiko* are spicy.

Availability: Our *tobbiko* come from Japan. These are available year-round at nearly every sushi restaurant.

Price: $$

Additional Info: *Tobbiko gunkan-maki* is often served with a quail egg (*uzura*) on top. To prepare it in this style, the chef will create a small pit in the *tobbiko* and place the *uzura* yolk in the center.

GREEN TOBBIKO GETS COLOR AND SPICINESS FROM SOAKING IN WASABI

TOBBIKO IS GENERALLY RED TO ORANGE

NORI

SHARI INSIDE

Some creative chefs use both colors of tobbiko *and a quail egg to create a* gunkan-maki *called a "stoplight."*

Kazunoko (Herring Roe)

Origin: Herring come from the cold waters of northern Japan, Alaska, Canada, and Norway. Their roe are held in a sack within the belly of the female fish, and these sacks are used for sushi.

Distinguishing Characteristics: The egg sack these tiny eggs come in is very firm. The roe are yellow and the sacks are usually four to five inches in length and are shaped like a finger.

Presentation: *Kazunoko* are usually served *nigiri*-style, sometimes topped with bonito flakes (*katsu-bushi*), although some people may enjoy these as a sashimi side dish with a bit of sake.

Taste & Texture: These are generally marinated in a salt-and-sake mixture, so you will taste these flavors first, but as you bite into *kazunoko,* a fishy flavor is released. The roe are very crunchy, and the sack is so firm that you can literally break it in half.

Availability: Winter is the best season to enjoy *kazunoko,* because the fish spawn in fall and winter. Generally you will see these more during the wintertime, and they will be available at many *sushi-ya* throughout the sushi world.

Price: $$$

Additional Info: In Japan, *kazunoko* is said to bring good fortune; it is often served at New Year's festivities to bring good luck for the coming year.

数の子

RIGID EGG SACK

BONITO FLAKES

LIGHT YELLOW EGGS

NORI BELT

SHARI

SHAPED LIKE A FINGER

Bonito flakes are shaved off of preserved and dried pieces of bonito that are nearly rock hard.

Tarako (Cod Roe, Pollock Roe)

ORIGIN: *Tarako* are the roe taken from cod or pollock. These roe come in a small sack shaped like a finger, usually between three to four inches long.

DISTINGUISHING CHARACTERISTICS: The color of these eggs ranges from pink to light red, and the sack is transparent.

PRESENTATION: These will most often be served *nigiri*-style, but the chef may also open the sack and scrape the eggs out to use in *maki-mono*.

TASTE & TEXTURE: As with other fish eggs, the flavor of *tarako* is salty, but they also have a slight fishy taste. They are soft and pasty in texture and can be a fun challenge to eat if you've never tried them before.

AVAILABILITY: This is not a popular item in North America, so you only see this at a *sushi-ya* every once in a while. In Asia, however, this is a very well-known sushi item you can get almost anywhere.

PRICE: $$

ADDITIONAL INFO: In Japan, *tarako* are used often in *onigiri* (wrapped rice balls) or *ochazuke* (tea over rice), which is a traditional dish. Even though the U. S. is the largest exporter of *tarako* to Asia, there is only a very small market for it here. Seattle, Washington, is the biggest port in the world for buying and selling *tarako*.

THOUSANDS OF TINY EGGS MAKE UP A PIECE OF SUSHI

SHARI

COLOR RANGES FROM PINK TO RED

Like ankimo *and* tobbiko, tarako *are served as sushi even though cod is not.*

Komochi Konbu, Kazunoko Konbu, Komochi Wakame (Herring Roe on Kelp and Seaweed)

Origin: During spawning, female herring lay their eggs on kelp leaves or seaweed, and the male herring come around and release their sperm onto the eggs, which causes the eggs to firm up and stick to the kelp or seaweed. The leaves are then cut away by harvesters, with the eggs intact, and this is what is served as *komochi konbu* or *wakame.*

Distinguishing Characteristics: *Komochi konbu* and *wakame* look like leaves with a blanket of yellow herring roe on both sides.

Presentation: The large leaves are cut into little pieces and served *nigiri*-style or as sashimi.

Taste & Texture: The taste is like the ocean, a bit salty with a slight bitterness in the flavor from the kelp or seaweed. The texture is crunchy.

Availability: In Japan, *komochi konbu* is a delicacy, but it is not popular in North America and is only served occasionally.

Price: $$$$

Additional Info: As with *kazunoko,* eating *komochi konbu* and *wakame* is said to bring good luck because the roe represent vitality and new life.

SEAWEED

BONITO FLAKES

NORI BELT

HERRING EGGS

SHARI

The highest quality komochi konbu *has a thick layer of eggs on both sides of the seaweed.*

Masago (Smelt Roe)

Origin: *Masago* are tiny eggs like *tobbiko,* and some *sushi-ya* may serve *masago* instead of *tobbiko.*

Distinguishing Characteristics: These look like bright orange caviar, just like *tobbiko.*

Presentation: *Masago* are served as a *gunkan-maki,* and are also used as decorative garnish for *maki-mono,* sashimi, and *nigiri-zushi.*

Taste & Texture: The flavor and feel of *masago* are just like *tobbiko*—they are virtually interchangeable.

Availability: *Masago* usually come from Japan, but there are other places around the world that produce them. Some of the *masago* available in the United States comes from Iceland. Since *masago* and *tobbiko* are virtually the same item used for the same things, many places will have one or the other.

Price: $$

Additional Info: Cod roe (*tarako*), shrimp roe (*ebiko*), or crab roe (*kaniko*), are also used as a substitute for *tobikko* or *masago.*

真子

This alternative to tobbiko *is often used as a garnish because it is stickier.*

Maki-Mono (Rolls)

The Most Popular and Common Rolls

Rolls have been around for a very long time in sushi, their origins dating back hundreds of years to the period when Kyoto was the political capital of Japan.

There are three styles of *maki-mono* served today. *Hoso-maki-zushi,* or thin roll sushi, is made by rolling *shari* and one or two ingredients in a half-sheet of nori. *Futo-maki-zushi,* or large roll sushi, uses a full sheet of nori, allowing a number of ingredients to be rolled together. *Ura-maki-zushi* is a style in which the half-sheet of nori is on the inside of the roll between the *shari* and the fish or other ingredients at the very center. These are referred to as "inside-out" rolls in English, and are the most popular style of roll served in North America. The ubiquitous California roll is made in this style.

Te-maki-zushi, or hand-rolled sushi, is probably the newest style of *maki-mono.* It started as a quick snack made by and for sushi chefs as they worked. To make it, they grab a half-sheet of nori, put a little sushi rice onto it, add some tuna or yellowtail or whatever other ingredients they want, quickly roll the seaweed into a cone in their hands, and eat it.

巻き物

Tekka-Maki (Tuna Roll)

ORIGIN: *Tekka-maki* is a basic item that has been around roughly two hundred years, since the Edo period.

INGREDIENTS: Nori, *shari*, wasabi, and *akami*. You can also request a roll made with *chutoro, toro,* or *otoro.*

PRESENTATION: *Tekka-maki* is commonly served as a *hoso-maki.* A small bit of wasabi is added between the rice and tuna. *Tekka-maki* appears dark green or black on the outside, and the raw tuna gives it a red center.

TASTE & TEXTURE: The taste of tuna combines excellently with rice and seaweed. None of the flavors are too strong, and the result is a simple roll that is great for dipping in soy sauce and is uncomplicated to the palate.

PRICE: $$

ADDITIONAL INFO: *Tekka-maki* gets its name from a gambling place called Tekka-Ba. Gamblers wanted something to eat without getting their hands messy, so the chefs created the simple but delicious tuna roll and named it after the gambling spot.

鉄火巻

Tekka-maki, *a simple roll, is a great item to use to introduce children to* maki-mono.

Kappa-Maki (Cucumber Roll)

Origin: *Kappa-maki* is another basic sushi item that has been around a long time. Traditionally these were made by rolling a whole thin Japanese cucumber into the center of a roll. Now you are likely to see this served with regular cucumber at the center. This roll is a popular one with kids and is a good introduction to sushi for people who are not used to raw fish.

Ingredients: Nori, *shari,* sesame seeds, wasabi, and cucumber.

Presentation: This is made as a *hoso-maki,* so it will be fairly thin. It's black on the outside and white on the inside, with a green center.

Taste & Texture: The taste is a mixture of seaweed, rice, and cucumber. You will also taste the sesame slightly, as it adds a bit of a smoky flavor. The texture is on the crunchy side because of the cucumber.

Price: $

Additional Info: *Kappa-maki* got its name from a fictional creature called Kappa that is said to live in swampy areas and is green with a flat top. *Kappa-maki,* when cut, has a flat, green top.

河童巻

Instead of large chunks of cucumber a chef might julienne a cucumber to enhance the texture and appearance of kappa maki.

Kampyo-Maki (Gourd Roll)

ORIGIN: *Kampyo* is a vegetable that has been used in Japan for a long time. It is sold dried in long strips. Chefs prepare it by softening it in water for several hours and then cooking it in a soy-based broth.

INGREDIENTS: Nori, *shari,* wasabi, and *kampyo.*

PRESENTATION: *Kampyo-maki* is a *hoso-maki.* The *kampyo* turns brown when it is cooked, so this roll is black on the outside, white on the inside, and has a brown center.

TASTE & TEXTURE: The taste of *kampyo-maki* is a pleasant, mellow, sweet soy flavor. When the gourd is cooked it softens, so this roll will feel very soft in your mouth.

PRICE: $

ADDITIONAL INFO: *Kampyo* is often used creatively in Japanese cooking—a chef might use it to hold things together, or cook strips of *kampyo* in various broths and then use the *kampyo* as multicolored garnish. It is also added to other rolls such as *futo-maki* (see page 152) or vegetarian rolls (see page 178).

Whereas many maki-mono *are cut into six or eight pieces,* kampyo-maki *is usually cut into four longer segments.*

California Roll

Origin: This sushi creation has a "Made in America" stamp on it. The avocado is a big product of California. Every U. S. sushi restaurant has its own version of the California roll.

Ingredients: Nori, *shari,* avocado, *kani,* and often sesame seeds, cucumber, and *tobbiko.*

Presentation: California rolls are served as an *ura-maki*, so they are white on the outside, though a chef might cover these in *tobbiko,* giving them an orange exterior. Inside this roll is crab, avocado, and perhaps some cucumber or another vegetable. *Tobbiko* is often included inside with the crab and avocado for color, and cucumber can be added to give the roll a little more texture and crunch.

Taste & Texture: The match of avocado with crab is excellent—creamy because of the avocado, sweet due to the crab flavor. The softness of the avocado and the meatiness of the crab are great together.

Price: $$

Additional Info: This item is the number-one seller in America and is an excellent item for people who are first learning about sushi.

Although the pictured roll has tobbiko *on the inside, chefs will often roll this in* roe, *coating the outside.*

Oshinko-Maki (Pickle Roll)

ORIGIN: *Oshinko-maki* generally uses pickled daikon radish. Farmers salt and dry the radish to soften it up, and then pickle it in sweet vinegar. *Oshinko* is used not only for *maki,* but also as a side dish in sushi.

INGREDIENTS: Nori, *shari,* wasabi, sesame seeds, and *oshinko*.

PRESENTATION: *Oshinko-maki* is made in the *hoso-maki* style. It's black on the outside and white on the inside. The center might be yellow or white, depending on the way the radish was pickled. At times other types of pickled vegetables are used, so the center of the roll might be orange, brown, or purple.

TASTE & TEXTURE: The taste is usually a bit salty with a slight sweetness. The pickle goes well with the rice and seaweed. The texture of *oshinko-maki* is slightly crunchy.

PRICE: $

ADDITIONAL INFO: This a traditional roll, particularly popular with Asian people because of the pickled radish. The Japanese eat pickled vegetables as a side dish at almost every meal. There are even specialty stores that sell all different types of pickled vegetables.

Yama-gobo, *or burdock root, is another popular pickled item that is used in* oshinko-maki.

Spicy Tuna Roll

Origin: This mixture of tuna, spices, and mayonnaise is an American creation owing to the use of mayonnaise in the United States. Chefs in Japan have begun serving this roll, and it is becoming popular there.

Ingredients: Every place has its own recipe for this roll. The basic ingredients are mayonnaise, soy sauce, and a chile oil called *rayu.* Small amounts of these items are mixed with the tuna, some sesame seeds, and a bit of chopped scallion. It is then rolled with *shari,* nori, and a little wasabi.

Presentation: This roll usually comes as an *ura-maki*, so it is white on the outside with the black line of the seaweed surrounding the reddish or white (if albacore is used) tuna mixture in the center.

Taste & Texture: The tuna and mayonnaise give this a creamy and tangy flavor, and the spiciness is generally fairly mild. This is a soft roll, although there may be a bit of a crunch if the chef used scallion in the tuna mixture.

Price: $$$

Additional Info: This is a great roll for anyone who loves tuna. You can also ask for spicy tuna as a *te-maki* or *hoso-maki.*

スパイス鮪巻

It is common for other types of fish to be served with this spicy sauce recipe.

Ume-Shiso-Maki (Sour Plum Paste with Beefsteak Leaf Roll)

ORIGIN: *Umeboshi* (sour plum paste) is made from plums that are picked and pickled before they ripen. To make *umeboshi,* pickled plums are soaked in brine with red *shiso* leaves, which gives them their pinkish color. The fruit is then processed to produce the paste. *Shiso* is the jagged leaf of the beefsteak plant, which is part of the mint and basil family.

INGREDIENTS: Nori, *shari, shiso,* and *umeboshi.*

PRESENTATION: The plum paste is pinkish-purple or sometimes orange in color, and the *shiso* is green. This is prepared in the *hoso-maki* style.

TASTE & TEXTURE: Since *umeboshi* and *shiso* are such important items in Japanese cuisine, tasting this roll is like tasting Japan. The sourness of the plum paste and the basil-like flavor of the beefsteak leaves can be an acquired taste, but this traditional soft and sour roll is quite excellent.

PRICE: $

ADDITIONAL INFO: Some people like to finish their meals with this roll in order to leave a refreshing taste in their mouths. *Umeboshi* is extremely popular in Japan as one of the main condiments in its cuisine. Many people eat it for breakfast.

SHISO LEAVES

SHARI

SESAME SEEDS

SOUR PLUM PASTE

NORI OUTSIDE

Chefs often serve this as the last item in a chef's choice or between courses as a palate cleanser.

Spider Roll

Origin: This, yet again, is a U. S. creation. It is likely that Japanese sushi chefs on the east coast of the United States originated this roll because the blue, or soft-shell, crab is native to that area.

Ingredients: Nori, *shari,* fried soft-shell crab legs, avocado, cucumber, sesame seeds, *tobbiko,* and *kaiware* (radish sprouts).

Presentation: The spider roll is an *ura-maki*, and usually comes with the crab legs sticking out of the roll to make it look like a spider. Often avocado and *tobbiko* are used in the center of this roll to add to the flavor and to enhance its appearance.

Taste & Texture: The flavor is like a mixture of a crab sandwich and crab salad with rice. The texture is on the crunchy side because the crab is deep-fried.

Price: $$$

Additional Info: Spider rolls have become a very standard item served in U. S. *sushi-ya*, and you may see this served with a number of different ingredients accompanying the crab legs in the center of it.

FRIED SOFT-SHELL CRAB LEGS

KAIWARE

TOBBIKO

AVOCADO

NORI

SESAME

SHARI OUTSIDE

CUCUMBER

Kaiware *are added to spider rolls because they enhance the presentation.*

Avocado-Maki (Avocado Roll)

Origin: Like the California roll, the avocado-*maki* is the result of sushi's growing popularity in the United States, and the availability of avocado to sushi chefs. This is a new take on the basic, traditional Japanese rolls in the *hoso-maki* style, such as *tekka-maki* and *kappa-maki*.

Ingredients: Nori, *shari,* sesame seeds, wasabi, and avocado.

Presentation: This roll is black on the outside and white on the inside, with a green center. The sesame seeds are mixed into the rice.

Taste & Texture: As *maki-mono* go, this roll is on the simple side. If you like avocado, you will like this roll, because avocado is the main flavor. Avocado-*maki* is soft and creamy.

Price: $

Additional Info: While avocado is widely used for sushi in North America and people here often think of it as a main ingredient in sushi, this fruit is used very little for sushi in Japan, although its popularity is starting to increase there.

アボカド巻き

This is a very healthy roll because avocado contains non-saturated or "good" fats.

Negi Hama-Maki

(Yellowtail with Scallion Roll)

ORIGIN: This roll is a Japanese invention. The style of mixing the fish and scallions together is used very widely in Japan. The flavor of the onions counteracts the fishy smell often present in richer fish such as yellowtail, allowing people to concentrate on the flavor of the fish.

INGREDIENTS: Nori, *shari*, wasabi, sesame seeds, scallions, and *hamachi*.

PRESENTATION: Usually this is served as an *ura-maki*, so it is white on the outside, and tan and green on the inside.

TASTE & TEXTURE: If you like *hamachi*, you will love this roll. The taste of the yellowtail is greatly enhanced by the addition of scallion for a great harmony of flavors.

PRICE: $$

ADDITIONAL INFO: Although you will often see scallion combined with *hamachi*, many other rich-flavored fish are served in this style. If you like it, try scallions with different fish such as *maguro* or *karei*.

ネギハマ巻

This roll is served in the hoso-maki *style at* sushi-ya *in Japan. The "inside out" style is not widely used there for any rolls.*

Futo-Maki (Large Roll, Fat Roll)

Origin: *Futo-maki,* one of the basic rolls, has been around for over two hundred years. It is very popular in Japan and is traditionally served at family functions or celebrations such as New Year's because it is so colorful and hearty.

Ingredients: Nori, *shari, tamago,* wasabi, *oboro* (sweet fish powder), and a number of cooked or pickled vegetables and sometimes fish.

Presentation: This roll is served with the seaweed on the outside, like a giant sushi burrito.

Taste & Texture: As rolls go, this is going to be one of the most complex combinations of flavors and textures, due to the number of ingredients. Ask the chef what goes into his *futo-maki.* The texture can be soft, chewy, or crunchy, depending on what is inside.

Price: $$$

Additional Info: There is a variation of the *futo-maki* style called *date-maki* or "dandy-rolls" due to their variety of colors and their showiness. *Date-maki* is essentially a *futo-maki* rolled in *tamago,* although the ingredients inside may vary slightly from those traditionally found in *futo-maki.* These rolls are not served often, but remain a popular treat for special occasions in Japan.

TAMAGO

SHARI

OBORO INSIDE

NORI OUTSIDE

PICKLED AND COOKED VEGETABLES

Oboro *is used in sushi only for* futo-maki. *Some people ask for* oboro *on the side and enjoy its sweet flavor.*

Una-Kyu-Maki
(Eel and Cucumber Roll)

ORIGIN: This traditional roll is a Japanese product that caters to the people there who really enjoy *unagi*.

INGREDIENTS: Nori, *shari*, wasabi, sesame seeds, *unagi*, and cucumber.

PRESENTATION: This roll is served inside out, with the rice on the outside and the *unagi* and cucumber inside. Often this will have *nitsume* served over the top of it, adding a brown color to the mix.

TASTE & TEXTURE: This roll has a very strong *unagi* flavor, especially when it's served with *nitsume*. The soft eel with the fresh, crunchy cucumber makes an excellent combination of textures.

PRICE: $$

ADDITIONAL INFO: *Una-kyu-maki* is a popular roll because the eel is cooked and the flavor is sweet, like a teriyaki flavor. I think this is a great roll for people who are scared to try anything new. I tell novice sushi eaters to try it because *unagi* tastes like chicken. They usually like it and begin to explore other sushi items.

うなぎ巻

Not traditionally used in this roll, chefs may choose to include avocado to add richness and creaminess.

Te-Maki (Hand Roll)

Origin: *Te-maki* was invented at the sushi counter by chefs who needed a quick meal that they could eat while they worked.

Ingredients: You can generally ask for any *hoso-maki* or *ura-maki* roll on the menu to be made in this style. Most chefs will also let you choose your own ingredients.

Presentation: *Te-maki* is shaped like a cone, with the different ingredients emerging from its top like colorful flowers from a bouquet.

Taste & Texture: The flavors will vary with the ingredients.

Price: Varies with ingredients.

Additional Info: When you get your hand roll, you should eat it right away before the seaweed gets moist from the rice and becomes chewy. *Te-maki* are very popular because they allow you to have a taste of the flavors of certain rolls without having to order the whole roll. If you want to try something you've never had, try it in the *te-maki* style. This will allow you to sample the flavors and judge your interest.

手巻き

CONE-SHAPED NORI

SHARI AND OTHER INGREDIENTS

ASK FOR ANY ROLL IN THIS STYLE OR CREATE YOUR OWN

A skilled sushi chef can often roll te-maki *using only one hand.*

Sake-Maki (Salmon Roll)

Origin: This is a traditionally Japanese preparation in which the fish is mixed with scallions to add a bit of kick to the flavor of the roll, but the use of *sake* is the result of sushi's popularity outside of Japan, in areas where salmon are caught fresh locally.

Ingredients: Nori, *shari, sake,* wasabi, scallions, sesame seeds, and cucumber.

Presentation: This is an *ura-maki* that looks like the *hinomaru*: the Japanese flag.

Taste & Texture: The texture is pleasant, and the taste changes depending on what kind of salmon is used. We use smoked salmon with some cucumber and scallion for a strong salmon flavor. Other sushi restaurants may use raw salmon for a mellower taste.

Price: $$

Additional Info: Another roll using *sake* that you may see is the "salmon skin roll," in which grilled salmon skin is the main ingredient. This may sound a bit unappealing, but it is actually very popular because salmon skin is quite tasty.

Sake is also great mixed with the same sauce as that on the spicy tuna roll (see page 142).

Creative Rolls

Examples of How Local Ingredients Have Inspired Chefs

One of the greatest things about sushi's growing popularity is the number of different ingredients available to chefs all over the world, and the variety of tastes and flavors that people from different areas of the globe enjoy. The result has been an escalation in the creativity of sushi chefs as they combine the tastes of the world into their cuisine. This creativity is perhaps most evident in the development of *maki-mono*.

In the following pages I've included a few of the creative rolls that have caught on, along with a few of the rolls I've created in my time as a chef. I encourage you to try the rolls that are particular to the *sushi-ya* you are visiting, so you can appreciate the artistry and skill of the chef.

独創的

Caterpillar Roll

Origin: As we have seen with other rolls using avocado, this was developed by sushi chefs in America. Avocado is still rare in Japan, but people are starting to enjoy it more and more.

Ingredients: The ingredients that make this a caterpillar roll are avocado and *nitsume*. What comes on the inside of the roll will vary depending on the chef. We use eel and cucumber on the inside of our caterpillar roll.

Presentation: This *ura-maki* roll resembles a caterpillar because of the green color of the avocado along with the brown of the *nitsume*.

Taste & Texture: The avocado and *nitsume* add a creamy texture and sweet flavor that make almost any roll better.

Price: $$$

Additional Info: Because of this roll's popularity in the U. S., most sushi chefs throughout the world will know how to make a caterpillar roll, even if it isn't on the menu. Ask your local chef about it if you don't see it.

キャタピラ巻

The insides of a caterpillar roll vary with the chef, as will the amount of creativity put into the appearance.

California Crunch

Origin: The "crunch" is a new fusion style of *maki-mono*. Many *sushi-ya* have some type of crunch roll. We took the popular California roll and made it a bit better by adding *temp-kasu* (tempura crumbs) to give it a crunch.

Ingredients: California roll plus tempura crumbs. Tempura crumbs are made from deep-fried tempura batter. Recipes for tempura batter will vary, but flour, cornstarch, eggs, baking powder, and water are the main ingredients, with spices added to enhance the flavor.

Presentation: The tempura crumbs on the outside give this roll a light brown to golden yellow color, with the green of avocado, the orange of *tobbiko,* and the milky color of crabmeat decorating the center.

Taste & Texture: The taste and texture of this roll are amazing! The *temp-kasu* enhance the flavor of the crab and make the roll crunch as you eat it.

Price: $$

Additional Info: This roll was a hit from the day it got on the menu. As a chef, sometimes you don't know if your new creations will sell, but when people like it enough to order another, you know it's good. You will see tempura vegetables or shrimp tempura used in a number of rolls these days, and you may also see entire rolls coated in tempura batter and deep-fried.

カルフォニヤ
クランチ

AVOCADO

CRAB

SESAME SEEDS

LIGHT BROWN
TEMPURA CRUMBS

This roll has the crunch of tempura but is healthier than many other tempura rolls because it uses less batter.

Yokozuna-Maki
(Grand Champion Roll)

Origin: I created this roll for myself while I was training for sumo. I used to have this enormous roll for dinner once a week.

Ingredients: Nori, *shari, tobikko,* wasabi, and six to eight different types of seafood.

Presentation: The *yokozuna* roll is made in the *futo-maki* style, with a whole sheet of seaweed enclosing the mass of ingredients. Inside this roll a variety of seafood is used, so the colors might be a mixture of red, white, orange, brown, and green. I also use *tobbiko* to add to the appearance.

Taste & Texture: The taste and texture of this roll are amazing. Some parts are soft, some chewy, all inside your mouth at once. The flavor of all of the different items together is very good, especially with a bit of soy.

Price: $$$

Additional Info: I named this roll after the ultimate goal of the sumo wrestler: to be the *yokozuna* (grand champion) at sumo tournaments.

横綱巻

When chefs create their signature rolls they think both in terms of taste and appearance.

Rainbow Roll

ORIGIN: This is a creative roll that originated in Japan. The many different types of fish used for the rainbow roll give it its name.

INGREDIENTS: Nori, *shari,* wasabi, and one or two other ingredients in the center of the roll, along with a variety of fish.

PRESENTATION: This *ura-maki* has a variety of fish wrapped over the outside of it. There is great beauty in the colorful arrangement of the fish, and how it's cut and presented. The ingredients on the inside are generally very simple, so the focus is on the fish.

TASTE & TEXTURE: The taste and texture change with each bite, as different fish combine with the filling of the roll.

PRICE: $$$

ADDITIONAL INFO: Beautiful to look at and great-tasting, this roll is popular nearly everywhere. The name might differ, depending on where you are. Don't hesitate to ask the chef if he or she serves a rainbow roll—everyone knows how to make this.

レンボー巻き

DIFFERENT TYPES OF FISH MAKE THIS ROLL A RAINBOW OF COLORS

SHARI OUTSIDE

INGREDIENTS ON THE INSIDE VARY; HERE YOU SEE CRAB AND AVOCADO

The key to creating a great rainbow roll is not the variety of fish, but the variety of colors.

Vegetarian Sushi

Delicious Items for the Veggie-Lover

One of the major reasons sushi has become so popular worldwide is that it is healthy. People who do not eat red meat enjoy sushi because it is based entirely on seafood. And even those who do not eat meat at all can find great vegetarian options at a *sushi-ya.*

This section covers some of the vegetarian items most commonly found, but certainly these will differ from restaurant to restaurant. A number of vegetarian options have also already been mentioned in previous sections, so be sure to look for *inari-zushi* (see page 112), *kappa-maki* (page 134), *kampyo-maki* (see page 136), *oshinko-maki* (see page 140), *ume-shiso-maki* (see page 144), and avocado-*maki* (see page 148) at your local *sushi-ya.*

ベジタリアン

Avocado Nigiri

Origin: Avocado *nigiri* was developed by an American sushi chef as a vegetarian item. Avocados are packed with vitamins, nutrients, and are extremely low in saturated fats. They are among the healthiest fruits you can eat, so their prominent role in sushi restaurants outside of Japan has added another very healthy aspect to this cuisine.

Ingredients: This is a simple sushi item—one or two slices of avocado over *shari* with a little nori belt.

Taste & Texture: The texture of the creamy avocado with the sushi rice is simple and delicious.

Price: $

Additional Info: Generally only sushi chefs outside Japan develop sushi items with vegetarians in mind. Not many people in Japan are vegetarian because the food is based on fish, so many of the health concerns arising in other cultures as a result of red meat consumption do not cause people to become vegetarians.

アポカド
ニギリ

A chef uses either one large chunk or two or three smaller slices of avocado to make this.

Kaiware-Nigiri (Radish Sprout Nigiri)

ORIGIN: *Kaiware daikon* are the sprouts of the daikon radish, and are a very basic and widely used ingredient in sushi, often included in a chef's selection of *nigiri*.

PRESENTATION: Daikon radish sprouts are white stems with little green leaves at the tips. Usually this sushi item will have a little band of nori wrapped around it to hold it together.

TASTE & TEXTURE: *Kaiwarina* has a crispy crunch from the fresh daikon sprouts, which are lightly flavored and a bit spicy.

PRICE: $

ADDITIONAL INFO: *Kaiware* is a great item to order at the very end of a sushi meal, or to have as a cleanser in between pieces of *nigiri* or sashimi. It is also added to a number of rolls such as Spider rolls (see page 146) and vegetarian rolls (see page 180). If you enjoy the spice of *kaiware* you might try asking the chef to include it in another type of roll to add a bit of kick.

This item is often included in a chef's choice as a palate cleanser.

Nattō-Maki (Fermented Soybean Roll)

ORIGIN: *Nattō* is a very Japanese item that is made by fermenting soybeans with bacteria. It is packaged and sold widely in food stores in Japan, where it is often eaten over rice or mixed with a raw egg for breakfast. Other popular *nattō* dishes are *nattō miso* soup and *nattō tempura.*

INGREDIENTS: Nori, *shari*, wasabi, scallions, and *nattō.*

PRESENTATION: *Nattō-maki* is served in the *hoso-maki* style, with the light brown-colored *nattō* at the center.

TASTE & TEXTURE: The texture is slimy and the taste is an acquired one. If you're looking for something healthy, this is it, but I would not suggest this to someone who is just starting to eat sushi—*nattō-maki* has the potential to turn them off sushi completely. Often a chef will add sugar to *nattō* to sweeten it and make it easier to eat.

PRICE: $

ADDITIONAL INFO: The bacteria from the fermented soybean is said to be very good for you, so this is an excellent item for vegetarians. When *nattō* ferments, it gives off a very pungent smell. Those who like *nattō* grow to like this smell very much, but it is as off-putting as the flavor to people who don't know *nattō*. If you do develop a taste for it, it is also very good with fish in a roll.

People who like nattō *often ask for it to be added to other rolls.*

Vegetarian Roll

ORIGIN: This roll was created in America with vegetarians in mind.

INGREDIENTS: Vegetarian rolls can contain any variety of fresh or pickled veggies along with nori, *shari,* and wasabi. The ingredients included in the roll pictured here are *kaiware, kampyo,* carrot, *oshinko,* and cucumber.

PRESENTATION: This *ura-maki* looks like a salad rolled in *shari* and nori.

TASTE & TEXTURE: The taste is refreshing and the texture is both crunchy and soft, like a salad with rice.

PRICE: $

ADDITIONAL INFO: This roll is also very nice in the *te-maki* style—like a vegetable ice cream cone!

ベゲタリアン

RADISH SPROUTS

NORI

KAMPYO

CARROT

PICKLED DAIKON

SESAME SEEDS

CUCUMBER

SHARI OUTSIDE

Like spider rolls, veggie rolls are served with the ingredients bursting out of the roll, enhancing the appearance.

Other Sushi Dishes

Additional Preparations Commonly Found in a Sushi-Ya

In this section are a few traditional sushi preparations, while some of the following items allow the chef to choose the best and freshest ingredients of the day and present them to you. When you're not sure what to order, try a chef's choice plate.

Variety dishes involve a number of different ingredients and garnishes and offer the most visually pleasing sushi experience. The chef will always do his most creative work presenting these. Once you are ready to try anything, order one—you'll appreciate the artistry and variety of sushi at its absolute best.

盛合せ

Hako-Zushi, Oshi-Zushi
(Box Sushi)

ORIGIN: *Hako-zushi* is a style that has come a long way, originating as the first combination of fish and rice eaten together. *Hako-zushi* mimics the old method of preserving fish that the Chinese originated. The *Edomae* style of *nigiri-zushi* was developed from the principles of this preparation.

INGREDIENTS: *Shari* and any kind of fish.

PRESENTATION: *Oshi bako* (press boxes) are used to form this type of sushi. The fish is laid in the bottom of the box, and rice is added over the top of the fish. The chef then puts the lid on and presses it down to compact the fish and rice into a rectangular loaf that is removed and cut into smaller rectangular pieces.

TASTE & TEXTURE: This is the sushi in which you can taste the past. The flavor of the fish with the texture of the pressed rice is solid and pleasant.

PRICE: $$$

ADDITIONAL INFO: It is said that *oshi-zushi* was developed by rice merchants in Osaka, Japan.

There are usually six pieces in a portion of hako-zushi, *because of the size of the press box.*

Tekka Domburi (Tuna Bowl)

ORIGIN: *Tekka domburi* is from the *Edomae* sushi style. This dish is a very popular item in the U. S. as well as Japan.

INGREDIENTS: *Shari,* wasabi, *shiso, tamago,* and *akami.* Other garnishes such as cucumber or shredded nori may also be added.

PRESENTATION: This dish is a bowl of sushi rice with tuna arranged artistically over the top, and everything else adding color as a garnish. It may appear that the chef has made slices in each of the pieces of fish, but these are just the natural layers that exist in tuna, revealed by the chef through a technique of cutting the meat "against the grain."

TASTE & TEXTURE: This dish is for the tuna lovers. The tuna flavors and textures are the focus.

PRICE: $$$

ADDITIONAL INFO: You can order other *domburi* dishes, with whatever topping you'd like. For instance, *hamachi domburi* is a popular item. You may also see *tekka-hama domburi,* a mixture of tuna and yellowtail.

A chef will often arrange a piece of fish in a domburi *to look like a flower, as you see here.*

鉄火丼

Chirashi-Zushi
(Assorted Raw Fish over Rice)

ORIGIN: This is from the Edo period and is the result of the artistry of one of the Tokyo chefs.

INGREDIENTS: Assorted raw fish and *shari,* along with any number of garnishes such as *tamago, shiso,* or *gari.* The ingredients in this particular *chirashi-zushi* are *akami, karei, bincho, madai, ikura, ika, ebi, hokkigai, tako, suzuki, saba, kanpachi,* and *sake.*

PRESENTATION: The concept used by chefs when presenting this dish is to make it appear to be a small garden, with a bouquet of vibrant shapes and colors.

TASTE & TEXTURE: This is a great way to explore the many flavors and textures of different fish as if you were conducting a taste test.

PRICE: $$$-$$$$

ADDITIONAL INFO: *Chirashi* is a dish developed in the Edo period as a derivative of the Kansai-style preparation called *bara-zushi*, in which all the ingredients are cooked and mixed into the sushi rice, like a jumbalaya.

ちらし寿し

Chirashi *give the chef an opportunity to show the variety of fish available at the* sushi-ya.

Sashimi Moriawase
(Chef's Choice Sashimi Plate)

ORIGIN: This is another dish that was born out of the creativity of Japanese sushi chefs.

INGREDIENTS: As with other "chef's choice" plates, *sashimi moriawase* includes the freshest fish of the day presented with garnishes such as *shiso* or shredded *kaiware*, as well as wasabi and *gari*. Pictured in this selection are *suzuki, tai, sake, akami, mirugai, kanpachi,* and *saba.*

PRESENTATION: Various types of fish are sliced and arranged with a variety of garnishes, exhibiting a wide variety of colors and shapes. Generally these will come with three or four pieces of each fish used.

TASTE & TEXTURE: As with all of the "chef's choice" dishes, this is a great way to make sure that you are getting the freshest and best fish available.

PRICE: $$$

ADDITIONAL INFO: Often the chef will serve certain pieces of sashimi on *shiso* (perilla leaves). This plant from the mint family has a great flavor, and you will often see these leaves used for sushi. If you do get *shiso* with your *sashimi moriawase,* be sure to try one of the pieces of fish wrapped in a leaf.

Shiso leaves and grated daikon radish are often used to make a sashimi plate resemble a garden.

Sushi Moriawase
(Chef's Choice Sushi Plate)

ORIGIN: Serving a variety of *nigiri-zushi* arranged together is, again, an old Japanese style of presentation, but local ingredients and creativity ensure that no two *moriawase* are the same.

INGREDIENTS: This particular *sushi moriawase* includes *akami, suzuki, ebi, hotategai, hokkigai, madai, sake, bincho,* and *karei,* along with half of a California roll and half of a *kampyo-maki.*

PRESENTATION: This assortment of *nigiri-zushi* often comes with one full *maki-mono,* or halves of two types of roll. It will also often include a vegetarian *nigiri* item, or perhaps a piece of *tamago nigiri.*

TASTE & TEXTURE: This is a great dish for people who have not had the chance to try all different types of fish. The textures will vary from mild to chewy, depending on the fish. The tastes are all a little different also.

PRICE: $$$

ADDITIONAL INFO: It is not uncommon for people who order these dishes to do so as a way to sample what is best at a *sushi-ya* on a given day. Once they are finished, they will order more of what they liked.

SERVED WITH ONE FULL ROLL OR HALVES OF TWO ROLLS

GARI TO CLEANSE THE PALATE

WASABI

AN ASSORTMENT OF THE CHEF'S BEST NIGIRI

In Japan, one sushi moriawase *is traditionally only eight pieces of* nigiri *and one roll.*

Acknowledgments

I dedicate this book to my mother, Betty Etsuko Suetsugu, who passed in April of 2003. She really loved sushi—the last food she ate was tuna sushi. She was from Kyoto, where she learned to make *saba-zushi.* My first taste of sushi was from the *saba-zushi* she made.

To my father, George Sadao Suetsugu, I would like to say thanks for his love and support, and for providing the Japanese characters you see throughout this book. He is a master calligrapher.

To my brothers and sisters, thanks for the laughter and tears we share in life.

Special thanks to Leighton Armitage for his expertise, educational support, knowledge, and his friendship.

And last of all, thanks to the two people closest to me—my wife, Bing, who gives me all her loving support, and my daughter, Aiko, for being the inspiration of my life.

About the Author

Robert Suetsugu, a former sumo wrestler, studied the time-honored art of sushi in Tokyo under master chef Yoshio Takasaki, and perfected his skills in restaurants in Hokkaido, Japan, New York City, and Seattle. He is the proprietor of Sushiman, a Japanese restaurant he established in 1990 in Issaquah, a suburb of Seattle, Washington. He lives in the Seattle area with his wife and daughter.

Glossary: Definitions and Pronunciations of the Japanese Words Used In This Book

An understanding of the sounds of Japanese vowels is the easy first step to correct pronunciation:

A= ah
I= ee
U= oo
E= eh
O= oh

A

Aji: (ah-jee) horse mackerel
Ajino tataki: (ah-jee-NO tah-tah-KEE) a presentation using aji in which the meat is chopped into small pieces and arranged with ginger and scallions
Akagai: (ah-kah-GUY) red clam; also known as the ark shell
Akami: (ah-kah-MEE) red meat tuna
Ama ebi: (ah-MAH eh-BEE) sweet shrimp
Anago: (ah-nah-GO) sea or conger eel
An-kimo: (ahn-kee-MO) monkfish liver
Avocado-maki: (ah-vo-KAH-do mah-KEE) avocado roll
Awabi: (ah-wah-BEE) shellfish with only the top shell

B

Bafun uni: (bah-FOON oo-NEE) green urchin
Bakagai: (bah-kah-GUY) technical name for aoyagi
Bincho: (been-CHO) albacore tuna
Botan ebi: (bo-TAN eh-BEE) spot prawn, the largest of the shrimp used for *ama ebi*
Buri: (boo-ree) yellowtail over ten pounds

C

Chirashi-zushi: (che-RAH-she) assorted raw fish served over rice
Chu-toro: (choo-TOW-ro) medium tuna

E

Ebi: (eh-BEE) common term for shrimp or prawn
Edomae: (eh-do-MY) sushi style with fresh fish served on rice; also known as Kanto-style
Engawa: (en-gah-WAH) the edge of a flatfish

F

Futo-maki: (foo-TOW-mah-KEE) large sushi roll with a combination of cooked and fresh vegetables and usually a piece of egg

G

Gari: (gah-ree) pickled ginger
Geso: (guess-so) squid tentacles
Gohan: (GO-hon) cooked rice

H

Hako-zushi: (hah-KO zoo-shee) sushi style formed with press boxes, also known as *oshi-zushi*
Hamachi: (hah-mah-CHEE) yellowtail, usually eight to ten pounds
Hikari-mono: (hik-ah-REE-mo-no) smaller fish that have silvery, shiny skin
Himo (HE-mo): thread-like filament that connects a clam's body to its shell
Hirame: (hee-rah-MAY) sole or flounder
Hiramasa: (hee-RAH-mah-SAH) a yellowtail relative fished exclusively in the waters of Japan
Hokkigai: (ho-KEE-guy) surf clam
Hokoku aka ebi: (ho-ko-koo ah-KAH eh-BEE) northern red shrimp
Hon Maguro: (hone mah-goo-RO) bluefin tuna from the Atlantic Ocean
Hoso-maki: (ho-so-mah-KEE) thin roll
Hotategai: (ho-TAH-tay-GUY) scallop

I

Ika: (ee-KAH) squid or cuttlefish
Ikura: (ee-koo-rah) salmon eggs
Inada: (ee-nah-dah) yellowtail less than eight pounds
Inari sushi: (ee-nah-REE soo-shee) sushi using small, deep-fried pouches of tofu cooked in sweet soy sauce
Inari age: (ee-nah-REE ah-GEH) small, deep-fried pouches of tofu cooked in sweet soy sauce

K

Kabayaki: (kah-BAH-yah-KEE) barbecue style
Kai: (ky) general term for shellfish
Kaiware nigiri: (ky-wah-REH nee-gee-REE) radish sprout nigiri
Kajiki maguro: (kah-jee-KEE mah-goo-RO) swordfish
Kampyo-maki: (kamp-YO mah-KEE) gourd roll
Kani: (kah-NEE) crab
Kanpachi: (kan-pah-CHEE) amberjack
Kansai: (kan-SI) western region of Japan, where sushi originated
Kanto: (kan-TOW) eastern region of Japan, the common style of sushi
Kappa-maki: (kah-PAH-mah-KEE) cucumber roll
Karei: (kah-REH-ee) the general term for a flatfish with eyes on the right side of its head
Katsuo: (kat-SOO-o) bonito, a red meat fish related to tuna and mackerel
Katsu bushi (cot-sue boo-she): bonito flakes
Kasugo: (kah-SOO-go) young sea bream
Kazunoko: (kah-ZOO-no-KO) herring roe
Kihada maguro: (kee-HA-dah mah-goo-RO) yellowfin tuna
Kodai: (ko-die) baby snapper
Kohada: (ko-hah-DAH) gizzard shad

Kome: (ko-MAY) uncooked short grain rice
Komochi konbu: (ko-muh-chee kon-boo) herring eggs on kelp
Komochi wakame: (ko-muh-chee wah-kah-may) herring eggs on seaweed
Kuro maguro: (koo-ro mah-goo-ro) bluefin tuna from the Pacific Ocean
Kuruma ebi: (koo-roo-MAH eh-BEE) wheel shrimp or prawns
Kyu bon: (cue-BAHN) octopus tentacles

M

Madai: (mah-DIE) red sea bream, also called red snapper
Maguro: (mah-goo-RO) tuna
Maki-mono: (mah-KEE-mo-NO) rolled sushi
Masago: (mah-sah-go) smelt eggs
Matsubagani: (mat-soo-BAH-gah-nee) snow crab also known as zuwai gani
Mebachi Maguro: (meh-bah-CHEE mah-goo-RO) bigeye tuna
Minami Maguro: (mee-nah-MEE mah-goo-RO) southern tuna
Mirugai: (mee-roo-GUY) some of the largest clams used for sushi, including geoduck, horse neck clam, and giant clam
Murasaki uni: (moo-RAH-sah-KEE oo-nee) purple urchin

N

Nabe: (nah-BAY) hot pots
Natto-maki: (nah-tow-mah-kee) fermented soybean roll
Negi Hama-maki: (neh-GEE hah-MAH-mah-KEE) yellowtail with scallion roll
Nigiri-zushi: (nee-gee-REE zoo-SHE) hand-formed sushi
Nimono neta: (nee-mo-NO neh-TAH) a cooked item
Nori: (no-REE) dried seaweed

O

Oboro (oh-BOH-ro) fish powder
Odori ebi: (o-do-REE eh-BEE) kuruma ebi served alive, also known as "dancing shrimp"
Oshinko-maki: (o-SHEEN-ko-mah-KEE) pickle roll
Oshi bako (oh-SHE BAH-koh) press box
Otoro: (o-TOW-RO) very fatty tuna

R

Rayu: (rah-YOO) a type of chile oil

S

Sake: (sah-keh) salmon
Sake-maki: (sah-keh-mah-kee) salmon roll
Sashimi: (sah-shee-MEE) sliced raw fish or other seafood
Sashimi moriawase: (sah-shee-MEE mo-ree-AH-wah-SEH) chef's choice sashimi plate
Shakko: (shah-ko) mantis shrimp

Shima aji: (shee-MAH ah-jee) yellow jack fish, from the yellowtail family
Shime saba: (shee-meh sah-bah) pickled mackerel
Shiromi: (shee-ro-MEE) white meat fish, low in fat and light tasting
Shiso: (shee-so) perilla leaves
Shōyu: (sho-YOO) soy sauce
Su: (soo) rice vinegar
Sunomono: (soo-no-mo-no) salad with a vinaigrette sauce
Sushi moriawase: (soo-shee mo-ree-AH-wah-SEH) chef's choice sushi plate
Suzuki: (soo-zoo-KEE) sea bass

T
Tairagai: (tie-rah-GUY) razor clam
Tako: (tah-ko) octopus
Tamago: (tah-mah-go) sushi omelet made from chicken eggs
Taraba gani: (tah-rah-BAH gah-NEE) king crab
Tarako: (tah-rah-KO) eggs from cod or pollock
Tekka domburi: (teh-kah dom-boo-ree) tuna bowl
Tekka-maki: (teh-kah-mah-KEE) tuna roll
Te-maki: (teh-mah-KEE) hand-rolled sushi
Temp-kasu: (temp-kah-SOO) tempura crumbs
Tobikko: (tow-bee-KO) flying fish eggs, also known as tobiuo-noko
Tobiuo: (tow-BEE-yoo-O) flying fish
Torigai: (tow-ree-GUY) cockle clam
Toro: (tow-RO) fatty tuna

U
Ubagai: (oo-bah-guy) formal name for hokkigai
Uchikawa (oo-chi-KAH-wah): The often shiny layer just beneath the skin of fish
Ume-shiso-maki: (oo-MEH-shee-SO-mah-KEE) sour plum paste with beefsteak leaf roll
Unagi: (oo-nah-GEE) freshwater eel
Una-kyu-maki: (oo-nah-CUE-mah-KEE) eel-and-cucumber roll
Uni: (oo-nee) sea urchin
Ura-maki: (oo-RAH-mah-KEE) style of sushi roll in which a half-sheet of nori is on the inside of the roll between the fish and other ingredients

W
Wasabi: (wah-SAH-BEE) Japanese horseradish

Y
Yokozuna-maki: (yo-ko-ZOO-nah-mah-KEE) grand champion roll

Z
Zuke: (zoo-KAY) fish
Zuwai gani: (zoo-WAH-ee gah-NEE) snow crab, also known as matsubagai

Index (Japanese and English)

Southern California's

Best Beach Dives

BY DALE & KIM SHECKLER

PUBLISHED BY
SAINT BRENDAN CORP.
HOME OF CALIFORNIA DIVING news

First Edition 1986
Second Edition 1991 (2 printings)
Third Edition 2001 (2 printings)

Saint Brendan Corporation, P.O. Box 11231, Torrance, CA 90510
(310) 792-2333, FAX (310) 792-2336, website: www.saintbrendan.com

Printed in the USA by Rodgers & McDonald Graphics, Carson, CA

SPECIAL NOTE: The descriptions in this book are not scientific facts. The diver's final decisions and actions are their responsibility. The publishers and author of this book assume no responsibility of any mishap claimed to be a result of this book.

Special Thanks to:

Dive stores and dive clubs of Southern California
Greater Los Angeles Council of Divers (GLACD)
San Diego Council of Divers
Los Angeles Underwater Instructor's Association
Corky and Mary Lou Reed

Dedication:

To our boys, Christopher, Reed and Eric - May they always delight in the sea

ISBN 978-0-9628600-4-1

Contents

Introduction

Beach diving in Southern California can be rewarding, exciting and just plain fun. You simply need to know where to go. Much of the coastline along Southern California is neither fit nor fun to dive. Then again, many locations offer excellent diving in clear, life-filled waters and are very easy to reach. To repeat: You simply need to know where to go. That is the purpose of this book. It is meant to be a highly detailed dive guide of the best beach diving along the Southern California coastline.

The criteria for a beach location to be considered a "best beach dive" are simple: First, the dive spot must have consistently fair to good visibility. If it averages 10 to 15 feet or better year round, it is a good standard. Many locations along the coast will reach and exceed that standard from time to time, but if the water clarity is unpredictable, the dive spot does not qualify. If you are like most sport divers in California, water visibility need not be spectacular to have a good time, but you probably need a minimum of 10 feet to make the dive an enjoyable one. You will find, however, a few exceptions have been made.

Rockfish face

Secondly, there must be a wide variety of things to see and do at the dive spot. Fifty-foot visibility is great, but if there is nothing to see but sand, the dive can get boring quickly. While not all dive spots described in this book are open to hunting (some fall into marine or ecological preserves), the underwater photographer, explorer, or general sightseer will enjoy most of them.

Almost all of the dive spots that have been reviewed are within 100 to 200 yards off shore; many are very close to the water's edge. Long swims are not necessary to find excellent diving along the Southern California coastline; however, most of these dive spots do have good diving farther out for those who choose to dive the more remote reefs and locations.

Easy access to the shore is another important consideration, but a few exceptions have been made. Several of the locations along Palos Verdes, for example, have poor access but the diving off these spots is so good that their attention is warranted. At some of the locations, driving your car almost to water's edge is possible, where others require some climbing on steep but safe trails and stairs. Ultimately, only you can best judge your climbing ability.

Some final considerations in qualifying a shore location as a "best beach dive" can include crowds (or lack thereof), facilities, game, currents, average surf conditions, and how well the location is known. Several locations such as 1,000 Steps in Orange County and El Matador Beach in Los Angeles County are only known to the local divers, yet these spots offer superb diving that is

Giant spined star

well worth the drive from outside the area.

Almost all of these dive spots are worth the drive of a few hours. Many of the locations are very unusual. The vertical drops of La Jolla Canyon and the tall, life-covered pilings at Old Redondo Pier #3 are good examples of underwater terrain that is hard to find elsewhere along the coast.

Almost all known dive spots—good or bad—are listed in the introduction sections of each county. If you are a more advanced diver, many of the locations not described may be rewarding to you. With the large number of dive spots detailed in this book, you could dive a different location every other weekend for two years. You can explore several of the dive sites over and over again and never cover the same area twice.

There are some important things to remember about this book. As good as many of these spots are all are subject to local ocean and weather conditions. The dive spots listed in this book will, more often than not, have good diving, but all spots along the coast have their bad days. Water will be dirty after rain in most spots, and high surf will pound good dive spots along with the bad. To avoid wasted trips, always call the surf report or consult online surf reports before leaving home and have an alternate dive site in mind.

The final decision to make the dive or not is yours. KNOW YOUR LIMITATIONS! Many of the dive spots in this book are very easy to dive, but all require some degree of skill. Only you can judge your ability to deal with surf and local conditions.

Finally, this book is as accurate as possible. Underwater features are close approximates at best. Storms and time change the face of the coastline and ocean bottom constantly. Facilities can also change through additions or renovations. This is the most detailed dive guide of this type ever attempted, but keep the changes of time in mind.

Armed with this book you will have years of excellent beach diving ahead of you. Dive safe and enjoy!

Garibaldi

Octopus

Beach Diving Tips

Beach diving in Southern California can and should be an enjoyable experience, with some of the world's finest diving lying off this coastline. Of course, beach diving cannot beat the ease, convenience and quality of boat diving; however, beach diving does have some advantages over boat diving. It's cheap and you can dive when you want to and as long as you wish. To make beach diving just as enjoyable as boat diving, a few simple steps in preparation and diving techniques are needed, none of which requires a great deal of time or expense.

PREPARATION

Physical Conditioning

The first step in preparation should be awareness of your physical conditioning. It doesn't take a great deal of physical prowess to beach dive in Southern California, but you should be able to run around the block a couple of times without a problem. Most of the dive sites in this book are easy with short swims of 150 yards or less. The best way to get into shape for beach diving is some kind of aerobic exercise: running, cycling, dance, or preferably swimming. Try to do a lot of just plain hard kicking with fins. Emphasizing again, it does not take a lot of physical strength to make a beach dive in calm conditions, but you must have enough stamina to get you in and out of the water, get you to your offshore destination, and adequately handle any emergency that may arise. You are the final judge of your capabilities.

Gear

The next step of preparation takes place before ever leaving home. Check your gear thoroughly. Make sure mask and fin straps are in good condition and fit snugly. Weight belt buckles should secure the weight belt tightly as well. Check your regulator for ruptures in the mouthpiece (a frequently overlooked problem.) These are good points to check for any type of diving. For beach diving it's also important to check your tank fill and regulator function. Should you discover your tank is empty on the beach you will have no choice but to drag it back to the nearest dive store. All equipment checks should be done prior to the day of the planned dive to allow for enough time for a visit to the local dive store, if needed.

Extra pieces of gear to consider carrying on a beach dive include a flag and float, spare fresh water, towel, and a blanket, tarp or sheet to lay across the sand to place your gear.

Planning

Always check online or call the surf and/or dive report before leaving home. This will give you a general idea as to what to expect on arriving at the beach. If the surf is up at one beach, it may be almost nothing at another. Southern California diving has the great advantage of beaches that face several different directions. A fine example is when the southerly swells are hitting Laguna Beach and Malibu hard, the west-facing (Torrance and Redondo Beach) beaches in Santa Monica Bay are often well protected and fairly calm. Some of the "surf/dive" report sources are very complete, offering reports on visibility and surge conditions.

Keep your ears glued to weather reports for "Santa Ana" wind conditions. Santa Ana Winds blow from the northeast or, in other words, from the land out to sea. These winds blow dirty near shore waters out to sea to be replaced with cool, clean waters from the depths in an effect known as upwelling. The winds also tend to lay moderate surf down (an adverse effect, however, is to "wall up" large surf). The results of several days of Santa Ana Winds is usually flat, calm, clear waters—in short, excellent diving conditions with water visibility that can exceed 50 feet. Santa Ana Winds are the most common in late fall through winter.

Try to plan your dives in the mornings. The seas tend to be calmer this time of day and the crowds thinner. Also try to plan dives during periods of high or incoming tides. The incoming tides bring in the clear offshore water creating better visibility. The higher water may also help in getting by any shallow reef on your swim out to the dive site. The rule of diving with the high tide does have its exceptions. Some beaches are impassable during high tide, and the surf may be more difficult to deal with. Use these rules as a guideline, but don't revolve your dive plans around them.

Observation

Upon arrival at the beach, take the time to observe conditions carefully. Many dive sites offer high vantage points in which to observe ocean conditions below. Before ever putting on any gear, scout the dive site carefully. Bring a pair of binoculars, if available; they may reveal hidden reefs or kelp. Watch the surf carefully. Surf will often come in "sets" of three to eight big waves followed by periods of two to ten minutes of small waves. Time these sets. Wave set consistency is remarkable but not 100 percent accurate. Only dive if you can handle the largest wave you observe.

Look for rip currents. A rip current is a free ticket offshore if you use it properly. Personally, I do not like rips because they take dirty water near shore and deposit it on my dive site. But you do need to consider them even if you choose not to use them as they could affect your planned exit adversely. Some rocky coves have a "prevailing rip" that is generally predictable, usually out down the middle of the cove, but at other sites, such as sand beaches, the rips are unpredictable and can shift.

Another water current of possible concern is the longshore current. Waves rarely hit a beach head on. Waves hitting the beach at an angle will tend to drive the water mass along the beach in the surf zone and just a bit beyond. This needs to be considered as you could find yourself thrown off course in traversing a surf zone with a heavy longshore current.

Offshore oceanic type currents rarely affect coastal beach diving. There are, however, exceptions near points such as Point Dume and Point Vicente. Look at the way the kelp is laying or debris floating on the water; this is a good indication of currents.

Carefully check entry and exit points and always have an alternate. Also know your surrounding coastline well enough that, should the worst happen and getting back to your original cove or beach be impossible, you have in mind more protected spots as options, even if it means a swim of several hundred yards.

In choosing your entry points, consider making a rock entry as opposed to a sand beach entry; it may save a lot of swimming.

You will decide at this point, before you put on any dive gear, if this particular dive spot and present conditions are for you. KNOW YOUR LIMITATIONS! You must ask yourself, "Will I enjoy a dive here today?" If not, seek an alternate dive spot or activity. Struggling in conditions that are past your comfort level will not be fun, and at worst, may also be dangerous. A beach diver's best companion sport may be surfing.

Pre-Dive Preparation

Unless you have a long walk to the beach and plan to rest before entering the water, dress completely at the car, mask and fins excluded. If you don't, you will merely have to dress again on the beach, wasting time and energy. Complete dress-in at the car also assures that you have forgotten nothing before you make the sometimes long trek. Use caution in your descent to the beach. Even safe-looking stairs can be hazardous with a lot of extra gear on.

On the beach, once again scope out the conditions. Take a look at the slope of the beach and shape of the waves. With a steep beach slope, waves will build quickly and plunge hard. The surf zone will be narrower but the waves less forgiving. A gently sloping beach will have a wider surf zone; the waves will not be quite as powerful, but you may have to endure more waves. Again, assess your ability to dive this particular situation on this particular day. It's not too late to back out and go body surfing instead.

Water Entry

Carefully discuss again the dive plan with your buddy. Agree on entry and exit points, alternate exit point, etc. Check each other's gear thoroughly. Make sure air is on. Get all gear completely in place; that means fins on your feet and mask on your face. Without fins on, should a wave knock you down, you are without power and propulsion. The ONLY exception to this rule is if the surf is completely calm. Then and only then can you put fins on in the water. To go into the surf without fins on and mask on your face means almost certain loss of gear and maybe worse.

Always have all gear in place before entering the water. Assuming that you are properly weighted (neutral with all the air removed from your BCD), you will most likely want just a bit of air in your BC to make you slightly buoyant, although this is personal preference. You definitely do not want to have your BCD fully inflated. The drag through the surf would be tremendous and positive buoyancy would allow you to be tossed to and fro by the waves.

Whether you'll have your regulator in your mouth or your snorkel is again personal preference, but you need some kind of breathing aid. More cautious divers prefer the regulator (with air supply on, of course). If you choose a snorkel, have your regulator in your hand.

Time the wave "sets" again; also time the wave "interval." Waves will come in intervals of 5 to 20 seconds. You will want to enter the water between the "sets" and during the wave "interval." Properly done, it is not unusual to be able to get past a short surf zone without ever being touched by a wave.

In timing, enter the water at the end of a set, between waves. Fins, of course, prevent walking straight ahead, but a backward shuffle means you must turn your back to the sea. Instead, use a sideways shuffle. This allows you to turn your head to look at the incoming surf and, at the same time, brace yourself against a wave. In taking a wave, try to put one hand over your mask (fingers spread so you can see at least a little) and the other over your weight belt. These are the most likely items to be knocked loose on impact by a wave.

When entering the surf zone, waste no time. Do not stop to adjust gear or look back. You can turn and swim in as little as knee-deep water and swimming is definitely faster than shuffling. If you get knocked down, stay down and swim out. A wave's rush forward onto the beach is always matched by a flow back of water under the waves. Ducking under the waves not only avoids the force of the wave but also allows you to take advantage of this

Sea hare

outward flow. Again, get through the surf zone as quickly as possible. Swim out just past the surf, then rest.

The buddy system does not work well in the surf zone. Never hold hands. The best method I have seen and used is for one buddy to stand on the beach, fully dressed in and ready to go while the other traverses the surf zone. Should the buddy in the surf zone get into trouble, the buddy on the beach can drop their heavy gear and head on out to provide assistance. Once through the surf zone, the second buddy follows. Again, if the second buddy gets into trouble the first buddy can ditch their heavy gear beyond the surf zone and move in toward the beach to help the buddy in distress. The same kind of arrangement works well in reverse for exiting the water.

Water Exit

Exiting the water is a reverse of the above. Approach the seaward side of the surf zone as close as possible and wait there. Relax and catch your breath. To repeat, time the waves. Between wave sets and in the interval is the time to go for shore. Waste no time and don't stop. Again, if done properly, you may reach shore and never be touched by a wave. When you reach waist-deep water, stand up and back out the remainder of the way, keeping your eye on the surf. If you get knocked down or can't get up, stay down and crawl in.

Rock Surf Entry and Exit

Your may want to consider making a rock entry and/or exit. It can sometimes save a lot of swimming. With the proper conditions, a rock entry is nearly as simple as getting off a boat. This kind of entry does require training by an experienced instructor and an advanced class is highly recommended. Another recommended course is the 3Rs classes (Rocks, Reefs, and Rips). The trick with a rock surf entry is to find quick access to deep water. You will want to fall off a rock into three to four feet of water or deeper and quickly swim out. You can also find a surge channel between rocks. As a wave surges up, you drop into the water and let the receding water carry you out.

Horn shark

If you can jump from a vertical drop into six feet of water or more, try this. Getting out of the water is a bit more difficult and will require crawling usually with fins off. Needless to say, conditions have to be very calm for this kind of water entry and exit.

Nobody likes to get rolled over in the surf when beach diving. It is probably what keeps most people away from shore diving. It shouldn't. Key is planning, observation, and to go with the flow. Rather than fighting it, use the force of the ocean to take you where you want to go.

With a little experience, guidance, and by diving the best spots (that's what this book is all about), you will find yourself becoming an avid and regular beach diver. Why? Because beach diving is fun and enjoyable.

	VISIBILITY	PHOTOGRAPHY	GAME	FACILITIES	ACCESS	ENTRY	SNORKELING
SANTA BARBARA CO.							
Gaviota Beach	G	P	G	T/S/C	E	E	F
Tajiguas	G	G	F	N	E	E	G
Refugio	G	G	F	T/S/C	E	E	G
El Capitan	F	F	F	T/S/C	E	E	F
Isla Vista	F	P	G	N	M	M	P
Goleta Beach	P	P	F	T/S	E	E	F
Arroyo Burro State Beach	F	F	P	T	E	E	F
Mesa Lane	VG	F	G	N	D	E	G
Santa Cruz Boulevard	G	G	F	N	D	M	G
Leadbetter Beach	P	P	P	T/S	W	E	P
Biltmore Steps	F	G	F	N	E	E	G
VENTURA COUNTY							
Punta Gorda	P	P	F	N	E	D	P
Silver Strand	P	P	G	N	E	M	P
La Jennelle	G	G	F	N	E	D	F
Deer Creek Road	F	G	G	N	E	E	F
LOS ANGELES COUNTY							
Leo Carrillo/North Beach	F	F	F	T/S	E	M	F
Leo Carrillo/Sequit Point	G	G	G	T/S	E	E	G
El Matador State Beach	G	G	VG	T	D	E	F
Zuma	F	P	G	T/S	E	M	P
Point Dume	VG	G	G	T/S	E/D	E/D	P
Escondido Beach	P	P	F	N	E	E	P
Corral Beach	F	F	F	T	M	M	F
Malibu Road	F	F	F	N	M	E	F
Big Rock	F	F	F	N	E	M	F
Las Tunas	F	F	F	N	E	E	F
Gladstone's	P	P	F	T	E	E	F
Redondo Breakwater	F	F	G	N	M	D	F
Redondo Submarine Canyon	G	G	P	T/S	E	E	P
Old Redondo Pier #3	G	G	P	T/S	M	E	F
R.A.T. Beach Reefs	P	P	F	N	M	M	F
Malaga Cove	F	G	G	N	E	M	G
Haggerty's	G	F	G	N	VD	D	G
Flat Rock	G	G	VG	N	VD	D	G
Margate	G	G	G	N	VD	D	G
Christmas Tree Cove	VG	G	G	N	VD	D	G
Point Vicente Fishing Access	F	G	F	T	D	D	G
Terrenea Resort	G	G	F	N	M	M	G
White Point	F	G	P	T	E	E	G
Point Fermin West	P	P	F	T	E	D	P
Cabrillo Beach	P	P	P/R	T/S	E	E	P

	VISIBILITY	PHOTOGRAPHY	GAME	FACILITIES	ACCESS	ENTRY	SNORKELING
ORANGE COUNTY							
Newport Pier	F	G	P	T/S	E	E	F
Corona Del Mar Breakwater	F	G	F	T/S	E	E	G
Corona Del Mar, Inspiration Pt.	G	G	F	T/S	M	E	G
Little Corona	G	G	G	T/S	M	E	G
Reef Point	G	G	G	T/S	M	E	G
Seal Rocks/Crescent Bay	G	G	F	T/S	M	E	G
Deadman's Reef	G	G	F	T/S	M	E	P
Shaw's Cove	G	G	P	N	M	E	G
Fisherman's Cove	G	G	F	N	E	E	G
Diver's Cove	G	G	R	N	E	E	G
Picnic Beach	G	G	R	T/S	M	E	G
Rocky Beach	G	G	R	T/S	M	M	G
Main Beach	F	G	R	T/S	M	M	G
Cleo Street Wreck	F	G	F	N	M	M	P
Cress Street	F	G	G	N	E	M	G
Woods Cove	G	G	G	N	M	E	G
Moss Street	G	G	G	N	M	E	G
Montage Resort	G	G	F	T/S	E	E	F
Aliso Beach	F	F	G	T/S	E/M	M	F
1,000 Steps	F	F	G	T/S	D	M	G
Dana Point	F	F	P	T	M	M	F
SAN DIEGO COUNTY							
San Elijo	P	P	G	T/S/C	D	D	P
La Jolla Submarine Canyon	G	G	R	T/S	E	E	P
Marine Room	F	G	R	N	E	E	G
Goldfish Point	G	G	R	N	D	M	G
La Jolla Cove	G	G	R	T/S	M	E	G
Children's Pool	G	G	F	T/S	E	E	G
North Bird Rock	F	F	G	N	M	M	F
North Mission Beach Jetty	F	P	G	T/S	E	D	F

P: Poor
F: Fair
G: Good
VG: Very Good
R: Ecological Reserve, no game to be taken

E: Easy
M: Moderate
D: Difficult
VD: Very Difficult

N: None
T: Toilets
S: Showers
C: Camping

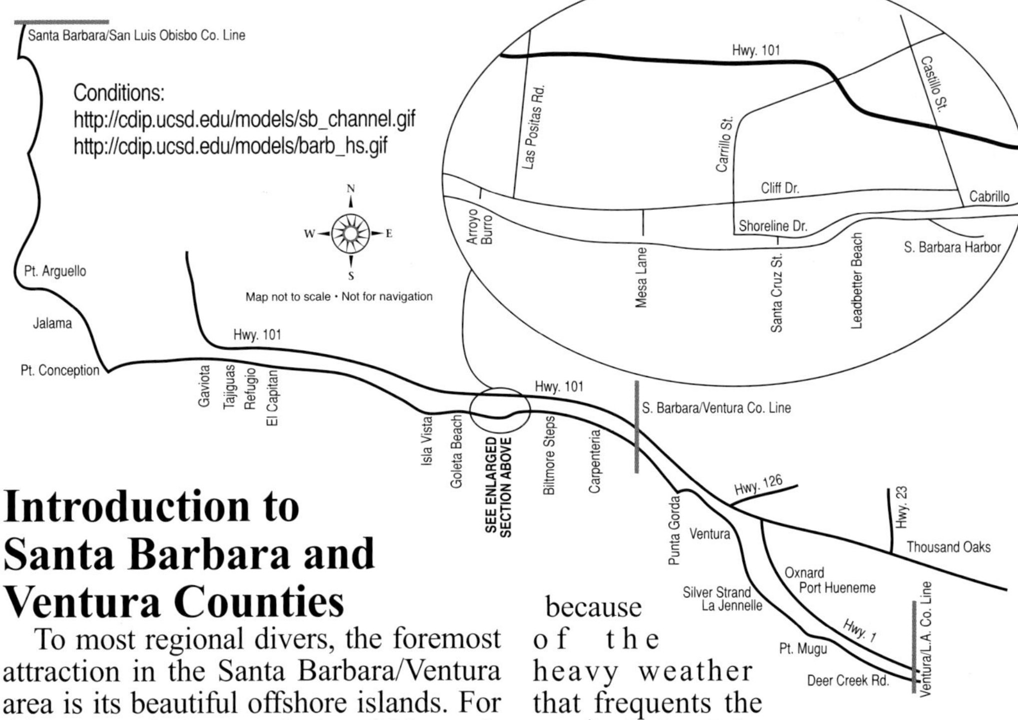

Introduction to Santa Barbara and Ventura Counties

To most regional divers, the foremost attraction in the Santa Barbara/Ventura area is its beautiful offshore islands. For this reason, the large majority of this area's shore-diving spots are somewhat ignored. These locations offer easy accessibility, superb diving conditions, plentiful game, and beautiful underwater scenery. If you have only a few hours to spare or you don't want to spend the money on a boat trip, these dive spots are worth looking into. If you aren't from the Santa Barbara/Ventura County area, you might consider exploring these spots. They are well worth the trip.

Diving the Santa Barbara County coastline can be quite different from coastal diving farther south. Perhaps the largest noticeable difference is in the types and varieties of sea life. Colors and sizes are more varied, and every crevice and rock seems to hold a surprise.

From the San Luis Obispo/Santa Barbara County line southward, around Point Arguello and Point Conception, there is little or no coastal access with the exception of Jalama Beach County Park, north of Point Conception. Point Conception has been called the "Cape Horn of the Pacific" because of the heavy weather that frequents the area including Jalama Beach. Around the "horn" of Point Conception is Gaviota Beach. Here the beach access is good but diving is over mostly sand. Halibut hunting, however, can be quite good here.

Kelp crab

Down the coast from Gaviota, the next good beach access is at Tajiguas. This small sandy cove offers easy entry, good diving and escape from crowds. Only a mile or so farther south is Refugio State Beach with excellent facilities and good diving on both sides of a sandy cove beach.

Continuing southward the diving runs into dirtier water. El Capitan State Beach, like Refugio, has excellent facilities but only average diving. The next nearest shore access is in the Isla Vista and Goleta Beach area, but water visibility is only fair and the water is sometimes covered with oil from a natural seepage from nearby Coal Oil Point.

Arroyo Burro State Beach has cleaner water and good access. Although facilities at Arroyo are very good, they are lacking at Mesa Lane and Santa Cruz Street. The beach diving at these sites is some of the best Santa Barbara County has to offer but you'll have to work for it as each of these points have many stairs. Farther toward the harbor, there are other access points but water becomes progressively less clean. Leadbetter Beach, adjacent to the harbor breakwater, has some interesting reefs and good facilities but poorer visibility.

South of Santa Barbara Harbor, diving spots become scarcer. Patches of kelp mark small reefs along the coast. Hidden away from sight of the heaviest beach crowds is the Biltmore Steps dive site with easy access and entry. More patch reefs and kelp can be found off Montecito where access is limited. Carpenteria Beach holds a larger reef but the best diving is a very long swim away. At the Ventura County line is Rincon Beach Park for diving in generally poor visibility.

Most of the diving from Rincon southward to the city of Ventura is in poor visibility. But possible dive spots in this area include Punta Gorda, offering diving with easy access on the pier that extends to the offshore artificial oil island. More oil piers to the south and offshore kelp present more diving opportunities.

Pierpoint Bay off the City of Ventura has little diving. The bottom is a gently sloping sand bottom and heavy surf is common. The sand beaches here and south of the harbor mouth offer diving for halibut and pismo clams only. Silver Strand beach between Channel Islands Harbor and Port Hueneme holds a very large pismo clam bed.

Proceeding southward after the mouth of Channel Islands Harbor is the mouth of Port Hueneme. Here lies the ill-fated

Copper rockfish

luxury ship *La Jenelle*. The wreck was filled in with rock and, lying at the edge of Hueneme Submarine Canyon.

South of Port Hueneme, access is limited and diving is mainly over sand until reaching Point Mugu. From Point Mugu, there are spotty offshore reefs, many of which are long swims. The one exception is at Deer Creek Road. Access here is easy and the kelp comes within 30 yards of shore.

Just before the Los Angeles County line and the Malibu area is another close-in reef near the intersection of Yerba Buena Road. However, this reef is more exposed to surf than the Deer Creek Road location and subject to heavy surge and thus many surfers.

A short distance down the road is Harrison's (County Line) Reef. Lying 300 yards offshore from the blue-roofed apartment buildings, a dive here is only for the good swimmer.

Gaviota Beach

Spring and early summer is the season when tasty halibut or "flatties" move into shallow waters. For shore divers, the trick is not so much to find that secret spot, but rather to find the spot with less diver traffic. Gaviota might just be that spot. And Gaviota offers access to rarely visited dive sites just up the coast.

Leaving Santa Barbara, traveling north on 101, the highway follows along the coast, approaching ever closer to the bluffs as the mountains increasingly crowd the ocean. There are the great dives at El Capitan and Refugio State Beaches and Tajiguas, but after those sites, access to the sea becomes difficult, down steep bluffs with no trails. Then the mountains finally crowd the ocean too close, and the highway must make a 90-degree turn inland, to the north and away from the sea. It is at this point you'll find the last in a string of state parks, Gaviota.

Human activity is not new to Gaviota. Remains of a Chumash Indian village have been found here. In 1542 the famous explorer Cabrillo visited and then again in 1769 by Portola. In his diary, one of his soldiers shot a seagull, or gaviota, hence the name.

Gaviota is now a state park and contains more than just five and one-half miles of beautiful coast. There is a pretty and lush canyon stream, hiking trails, and a hot spring. An improved campground is located just back from the beach and beside the stream.

The campground, however, is rarely as crowded as Refugio and El Capitan to the east. Gaviota is a bit barren and nearly always windy. But there is access to a quiet, secluded beach and because the winds are almost always offshore, the waters here are clear and often quite calm.

Directly out from the main beach is a sloping sand bottom. To the east there are sporadic low-lying reefs but nothing with any substance to harbor marine life, except for halibut that like to lie in wait for the schools of baitfish that frequent the shallows. This is your halibut hunting ground.

On the west side of the beach is a long pier with a launch hoist for small boats. Diving under or around the pier is prohibited. If the hoist is functioning, boaters can disconnect their trailered small boats from their vehicles at the base of the pier and wheel them out to the hoist for launching. Experienced boaters can launch small inflatable boats from the beach. From here it is only a short run to the west for remote reefs not often visited by divers. For the sightseer and photographer, this is your best bet, as directly off Gaviota has little to offer. Kelp will mark the larger reefs with beds extending far offshore. In these kelp forests you will find rockfish, cabezon, and sheephead, all of respectable size. There are also spotty kelp patches to the east but with less fish.

The kayaking diver can also use Gaviota as a jumping-off point for reefs to the east and west. A word of caution, however: winds here are usually strong and blow out to sea. Kayaks can be very difficult to control in a strong wind.

White-spotted rose anemone

Tajiguas

Diving and other leisure activities abound at the state beaches along the coast north of Santa Barbara. It's easy to understand why. The state beaches offer excellent facilities including restrooms, camping, showers, and food services. Unfortunately, large crowds often come with the comforts. If you want to escape the crowds and enjoy fine diving north of Santa Barbara, try Tajiguas.

Diving from the small sandy cove can be very rewarding. Rocky ledges lie directly off the beach and extend around the point to the west. The ledges begin in shallow water and extend into water over 40-feet deep running parallel to shore. Most of the rocks are low-lying, rising from the bottom three to five feet. What make them interesting are the sometimes large overhangs they create. Some of these slabs of rock stick out as much as five feet creating homes for many colorful types of marine life in the underside and tops of these ledges.

Invertebrates are the most common. Corynactis anemones are in several clumps with hues ranging from yellow to pink to lavender. Other types of anemones include the white-spotted rose anemone with its striking red body and tentacles or the

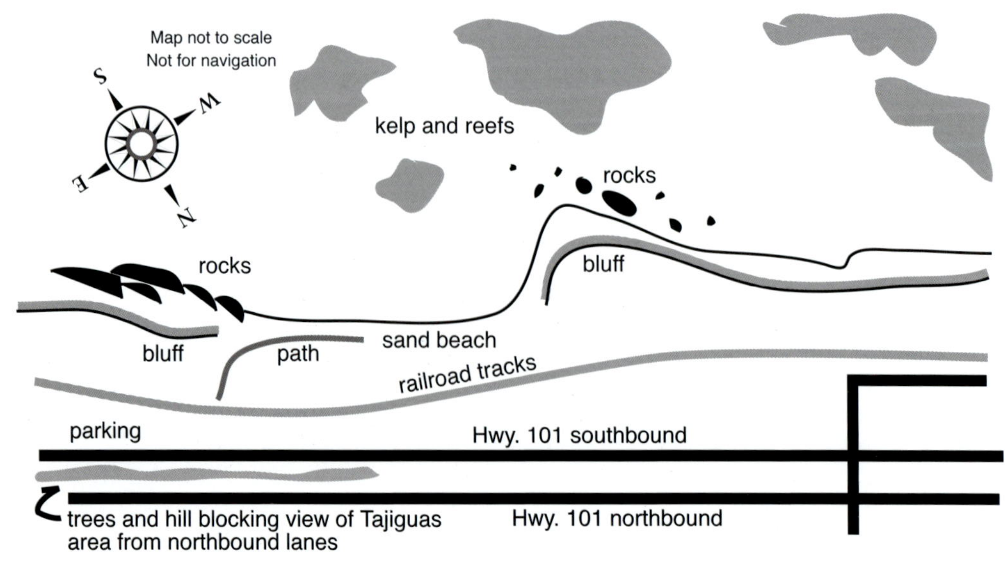

large rose anemone with white tentacles and deep red body. All of these make for excellent macro-photo material. Red and brown and California golden gorgonian are also present on the deeper reefs, but not in large numbers. The brilliant orange and blue Spanish shawl and white and gold-horned nudibranchs make for interesting observation. One of the more fun creatures for photography is the kelp crab often seen hanging from the kelp stalks.

Fish are a little sparse in the area, but various rockfish find cover under the ledges, and some game fish find cover in the kelp canopy.

Hunters will find little here. There are occasionally lobster present, but the area is usually well worked over. Scallops can be found on the deeper and less-accessible reefs.

Access to the beach is easy off the southbound side of Highway 101. Parking and access is not visible from the northbound lanes. If traveling on the northbound lanes, turn around two miles north of Refugio State Beach. There is parking alongside of the highway on a dirt area. Access to the beach is via a dirt trail across the railroad tracks. The dirt path is gentle and safe. There are no facilities on the beach or near the parking area.

The best diving and entry is on the west end (far end) of the beach. Surfers congregate at the east end. Although most of the beach is sand, there are cobblestones in the surf, particularly in the winter.

Water conditions for Tajiguas are usually good. Visibility averages 10 feet and is often cleaner than beaches to the south due to a common mild current.

There is also access farther west on the road that leads to the west side of the point. Access here is steeper and more treacherous but the swim to some of the outer kelp is shortened.

Refugio

Refugio Beach beckons the leisure seeker. Under swaying palm trees, this secluded beach offers peaceful picnic facilities, excellent camping areas and good diving.

Refugio Beach is a state park complete with facilities such as 85 campsites, restrooms, showers and food. One could come here and have a thoroughly enjoyable time without ever touching the water. But the water is why local divers make this a favorite spot.

Reefs and kelp lie off the beach only 50 yards out. The reefs offer a variety of terrain and sea life that will delight almost every diver. On the southeast end of the beach kelp beds grow on a rock bottom from 10 to 20 feet deep. In calm weather, this area can be excellent for snorkeling. Beyond the kelp is a series of jagged rock ledges running parallel to shore. These ledges rise 12 feet from the bottom in spots and create interesting

California spiny lobster

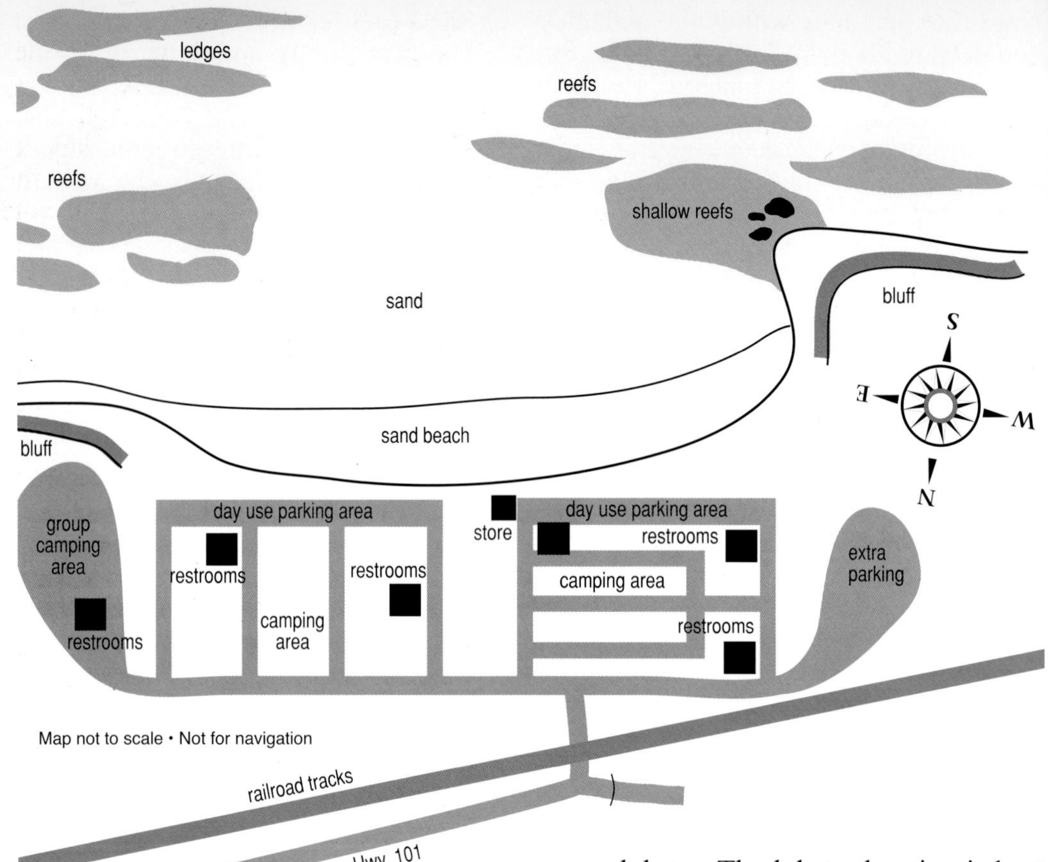

overhangs. These ridges extend far down the beach to the east.

On these reefs are a wide variety of invertebrates, some of which may not be readily recognized by the diver from the southern coastal waters. Nudibranchs are present in large numbers. Sea pansies dot the sand bottom and the odd sea porcupine or sea mouse can be found crawling about. Sea hares (sea slugs) are everywhere. Colorful anemones splash the reefs with color. In short, the rock ledges are a good area for the macro-photographer and sightseer.

In the kelp, only a few fish can be found. This is not a good area for spearfishing. Kelp bass in this area are skittish and difficult to approach. There are some rockfish but most are small. There are, however, some lobster. The lobster hunting is best down the beach, a quarter mile or more.

Off the point and around the corner to the west is a completely different diving area. Kelp is attached to low-lying reefs sometimes silted in with sand. The depths of these reefs are between 15 and 25 feet. In the sections that are large enough to support them, an occasional lobster can be found, but most are small. The long swim from the beach or hike to the point definitely requires a diver to be in good physical condition. Spearfishing at the reefs off the point is better with some barred sand bass, calicos and halibut in the nearby sand.

These and other nearby reefs can also be reached by inflatable boat or kayak, which can be easily launched from the beach in calm weather. Most of the parking is only a few gently sloping yards from the beach.

Although the beach is somewhat protected from the northwest, it is a good idea to call ahead to check conditions.

Refugio State Beach is approximately 25 miles north of Santa Barbara, just off Highway 101. Exit 101 on the ramp indicating Refugio Beach. There is a day-use and camping fee. A group site, overlooking the east reefs, is available. For camping reservations call 1-800-444-7275 or visit www.reserveamerica.com on the web. Proceed through the gate and, after passing under the railroad tracks, turn right for the northwest end of the beach and right for the southeast. There is ample parking close to water's edge.

In the summer, the burger stand is open for a between-dive snack. A bike path leads to El Capitan State Beach. The only disadvantage of this spot is summer crowds. On busy summer weekends, even the day use area fills up and you could be turned away. If camping is in your plans, get reservations early.

El Capitan State Beach

California coastal camping is such a delight. Waking up in the morning with the beach at my bedside is one of my favorite things to do. I wipe the sleep from my eyes, strap on my dive gear and commune with underwater nature. The coastline northwest of Santa Barbara has a few locations that fit the bill quite well.

Hands down, Refugio State Beach is the best for divers. Reefs on both sides of the cove are within easy beach-diving range. The beach is also a good place to launch inflatable boats or kayaks for exploring reefs up and down the coast. Camping, however, although quite pleasant, is often crowded with sites that are closely packed together. Such is the case at Refugio. And getting a campsite without a reservation is difficult.

El Capitan State Beach lies just to the southeast of Refugio. It is a much larger campground set inland slightly, up in the woods for a more pleasant, and private, camping experience. While not as nice as Refugio, the reefs here are quite divable.

A large point divides the park with a southwest facing beach and a cove that faces southeast (most commonly referred to as South Cove). There are a few small divable reefs off the point, the beach near the point, and in South Cove. The point and beach are open to the prevailing weather. Surf and surge are common, but for those wishing to brave the waves there are small scattered reefs with lobster. The reef structure is mostly boulders, some quite large. It is under the shelter of these large rocks that lobster can be found. Lobster seem to be a bit more abundant here than Refugio because there is less pressure from divers. The most productive reefs lie in 15 to 25 feet of water. Kelp sometimes marks the rocks but

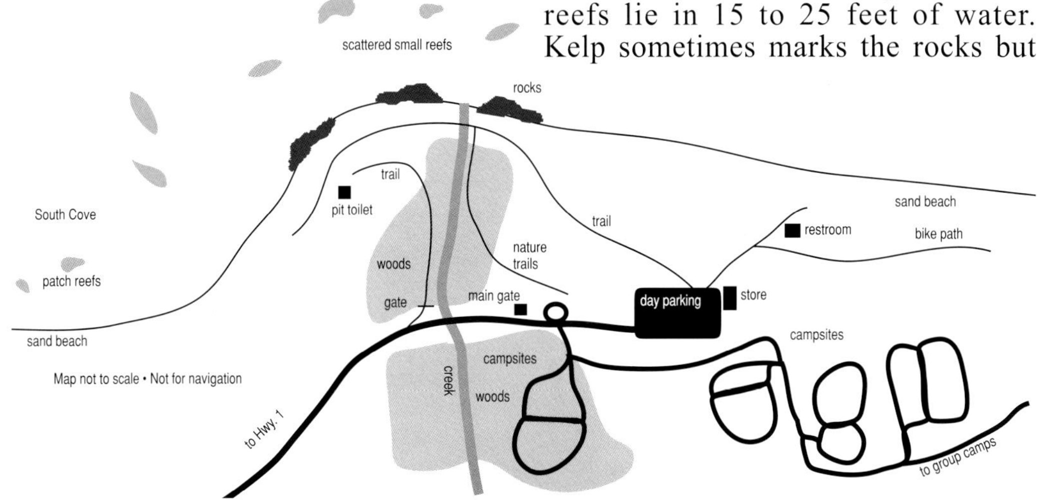

is often gone. Visibility is poor due to the common surge and runoff from the stream that empties into the seas near the point. Access to the beach and point is easiest from the day-use parking area.

South Cove is more protected but a bit more of a hike. There are scattered rock reefs off the inside of the point and also some within the cove itself. Much of the cove, however, is sand bottom that slopes gently to 25 feet deep 200 yards out. In the cove are clams, halibut, rays and abundant crabs. Look for the especially large kelp crabs grazing atop the shallow rocks.

The quickest and most enjoyable way to reach the South Cove is by way of the nature trail just of the loop next to the main gate. The trail winds about a quarter mile through beautiful woodland and along the stream. At the ocean, turn left, cross the stream and the cove will be ahead of you. (Because of the stream, do not dive here during or after a heavy rain.)

The facilities are excellent at El Capitan. There is plenty of day parking (there is a day-use fee), a small store, a bike path, restrooms, showers, and picnic areas with barbecues right on the beach. This is a shining example of the state park system at its best. Bring the family to camp and dive. Spend some time lounging on the beach, wading in the stream and hiking in the woods.

Isla Vista

One of the most extensive kelp forests off the coastline of Santa Barbara is in the section known as Isla Vista between Coal Oil Point and Goleta Point. This has always been a popular game dive and game life is abundant. Spearfishing is good for calico and barred sand bass, as well as halibut and, occasionally,

Hermit crab

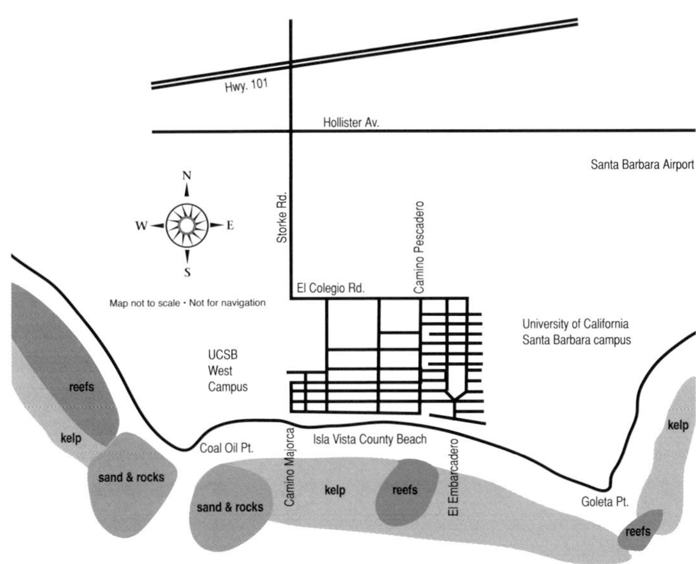

yellowtail and white sea bass.

Easy beach access can be found at (west to east) Camino Majorca, Camino Pescadero, and El Embarcadero. While the beach access is easy, this can be a tough beach dive. Surf is not usually large, but the beach is a gently sloping mixed sand and rock bottom. Depending on the tide, you'll have to swim a long way through often very thick kelp to get to decent diving waters. A 200-to 300-yard swim is not unusual. Even so, if you're a strong swimmer, this can be a rewarding dive.

If it is a good day, and you are comfortable in the thick kelp, the shallows close to shore can be a lot of fun. The reefs are low-lying ridges with an occasional overhang holding lobster hidden by abundant eelgrass and feather boa kelp.

Out about 200 yards, the water clears and bottom becomes broken reefs and boulders. The kelp thins, making it easier to move about. None of the reefs are particularly tall or large, but each is substantial enough to hold nudibranchs, urchins, stars and snails. This was once prime abalone hunting ground for the south coast. While they are few and far between nowadays, it is still possible to stumble across one here. Now protected south of San Francisco, do not disturb this noble but simple mollusk. Someday they may return in numbers at this place.

Between the rocks and reefs is where you will find the halibut. This is excellent

The Free Dive

Underwater it's quiet.
Ever feel the ends of kelp fronds
tickle your face as you glide
through a thick patch of kelp?
With no rush of air through my lungs,
my visit here is short.
The fish are brighter, closer. . .
and I hear them speak.

One says "Whoa! Where did you come from?
I didn't hear you coming!"

I can almost hear the light dancing
on the bottom.

The sea moves, but time doesn't.
I am a creature of the sea,
. . .only for a moment,
. . . only for eternity.

And it is only until eternity has passed
that I realize I must rise for air.

halibut hunting territory. Waters are not too deep, so a tank of air will last longer. Free-divers will enjoy hunting white sea bass, yellowtail, and calico bass here.

Closer to Coal Oil Point the bottom drops away a bit faster. The name of this spot is derived from natural oil seepage coming from the bluffs and even the sea floor. An oil sheen can often be seen on the surface of the water; it smells, and can even foul up gear. But don't worry, this is nature. There is no direct shore access to Coal Oil Point. Reaching this site requires either a long swim or long hike up the beach.

For Santa Barbara divers, Isla Vista offers numerous dives that can keep the underwater explorer busy, particularly spearfishers.

Goleta Beach

A poor visibility dive need not necessarily be a bad dive. Goleta Beach is one example. Water clarity here is never above 10 feet and is often as little as 5. Even so, there is an exceptional amount of marine life to see, it is an easy beach entry, and beachside facilities are great.

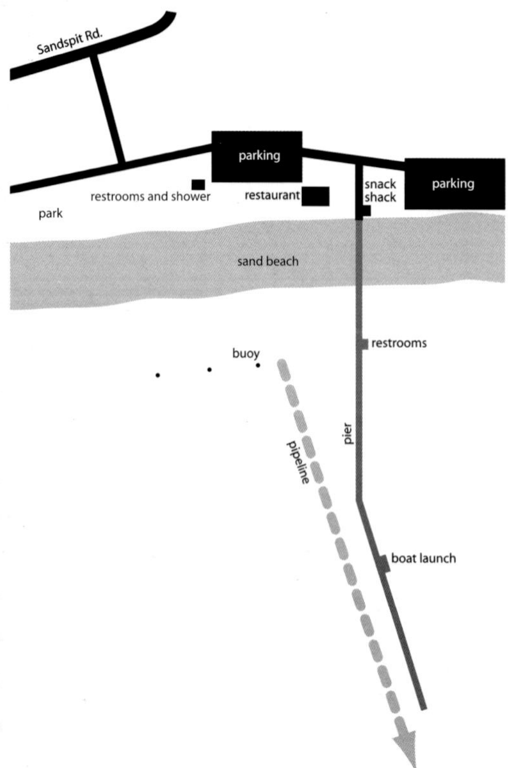

The underwater attraction here is the sewer outfall pipeline that parallels the pier. If you are concerned about health issues, the treated effluent is dumped about a mile offshore in 95 feet of water. There has been controversy that this effluent is not treated properly. If this bothers you, do not dive here.

The pipeline cannot be seen from shore as it buried under the sand. Just a short distance from the beach, however, this pipeline makes itself known by a thin veil of kelp. The length of the pipeline heading out to sea is covered by armor rock for protection. Because the kelp is easily visible from the pier take a short hike out along the pier before you dive to scope out the site. The pipeline is just to the west of the pier, directly out from the restaurant. The rocks start from the swimming buoys a short distance from the shoreline. Diving under the pier is prohibited.

Depths at this dive are from 10 feet to about 25 feet and you have to swim a long way to get to 25 feet. The structure of pipeline and covering rock rises about 10 feet above the bottom and is about 10 feet wide. Underwater navigation is a cinch; just follow the pipeline out and back again. Due to the close proximity to the pier, fishing line is common so bring a sharp knife or snips.

The rocks hold an abundance of marine life including octopus, giant keyhole limpets, large pisaster stars, nudibranchs, and sheep crabs. Of note to the hunters is a good population of lobster. Fish life includes small schools of perch, small lingcod and an occasional rockfish.

Water entry is amazingly simple and easy. Parking is free. Park on the west side of the restaurant and enter off and

sand beach just steps away. Sheltered from the prevailing winds and waves from the northwest and protection from south swells by the Channel Islands, surf here is almost always small.

Facilities include clean restrooms, showers and picnic area. The restaurant is mildly upscale, but there is a small snack shop at the base of the pier. A four-ton boat launch can be found at the end of the pier for those wanting to launch small vessels for excursions to offshore reefs to the east and west. To reach the beach, head south on Fairview Ave. Follow Fairview as it turns into Fowler and then as it curves into Moffit and then to Sandspit Road and turn toward the beach at the sign.

Arroyo Burro (a.k.a. Hendry's Beach)

Probably the best combination of good diving and easy access around the city of Santa Barbara is off Arroyo Burro Beach. This beach lies neatly tucked into a small canyon about four miles north of the Santa Barbara Harbor. The beach is quite pleasant with picnic tables, restrooms, and even a small restaurant and snack bar. These amenities, along with plenty of parking, can at times attract heavy crowds. The beach is also used often by local instructors for checkout dives.

The best diving lies to the southeast off South Point. Diving off this point will require some walking, but the beach is mainly sand, making the walk a pleasant one. Directly off the beach is mostly sand bottom. Offshore from South Point are

Urchins

rocky ledges beginning as close as 25 to 50 yards out in 10 to 15 feet of water.

In deeper water, the ledges can become very colorful with anemones, nudibranchs and other invertebrates. Fish life includes occasional garibaldi, lingcod, sheephead, calico bass, and halibut. Other game is scarce.

Divers frequently use this area as a jumping-off point to reach Mohawk Reef, a large reef structure beginning at South Point and extending south past the Mesa Lane beach area. The best sections of this reef are, however, a long swim away. Because of Mohawk Reef, water clarity is usually best to the south with visibility averaging 15 feet.

There is no use fee or parking fee but the parking can fill up fast on busy weekends.

Mesa Lane

To find beach diving with the best visibility off the city of Santa Barbara you will have to expend some energy. Because of an excellent reef structure, the diving off Mesa Lane is some of the best in the county, but until just a few years ago access to the diving here was limited to boats or mountain-goat divers who risked the steep, treacherous path that was once the only way to get to the beach. That path was replaced a several years ago by a large number of safe, but long, steep stairs.

From the top of the stairs, an excellent view is offered of the diving area below. The beach is sand and rocks with a number of different entry and exit points. Offshore are kelp beds marking the best reefs to the east and west. The large Mohawk Reef extends, in sections, up and down the coast.

Along the shore is a thin sand beach that can disappear in the winter or during high tides and surf. Small reefs begin within 25 to 50 yards of shore and extend in both directions along the coast. Kelp and more substantial reefs are 50 to 100 yards farther out.

All of the reefs in the area offer excellent underwater exploration. Small caves, huge rocks, large ledges

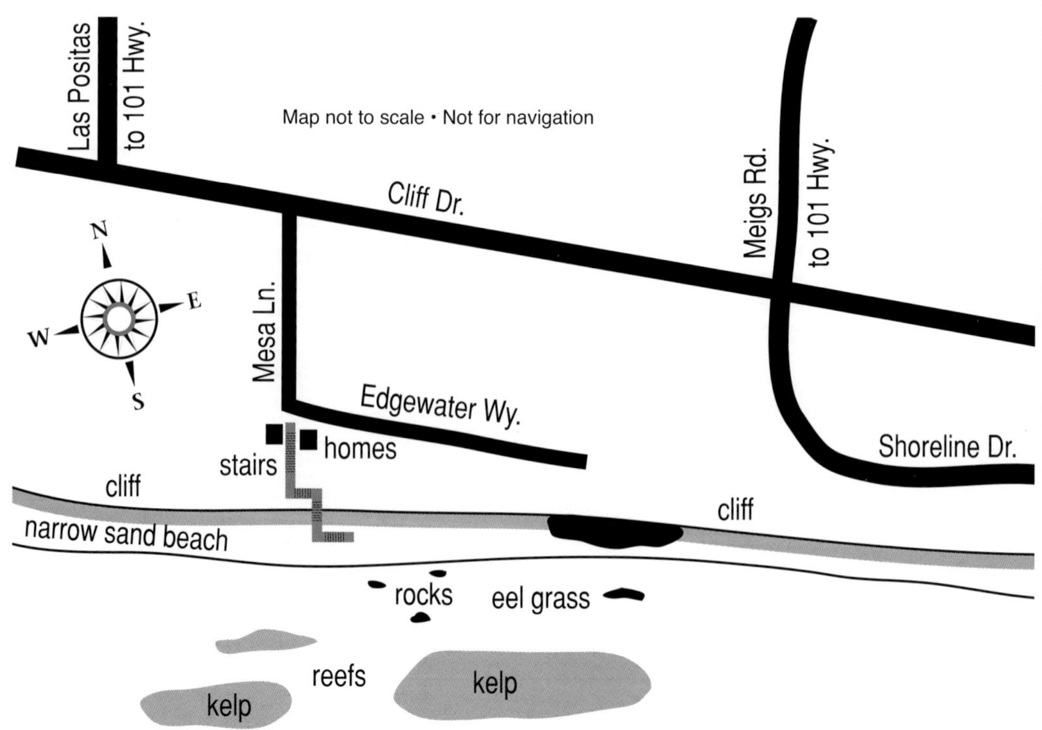

and overhangs are common. Depths on the reefs vary from 10 to 15 feet on top to 25 to 30 feet on the bottom. Just outside the kelp, depths reach 40 feet. On the rocks and under the kelp is a large variety of sea life to delight the photographer and sightseer. The usually excellent water clarity also helps with photography and exploring. Visibility averages 15 to 20 feet and can reach 35 feet under the right conditions.

Hunters will enjoy this location as well. Game fish such as lingcod, large sheephead, and calico bass are common. Scallops and lobster also can be found.

Access begins at the end of Mesa Lane. There are no facilities.

Santa Cruz Boulevard (a.k.a. 1,000 Steps)

Tall, lush stands of kelp are broken up with patches and stretches of ivory sand. The rocky ledges are dotted with sprigs of color. Plenty of blue and purple color is provided by the urchins, so thick in spots, that from a distance, their spines give the illusion of a shag carpet stretching out across the reef.

Here and there, splotches of nature's bright blanket seem to be placed ever so carefully in order to provide delightful dashes of color. Donating the color are a variety of sea stars, nudibranchs, and an occasional patch of anemones. Movement is provided by rockfish and thin señorita fish passing through the sunbeams like birds in a forest.

The walls of this magnificent room are the kelp. In places, solitary stands of kelp, regularly spaced from each other, appear as columns reaching for and supporting the amber translucent ceiling above. In reality the ceiling is floating and supporting the walls and columns. It is here, on clear, calm days, that the kelp forest in the shallow waters off Santa Cruz Boulevard in Santa Barbara provides one of the most beautiful coastal spots in Southern California.

Access to the beach is via 140 steps at the end of Santa Cruz Boulevard. Unfortunately, 140 steps can take on an ominous appearance to divers with 40 pounds of gear on their backs; consequently, the dive site has earned the nickname "1,000 steps." It's not as bad as it sounds, however, and very much worth it.

Limited parking can be found at the end of Santa Cruz Boulevard. There are no facilities here and private property abuts the stairway. Please be quiet and considerate of the residents. Public restrooms are available at Shoreline Park a block or so east on Shoreline Drive.

There is an excellent vantage point overlooking the kelp on the bluff. From there, ocean conditions can be assessed and a dive plan considered.

While overlooking the dive site, note the shallow reefs near the surf zone. Because of these rocks, this dive site is best during a high tide. Be aware, however, the beach here is very narrow and disappears entirely during an extreme high tide.

The shallow rocks are

covered with thick eelgrass that reaches to the surface. Swim through open channels on your way out to kelp to avoid entanglement.

From the beach, the bottom drops away at a gentle pace. Because this is a gently sloping bottom and a relatively shallow dive (10 - 25 feet deep), surf conditions can heavily affect the bottom. Surge is common. Call the local surf report phone number before heading for the beach. If the surf is three feet or larger, you'd be better off seeking out another deeper, more protected dive site.

But during calm days of little surf, particularly during the Santa Ana wind conditions, diving here can be superb. The Santa Anas are the winds that blow from the shore out to sea. They push the dirty surface water close to shore outward. Cool, clear deep waters move in to replace it. The result is low surf and visibility that can exceed 50 feet. The Santa Ana winds are most common during late fall and winter. During these conditions visibility at Santa Cruz Boulevard runs between 30 and 50 feet. During other times of small or calm surf, visibility averages about 15 to 20 feet.

Regardless of the water clarity, you will find a lot to explore in this kelp forest. The bottom is varied with plenty of rocks, boulders and sand. An occasional rocky spire rises from the bottom providing interesting overhangs and mini-walls covered with life. Sand channels break up the kelp, allowing sunlight to stream in here and there.

Hunting at this site is only fair. Spearfishers will do well stalking rockfish on the reef and calico bass up among the kelp fronds. Halibut are less abundant but still available. Gathering on the bottom is less productive. Although there are rock scallops and lobster, they are not abundant.

This is more of a site for sightseers and photographers. Photographers are often reluctant to carry their cameras on through the surf but, with proper precautions, a camera can be safely taken on beach dives. This dive site is good for both wide-angle and macro shots. The kelp and fish provide good backdrops and subject material for wide-angle work, while patches of corynactis anemones, octopus, nudibranchs, and other invertebrates make for excellent close-up photo material.

Tube anemone

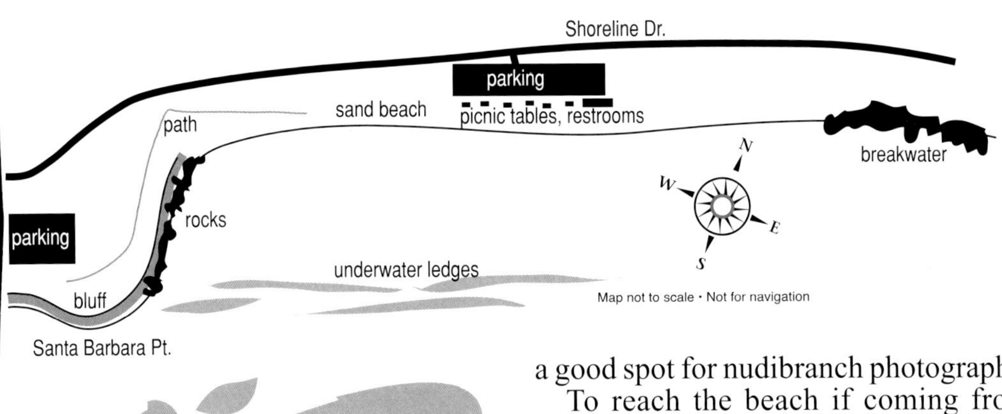

Leadbetter Beach

Leadbetter Beach in Santa Barbara is popular for sunbathers and vacationers in the summer and lends itself to some fair diving almost any time of year.

Extending from Santa Barbara Point southward, parallel to the beach, are a series of rocky ledges. The ledges lie in 20 to 30 feet of water. Making their home on the ledges are scallops, sponges, a variety of fish, and, to a lesser degree, lobster. Halibut can also be found in the sand.

Conditions can be easily observed from Shoreline Park on Santa Barbara Point to the north. From here the small reefs can sometimes be spotted by kelp rising to the surface. Approximately 200 to 300 yards out from shore, larger kelp beds can be spotted. These offer somewhat better diving but necessitate a long swim.

The facilities at the beach are top-notch with plenty of parking available. Picnic benches and barbecues are at your disposal. Adjacent to the parking area are restrooms and a burger stand.

The major setback of the spot is its usually poor visibility. Averaging five feet, the visibility improves slightly toward the point. On better days, 10 to 15 feet is not unusual.

For the photographer, there is colorful subject matter but poor visibility limits photography to close-ups at best. This is a good spot for nudibranch photography.

To reach the beach if coming from the south, exit at Cabrillo Blvd. from Highway 101. Cabrillo Blvd. will take you past the beautiful beaches and harbor area of Santa Barbara before turning into Shoreline Drive. The parking entrance to Leadbetter Beach lies 1/4 mile north of the harbor.

Biltmore Steps

Built in 1927, the Biltmore Hotel has long been an elegant landmark on the Santa Barbara landscape. Overlooking the Santa Barbara Channel and the Northern Channel Islands beyond, the Santa Barbara Biltmore Hotel is one of the premier hotels of Southern California due mainly to its excellent location. It is even somewhat secluded from much of usual Santa Barbara tourist crowd.

Directly in front of the hotel, just on the other side of Channel Drive, is a thin sand beach where hotel guests and honeymooners frequently stroll. But what many of them don't notice is the kelp bed lying offshore to the east.

The dive site at the Biltmore Hotel has easy access and good diving, but is not well known outside the local Santa Barbara diving community. While this is certainly not the most exciting dive site along the Santa Barbara coastline, its removal from the crowds of the main beaches makes it an attractive alternative to other more popular and crowded dive sites.

The best diving lies at the extreme east end of the beach, out from the historic Coral Casino (also owned by the hotel). There are two main reefs: an inner reef very close to shore and an outer kelp bed 100 to 200 yards out.

The sand beach here drops off quickly in depth to 15 feet. Because of this, the surf zone is narrow and the breakers are powerful plungers. This type of wave is good in that the surf zone is short and, with proper timing, it's easy to get out with little trouble. The bad news about plunging waves is they carry much more of a wallop—picking divers up and dropping them suddenly to the beach. Time your water entries and exit carefully to coincide with wave sets and intervals.

The inner reef begins just beyond the surf line. The bottom is strewn with various-sized boulders covered with a mixture of eelgrass and feather boa kelp. Eelgrass and feather boa kelp does not break as easily as giant kelp, so use caution in passage. There is some giant kelp on this inner reef, but its presence and abundance is dictated by water conditions and recent storms.

Among these marine plants are large schools of surfperch and opaleye. For the spearfishing enthusiast, both calico and sand bass are abundant and large. Halibut can sometimes be found in the sand adjacent to the reef. Other fish filling the waters around this inner reef include señoritas, kelpfish, and gobies.

Frankly, the rocks on this inner reef are not terribly exciting. For observing reef life, the outer kelp bed is much more interesting.

The outer kelp is a bit of a swim but worth it. Use caution on the swim out as boat traffic can occasionally be heavy. A suggested dive plan is to first descend on the inner reef after taking a compass heading for the outer kelp. Swim over to the outer kelp underwater. The sand flats between the two reefs are by no means dull. Marine life to be observed include thornback rays, halibut, sea pens, and sand stars. An occasional random boulder dots the sand flat.

The outer reef depths fall in the 20- to 25-foot range. Giant kelp is usually abundant and thick. Lucky divers may spot lobster among the crevices. Color is provided by small stands of golden gorgonian sea fans and bat stars. As with the inner reef, schools of perch, and some rather large opaleye, cruise the kelp trees.

Water conditions at this site are consistent but usually only fair. Visibility averages 10 to 15 feet. As the dive is relatively shallow, surf of three feet or over can stir up the bottom with surge. Plankton blooms can also affect visibility adversely. With the exception of the surge, currents are rare.

The easiest way to reach the somewhat hidden Biltmore is to exit the 101 Freeway at Olive Mill Road and head south to the beach. This road will curve around to the west becoming Channel Drive running parallel to the beach. The beach is long and narrow with the most interesting diving at the east end adjacent to the Coral Casino. Parking is limited along the street and free. A few steps lead to the beach.

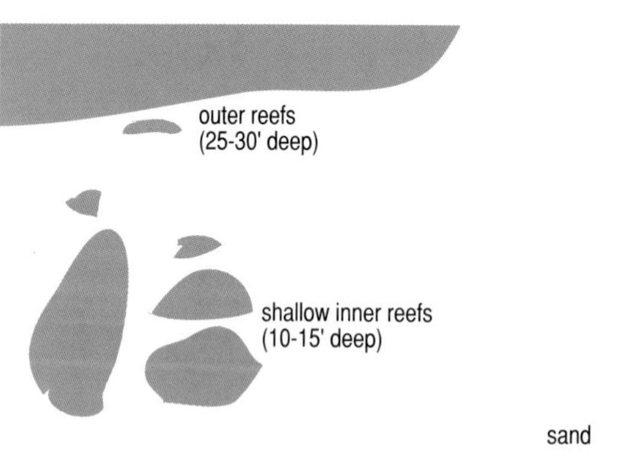

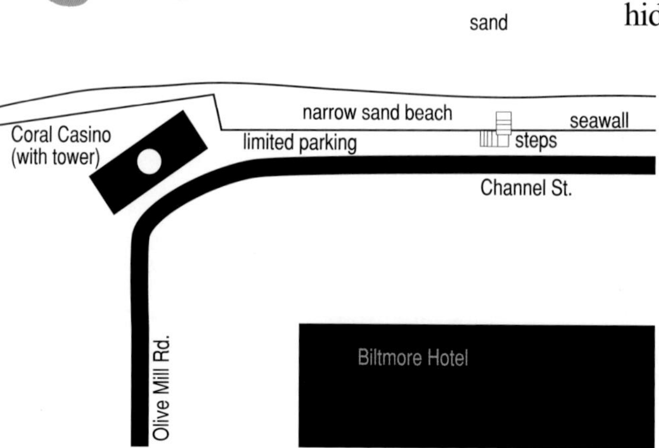

Discovering New Dive Sites

The California ocean is like a giant veil, hiding underwater sights from eyes that peer from the surface. A lot of divers have spent a great deal of their life exploring and discovering these unique features. Some of these special underwater features have become very popular dive sites. There are hundreds, if not thousands, of great known dive sites, up and down our coastline. Resources for learning about these dive sites include this book, magazines, and guidance from dive stores, dive boats and scuba instructors.

But what about those undiscovered dive sites? Are there any left? Speaking from over 30 years experience in exploring the California coastline, I can say without hesitation that there is a great deal left. Not a month goes by where I don't hear about or discover new and unique underwater locations. Discovering them is not as hard as you might think. There are relatively few underwater sites that have not seen the flick of a diver's fin, but there are a great deal of spots that are relatively unknown, not talked about, and rarely visited.

There's nothing quite as thrilling as making your own underwater discovery and finding a dive site you can call your own. There are a number of resources that will assist you in your underwater search.

Start with known popular dive sites. With this approach you will be dealing with, at least, some familiar territory including access, parking, facilities, and that sort of thing. The problem about most popular dive sites is that most people will head directly towards the most popular areas. At Shaw's Cove (Laguna Beach), for example, 90 percent of the divers visiting there immediately head for the area known as "The Crevice." While this underwater feature is spectacular in itself, there are a number of interesting reefs close by. As you explore popular, known destinations, head in the opposite direction of the other divers or at a 90-degree angle. Head out across the sand flat, beyond the popular underwater landmark. By venturing farther out, you will discover underwater terrain infrequently seen. Going out across the sand flats may result only in just an interesting dive, observing sand bottom marine life, but you might also come across an interesting small patch reef, a random rock, or even a small wreck. Many airplane wrecks have been discovered in this fashion. There are a number of airplane wrecks off of the popular dive sites of Laguna Beach, which were discovered by divers simply heading off into the sand plains. Some of these locations are closely guarded secrets.

Another way of discovering new dive sites is to take a little bit of extra time going to and from your favorite dive destinations. Carry binoculars. Stop along the bluffs overlooking the ocean, and peer down looking for random patches of kelp or other telltale signs of reefs that may lie below. Telltale signs include kelp, areas where incoming waves seem to be disturbed, or bird activity. Seabirds tend to congregate over reef areas where fish can be found. While this is not a very reliable clue, it can be combined with other clues to help you find an uncharted reef.

Speaking of charts, the charts prepared by the U.S. Geological Survey are another great resource. While they are wracked with errors and inaccuracies, and actually quite old in terms of their data, they can be interesting for browsing and planning and scheming at home.

But bar none, the best source for leads for rarely dived sites is scuttlebutt. Scuttlebutt is the chitchat that goes on amongst diving enthusiasts at dive clubs, dive stores, and consumer dive shows. The only thing divers seem to love as much as diving is talking about it, particularly talking about their discoveries. Often a lead has worked its way down through three or four people, has been twisted and even perverted, but sometimes those are the best and most fun to follow-up on. You go to a dive club meeting, and Joe will have heard from Sam who talked to Sue, who said they heard about a great lobster hole off this point to the left and to the south in about 45 feet of water. While it may take a few dives to discover that it was to the right and to the north, there is nothing quite as fun as when you come across that small rock in the middle of nowhere with lobsters all crammed around underneath it.

Another popular place for this kind of discussion and talk is around air fill stations at dive stores. Sometimes you just have to stand there and listen carefully. Other times you can be inquisitive. But be prepared for the fact that seasoned divers will be reluctant to give up cherished information.

And finally there is the internet. Boards are the best but just remember that you are not the only one reading this material. It is likely that hundreds of others are looking of this information about a "secret" dive site.

Diving is about exploration and discovery. With a bit of effort, persistence and some smarts, you, too, can be an explorer with a discovery under your belt.

Punta Gorda (a.k.a. Mussel Shoals)

Traveling divers passing along the coast between Ventura and Santa Barbara have probably seen the artificial oil island and long connecting pier to the shore at Punta Gorda (a.k.a. Mussel Shoals) and wondered if the area held good diving. The access to the shore is very good and crowds along the beach are small. The diving, however, is on the fair side.

The bottom is fine-grain sand and slopes gently to 30 feet deep about 300 yards out at the center of the pier. Under the pier, scattered rocks and boulders break up the sandy bottom.

On the pier pilings and rocks are mussels, ochre stars, and anemones. Variety and color are not abundant, but there is enough here to interest the sightseer and macro photographer. Other colorful life here includes an occasional nudibranch and some colorful sponge growths. Fish are scarce but sheep crab are to be found sometimes on the bottom.

Hunters will find only halibut on the sandy bottom. Rincon Island at the end of the pier is quite good for hunting other game but is much too far for a beach swim. For those who choose to approach the island by boat, always respect the oil company's restrictions and requests to stay clear if so directed. Immediately to the south of the island is an artificial reef made up of old tires in about 40 feet of water. Visibility out here is only fair to poor and currents can come up.

Punta Gorda's main setback is generally poor conditions. Visibility averages only 5 to 10 feet and rarely gets better. Due to the gentle beach slope and the point's lack of protection, surf and surge conditions can be a problem. The frequent surge stirs up the fine-sand bottom easily.

On calm days, the access and entry is enjoyably easy. Punta Gorda lies about eight miles north of Ventura just off Highway 101. If approaching from the north, exit at sign marked as Mussel Shoals; if from the south, exit at Ocean Ave adjacent to the Cliff House Hotel. Ocean Ave. will turn to the right and then to the left toward the sea. You can park on either side of the road just before the gate on the pier, but stay out of areas where parking is marked prohibited. Only authorized personnel are allowed on the pier; do not trespass. Also respect the private residences in the area and don't violate their "no trespassing" signs. Entry can be made on either side of the pier depending on the direction of the swells, although the south side tends to be best. If conditions are marginal, try elsewhere on the coast. Otherwise, Punta Gorda may be a new alternative for your beach diving agenda.

Silver Strand

Those heading for Silver Strand Beach do so most often to surf the ocean or sun their bodies. Diving activity is limited and usually confined to the southeast end of the beach at La Jenelle Park, including the rocks and nearby submarine canyon. But divers with a fetish for Pismo clams know Silver Strand to be a gold mine.

Extending from the rocks at La Jenelle all the way to the breakwater at Channel Islands Harbor is one of the most abundant and productive beds of Pismo clams in Southern California. Better yet, they are the most meaty and tasty of the clams available in the southern half of the state. They make fantastic chowder with nearly the entire contents being usable. The clam bed at Silver Strand lies 50 to 100 yards out in 10 to 25 of water. Depths of 15 to 20 feet seem to be the most productive.

This is how you find them: look for two fleshy tubes or holes, right next to each other, in an indentation in the sand. What looks like coagulated sand—actually slime from the clam—will surround the siphons. Frequently, a small part of the clam will protrude from the sand. Dig quickly, as Pismo clams can be fast,

A sand star nestles in a bed of sand dollars.

strong diggers. Usually, only a large dive knife is needed as a probing and digging tool. The only other special gear needed includes a measuring device and a bag. Ten Pismo clams (the legal limit) can, however, be quite heavy. Some divers choose to use a float or lift bag to get their clams through the surf and to shore.

Surf here, by the way, can be a problem. The beach is rarely calm. This is a beach dive only for the experienced. The only semi-protected entry and exit is the small cove at La Jenelle Park. This, however, can be quite deceptive. The water in the cove is shallow and often simply makes for a wider surf zone. Also, there is a prevailing rip current off the end of the rocks that can make for confusion both on entry and exit. I often find the more efficient approach is just to head straight out from the beach.

The clams will run in patches. Once you have found one or two, there will be dozens. The last two times I've dived here I've had my limit in less than 15 minutes. Most of the clams are about the same size, so there's not much point of picking and choosing. Minimum legal size for Pismo clams (south of Point Conception) is 4 1/2 inches at the widest

Cleaning Pismo Clams

As tasty and meaty as they are, pismo clams can be a bear to get open. They have the thickest shell of all the popular clams. And they close up tight!

Working over a pan to collect the clam's juices, use a thin sharp knife to insert at the hinge. While the hinge is tough, it can be penetrated and cut. Sweep the knife in a full arch to cut both adductor muscles that hold the shells closed. The adductor muscles are in the upper right and left sides of the shell. With the muscles cut, the clam will open enough to pry open the remainder of the way. Remember to save the juices!

Nearly all the meat is usable. Discard the darkest portions. Scrape the adductor muscles from the shell. Drain the juices to save for later and then rinse the meat of sand thoroughly. Filter the juices clean of sand and other debris with cheesecloth and save.

Pismo clams make excellent clam chowder. Pick your favorite recipe, making sure to use the juices for full flavor.

point. Most of the clams at Silver Strand are 5 to 5 1/2 inches, rarely bigger. You'll need a measuring device that is sometimes hard to come by. If you can't find one, cut a 4 1/2 inch gap in a plastic slate.

As much as I like to dive here for clams, it can be a bit of a boring dive. Once I have my limit, there is little else to do or to see! One additional option is halibut hunting. The sand dollar beds can be interesting to explore, harboring an occasional fish, sea star or crab, but it's hardly enough to burn up an entire tank of air in 20 feet of water. I generally just like to head back to the beach using my energy to drag a load of clams back through the surf.

La Jenelle

I am a gorgonian freak. I just love these sea fans that are actually a soft coral. Thousands of tiny polyp animals make up each stand that sways gently in the surge. They align themselves with prevailing currents and surge to take maximum advantage of water movement. Seawater bearing food is filtered of nutrition by the tiny polyps on the gorgonian's branches. They pluck microscopic plants and animals from the liquid suspension.

The branches of the gorgonian come in gold, yellow, pink, red, and even purple. They make great backdrops and foregrounds for wide-angle photos. And the macro photographer can zoom in on small animals that call the branches home or on the little polyps themselves.

As a gorgonian nut, I have carefully noted in my logbook all the great gorgonian dives Southern California has to offer. Most of these gorgonian-rich sites lie offshore at the Channel Islands, but there are a few really good beach dives for frolicking among the fields of gold. One of these sites is at the mouth of the Hueneme Submarine Canyon, off a small rocky peninsula known as La Jenelle Park.

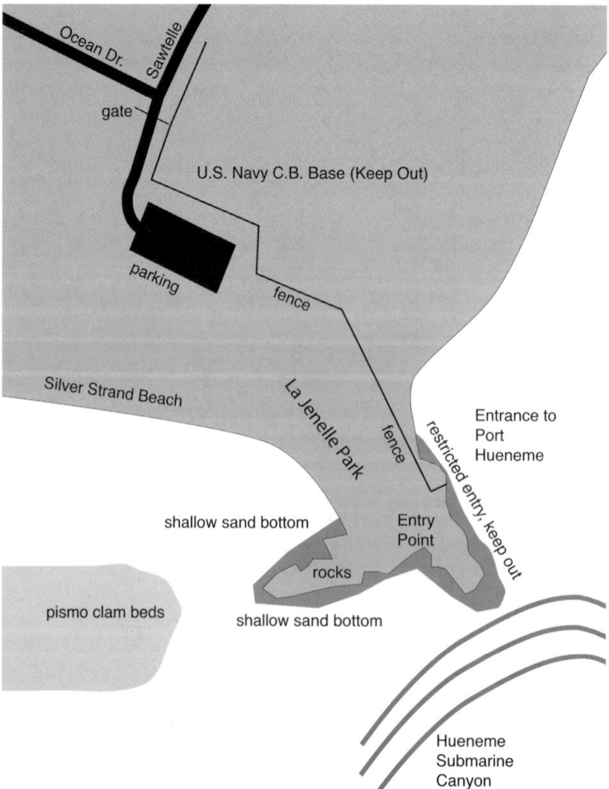

The name was gained from the misfortunes of a luxury passenger liner that ran aground here in 1970. The ship La Jenelle floundered on the sand shore near the mouth of the present day Port Hueneme. Hard aground and unsalvageable, the superstructure of the ship was removed and the hull filled in with rock, forming the rocky peninsula that exists today. Only small portions of the original hull can be seen above water. Underwater, only the rocks are of interest to divers.

The rocks filling the wreckage adjoin the breakwater at the mouth of Port Hueneme. It is this breakwater that runs out to the end of the submarine canyon. The rocks, proximity to the canyon, and constant surge make ideal conditions for growing gorgonian.

Unfortunately, access to the water at this dive site is not as

have been cited and sometimes arrested.

Water entry is now best done in the small rocky cove at the base of the breakwater. Entry and exit is from the rocks; it can be tricky, and should be attempted only when calm and by the experienced. The water immediately drops off to 20 feet around the boulders. The sand bottom is at 25 feet. Heading toward the tip of the breakwater will bring you into deeper water,

good as it once was. The park borders on the Port Hueneme Naval CB (Seabee) Base. In the '80s and again after 9/11, security for the base was beefed up. This included the rebuilding of the dilapidated fence along the park. This removed access to the most protected portion for water entry. Although individuals eager for the old days have cut holes in the fence, entry into this section is trespassing, and divers

the head of the submarine canyon, and the best diving—including gorgonian galore.

The rocks reach out to a steeply sloping sand bottom at 45 feet at the end of the breakwater. The gorgonian are abundant and healthy. Gold is the predominant color, but red gorgonian, appearing pink with their white polyps extended, are also plentiful.

Bottom fish use the gorgonian stands for cover. Rockfish, lingcod, and scorpionfish are common. Calico and barred sand bass use the rocks for cover. Invertebrates include the large sheep crab, a variety of nudibranchs, and, in the shelter of the boulders, lobster. Schooling fish, in particular, like the tip of the rocks. Blacksmith, sargo, opaleye and a selection of perch hover over the rocks. This is also a good spot to play

Cabezon

with the not-so-shy orange garibaldi.

No underwater trip here would be complete without an excursion into the submarine canyon. The sand bottom slopes quickly to 80 feet and then more gently to depths farther than I'd like to go. You'll see more in the Redondo or La Jolla Submarine canyons, but the excursion into these depths is worth it just for the thrill of being this deep this close to the mainland shore.

Deer Creek Road

On the extreme southern coastline of Ventura County, near Point Mugu, the shore becomes rugged and rocky with some small coves and stretches of sand beaches. Highway 1 comes very close to the water's edge in places but access is still limited. Where Deer Creek Road intersects with the highway, kelp beds reach close to shore, and there is easy stairway access to a sandy beach.

Thick kelp and lush reefs lie close to shore at this easy access location. A mere 27 concrete steps lead down to a sandy beach entry. One of the few disadvantages of this location, however, is its exposure to the open sea. Diving here in any more than a two-foot shore break is risking a pounding.

The bottom drops away quickly to a surge-swept sand bottom interspersed with rocks. Watch out for rocks in the surf zone. Look for corbina and halibut in the shallow area just beyond the breakers. The kelp starts in 20 feet of water close to shore and extends out to depths of 30-35 feet over 200 yards out.

Giant kelpfish

But the real action—lobster—lies within the outer reefs to the right and left. The reefs directly out from the beach are interesting but lack significant crevices for the shy crustacean. The outer reef, particularly to the right side of the beach, holds boulders, crevices, and cracks where lobster can be found. It's a bit of a swim, but it may pay off in a lobster dinner.

Lobster is not the only quarry available to the underwater hunter. Halibut can be found in the sand channels between the reefs, particularly in shallow water. Fair size calicos cruise the kelp stalks all across the reef, but spearfishers will have the best luck on the outer fringes or up and down the beach.

Seafood hunting is by no means the only attraction of this dive site. When conditions are right, the sightseer and photographer will enjoy the color provided by gorgonian in a handful of varieties, bat stars, and extra large pisaster stars.

On one dive, I had the rare opportunity to photograph ringed nudibranchs in what appeared to be a mating ritual (you have to be patient to watch sea slugs mate). On the same dive, I also photographed the brilliant purple and orange Spanish shawl nudibranch, and the bright yellow sea lemon. Just as interesting but much duller in color, the sea hare slug is also common at Deer Creek Road.

Other underwater playmates and photo subjects include rays, sheep crab, an occasional garibaldi, and schools of blacksmith fish that dance in the sunbeams streaming through the thick kelp canopy. Lucky divers may also encounter dolphins, seals or even migrating gray whales on the seaward side of the reef.

Visibility here is generally good, running about 10-15 feet inside the kelp and 20 to 30 feet outside the reef.

Although access to the beach is easy, there are no facilities here. Parking is along the highway with camping not far away. Remember to always check the surf report before diving this location because of the site's lack of protection from wave action.

Opaleye

Hermissenda nudibranch

Conditions: Malibu (310) 457-9701, South Bay (310) 379-8471, Cabrillo Beach (310) 832-1130
http://cdip.ucsd.edu/models/santa_monica.gif, http://cdip.ucsd.edu/models/spc.gif

Introduction to Los Angeles County

From the Ventura/Los Angeles County line, kelp beds become increasingly more common indicating offshore reefs. About a quarter of a mile from the county line is Harrison's Reef. Lying 300 yards offshore, Harrison's Reef is a dive for those who don't mind the longer swim. This kelp bed blends into, and marks the beginning of the reefs that lie parallel to Leo Carrillo State Beach. At **Leo Carrillo's North Beach** the kelp comes to within 25 yards of the sandy shore with a parking lot and excellent facilities. The best part of the **Leo Carrillo State Beach** for diving is off **Sequit Point**. Off Sequit Point, the bottom is varied with many tall reefs that support healthy kelp and much sea life. Because most of the bottom is rock, visibility is usually good as well.

Farther south, the kelp begins again at Nicolas Canyon. Access is good but quite long and arduous. The swim to the kelp can also be a little too long. Access at El Pescador Beach is not as good and the swim can still be long through dirty water. A lesser-known but good spot is at **El Matador Beach**. Access is not as easy as at Leo Carrillo, but it is safe. Kelp comes to within a few yards of the beach. Underneath the kelp, farther out, is an interesting reef in moderately clean water. From here southward, there are many diving spots that are good but not consistently so. Trancas Beach is the next access point and is excellent for halibut hunting but little else. **Zuma**

Crevice kelpfish

Beach, as well as Westward Beach, are fun dives with large sand dollar beds, Pismo clams, but often large surf.

Point Dume is excellent diving with a submarine canyon bringing clear water and much life, but the dive is only for the experienced as treacherous currents can plague the area.

Point Dume deflects the cleaning oceanic currents, so everything east of here suffers in water clarity. Paradise Cove can be a fun dive, but the private beach holds an expensive entry fee and poor visibility. **Escondido Beach** visibility is also only fair but access is easy and free. There are some small but interesting reefs at **Corral Beach,** which is frequently used by instructors as a spot for checkout dives. Visibility, however, is, again, only fair.

Off the beaten path and less known are tiny access points off **Malibu Road**. Three of these less frequented access points offer good diving in a kelp forest attached to a rocky reef.

Shore access, water clarity and reef structure improves beginning at the **Big Rock Reef**. Adjacent to Big Rock is **Las Tunas Beach**. Water clarity is better with some sea life, and an extensive reef area. The last patch of reef before the long sand beaches of the Santa Monica Bay is at the end of Sunset Blvd., just offshore from a restaurant known as **Gladstone's**.

The Santa Monica Bay is a long, almost unbroken stretch of beautiful sand beaches. Interesting diving can sometimes be done due to some of the piers, but don't go in if prohibited. Artificial reefs present another alternative. Most require a boat to dive. There are some rocks north of the Santa Monica Pier, remnants of a former breakwater. A lesser-known artificial reef at 24th Street in Hermosa Beach is within 200 yards of shore; there is, however, little left of it. A dive off the outside of the large **Redondo Breakwater** may reward you with some lobster, but heavy surge and a walk over large boulders can be a problem. Diving near the present-day pier

Sea hare

or near the harbor mouth is prohibited.

Early in the century, a total of three piers were built off Redondo Beach for ships to take advantage of deep waters close to shore provided by the **Redondo Submarine Canyon**. The canyon comes very close to shore and makes for an interesting dive. The remains of **Old Redondo Pier #3** can be seen today on the ocean floor off Topaz Street. At both the canyon and the old pier, visibility is usually good and the anemone-encrusted pier pilings make for interesting diving. Rumored to be off Ave. C in Redondo Beach is a series of small reef ledges in 35 feet of water that are reported to be good for lobster hunting early in the season.

The sand beaches continue southward until Torrance Beach. Here, there is a little known reef out from the white cliffs at a place the locals call **RAT Beach**. RAT Beach and surrounding waters have long been noted as excellent halibut hunting grounds. The beach becomes much more rocky at the southward end of Torrance Beach where the shore turns westward to form **Malaga Cove**. This cove really marks the beginning of the excellent diving that the Palos Verdes area has to offer.

Palos Verdes is, unfortunately, also surrounded by cliffs making access to the water sometimes very difficult. At **Malaga Cove** there is good access on a steep paved path and good diving over parallel reefs. From the same access at Malaga Cove you can make the trek west to the beautiful kelp forests off **Haggerty's**. Turning the corner at **Flat Rock Point** brings you even better diving, but increasingly difficult access. Across Bluff or Paddleboard Cove is the cliff area known as **Margate**. The trails are tough, and the beach is exposed, but the lobster hunting is excellent. A few more coves southward is the small **Christmas Tree Cove**. Excellent diving in Palos Verdes' clearest water can be difficult to reach but usually worth it. Shore access from Christmas Tree to Point Vicente is spotty and dangerous at best. Around the corner is **Point Vicente Fishing Access**. Made infamous by "Cardiac Hill," the very steep and long but safe path leading to the water's edge, Point Vicente Fishing Access has some very good diving in nearby kelp.

Terrenea Resort (a.k.a. Long Point or "Old Marineland") is the site of a now developing extensive resort complex. Temporary public access is provided during construction and more is promised when completed. Most importantly, the diving is great. Shore access farther to the east becomes increasingly sparse. A very long walk will bring you to good diving at Abalone Cove, a protected beach with good facilities and marine preserve.

White Point is the only place around Palos Verdes where you can actually drive your car to the water's edge. You'll find a lot of divers at White Point but it's still an enjoyable excursion. A little over a half a mile down the road is shore access on the west side of **Point Fermin** where there is access but the water visibility is generally poor. **Cabrillo Beach** near Los Angeles Harbor has good access, excellent facilities, but again poor water clarity. The harbor prevents any diving until you reach the sand beaches of Orange County.

Green anemone

Leo Carrillo/ North Beach

The beauty of Leo Carrillo State Beach has attracted humans for thousands of years. Chumash Indians had an extensive settlement at this location for centuries prior to the arrival of the white man.

A famous actor, Leo Carrillo, also loved this place. His most famous role was as Pancho, Cisco Kid's sidekick, in the early television series. Leo Carrillo wanted the site preserved for future generations and led the drive to acquire the land for the state park system. Today, Leo Carrillo State Beach is one of the crown jewels in the state park system.

The beach at Leo Carrillo can be divided into three sections. Each section has excellent diving opportunities directly offshore, but each section has its own particular underwater terrain and diving concerns. The mile-long beach front of the park is divided by Sequit Point. To one side is South Beach. Easily reached from Pacific Coast Highway, South Beach is probably the most heavily used section of coastline in the park. Access to South Beach and Sequit Point is available without the day use fee by parking on Pacific Coast Highway. The cove at South Beach is used frequently by surfers and wind surfers. When the wind or surf is up, it is not a safe place for divers. When conditions are calm, there is a kelp forest offshore that is an extension of the reef system off Sequit Point.

Giant kelp

No doubt about it, North Beach has its advantages. A large parking lot lies right on the beach. There are excellent facilities with restrooms and showers. Access to the water is easy, and there are kelp patches a stone's throw from water's edge.

North Beach has a steep face. Although the surf zone is narrow, the waves build up tall and break hard. Check the surf report ahead of time and if waves in the Malibu area are breaking three feet or larger, try other sections of Leo Carrillo, or Malibu, for diving.

Once out beyond the narrow surf zone, the bottom drops

away quickly to 10 to 15 feet. Sand is interspersed with boulders and small reefs. In the channels between the rocks, guitarfish, rays, and halibut lounge, waiting for a tiny fishmeal to be swept off the rocks by the sometimes heavy surge.

Under the kelp patches are more extensive reefs with marine life to match. The kelp is thick and lush with plentiful, fat calico bass up among the fronds. Because of the easy access for spearfisher, big bass are skittish but present, usually on the edge of visibility. Stealthy hunters that free dive may also be privileged to see white sea bass on outer edges of the kelp. Other quarry available to the spearfishing enthusiast includes halibut and sheephead.

Underwater hunting is allowed in this state park, but with specific regulations. In general, the taking of "normal" game follows California Fish and Game rules and regulations. Consult with the State Park Ranger for more specific regulations.

Lobsters are present on the reefs off North Beach, but this is by no means the best bug hunting in the North Los Angeles County area. Most of the lobsters of North Beach are spread thin and on the short side. For better luck, try off Sequit Point where there are more deep crevices for the shy crustaceans.

Water visibility is best within the stalks of kelp that dampen the effects of the common surge. Water clarity at the North Beach is usually better than that of South Beach, but worse than off Sequit Point. If the surf is up, or there has been a recent rain, visibility suffers considerably.

Within the stalks of kelp, schools of opaleye and various types of perch are common. On the reef you will also find abundant rockfish. There is no shortage of fish at any section of Leo Carrillo State Beach.

On the outer edges of the kelp, water depths reach 35 feet. Ivory sand stretches seaward dotted with sea pansies, spiny sand stars and sea pens. Along the reef edges and in the shallow channels, gold gorgonian fans have set themselves up to take maximum benefits for filter feeding in the surge and currents. The shallow channels, dips in the reef, and clearings in the kelp seem to hold the most abundant marine life. Sea stars, nudibranchs, and algae dot the rocks in a mosaic of color.

Facilities at Leo Carrillo State Beach are excellent. The day-use parking lot at North Beach uses pit toilets, and picnic tables are available. There is also a visitor center at North Beach. The camping area has flush toilets and fresh-water showers available. There is a fee for day-use and camping. The North Beach camping area is entirely asphalt. Reservations are recommended and can be made by calling 800-444-PARK or visiting www.reserveamerica.com on the web.

There is also a camping area in the canyon slightly inland. While not right on the beach, it's a beautiful wooded area. Unfortunately, when making reservations, you cannot specify desired area.

Access to North Beach is sometimes closed due to heavy rains and subsequent run-off, closing the road. Call (805) 488-5223 for current road status. Additional beach camping is available just north at Sycamore Canyon and Thornhill Broome.

Corynactis anemones

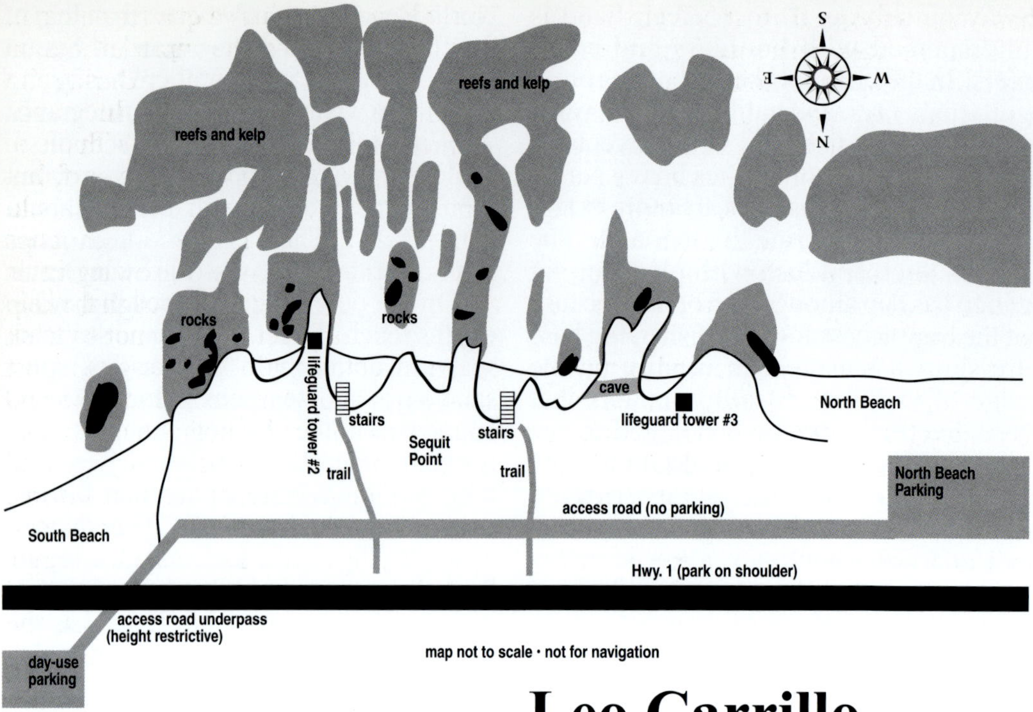

reefs and kelp
reefs and kelp
rocks
rocks
lifeguard tower #2
stairs
stairs
Sequit Point
cave
lifeguard tower #3
North Beach
trail
trail
North Beach Parking
access road (no parking)
South Beach
Hwy. 1 (park on shoulder)
access road underpass (height restrictive)
day-use parking
map not to scale · not for navigation

Leo Carrillo

One of the most prolific yet easily accessible kelp beds along the Southern California coastline lies as close as 20 yards off Leo Carrillo State Beach in west Los Angeles County. The shoreline runs east-west, with two beaches being separated by rocky Sequit Point.

Sequit Point provides probably the best diving with kelp beds the size of several football fields. The reefs that stretch out from the rocky point support a wide variety of sea life. Many urchins, numerous species of sea stars and anemones, as well as nudibranchs, mollusks, and small sponges attach themselves on the rocks under the kelp canopy. Photographers will enjoy the multitude of subjects available. Of particular note are the large numbers of colorful gorgonians that lie on the outer edges of the reefs. Big octopuses are also not unusual here.

Octopus

For hunters, the rocks conceal a few lobsters. The kelp cover attracts a wide variety of game fish including kelp bass and sheephead. On the sand between the reefs, halibut are common. For the experienced free-diver, even white sea bass can be found in this kelp forest.

This is a state beach and facilities are excellent. There is camping, showers, restrooms and lots of parking. Most of this is in the canyon and at the North Beach section up the coast from Sequit Point (see previous chapter). Access to the North Beach facilities is not always available. Winter storms sometimes wash out the access road that leads directly to the beach to the west of Sequit Point. When the roads are open, there is a fee for day use and camping.

For diving Sequit Point, your best bet is to park on the seaward side of Highway 1 near the sign "Mulholland Hwy." This will place you within a short walking distance down a gentle slope to the entry-exit areas on the point. There are trails leading from the highway out to the point.

The point is a fascinating collection of small rocky coves and caves. Immediately to the west of lifeguard tower #2 and to the east of tower #3 are stairs that lead to sandy coves between the rocks that are excellent for entry or exit. The large kelp beds are easily visible running in as close as 20 yards to as much as a quarter mile out. Rips and currents can be unpredictable, so observe conditions carefully. During the summer and on some holidays, lifeguards are present; it is wise to check with them.

There are some rocks in the surf, but careful observation before entry should prevent any problems. The bottom drops off moderately with kelp growing in as little as 10 feet of water. Although the kelp can be abundant, it is usually not so thick as to prevent underwater passage in most locations. On the bottom, the reefs rise up as much as 10 feet in spots. An occasional tall boulder can be found usually covered with a wide variety of feather worms, anemones, and other colorful invertebrates.

The diving area at Leo Carrillo is large. Because of this, alternate dive spots and entry/exit points can be found on the beaches on either side of the point. Each of these beaches faces the ocean differently, thus giving you a number of diving options. If it is exceptionally calm, it is even possible to enter the water directly off the rocky point near tower #3.

Female sheephead

Beach Diving With A Camera

Yes, I do take my camera on beach dives. Don't gasp in horror! It can be done, and quite successfully. In my nearly 35 years of beach diving (about 25 of those with a camera), I've learned a lot, much of it the hard way. I've often learned the expensive way, through flooded strobes, cameras, and housings. Yet, I still take my camera in on underwater excursions from shore, and I get some great photos in the ocean, five minutes from my house.

You, too, can get great underwater photos beach diving, but I don't want you to go through the same negative experiences I had, so listen up!

CLOSE-UP MACRO OR WIDE ANGLE?

I've had some beach dives with remarkably clear water, but it's no secret that diving from shore most often leads to less than great visibility. With that in mind, most think that macro (close-up) photography is the only option. Not so! The wide-angle lens is a remarkable tool in dirty water. With a wide angle you can get very close to a large subject and still get most, or all, in the frame. Close-focus, wide-angle photography takes some special techniques but can be very rewarding.

THE RIG

Diving from shore almost always involves swimming some distance. It also usually means a transit through the surf. Experienced beach divers will tell you that in order to avoid fatigue, the diver needs to be as streamlined as possible. The same goes for the camera. Small and compact are best.

In addition, beach diving requires that at least one hand be free. Avoid beach diving photo trips with those huge two-fisted camera rigs.

The first place to streamline is in the strobe arms. Keep them simple. It is possible to have arms that are compact, yet versatile. Also, seriously consider only one strobe. Unless you're experienced in how to use two strobes in dirty water, a single strobe is often better anyway. It's easier to control the light and limit backscatter. With a single strobe, shooting wide angle, use a simple, direct approach, exposing so the background will come in, and aiming the strobe from on high to imitate natural sunlight from above.

Use a small camera and compact, lightweight strobes. My camera of choice is a compact digital camera with a supplemental wide-angle lens that can be installed and remove underwater, small strobes, and arms that fold up the whole thing into a compact package.

WHERE TO DIVE/HOW TO DIVE

Lower your expectations when beach diving with a camera. If you can normally handle three-to four-foot surf without a camera, do only one-to two-foot surf with a camera. Also take the distance you'll need to swim into consideration. It's surprising how much even a moderate sized camera will slow you down.

Buddy cooperation is a must. Use only one camera per buddy team. As previously stated, the beach diver needs a free hand. With only one camera for two divers, at least some hands will be free.

Sandy beach entries are the easiest but the most dangerous for flooding. DO NOT place your camera in the sand, particularly where water can swirl around it. The camera's 'O' rings, essential for sealing out water, are not yet seated in place. This requires the pressure of surrounding water. Before pressurizing, sand can easily lodge in essential 'O' ring seats.

I like beach diving from a rocky beach because visibility is usually better and the reef closer. The problem is you usually get banged around just a bit getting in and out of the water. While the human body can absorb this, cameras cannot. I only do rocky beach dives with my camera when it is calm.

THE CLEANUP

Proper maintenance is the key to preventing flooding for the beach diving shutterbug. You have to be fanatical about cleaning and maintaining your camera equipment. As much as you try to avoid it, sand will work its way in. You have to get all of it out. Thoroughly clean and inspect all 'O' rings and their seats, and then clean them again. Do not over-lubricate 'O' rings as this will only attract and hold sand grains. Make sure ALL 'O' rings are properly maintained, including those around control knobs if possible.

Some of my best underwater photos have been taken while beach diving. Beach diving holds many opportunities for the underwater photographer. Carrying your camera while beach diving can be very rewarding and can be done successfully with a minimum amount of headaches.

El Matador Beach

Quite a few divers are already familiar with the good beach diving that northwest Los Angeles County has to offer. Most of this diving activity is concentrated in the Leo Carrillo State Beach area, which is understandable because Leo Carrillo offers good diving with a variety of underwater scenery and activities. What is not as well known by divers is that good diving can also be done nearby with fewer crowds. To the southeast of Leo Carrillo is a string of beaches, most of which are also part of the state beach system. They include Nicolas Canyon, El Pescador, La Piedra, and El Matador.

El Matador State Beach is the farthest southeast of these beaches. Although shore access and facilities are not as good as at Leo Carrillo, this beach offers some very good diving. Healthy kelp comes within 50 yards of shore. Rocky reefs extend out from the beach 150 yards, with most of the reefs consisting of very large boulders on a sand and rock bottom. Several of these boulders rise from the bottom as much as 15 feet.

Juvenile treefish

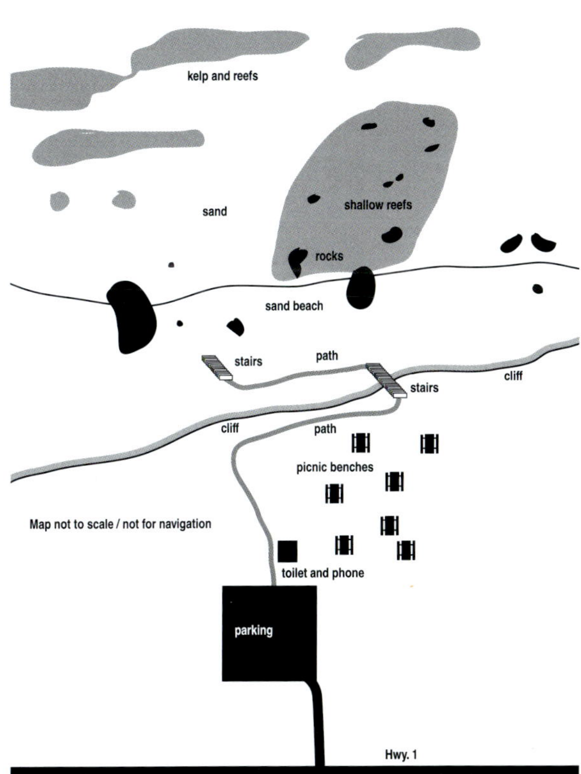

Attached to the boulders are bunches of gorgonian, corynactis, and giant keyhole limpets. Although this may not be the photographer's and sightseer's paradise, there is ample color and life here to fill the eye. Garibaldi, señoritas, and even a few bluebanded gobies dart about.

The hunter will find sheephead, rockfish and kelp bass. On the sand surrounding the reefs, an occasional halibut can be seen. Although the size of the game fish in this area is not particularly big, the quantity is sufficient. A fair number of lobsters are present in the right cracks and look close for scallops; they are there also.

Conditions at El Matador State beach are variable because the beach is open to the weather. A day or two of pounding surf or rain will reduce the visibility at the beach considerably, but on good days visibility averages 10 to 15 feet. Occasionally, it reaches 30 feet in calm Fall conditions or during Santa Ana winds. Currents are not much of a problem and usually only affect the outer edges of the kelp.

Locating the state beach is easy:

The turn off to the parking area is directly off Pacific Coast Highway (Highway 1). The beach is approximately four miles south of Leo Carrillo and two miles north of Trancas Beach. The turnoff is well marked with signs along the highway.

There is ample parking, chemical toilets, a pay phone, and picnic benches. No overnight camping is allowed and the park is open from 8 a.m. to sunset. There is a day-use fee, which is paid by using a self-service box. There is no running water.

The path to the beach begins at the toilets. The path is only moderately steep and is safe. The path is broken up by two sections of stairs for a total of about 80 steps.

Before descending the steps, take a good look at the beach. The first thing you will notice is the beauty of the beach. El Matador is one of the most attractive and secluded beaches in all of Los Angeles County. You may want to consider this beach for a picnic—with or without diving. Almost directly off the beach is a reef with rocks breaking the surface extending out about 75 yards. Depth on this reef runs between 10 to 20 feet. Although healthy kelp grows here, the visibility can be reduced due to surge. Snorkeling is also good when the surf is low. Looking out past the shallower reefs, you will see an additional bed of kelp extending 75 to- 150 yards out. These reefs hold the best diving with depths ranging between 25 and 35 feet. In addition, there are large kelp beds extending along the shoreline in both directions, creating a huge diving area that should satisfy everybody.

Zuma Beach

Divers traveling north along Highway 1 from Los Angeles have probably passed Zuma Beach several times on their way to better known spots like Leo Carrillo in north Los Angeles County. Connected with Westward Beach to the southeast (ending at Point Dume) and with Trancas Beach to the northwest, this is the longest stretch of unbroken sandy public beach in the Malibu area. During the summer, crowds of sunbathers, surfers and beachgoers crowd Zuma, making it one of the most popular beaches in Los Angeles County. But surprisingly few divers know of the underwater environment that lies on the sandy sea bottom off this beach.

Over a quarter century ago, the California Fish & Game department planted a colony of Pismo clams at Zuma. They were quite successful as Zuma Beach developed a large population of legal-sized pismo clams. Unfortunately, storms a few years ago reduced the population considerably. Although the clams have bounced back somewhat, they have never completely recovered and underwater hunting of the delicious clams is now hit or miss proposition.

There area a few other attractions for divers at Zuma. One of the most apparent is the massive beds of sand dollars that lie parallel to shore in 20 to 30 feet of water where it is not unusual to see crabs feeding on the numerous creatures. Also residing in the sand are halibut and moon snails, some reaching the size of your fist. There are a few spot reefs along the beach, but these are small, unproductive and often difficult to find.

Zuma is a dive spot for the intermediate or advanced diver. Conditions at the beach can be rough due to the beach being open and facing southwest, the direction of prevailing weather and surf. It is not unusual for Zuma to have one to three foot higher surf than other beaches only a few miles away. Surf at Zuma is rarely below three feet. The one consolation is the surf zone narrow at high tide. The shore break is sharp, however, creating waves that break hard and fast. The strong surf also creates riptide hazards. It is a good idea to check with the main lifeguard tower before entering the water.

There is also a strong southeast current that catches many divers by surprise. The current is at its strongest in the summer. Because the beach is long, many divers use the current to their advantage by drift diving. The beach-access road runs parallel to the beach. Some divers will choose to dive with the current and then, at the end of their dive, one buddy drops their gear on the beach to return to the car and drive to the exit point. One serious note of caution on this technique: the southeast current spreads out to sea as it approaches Point Dume. Do not venture far from shore.

The lifeguards at Zuma require divers to use a float and a flag. In using a float and flag, you should probably drag it behind you throughout the dive. Many divers have lost expensive flag assemblies in the strong current.

One benefit of the current is the usually good visibility. Considering the sea bottom is nearly all sand, the 12-foot-average visibility at Zuma is quite good.

Point Dume

One of the most consistently thrilling, yet hazardous beach dives along the Southern California coast is at Point Dume. Here the Dume Submarine Canyon comes very close to shore, closer than any other submarine canyon. Couple this with a powerful oceanic current that literally sideswipes the point and you have an exciting underwater combination. Whales, large sharks, pelagics and more pass by this point on a regular basis. But this is not a beach dive for the faint of heart.

It takes a careful eye to spot tricky currents and surf and then plan your dive accordingly. Access to the point is at the end of Westward Beach Road. Point Dume County Beach has a parking fee and is only open daylight hours. The beach ends at a large rock cliff face. (This location has been used in countless movies, TV shows and TV commercials.) Surf entry can be tough with a sharp shore break common.

The reefs off the first set of rocks peter out quickly into scattered boulders here and there over mostly sand. But then the bottom slopes quickly into the canyon. The slope is not as dramatic as La Jolla or Redondo Submarine Canyons but is steep enough that you can be in deep water rather quickly. At 75 feet, toward the point, you come across three large boulders with gorgonian, nudibranchs and large sheep crabs. Large halibut and big bat rays are common in the sand here.

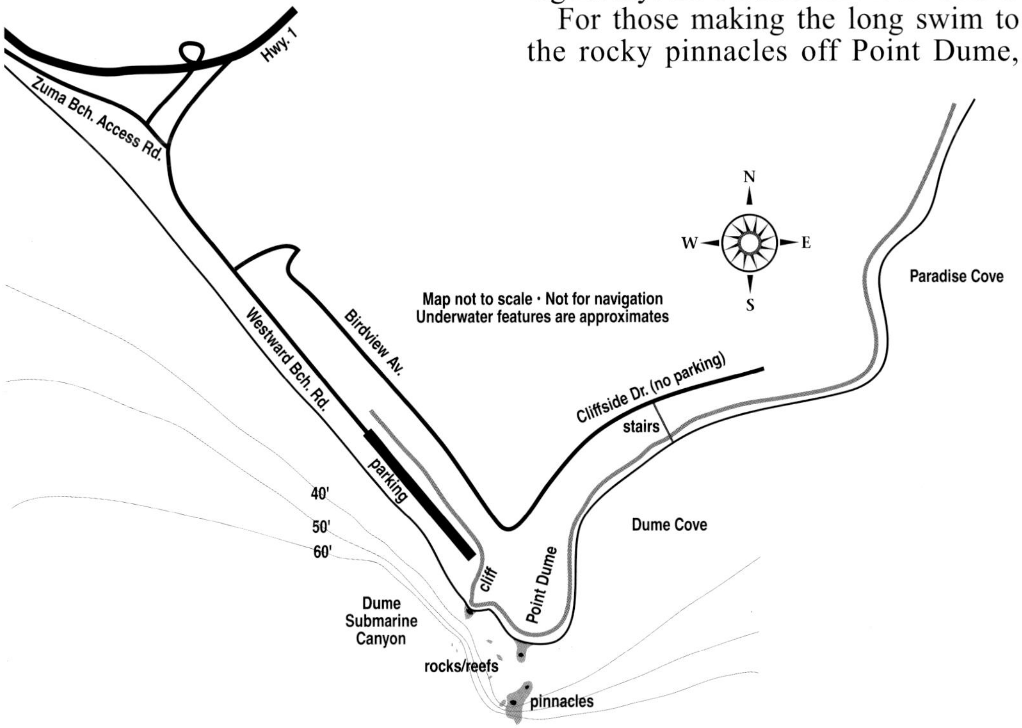

For those making the long swim to the rocky pinnacles off Point Dume, the reward will be a rock wall dropping vertically to 40 feet. More reefs and pinnacles slope into the canyon. Schools of barracuda and an occasional black sea bass can be seen here.

Visibility is generally very good because of the submarine canyon, lack of run-off and clean oceanic currents. A consistent 15 to 20 feet can be expected along the canyon slope. Out near the pinnacles, viz in the range of 25 to 30 feet is not unusual. The only exception is when plankton blooms, sometimes dropping water clarity.

In planning your dive, keep in mind prevailing currents here are from west to east, meaning you will be starting your dive *with* the current, breaking a rule of current diving. This is okay if you take three things into consideration: First, observe the conditions carefully. Try to get an estimation of the current's speed and then determine if you can handle it on the return swim. Second, plan your dive to return on the bottom hugging the shoreline where the current's effect is less. Leave enough air in your tank for the return trip. And finally, remember that should you not be able to return to

Sheep crab

Sea stars

your entry point at Westward Beach, you can always swim around the corner and exit down the coast at Dume Cove. While you'll have a long walk back to your car, it beats the alternative of being swept far out into the Santa Monica Bay. If all this isn't enough, sometimes there is a counter current. Keep a sharp eye and be ready to change your dive plans accordingly, even in the middle of the dive. Also, the prevailing direction of the waves, usually pushing along the beach from west to east, creates what is known as "long-shore current" in the surf zone. This is a net water movement in or near the surf zone pushing the water to the east, or in other words, onto the rocks. Again, plan accordingly.

Escondido Beach

Easy access points are rare in the Malibu area. Escondido beach is a small beach with very limited parking along the Coast Highway. As a consequence, crowds here are generally thin in comparison to Paradise Cove, a mile to the north and the other beaches to the south. Access to the beach is only a few steps from Highway 1. Parking is limited to the opposite side of the highway, 100 feet or so to the north. In addition, there are no other facilities. There is a chemical toilet but no lifeguards on duty.

Diving here is not as good as other parts of the Malibu area. The sand bottom drops off from shore to about 15 feet 25 yards from shore. The bottom then turns from sand to jumbled medium-sized stones. Out 75 yards or so, kelp grows on some of the larger boulders and rock outcroppings.

Fine sand surrounds and is intermixed within the rocks, which is easily stirred by surge and, consequently, reduces visibility to usually less than 10 feet. Toward the outer edges of the kelp, 250 to 300 yards out, the visibility does improve somewhat.

Spearfishers may fair well at Escondido Beach. The reduced visibility dares some fair-sized kelp and barred sand bass to approach closely. Halibut can also be found over the sand. Other game, such as lobsters and scallops, are rare or non-existent and only on the outer edges of the kelp.

The sightseer/photographer will unfortunately find little here in comparison to other areas of Malibu. An occasional sea star, urchin, or anemones are on the rocks. Small camouflaged crabs are common. The outer edges of the kelp may hold more interesting subject material such as a few gorgonians and nudibranchs.

Locals sometimes use the area to moor their boats and, on calm summer days, for waterskiing. Beware of boat activity and use a float and flag, if necessary.

Chestnut cowry

Corral Beach

Halibut

Corral Beach is a simple, easy dive. Local instructors have used this location for years as a check-out dive spot for their students and although easy, it is still an enjoyable dive as well. We have had a number of fun, relaxing dives here, including a close encounter with passing dolphins.

This quiet sandy beach is located in the Malibu area of Los Angeles County, being passed over frequently by divers from Los Angeles on the way up to more popular spots like Leo Carrillo State Beach. More precisely, Corral Beach is located about 2 1/2 miles east of Paradise Cove. Coral beach is popular in the summer with beach-goers and is sometimes crowded. On the extreme west end of the beach, out 30 to 75 yards, are small patches of kelp that reveal the location of submerged reefs and a good diving area.

Park just across from the Beaurivage Restaurant at 26035 Pacific Coast Highway, using caution to avoid the no-parking zones and fire hydrant. At this point on a small bluff above the beach, ocean conditions can be observed carefully. There is also an easy path to the beach here.

Water entry from the beach is usually easy; however, a southerly swell, sporadic in the summer, can create large breakers. The best time to dive here is

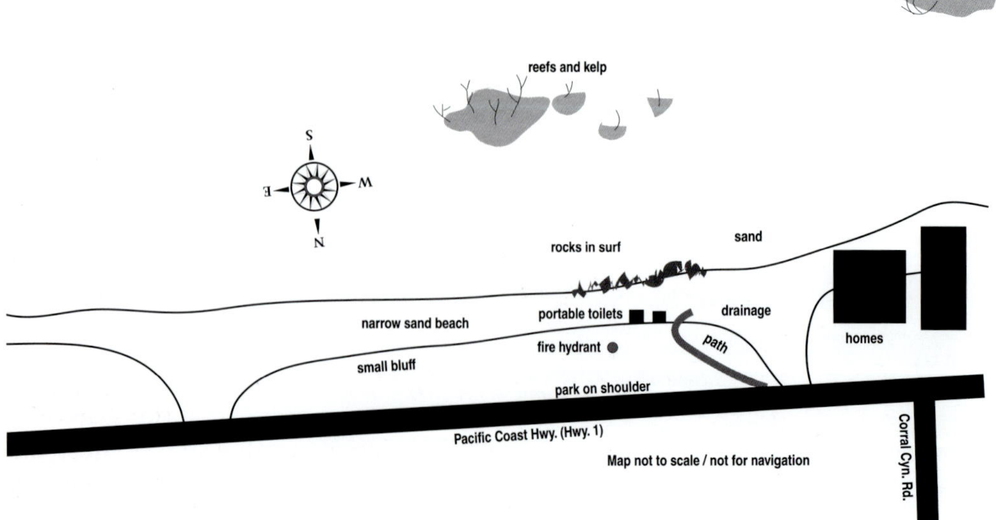

after a healthy blow of Santa Ana winds that gust from the land out to sea. Surf is generally small but always check with the surf report in advance. What can make the entry here tough, however, are the rocks in the surf zone. Pick your entry point carefully and watch your step! Out from the beach, the bottom drops off quickly to a rocky 10-to 15-foot deep bottom. This shallow area near shore is relatively barren but an occasional halibut and large boulder that can produce a lobster.

Slightly farther out is the bulk of the kelp growing from scattered boulders and small reefs. The largest boulder stands nearly 12 feet high and is covered with corynactis, gorgonian and a host of other creatures. On this and surrounding rocks, nudibranchs and starfish can be seen lazily grazing. Sheep crabs are common. Hiding in small holes of the reef are octopus. The fish around this small reef is abundant as well. The orange garibaldi is fiercely territorial and stakes his claim in several sections. Some species kelp bass and perch are present in sufficient quantities for fair spearfishing.

The spearfishers may also want to cruise over the vast sand bottom in search of halibut. Other than the aforementioned fish for spearing, the hunter will not find much to bag at Corral Beach. The few rocks support almost no scallops and, although there are some good cracks for lobster, bug hunting is largely a hit or miss proposition.

Giant kelp forest

There are larger, more dramatic reefs farther out and to the west, but you'll be in for a long swim if you want to visit this kelp forest. This outer reef is good for lobster hunting in season.

If you choose to take your camera to this spot, it would be best to use a macro lens. Visibility is limited at best, averaging only 5 to 15 feet. The poor visibility owes itself to two factors at this location: First is the creek drainage nearby, so avoid this location after heavy rains; second is the beach's protected position from water-cleaning currents. Due to Latigo Point to the west, very little clean ocean currents reach the small reefs to carry away accumulated sediment.

If you do not mind a little dirty water and are looking for an easy dive, Corral Beach may be an interesting spot to check out on your next beach dive outing.

Female sheephead

Beach Diving Security

On your latest beach dive, where did you park your car? Where did you keep your keys? Did you leave anything on the beach? Was it there when you got back?

While underwater on a beach dive, although you're actually only a couple hundred yards away, you might as well be on another planet. You're not going to hear your car alarm. Worse yet, your dive gear tells all the bad guys that you'll be well out of range for some time.

And what about the stuff you have to leave on the beach? Even if you saw the punk that tried on your super-diver patch jacket, you wouldn't be able to swim back to the beach in time to prevent its theft.

Beach divers are big, easy targets.

But there are things you can do to prevent you from becoming a crime victim while on a beach dive.

First, never, ever leave keys in, or on, your vehicle. "Secret" hiding places for keys are rarely secret to thieves. Lock your car securely, and take the keys with you. A key pocket on the inside of your wetsuit jacket is now common on some of the off-the-rack suits and a must-have option on custom suits. Another option is a simple lanyard around the neck.

A disadvantage of carrying your keys this way is that the salt and sand that coats your key will be inserted into your lock after the dive. The locking mechanism could be damaged. Rinse the key with freshwater before use. Or a quick trick is to simply suck off the salt and sand with your mouth before inserting the key. Better yet, use one of the small plastic watertight containers now on the market. Hang it around the neck to keep dry keys, I.D., fishing license, C-card, and a small amount of cash. These are a must for the new electronic keys standard on most cars these days. These small containers are inexpensive and available at most dive stores.

To further secure your vehicle, use "The Club" or similar steering wheel locking device. Car alarms lose their effectiveness because you're not around to respond to it (and you know how much others pay attention to alarms). A steering wheel locking device will deter or at least slow down a thief. You do, however, have the problem of another key to carry.

The simplest solution to prevent theft on the beach is to leave nothing on the beach to steal. If possible, dress in completely at your vehicle, except for your fins and mask, which you'll carry. This is also a good way to ensure that nothing is accidentally left at the car.

Don't leave anything of valuable visible in the car. Tanks, cameras, expensive jackets, wallets, etc. should be secured in the trunk or out of sight.

Often though, it is necessary to leave some items on the beach. You may wish to bring extra tanks, towels, freshwater, books, cash, or cameras. Small, loose, valuable items are easier to steal than a bulky nondescript item. Secure all of your possessions in a large bag or container that can be closed and, if possible, locked.

I sometimes use a wheeled trash can, with a hinged, locking lid (hinge and lock I installed). Locked trash on the beach is not very enticing to crooks. The wheels make for easy gear transport and all the wet, sandy gear is contained within the can, not contaminating the inside of my truck.

Every year, more and more beach divers become victims of thievery, some as minor as an expensive coat, others as major as an automobile. Normal theft deterrence methods are only partially effective when you're underwater. Only a few extra precautions on your part, some unusual or creative, will protect you and your valued possessions.

Treefish

Malibu Road

The large public beaches are common knowledge along Malibu, but what is not as well known is the handful of tiny access points. There are three such locations along Malibu Road in the area near Pepperdine University. These sites are rarely visited due to lack of facilities, very limited parking, and *very* limited amount of public beach.

While private property should always be respected and not trespassed upon, it's not a commonly known fact that all beach, from the high tide water mark out, is available to the public. Unfortunately, with many storms washing away valuable beachfront, many of the multi-million dollar homes now overlap this high-water mark. Such is the case at the locations along Malibu Road.

While it is lawful to traverse the beach to the water, it is unlawful to trespass on private property. And since there is so little beach left at Malibu Road, sunbathers and other more casual beach visitors very rarely visit this site. Yet directly off shore are some of Malibu's most beautiful kelp forests. The public access points at the 24318 and 24434 Malibu Road have probably the best diving of the three locations. There is also a substantial kelp forest and reef to the west of the access at 24714 Malibu Road.

To reach Malibu Road, turn towards the beach off of Pacific Coast Highway at Webb Way. At the intersection with Malibu Road, turn right. The two-lane road parallels the beach in this residential area. You'll need to proceed slowly along the road in order to spot the public access points, which are not much more than a gate leading to some stairs. A good visual clue to the public beach is a trashcan at the entrance to the gate. Park on the opposite side of the road well off the pavement. Do not park on private property. This area is continually patrolled by private security. The gates are open during normal daylight hours and leads to a mixed sand and rocky beach.

Beginning at 50 to 100 yards offshore and extending to 200 yards out are large, healthy kelp forests and extensive reef systems below. The beach has a moderate slope, and you should be able to enter the water either directly out from the stairs or just slightly to the right. Large loose

Spanish shawl nudibranch

boulders and swirling sand dominate the near-shore bottom. It's not unusual to see halibut or shovel nose sharks in this area.

The kelp canopy is thick and contains an abundant amount of fish. Calico bass hover just beneath the fronds. Rather large versions of this fish will often hang just at the edge of visibility. Schooling fish such as opaleye, rubberlip surfperch, and a variety of baitfish move in and out of the kelp.

The best visibility lies on the outer edges of the kelp and averages 15 to 20 feet. The seaward fringes of the kelp forest always seem to make the most interesting diving. Here you will sometimes see barracuda cruising the fronds for small fish that venture too far from protection. On the reef, color is provided by giant spined stars, bat stars, and a smattering of nudibranchs. Small stands of gold gorgonian and spots of corynactis anemones fill out the patchwork of color. Also delightful to the eye are a variety of reef fish, including garibaldi, rockfish, and an occasional bluebanded goby.

Hunters would do best to stick to spearfishing for halibut on the sand on the inside and outside of the reef, but may also want to look for the occasional lobster that can be found within crevices in the rocks.

When you consider your next beach dive adventure, consider diving off of some of the private beaches of the stars. They may have an exclusive view of the beach, but you have an even more exclusive view of the ocean.

Blackeye goby

Big Rock

Malibu is known for its recluse stars and celebrities, with much of its coastline taken up with private beach bungalows and mansions. Beach access is often difficult with the large amount of private property abutting the beach but it can be done; you need to know exactly where to look for public water access. Several of these out-of-the- way shore access points lead to large healthy kelp beds with wonderful beach diving.

A large block of private beachfront residences abuts the beach known to locals as Big Rock. Just up the beach from the more popular Las Tunas Beach, kelp beds at Big Rock are often admired from afar by divers who think there is no access to the beach. Just off the 20000 block of Pacific Coast Highway, however, is a small public access way that is easy to drive past even when you are looking for it. Look for the "Coastal Access" sign. There are only two parking spaces here. The small gate at the flashing yellow traffic light opens to a few steps leading to a rock and sand beach fronting on an extensive and healthy kelp bed. Although the water entry can be tough, the diving is great and, although certainly not virgin, relatively untouched.

Big Rock gains its name from the medium large rock pinnacle inside the surf zone. A road just east of the beach access also gains its name from the pinnacle. Most local divers use this pinnacle as the jumping-off point for great kelp diving.

The beach is a peculiar mix of rock and sand. Depending on the time of year, the tides, storm conditions, and the face and shape of the beach can vary dramatically. Rocky beach surf entry experience is a must for diving this location. There are several large and small boulders in the surf, so you must pick and choose entry and exit

points carefully. Also take time to study the surf. As previously stated, most divers choose to use "Big Rock" for protected entries and exits. Look for surge channels so that you may be pulled out over the reefs. The rock affords a number of points that offer some protection from small to moderate surf. Because of the large number of rocks and reef in the surf zone, this beach is best avoided when the surf reaches three feet or more.

Moray eel

Once out past the shallow reefs close to shore, the bottom drops away to 10 feet deep. Spot reefs support prolific growths of eelgrass and, out a little deeper, feather boa kelp. Heading out farther, the bottom becomes mostly sand 15 to 20 feet down. At about 70 yards out, the giant kelp growth begins over large boulders and low-lying reefs. These close-in reefs are good areas to hunt for halibut but little else as the surge tends to stir up the bottom making visibility poor.

The best reef for sightseeing and other hunting begins about 100 yards out in 25 feet of water. An extensive reef structure is crisscrossed with crevices and large stands of healthy kelp. Look under large boulders for an occasional lobster or moray eel. Across the rocks are tiny pink anemones and rock scallop here and there. Small stands of

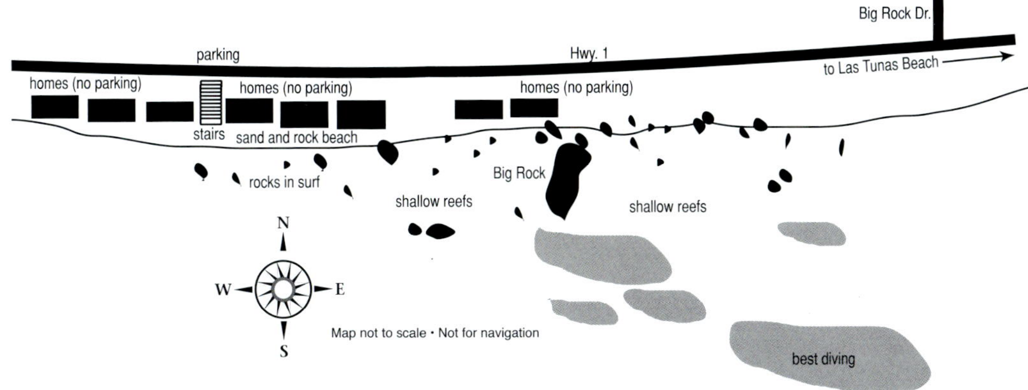

Cabezon

golden gorgonian color the bottom terrain.

Fish are plentiful with opaleye and perch being the most common. Up among the kelp fronds, spearfishers will find calico bass to stalk. Other fish worth stalking at this site include halibut usually found in the sand surrounding the kelp beds.

Water exits must be as cautious as water entries. Careful planning before the dive is a must. Have a primary and secondary exit sights planned in advance. Before passing back through the surf zone, time the wave sets carefully and exit on a lull between waves.

Those looking for the comforts of home at this dive sight had better forget it. There are no facilities here. The nearest public restrooms are over a mile away to the north or south. Parking here is poor as well. There is only one public parking space directly in front of the access gate. More parking is available on the opposite side of Highway 1, making crossing the highway in full dive gear the most hazardous part of the dive!

Although it's perfectly legal to dive here (daylight hours only), private property surrounds the beach. Do not trespass and respect the permanent resident's privacy and quiet. By the way, don't be surprised if angry dogs greet you as you walk on the beach. It's just another hazard of diving Malibu!

Las Tunas

Sometimes you just need a "quickie"! San Diego divers have La Jolla and Orange County Divers have Laguna Beach. Los Angeles divers have Palos Verdes and Malibu. The nearest major reefs for the heavily populated West Los Angeles, Santa Monica and San Fernando Valley areas are off Malibu. Heading west out of L.A. along Pacific Coast Highway (Highway 1), the first major reef you come to with easy public access is at Las Tunas Beach. As it's only a few minutes drive from the end of Sunset Boulevard, this is a great spot for a "quickie."

Rather than a dip in the hot tub after work, take a couple hours for a colorful dive along the coastline. With the long daylight hours of summer, you an easily get in a beach dive or two after work. And an added bonus is that dives can be made for only a few dollars for gas and air fill, and perhaps parking.

At Las Tunas Beach there is no parking fee! Parking is along the dirt shoulder on the ocean side of Pacific Coast Highway. Access to the water is only a few easy steps down a small bluff. Pause for a moment to first look over the conditions. The two-acre beach has a number of access points and beach faces.

In 1929, an erosion control program extended several metal and concrete groins into the surf designed to prevent sand from flowing away from the beach. While most of these submerged obstructions were removed a few years ago, some still remain. Carefully look over the surf and note their locations and use caution. The groins never properly did their job and the beach is heavily eroded in some locations.

Several spots are narrow sandy beaches while surf crashes on barren slippery rock in others. The small sand beaches are the best for water entry. The bottom drops off quickly to a depth of 10 to 15 feet, so the surf hitting the beach is frequently a sharp shore break, sometimes over rocks. Surf, however, is generally not a problem. The most popular water entry points for divers are on the extreme east end of the beach or near the middle next to the large rock. The large rock offers some shelter from waves. The path to the water here is short but slippery. The east end of the beach, known to the old-timers as "burnt-out house" because of a house that once caught fire here, offers a slightly larger area for parking and easier path. The swim out to the reefs is just a bit more, however.

Rubberlip seaperch

An extensive reef system extends from within 50 yards of shore to over 200 yards out. At one time this was one of the largest kelp beds off Malibu. Although nearly all other areas have recovered, Las Tunas has yet to do so for reasons unknown. The kelp forest here could recover at any time.

At about 100 yards out, in the middle of the reef, the rocky bottom becomes much more interesting and varied, pro-

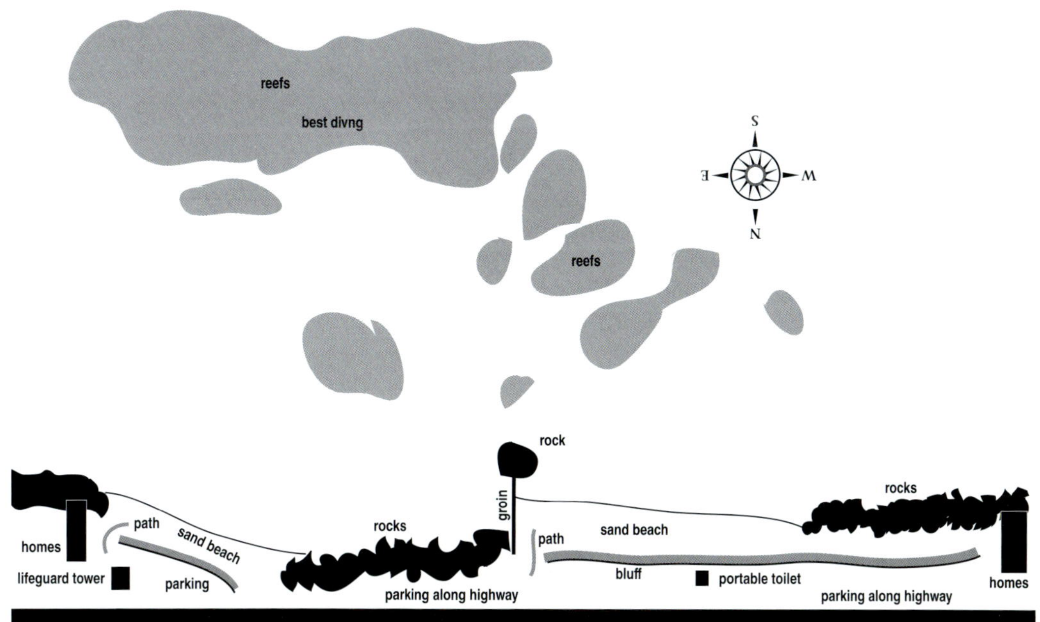

Green anemone

are plentiful. Don't come looking here for the bright orange garibaldi as they are curiously lacking. If the kelp recovers, even more fish will be back. (The name Las Tunas, by the way, has nothing to do with the fish but rather is Spanish for the prickly-pear cacti that use to be abundant on shore here.)

While this is by no means a photographer's heaven, the underwater shutterbug will find enough subject material to perhaps justify dragging a camera through the surf.

viding habitat for a wide variety of life. Groves of golden gorgonian are common. Adding to the splashes of color are patches of corynactis anemones and an occasional sea lemon or Spanish shawl nudibranchs. Other interesting reef creatures to be found here include sheep crabs, sea hares, feather duster worms and an unusual number of octopuses.

Las Tunas is plentiful with fish. Schools of large perch and salema cruise in and out of the cloudy waters. Large opaleye are also common and señoritas

The biggest deterrent to the underwater photographer is the visibility. Water visibility is only fair, averaging only 10 feet in the shoreward side of the kelp. It does improve somewhat to as much as 15 or 20 feet on the outer kelp edges, but this is too long of a swim for many divers.

Hunters, on the other hand, will definitely enjoy this location. Sand and kelp bass are bountiful, large, and relatively easy to approach. Halibut hunting is also good. The large flat fish can be spotted in the sand and gravel close to shore near the kelp stands. Lobster are present but not common. Most of the lobsters inhabit the outer reef. Scallops are also present but, again, not in plentiful numbers.

Be aware that this beach can become quite crowded on summer afternoons. The best time to dive here is in the early mornings because of the better conditions and lack of

California spiny lobster

crowds. In spite of its popularity, there are little facilities here. A lifeguard tower is staffed during the summer only and there are some portable toilets, nothing else.

If you live or work in the western half of Los Angeles County and have either a long lunch hour to kill, a weekend morning, or a need to escape the city tensions one summer evening, go to Las Tunas beach in Malibu for that "quickie."

Gladstone's

Almost everybody has heard of the famous Sunset Boulevard in Hollywood. But does anyone know where it ends? Running east-west, Sunset Boulevard ends on the west at the Pacific Ocean in an area of Los Angeles known as Pacific Palisades. The area is filthy with excellent seafood restaurants, but one eatery usually stands out in the minds of most locals—Gladstone's For Fish. Gladstone's is located at the very end of Sunset Boulevard, on Pacific Coast Highway and the Pacific Ocean.

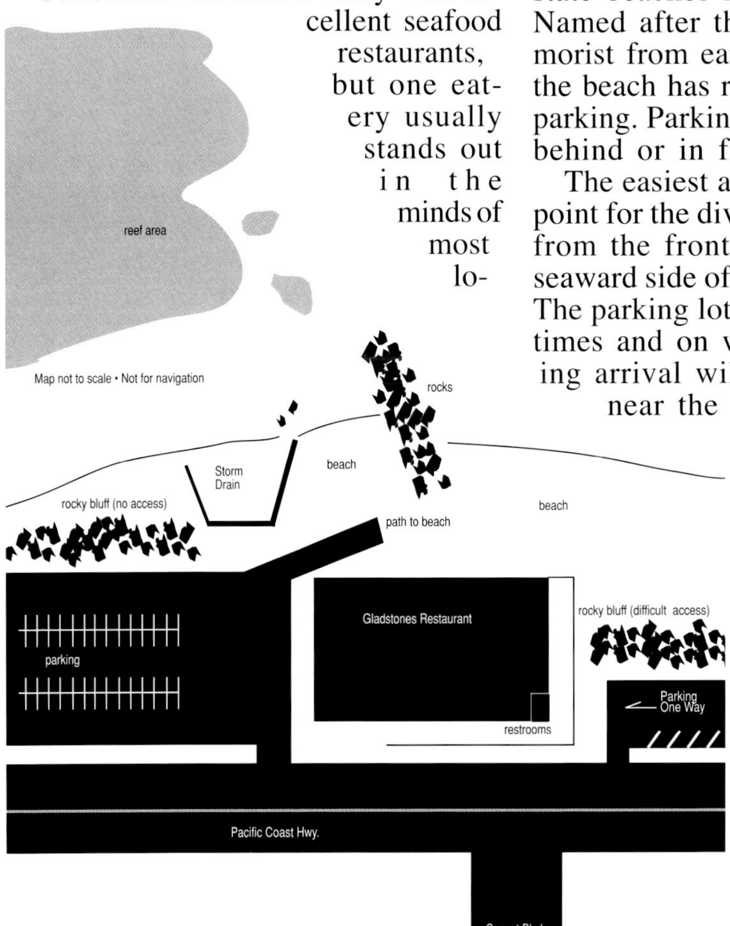

At almost any lunch or dinnertime, Gladstone's parking lot will be crammed with cars. It is a busy place. Hollywood stars frequent the eatery as well.

But rather than searching for celebrities, eyes of divers often turn seaward and wonder what is under the waves. Beyond the breakers, just below the restaurant a large reef area often covered by an extensive kelp forest. There is more seafood at this place than what is found in the restaurant. Lobster, halibut and other finfish can be found at this dive site.

Gladstone's is located on Will Rogers State Beach, one of the largest state beaches in Southern California. Named after the famous cowboy humorist from early in the 20th century, the beach has restrooms, showers, and parking. Parking (for a fee) is available behind or in front of the restaurant.

The easiest access to the water entry point for the dive site is the paved ramp from the front parking lot along the seaward side of the restaurant entrance. The parking lot fills up quickly at meal times and on weekends. Early morning arrival will assure a good space near the pathway to the beach.

Although extensive, most of the reef area is shallow, extending to only 25 feet deep at its outer edges. Surge can be a problem, so it is best to dive this site only in the calmest of conditions, preferably two-foot surf or less.

Water entry is done off a sandy beach at the base of the ramp. The walk down to the beach is easy and water entry simple when conditions are calm. You can use some of the rocks extending into the water for a bit of protection from the surf. The bottom drops off quickly from the surf line and almost immediately becomes rocky. Avoid the shallow areas as the surge stirs up plentiful silt, making visibility usually poor close in to shore.

Skirt along the outer edges of the kelp and pick a spot to descend. Again, this site isn't noted for its great visibility. Don't be disappointed with 10 to 15 feet of visibility; this is a good day at Gladstone's.

The outer edges of the reef are jumbled, low-lying boulders. The larger rocks are covered with giant kelp, feather boa kelp and a variety of other algae. The orange-mantled smooth turban snail can be observed munching on the kelp fronds. Wavy turban snails are common as well. Other abundant mollusks at this site include the small but colorful purple dwarf olives. About the size of a fingernail, the olives can be found in large groups buried in the sand. About the only other splash of color at this site is an occasional Spanish shawl nudibranch on the rocks.

Under some of the boulders lobster can be found but, frankly, most are below legal size. Look for the boulders with overhangs or deep pockets underneath.

You might have better luck with a speargun. Extensive sand swirling around the boulders is perfect hiding territory for halibut. Look carefully around rocks covered with kelp as halibut like to lie in wait for smaller fish to eat. Also search up in the reef in sand channels between rocks. Large fish can be frequently found in warm summer months in 10 feet of water or less. The populations of sand bass and calico bass are also good. Stealthy free divers are sometimes successful in stalking the illusive white sea bass.

Sightseers and photographers might be a bit disappointed diving at Gladstone's. Poor visibility, coupled with relatively barren reefs, make this somewhat drab reef. But the underwater hunter may do well at this spot.

Redondo Breakwater

As an answer to Redondo Beach's booming resort town, a small-craft harbor was built in 1939. This harbor was protected on the northwest by a half-mile long, arc-shaped breakwater. Problems of sand erosion and not enough protection for the harbor and municipal pier prompted the city to extend the breakwater another half-mile to the southeast and add a small jetty to the south end of the harbor in 1958.

It is the 100,000 tons of jumbled boulders on a sand bottom that created this dive site. The main diving attraction of the breakwater is its plentiful game. Several varieties of game fish are common and although their numbers have diminished, lobster is plentiful. Crab is also easily found.

The plentiful game is a result of the breakwater's large boulder construction, warm water dump from the nearby power plant, and the nearby submarine canyon. The power plant dumps its warmed cooling water from submerged towers around the breakwater. The warm seawater attracts and promotes growth of a variety of sea life. Nutrient rich upwellings from the canyon further enhance this mix.

These submerged towers are also used for seawater intake and may pose a hazard if approached; however, the towers are well clear of the breakwater. A diver has only to stay near the breakwater to avoid any danger.

The variety of marine life makes this an interesting if not intriguing site for the photographer. Short-spined sea stars so large they were not dwarfed by the huge boulders they were perched upon. Tucked in and about the boulders are various sponges, feather worms, anemones, and a variety of gorgonian. Even stands of the dead orange gorgonian make great diver photographs with its striking deep red colors.

The diving closer in to the breakwater is one continuous boulder field. Boulder upon boulder creates the perfect habitat for many a creature. Obviously the lobster loves this area and is a continuous catch all through lobster season, though odds are you'll not get your limit. You might get one per dive. This is due to the literally millions of holes and crevices created by the mile long breakwater. Many lobsters may never venture far enough out in the open to end up in your game bag.

The lobster are not the only thing you'll find lurking upon the boulders. Tucked back between large loosely packed boulders was the biggest cabezon I have ever seen. He peered out at me with a great big smile on his face—he was tucked back in such a way that we couldn't even get the camera into position.

As you move away from the breakwater and farther out to sea, the boulders will begin to give way to sand patches and then to a completely flat sand bottom. This is where you encounter sea pansies, large moon sails and halibut—another reason the breakwater is perfect for the underwater hunter.

Diving the breakwater from shore is possible but difficult. It should be attempted only on calm day by experienced divers. Access the breakwater from shore off Harbor Drive at Yacht Club Way. The road ends at the King Harbor Yacht Club (you'll have to pay for parking, if available). The boat docks will be on the left and the seawall to the right. Access to the breakwater is at the extreme west end of the lot. You'll have to park outside the Yacht Club parking lot and walk to the rocks.

Before donning gear, climb to the top of the breakwater and check the conditions. Diving here is often ruined by just a moderate swell. A three or four-foot swell can make entries hazardous, visibility poor, and movement on the bottom difficult in the surge. Call ahead for the surf report to check surf conditions. Diving is best in the early morning, when wind chop is at a minimum. Disregard the temptation of diving inside the harbor as this is illegal without a permit.

Although the best diving is at least 100 yards farther out along the breakwater, it's best to enter the water here and swim out, as walking along the breakwater is hazardous especially with scuba gear.

Water depth adjacent to the parking lot is 20 to 25 feet. Depths drop off slowly, moving south along the breakwater to a maximum of 45 feet at the tip.

Although some of the best diving is at the tip, it is either a long swim or a long walk. Generally, the best diving route is to enter near the parking lot, swim 100 yards south along the breakwater, descend and continue south underwater enjoying the scenery. To return, halfway or so through your tank, turn around and retrace north. Nooks, crannies and small caves are numerous all along the breakwater and many are filled with fascinating creatures. With luck, your dive will finish at or near your entry point.

Lingcod

Squid egg cases

Redondo Submarine Canyon

Along the Southern California coastline there are five submarine canyons that come close enough to shore to dive them from the beach. They are, from north to south, Hueneme, Dume, Redondo, Newport and La Jolla. Although not the most spectacular of the submarine canyons (that honor is owed to the La Jolla Canyon), the Redondo Canyon has probably the easiest access and best conditions.

Submarine canyons are a curious oceanographic phenomena. They are deep cuts into the continental shelf that transport ever shifting sands to the deep ocean floor and bring cold clear deep waters close to shore. Unusual marine life can be found in abundance in these canyons and Redondo is no exception.

Perhaps the most curious and interesting marine fauna that congregates here is the spawning market squid that

Sarcastic fringehead

Night Beach Diving

Night diving can lead to encounters with entirely different kinds of marine life. Beach diving has its advantages also. You can dive when you want to, for as long as you want to, and it's cheap. The near-shore underwater environment also holds some unique surprises of its own.

Can you combine night and beach diving? You bet! A few extra pieces of equipment, and some added diving techniques and procedures, and you'll be fully on your way to discovering a new, exciting and safe way to enjoy California's underwater world.

To the uninitiated, however, either beach or night diving alone can be a bit intimidating. Before you try doing both together, you'll want to be proficient and comfortable at both. Classes in night diving are readily available at most dive stores. They cover basic procedures and equipment. They also include your first night dive experience, usually off a boat and under the watchful eyes of an experienced instructor.

Classes in beach diving, however, are a little harder to come by. If it was not included with your basic course, you should seek training. Beach diving training can be often arranged through your local dive store, included with another course (such as an Advanced Diver course) or by participation in a "3Rs" course (Reefs, Rocks, Rips) which covers specific beach diving techniques for individual dive sites. The 3Rs are run regularly by various organizations in Southern California. A final way of learning beach diving is with an experienced beach diver. Dive clubs are great places to attach yourself to such a person.

In planning a night beach dive, always take yourself down one notch in experience level. Intermediate beach dives should be tried only by highly experienced divers at night. Dive sites that are considered "beginner" should be attempted at night, only by intermediate or advanced divers and so on. Prospective night beach sites should first be explored in daylight, both above and below the water. Be sure to check the posted beach hours as some beaches do not allow night activities. Also, remember your diver etiquette. After dark you'll want to be especially quiet on the beach and at your vehicle so as to not disturb neighbors.

On the night of your planned beach dive, just as you would with a daylight dive, check out the surf report first. You will, of course, want ideal conditions. Surf should be no more than one to two feet with little wind. Tides should be slack. High tide is usually best, but this often depends on the particular dive site. If possible, try to visit the site at dusk to check out current conditions or any last minute changes.

If you're a bit uncomfortable with your beach night dive, choose a site with a great deal of artificial lighting. Breakwaters near brightly lit harbors, sites near popular beaches or piers are often brightly illuminated with light spilling over the water. This lighting will aid in navigation and general orientation, both above and below the water.

Use the biggest and brightest dive light possible. A big light will help you study the surf before ever entering the water. For darker dive sites, place marker lights on shore for navigation purposes. Flashing lights are not a good choice as they could confuse boaters. Also avoid green or red marker lights as these are also used in boating navigation. Blue and Yellow are good choices. When diving from small coves or sites with many shallow reefs or rocks, you'll want to carefully mark on shore your intended water exit site as well as alternate exit point. Cylumes or chemical lights make excellent choices for marking as they are inexpensive and less likely to be stolen. For more complicated markings, use a combination of colors in distinctive patterns. Tie or tape your markers to fences, piers, or bring along small stakes. Avoid attachment to private property or vehicles, and always remove your markers on completion of the dive.

As with any night dive, carry a diver location light. Also carry a good quality back-up light tucked neatly into a BC pocket. While a good idea on any night dive, it is especially important on a beach dive as the odds of losing a primary light, or a breakdown due to sand or rough handling is greatly increased.

Surf entry should be done much as with a daylight dive. Using your most powerful light, check out the surf maximum height, time the sets and in wave intervals and go between sets and between waves. Use side shuffle with fins always keeping an eye (and light) on the surf, looking for any rogue waves. Get clear of the surf zone as quickly as possible.

Upon surfacing, use caution that you do not send confusing or conflicting signals with your light to nearby boats or those on shore. Try to keep your light low and out of other diver's faces. As you approach shore, you will, of course, want to illuminate the shoreline, but keep your light movements steady and with purpose. If you are signaling someone on shore, a slow circular movement indicates "OK." An erratic side-to-side rapid motion or flashing indicates problems. A whistle or air horn is highly recommended to signal problems. Short rapid bursts grab the most attention.

As with water entry, keep an eye and light on the surf as you exit the water. Don't be too proud to use the crawl exit if necessary.

invade the deep trench in winter. Moving in at night, the massive schools of deep-water squid rise to within just feet of the surface to spawn and lay their eggs. A winter night dive within the blizzard of mating squid can be exhilarating. Clusters of their egg cases can be found spread out across the sloping mud bottom like bouquets of snowy white flowers.

The squid also bring in predators. Blue sharks, huge schools of bonita, large rays, and sea lions are often seen while diving in the canyon during this special time of year.

Another curious occurrence is the congregation of decorator crabs. These interesting crustaceans vary in size from about the size of a golf ball up to six inches across. They get their name from their habit of camouflaging themselves by placing and growing a

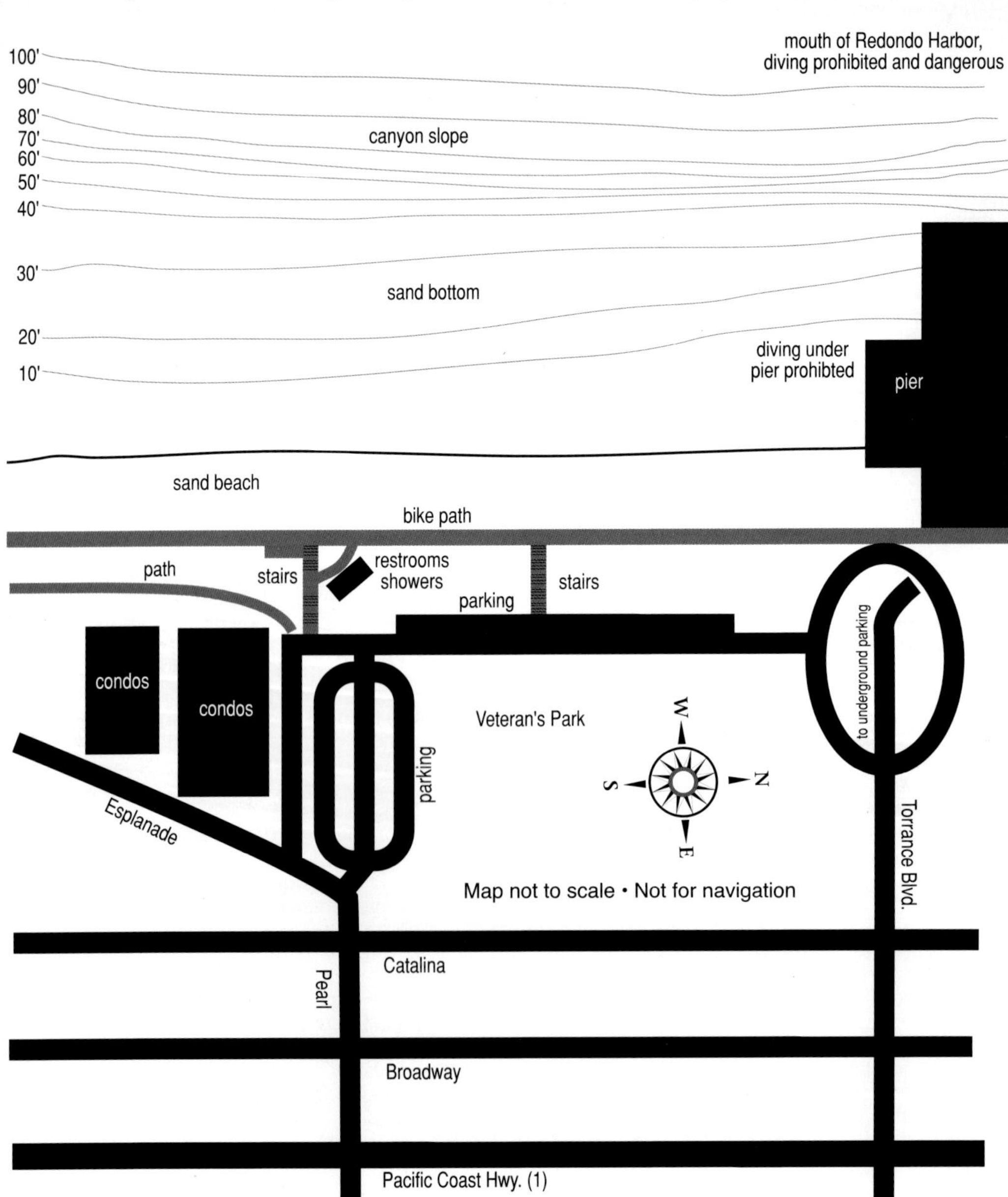

garden of algae on their shells. During the spring, hundreds of decorator crabs invade the canyon and group in piles of 10 to 50 in some sort of mating orgy. They appear as dark moving clumps on the bottom until you approach them; then they break up and scatter in a matter that is somewhat humorous. The similar looking but larger sheep crabs have also been reported to exhibit the same behavior in the area.

Sanddab

The Redondo Canyon is an easy dive; so easy, as a matter of fact, that many certification classes come to this beach for check-out dives. But they rarely descend into the canyon. And that's where you'll find the action.

The canyon head parallels the shore in front of the park, the parking area, and over to the pier. It's illegal to dive under the pier, so avoid that area. Most enter and exit directly off the stairs that lead to the restrooms and showers, but the stairs 100 feet to the north is another option. Due in part to the canyon, and part to the semi-protection from the jetty to the south and harbor to the north, the surf here is always half the size of nearby beaches. Even so, check out conditions from the bluff parking before gearing up. This is a west-facing beach and although rare, wicked surf can sometimes crash here.

It is only about a 70-yard swim to the canyon edge. Swim out until you are even with the end of the pier to the north. Submerge here and you'll be only a few fin kicks from the drop-off.

The sand bottom will drop rapidly from 35 feet to about 70 or 80 feet and taper off to a more moderate slope. It is the flats at the base of the steep slope that are the most interesting. Many critters make home here to benefit from the debris that slides down the slope. Wavy turban snails are common and their empty shells are popular homes with small octopus and a small fierce fish known as the sarcastic fringehead.

It is these fringeheads that are main target of interest for underwater photographers. They are fiercely territorial, guarding their seashell homes with an attitude worthy of a junkyard dog. They will react in one of two ways when you approach them: they will either cower into their shells or raise their dorsal fins and open their broad mouths in a defiant posture of attack. Shortly thereafter, you'll probably get bit. Although only four to eight inches in length, they can break skin on an ungloved hand. Their posturing makes for fascinating macro-photography.

Octopuses are also abundant, although never very large. Not only do they make their home in the turban shells, they can also be found in human debris such as bottles and cans. No doubt the octopus are here to feed on the abundant crab population. Swimming, rock, and hermit crabs are all well represented. Too big for the octopus, the sheep crabs roam freely about. A type of spider crab, they have a heavy shell and move slowly. Some can reach up to three feet across.

This is not a good fish dive except for those bay bottom type fish. Flatfish will be abundant, including sole and small halibut. The small flatfish will pose for your camera if you approach slowly. The shy barred sand bass, on the other hand, will stay just out of range. Rays can sometimes be seen on the canyon slope.

Big stars cruise the bottom. Pink pisaster stars are the most impressive, reaching up to two feet across. Their soft pale pink is in stark contrast to the spiny blue-gray of the sand star. They move at a surprisingly rapid pace across the sand bottom in search of food.

Pier piling

The farther you head out, the deeper it gets. It's very easy to get into over 90 feet of water. A bit further and you're beyond 100. Thermoclines are common at these depths and can be profound and bitingly cold. Be aware the further you head out, the more boat traffic you will encounter overhead from the nearby pleasure boat harbor. Use caution. For safety, avoid ascending from the canyon depths. Rather, finish your dive by heading up the canyon slope and heading toward shore before you surface.

The Redondo Submarine Canyon allows shore divers access to deep water and the deep-water environment that is so often hidden from our eyes. Exploring the depths of the canyon can be a unique, different and exciting experience that all divers should try.

Old Redondo Pier #3

Around the turn of the century, Redondo Beach was the hub of Los Angeles' maritime trade. The deep offshore submarine canyon, Redondo Canyon, allowed merchant ships to approach shore close in calm seas. In the late 19th century, piers were erected off the beach to service the growing merchant trade. Items carried on the ships included lumber from the Pacific Northwest and goods from the Far East. It was a prosperous time for that section of the coast. Much of it became a resort for Angelenos seeking a holiday from the daily worries of big-city living.

Eventually, a total of three piers were servicing the shipping business.

Pier #1 stood at Emerald Street, long since replaced, (several times) by the now famous Horseshoe Pier (itself heavily damaged by storms and fire in the late 1980s). Pier #1 was destroyed by a storm in 1914. At Ainsworth Court, next to Veteran's Park (then the luxurious Redondo Hotel) was the Y-shaped Pier #2. Reaching into the edge of the canyon, the pier was heavily damaged by a storm in 1915 and eventually was torn down, never to be rebuilt. The few underwater remains of Pier #2, just over the lip of the Redondo Canyon, disappeared in the late 1980s with winter storms.

The 480-foot long Pier #3, located between Sapphire and Topaz Streets, was also destroyed by a storm in 1926. From that time forward, the shipping boom for Redondo Beach was over as the new port at San Pedro was being constructed.

Pier #3 was the most prosperous of the three piers serving Redondo Beach and Los Angeles early in the century. The railroad ran to the length of the pier carrying cargo to and from merchant ships. The Pacific Steamship Company had a restaurant on the end of the pier as well. The storm of 1926 took much of that structure to the sea floor. Today, the only evidence of the pier's existence lies underwater.

The remaining pilings, numbering just over a dozen, are the main attraction of this dive spot. Jutting up from the bottom as high as twelve feet, they are covered with beautiful pink anemones which make excellent photo subjects.

Another attraction of this site is the artifacts that can be found on the bottom. Old bricks and broken dishes from the old restaurant are common. If you are lucky, you may find a bottle or a large piece of dish with an insignia.

The diving area can be reached by turning west on either Sapphire or Topaz off Pacific Coast Hwy. (Highway 1) in Redondo Beach. Both of these streets end at the Esplanade. Parking is along the street

Corynactis anemones

and access to the beach is via a pathway between the buildings at both locations.

The entry area is just to the north of the jetty. Facilities are good with showers at the lifeguard tower near the jetty and at the restrooms at the base of the path that leads to Sapphire Street.

Water entry is generally easy in light to moderate surf. The sand bottom slopes gently to approximately 35 feet deep 100 yards out. One way to locate the pier is to swim on the surface outward from the beach to just beyond the jetty. You should be directly out from the second set of condominiums just to the north of the jetty. Many divers locate the wreckage by swimming northwest across the bottom at a 45-degree angle from the end of the jetty. I like to enter farther to the north. Just beyond the jetty, I drop down and swim out until the bottom begins to drop away gently into the Redondo Submarine Canyon. At this point I follow the 35-foot contour to the south and out and I inevitably run into the first piling. In any event, don't give up quickly. The pier area is long and narrow, and it is very easy to be either too far north, south, or too close to shore. There is, by the way, an entire separate set of short pilings in only 10 to 15 feet of water

The area containing the most artifacts is closer to shore and is identified by the bricks scattered on the bottom. Digging in the sand here will produce broken fragments of dishes. The broken pilings are short and sometimes covered with stalks of kelp. Depending on the weather, the kelp may reach the surface in some locations, thus assisting the location of the dive site.

The tall pilings are seaward and more toward the north on the edge of the Redondo Canyon in about 40 to 45 feet of water. The Redondo Canyon begins

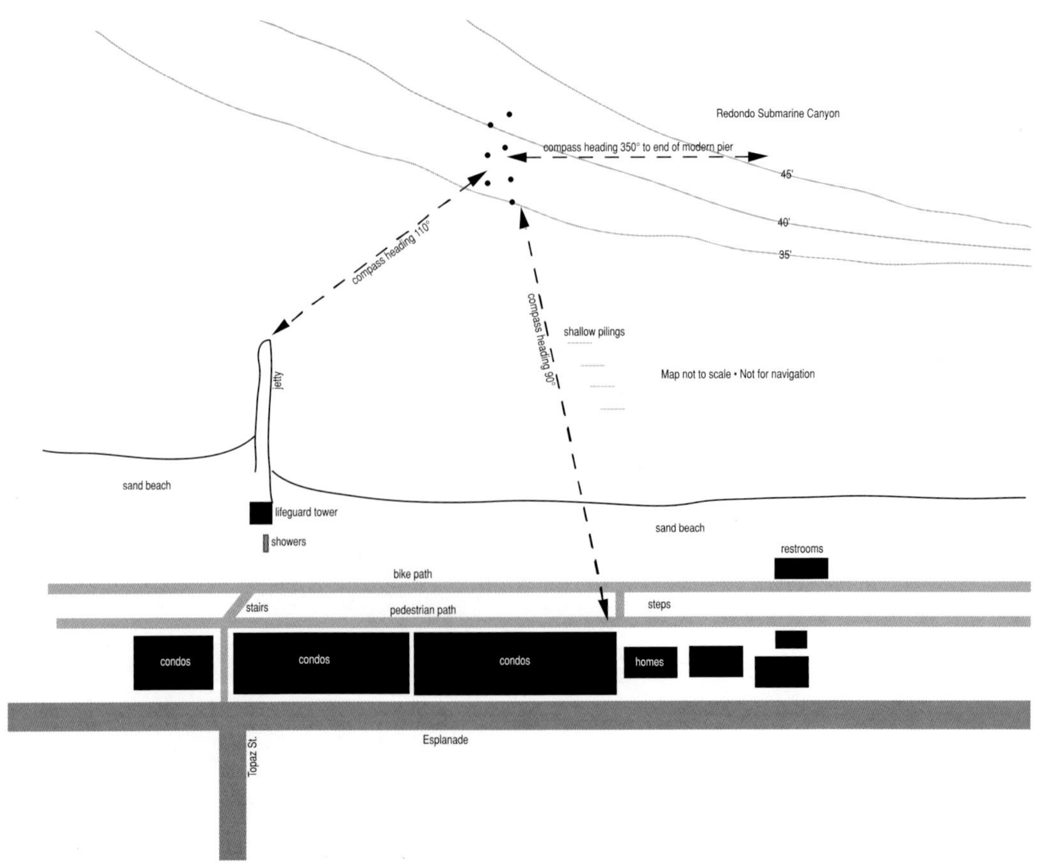

to drop off moderately just to the north. If, in your search, you find yourself dropping into the canyon, you are too far north. Head up the sloping bottom to the south to find the pilings. The pilings are generally just out of visibility range, so move around to spot them all. The outermost pilings are about 200 yards out from shore. Unfortunately storms have taken their toll on the pilings over the years and there are fewer than there once were so they are harder to find.

Ocean conditions at this dive sight are usually good. Visibility is consistent averaging between 10 and 20 feet. Upwelling from the nearby Redondo Canyon can increase visibility to the 30-foot range. Surf is little or no problem, particularly during the summer months when the west-facing beach is well protected from the predominately south swell. Prevailing westerlies during the winter can occasionally bring big surf while any current is almost nonexistent. The only real persistent hazard is the boat traffic from nearby Redondo Beach King Harbor, so a flag and float are recommended.

Hunting in the area is generally limited to good-sized halibut which are often taken in the sand surrounding the pilings. An occasional kelp bass can be spotted but is usually small. Sculpin or cabezon have been known to overrun the area from time to time.

Other sea life common around the pilings includes the often comical but always slow-moving sheep crab. This member of the spider crab family can grow to be quite large, averaging 18 inches across and as much as 24 inches. Octopus can be found cramped into small holes in the pilings, while on the sandy bottom, sea pens and sea pansies make their home.

RAT Beach Reefs

One of the most popular dive sites along the Palos Verdes Peninsula is Malaga Cove. This site is located along the Santa Monica Bay where the long, wide sandy beaches that are so famous in Los Angeles disappear into rocks and cliffs. It is also here that the beaches go from a north/south direction to a nearly westerly direction. What is created is a unique environment of kelp, sand and rocks which attracts an unusually bountiful variety of small sharks, rays, and other marine life.

Most divers hitting the waters of Malaga Cove head to the southwest and the lush kelp. But another, much less heavily visited site lies just 200 yards away off the sandy beach to the north. The locals know this beach as “RAT Beach.”

The term “RAT Beach” has nothing to do with local wildlife but rather is an acronym for “Right After Torrance.” A lot of people are unaware that Torrance even has a beach, which is a short stretch of sandy beach that extends from public parking, restrooms, and beach access in the north to just short of Malaga Cove on the south. What people call Rat Beach is really part of Torrance Beach but is less frequented by the crowds.

The easiest access to RAT Beach is from Malaga Cove. Unknown to most divers, intermittent reefs in 15 to 20 feet of water extend from Malaga Cove northward to a major reef off RAT Beach. On days of exceptional water visibility, these reefs can be spotted from the gazebo on the bluff at Malaga Cove.

Calico bass

While the reefs off RAT Beach are not as interesting as those at Malaga Cove, the life in waters surrounding these rocks is often superior.

Bat rays are quite common and it is not unusual to see several on one dive. Frequently they can be quite large with wingspans of over five feet. When you find bat rays, halibut are almost sure to follow. The halibut like to hide in the sand near the low-lying reefs. If you move quietly through the water, you may also spot the shy leopard and sand sharks.

Over the rocks, the fish life is plentiful. Kelp and sand bass are common and exceptionally large. Other common species include opaleye, surfperch, and halfmoons.

Life on the rocks, on the other hand, is sparse. Kelp is even sparser and eelgrass has trouble getting a hold on these rocks swept with surge.

The reefs here are shallow with depths running between 10-20 feet. Furthermore, the beach is exposed to a common westerly swell. All of this combines to create an environment that is intermittently swept with sand and brushed clean of all but the hardiest reef dwellers.

Visibility is poor, averaging 5 to 10 feet. But good days of visibility of 20 feet are frequent enough to consider this as an alternate dive site to Malaga Cove.

With the bountiful kelp bass, halibut and other fish, certainly this is a good site for the spearfisher. While lacking in colorful reefs and clear water, you may think this to be a poor spot for the sightseer and photographer. Not so. The presence of huge bat rays makes this an exciting dive for all.

Jumping off point for this shore dive is the same for Malaga Cove (follow the directions in the next chapter on how to reach Malaga Cove). There is adequate parking and a gazebo that overlooks the cove. From here, if you train your eyes up the beach to the north, you will spot a large light-colored section of the bluffs jutting from the darker bluffs. It is directly out from these white bluffs that the RAT Beach reefs lay. If the water is clear that day, you may be able to spot the reefs from the gazebo. They will appear as a dark section of water 30 to 50 yards from shore. They then extend sporadically to the north, just short of the southern most parking lot at Torrance Beach.

A short steep path leads down to Malaga Cove from the parking lot.

Water entry and getting to the reef can be done in one of two ways. The first option is to walk the 200-odd yards along the beach to the white bluffs, enter the water there, and swim directly to the reefs. Option two is to enter off the rocks at Malaga Cove and swim over, either by compass on scuba or with snorkel.

Swimming from Malaga Cove is recommended. The water off the rocks is frequently calmer and with scuba gear on your back, swimming is easier than walking. Most importantly, however, you will enjoy the stroll underwater. Between Malaga Cove and the RAT Beach reefs are several small intermittent reefs running parallel to each other and perpendicular to shore. It is in the sand between these reefs you will often see bat rays and halibut.

RAT Beach is a further attraction simply because it is a beautiful beach. With no direct access, it is frequently uncrowded even on hot summer weekends. With the attraction of the old favorite, Malaga Cove, and the new site, RAT Beach, you may want to bring two tanks.

Malaga Cove

At the southern regions of the Santa Monica Bay, the coastline takes a radical 90-degree turn from north-south to east-west. This is one of the few places where the California shoreline actually faces north. The sand beaches of the Santa Monica Bay meet the rocky cliffs of Palos Verdes at a place known as Malaga Cove. This meeting of rocky reefs and sandy plains is one of the most interesting underwater environments along the L.A. county coastline. More large and unusual marine life can be seen here on a consistent basis than any other dive site in the Santa Monica Bay. Divers frequently encounter leopard sharks, angel sharks, bat rays, black sea bass, and large schools of silvery barracuda.

The big plus for shore divers is the relatively easy beach access and water entry. Parking is on the bluff above the cove. Overlooking the diving area is a beautiful gazebo. From this vantage point the ocean conditions below can easily be observed. To the right of the gazebo, winding down the gully, a paved pathway leads to the beach. While the pathway is moderately steep, it is short and makes using wheeled transport of dive gear easy. Parking is free but is restricted to the hours of 6 a.m. to 10 p.m. There are no facilities and the nearest restrooms are a long way up the sandy beach at Torrance Beach.

Looking from the gazebo, stretched before you will be a beach of medium-sized boulders with shallow reefs just

Giant kelp forest

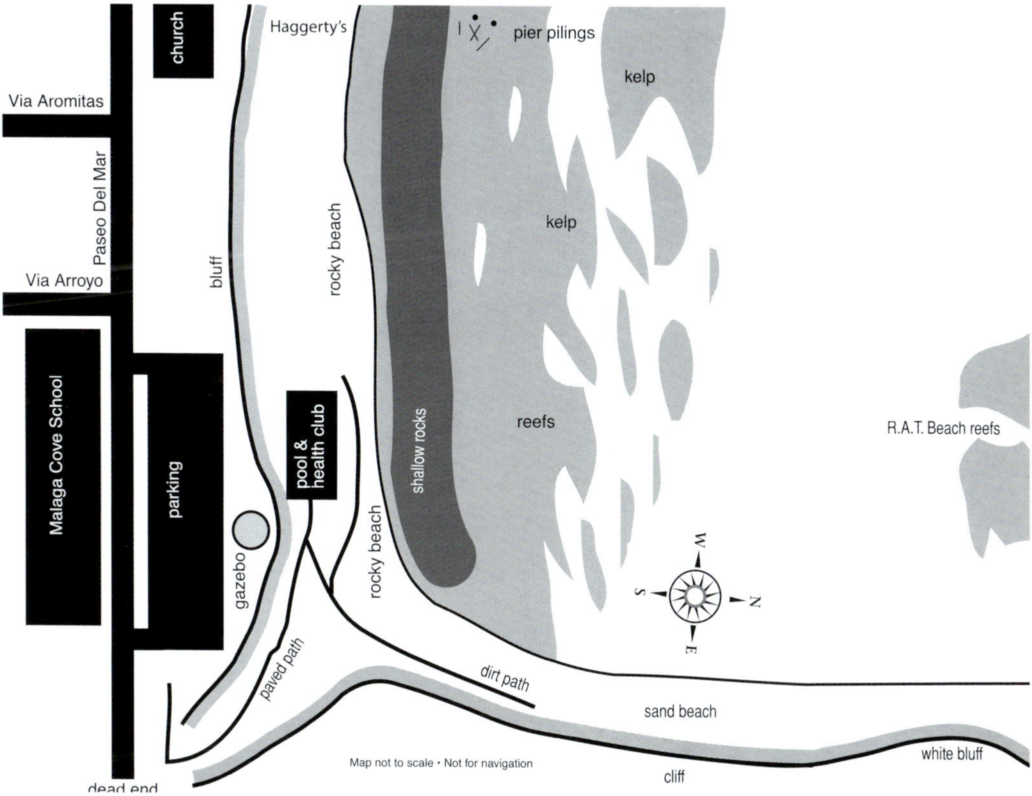

Octopus

off shore. To the right are the sandy beaches of the Santa Monica Bay. From the gazebo you'll be able to make an assessment of the surf conditions and water visibility. When diving conditions at Malaga Cove are good, they're usually great. When they are poor, however, they're often terrible. Malaga Cove is rarely in between. While the north-facing beach can be advantageous in certain situations, it often gets pounded from the prevailing west and northwest weather. In addition, the gully often dumps muddy rain run off onto near-shore reefs. With shallow water close to shore, and a high vantage point, water clarity can be estimated by simply looking into the water. Fortunately, for those poor days, there are many alternative dive sites close by, at Redondo Beach or around Palos Verdes.

Divers here have a choice of walking a few hundred feet and entering the water from a sandy beach or, if conditions permit, entering from the rocks for a shorter swim to the main diving area. While water entry off of the rocks shortens the swim distance to the more interesting reefs, conditions have to be right. There are numerous shallow reefs close to shore. Surf must be low and tide high to be able to swim safely across the jagged rocks.

When entering the water from the sandy beach, look carefully over the shallow rocks in the sand near shore. It is in this area that you will most often find large leopard sharks. Good-size halibut are also frequently spotted in the sand channels between these rock reefs. The bottom is gently sloping and reaches 20 feet deep about 100 yards out. There is almost always some sort of kelp growth. It became quite thin during El Niño, but most of the time it is thick and healthy. It becomes the thickest in summer and can actually become a problem when entering and exiting the water from the rocks. In the winter, kelp is quite thin or frequently reduced to only a few small stands.

When the kelp has thickened, the barracuda move in. A favorite food of black sea bass is the barracuda. The summer kelp of Malaga Cove can be an enchanted place when you're surrounded by silvery arrows of barracuda and the dark shadow of a black sea bass shows up.

The reefs fall in a pattern of ridges roughly parallel to shore. Some of these ledges can be quite tall, rising as much as six feet from the bottom. Along these ledges you'll find the most interesting bottom life. Octopuses are quite common here. The best way to spot the lair of an octopus is to look for its food debris outside of its hole. Feeding mostly on crabs and mollusks, an unusually large concentration of shells will indicate an octopus hole is near by.

The most abundant and obvious fish is the bright orange garibaldi. Because this is a popular dive site, they're quite accustomed to divers and will frequently gather around underwater visitors. Other abundant fish include the greenish opaleye, calico bass, and the thin señorita fish.

The more interesting reefs are directly off the health club and to the west. This is a good place for lobster hunting, particularly early in the season.

Hidden Places in a Kelp Forest

Kelpfish

It's very is easy to get caught up in the grandeur of a kelp forest. Tall stalks of kelp reach for the surface like many towering redwoods. Rocky reefs are covered in color, creating walls and a mosaic of underwater terrain that's exciting to explore and dazzling to the eye. In this kind of grandeur, it's often easy to ignore some of the smaller, more hidden pleasures. Also, we often find ourselves ignoring the reefs and kelp forests that perhaps on the surface appear dull and sparse of life. The persistent diver, however, need only have a bit more patience to slow down and look in the right places for exciting clusters of colorful marine life.

Whenever possible, carry a light on your dive. Even the smallest cracks and crevasses will often hold small fish, little invertebrates and tiny mollusks. Look under ledges and in holes. All that is needed to observe this marine life is to get close and use a bright penetrating light.

Similar kinds of marine life can be found on the under sides of rocks, which are often veritable nurseries of marine life harboring thousands of tiny animals. Turning over a small bolder will reveal brittle stars, baby mollusks, small sea stars, tiny worms and other critters. As a macro photographer, it presents an opportunity to photograph inaccessible animals that are often tucked neatly back into crevasses. However, when you're through photographing, carefully replace the rock back to its original position. The exposed juvenile animals and tiny creatures will quickly become prey to hungry fish if the rock is left exposed.

Another hidden, often overlooked place in the kelp forest is the holdfasts themselves. Kelp plants do not have roots per se, but rather cling to the bottom in a mass of tendrils that often engulf a small rock knob. Within these tendrils are numerous tiny cracks, crevasses and pockets in which small animals hide. Soft, amber hues of the holdfast make good background for photography of tiny animals that will peek out from the protected enclave of the kelp's "roots."

Many divers miss out by not looking carefully up among the kelp fronds. Undersides of the kelp "leaves" are often entire communities unto themselves. The kelp fronds can be covered with tiny bryozoans which in turn are fed on by small almost invisible invertebrates, which in turn become food for larger fish and animals. Many fish find shelter in the kelp fronds. There is the giant kelp fish that blends very effectively among the kelp stocks by imitating the shape and color of the kelp fronds. One of the more obvious residents of the kelp fronds is the Norris top snail. It can be easily spotted forging the leaves by its bright orange mantel. Another entertaining animal that feeds on the kelp fronds high above the ocean floor is the kelp crab.

Many kelp forest visitors often ignore the blue open water. Although really not hidden, one of the most exciting portions of the kelp forest is the outer edge that faces the open ocean. It is in this area that large pelagic fish will frequently cruise in hopes that a forest resident will stray too far from the protection and become a meal.

As you cruise the kelp, head towards the outer edges and peer off into the open ocean. A few divers will be treated to passing schools of fish. A marauding school of yellowtail can be quite exciting. In rare instances divers have encountered black and white sea bass, seals and sea lions, dolphins, sharks, and even whales.

Many California divers will agree that kelp diving can be the greatest underwater experience the world has to offer. To float among the tall stocks of kelp is to experience the freedom and weightlessness of floating through a giant enchanted forest. But the kelp forest has even more to offer in hidden nooks and crannies. One has only to take the time to slow down and look carefully.

Most are small but an occasional legal-size bug can be found. The shallower rocks seem to be the most productive.

Farther offshore sand channels break up the rock reefs. Isolated small reefs lie out across the sand flats. The adventure-some diver may wish to head out across the sand with the chance of spotting large halibut or a big angel shark. Even far from the reef, the depths rarely exceed 25 feet.

Because this section of the coastline faces mostly north, it can get the brunt of winter storms, but being a north-facing beach it does have its advantages. In the late summer through early fall, tropical storms far out in the Southern Pacific will throw up large southerly swells that hit such south facing beaches as Malibu and Laguna Beach. Malaga Cove, however, is usually unaffected.

Haggerty's

Rich people know how to pick 'em. It's a beautiful site overlooking the South Santa Monica Bay in an area known by the locals as the Queen's Necklace (how the shore looks at night from the lights). The rich man's name was Haggerty. Although he is long gone, and a church is now located at his mansion site, his name stuck to the location famous with surfers and divers. It's even mentioned in the Beach Boys ballad "Surfin' USA"!

Mr. Haggerty may have known at least a bit of the underwater treasures that were at his door step. Early in this century he built his mansion on the cliffs about as close to the water as anyone dared. Not content with that, a pier was extended from shore until the waves battered it back. Remains of the pier can still be seen today underwater. The main attraction for divers, however, is the rocky reefs on the bottom.

This shoreline is one of the few stretches of coast that actually faces somewhat north. Prevailing weather is from the northwest making this a favorite spot for surfers, but in the summer and fall, when the northwest weather calms and south swells pound the south facing beaches, the Haggerty's dive site is an excellent choice for underwater explorers.

Access to the site has, unfortunately, become more difficult. The short but steep trail that lead to the shore here washed away in storms and now the only way to reach it is by walking west from the same access at Malaga Cove. Enter the water over the rock at any place that looks good and head west as that is generally the best diving.

Rocky reefs start right from shore and so does the marine life. This has long been a good spot for lobster. While this is no secret, it is surprising how many lobster still come from this site considering the pressure it receives. Shallow reefs close to shore can make entry and exit tricky. Dive this site only when the surf is low and tide is high. It is these same shallow reefs and long eelgrass that provide shelter for

Pier pilings

Garibaldi with nest of eggs

lobster. This is a good place to free dive on a calm night during lobster season.

It is also in these shallows you'll find the remains of the old pier. The only two vertical pilings remaining are in 15 feet of water, directly out from the tower on the church. At low tide, the tops of the broken pilings can be seen protruding from the water. At the base of the pilings are more large cylindrical pilings lying horizontal on the bottom. These extend haphazard into 20 feet of water. Garibaldi dance around the fallen columns and, on calm clear days, make for interesting photography. And, again, it's not unusual to see lobster seeking refuge under the wreckage.

Beyond and out to 30 feet deep are more rock reefs eventually disappearing into sand. Along the outer edges are gorgonian, large barred sand bass, and, on the sand near the reefs, halibut. Huge sheep crab is perhaps the most dominant form of life on these reefs. Their size, slow movements and inability to cope with persistently curious divers make them enjoyable to watch. They can reach up to two feet across, and it is not unusual to see three or four in one dive. Sea hares or sea slugs are another readily available life form found under this kelp bed. Many are quite large reaching the size of soccer balls. Also look for the sea hare's clusters of yellow eggs. The kelp over the rocky reefs can be quite thick. Plan your dive with enough air left in your tank to return under the kelp canopy.

Flat Rock

Many divers agree that the west side of Palos Verdes offers some of the best coastal diving in Southern California; however, much of it has poor or no access. Flat Rock Point, which does offer access to good diving, marks the

California golden gorgonian

location where the coastline around Palos Verdes swings to the south again.

Flat Rock Point offers excellent diving on an interesting sea bottom. The bottom drops off quickly from shore to a 25 to 35 foot bottom made of boulders and reefs that run in the pattern of ridges rising from the bottom 5 to 10 feet. Between the ridges, small patches of ivory sand create clearings in the forests of healthy kelp that seem to grow almost everywhere.

The lush kelp and excellent reef formation support an excellent variety of fish life. Numerous garibaldi, señoritas, kelp bass, sheephead and other varieties are found here. The spearfishing enthusiast may be frustrated however; much of the game fish varieties are on the small side with the possible exception of the large halibut that pass over the small sand patches between the reefs.

Flat Rock Point has long been a consistent producer of lobster. Much of the near-shore reefs have been picked clean of the larger bugs, but outer waters, and sometimes the very shallow waters, can produce a big bug.

The photographers and sightseers will enjoy the usually good visibility. Averaging 15 to 20 feet, the kelp beds are ideal for exploring the underwater forest-like surroundings. On the bottom, colorful nudibranchs, sea stars, gorgonian and anemones make their home. Other invertebrates include an abundance of sea cucumbers, keyhole limpets, and sea hares. In the reef crevices, it is not unusual to find the yellow and black striped treefish, the small and shy bluebanded gobies or even an occasional horn shark. Urchins are common, so watch those knees!

Shore access to the point is difficult but not impossible. Flat Rock Point is located just down the road from other popular Palos Verdes dive spots such as Haggerty's and Malaga Cove. Proceed to the area via Pacific Coast Highway. In the city of Torrance, exit on Palos Verdes Blvd. proceeding south. Follow this

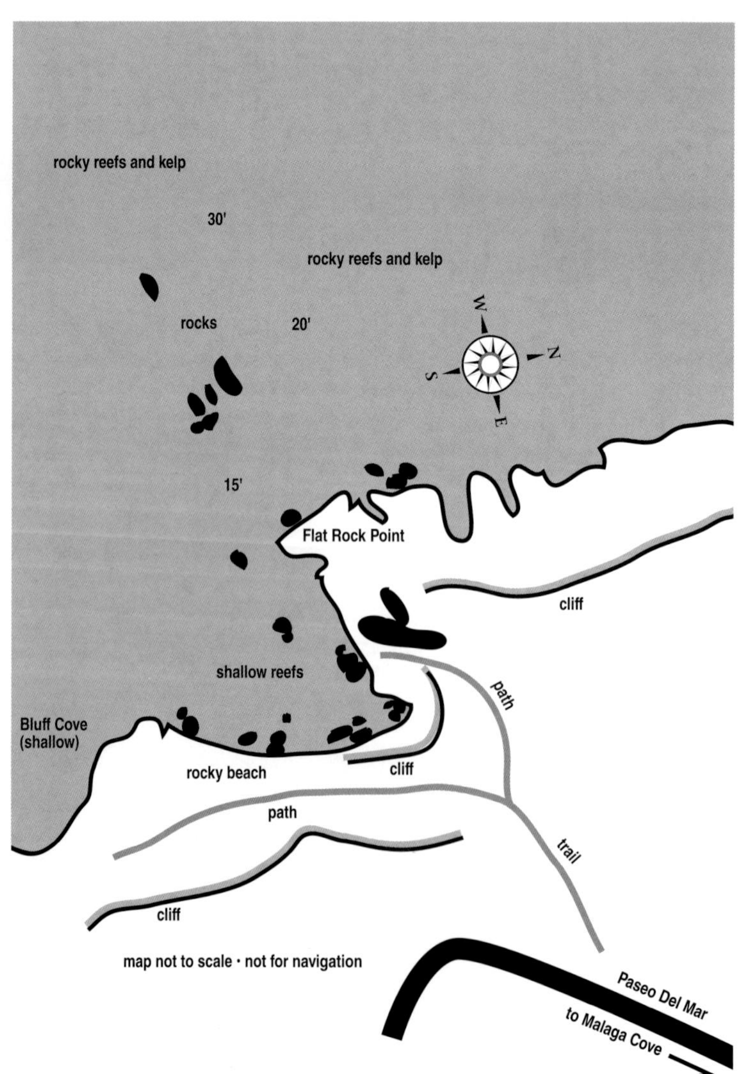

the name) on the point. Here, depending on the size and direction of the surf, entry is best made directly off the rock where it drops sharply to 12 feet of water or deeper. Experience in this type of entry/exit is important for shore diving this spot. There are also some small coves in the rocks to the northeast of the point that can be used if the surf is right.

Calico bass

road as it swings to the west into the town of Palos Verdes Estates and past beautiful Malaga Cove Plaza. Here you will turn right on Via Corta. Via Corta will turn into Via Almar as it swings to the left. After passing Via Arroyo, Via Aromitas and Via Media, you will come to Paseo Del Mar; turn left here. The head of the trail leading to Flat Rock Point will be directly ahead where the road rises sharply and begins to curve to the left at 600 Paseo Del Mar.

The trail to shore begins as an old dirt road (sorry, no vehicles). The trail then breaks off to a moderately steep, dirt path (avoid after a rain when the path will be muddy and very slippery; even when dry, the trail can be treacherous). Proceed with caution. Check it out before you strap on your dive gear to see if it manageable.

The trail ends at the flat rocks (hence

Margate

There are kelp beds that are scraggly, barely reaching the surface. There are kelp beds so thick that it is impossible to pass through them, and there are kelp beds that cover the surface so thoroughly as to block out the sun entirely. Most divers enjoy the kelp beds that are thick enough to provide a forest-like atmosphere with sunbeams streaking through the kelp fronds, yet not so thick as to prevent easy passage along the bottom. The kelp beds at Margate on the west side of the Palos Verdes Peninsula are considered some of the more beautiful in the area.

The Margate area of the Palos Verdes Peninsula is located south of Flat Rock Point and Bluff Cove. The bottom here is made up of ridges of rock that jut from the bottom as much as 15 feet and run at about a 30-degree angle to shore. Between the ridges are broken boulders and small patches of sand. In short, it is a perfect environment for healthy kelp and a wide variety of other marine life.

Sea slugs or sea hares (so named for their rabbit ear-like protrusions on the heads) are one of the more common forms of life. Other invertebrates found here include the giant keyhole limpet, sea cucumbers, and brittle stars. Some of the more colorful varieties of invertebrates are sparse but still present, with the majority of sea stars belonging to the brittle star variety.

Lobster, as well as scallops, can be found under some of the boulders. If it is very calm, this is an excellent area for lobster in water less than 10 feet deep. Spearfishing at Margate is fair. Keep to the outer edges of the kelp for the larger sheephead, kelp bass and halibut. For the free-diving spearfisher, this is a good spot for hunting white sea bass in the spring and summer.

Garibaldi

The shoreline is very rocky surrounded by cliffs and is open to westerly swells. There is shore access via a long steep dirt path at 1600 Paseo Del Mar. There are other paths to the shore but choose carefully; several are quite treacherous with full dive gear. Beach diving at Margate is best left for those with strong and steady legs and a good sense of balance.

Visibility averages 10 to 15 feet depending on the time of year and sea conditions. Currents are moderate and surge can be a problem when in shallow.

Blackeye goby

Christmas Tree Cove

The reefs at Christmas Tree Cove are, in spots, quite spectacular. In one location, a large section of the reef, the size of a bus, juts 18 feet from the bottom and drops vertically to a kelp bed below. Other areas of the reef have overhangs, channels, and huge boulders. Surrounding the reefs are lush kelp beds. All of this is waiting to be explored in water that has the best visibility for the area. Averaging 15 to 25 feet, the visibility here rarely drops below 10 feet and is frequently as much as 35 feet. In short, the diving here can rival Catalina Island.

The thick, healthy kelp and rugged bottom terrain provides a habitat for a large variety of sea life. A wide selection of sponges, anemones, and sea stars make the rocks their home. Many mollusks are in residence here also. Varieties such as the giant keyhole limpet, Norris top snail, Kellet's whelk, and shiny brown chestnut cowries are easily found. Splashes of brilliant color are provided by the red and blue Spanish shawl and bright yellow sea lemon nudibranchs. Watch out for those knees; urchins seem to be everywhere. Swimming above and around the abundance of life on the reefs are opaleye, rock wrasse, the ever-friendly garibaldi, and seemingly hundreds of señoritas. In the crevices, the shy striped treefish resides and the tiny, but colorful, bluebanded gobies dart about.

There is a good share in the game department also. Although not as plentiful as in other areas off Palos Verdes, game fish in good numbers are present here. In the sand that surrounds some of the kelp, halibut is occasionally present. Also in the kelp and on the rocks are kelp bass, sheephead and, in fewer numbers, rockfish. Scallops and lobster are also present but in limited numbers. And for the experienced free-diver, white sea bass are sometimes spotted off the points.

The biggest setback of this dive spot is the poor shore access which is via a steep dirt path along the north side of the cove. The path is for the sure-footed and stout-at-heart. This is a tough hike. In some spots, particularly after rain, the path can be hazardous.

The top of the path can be reached by

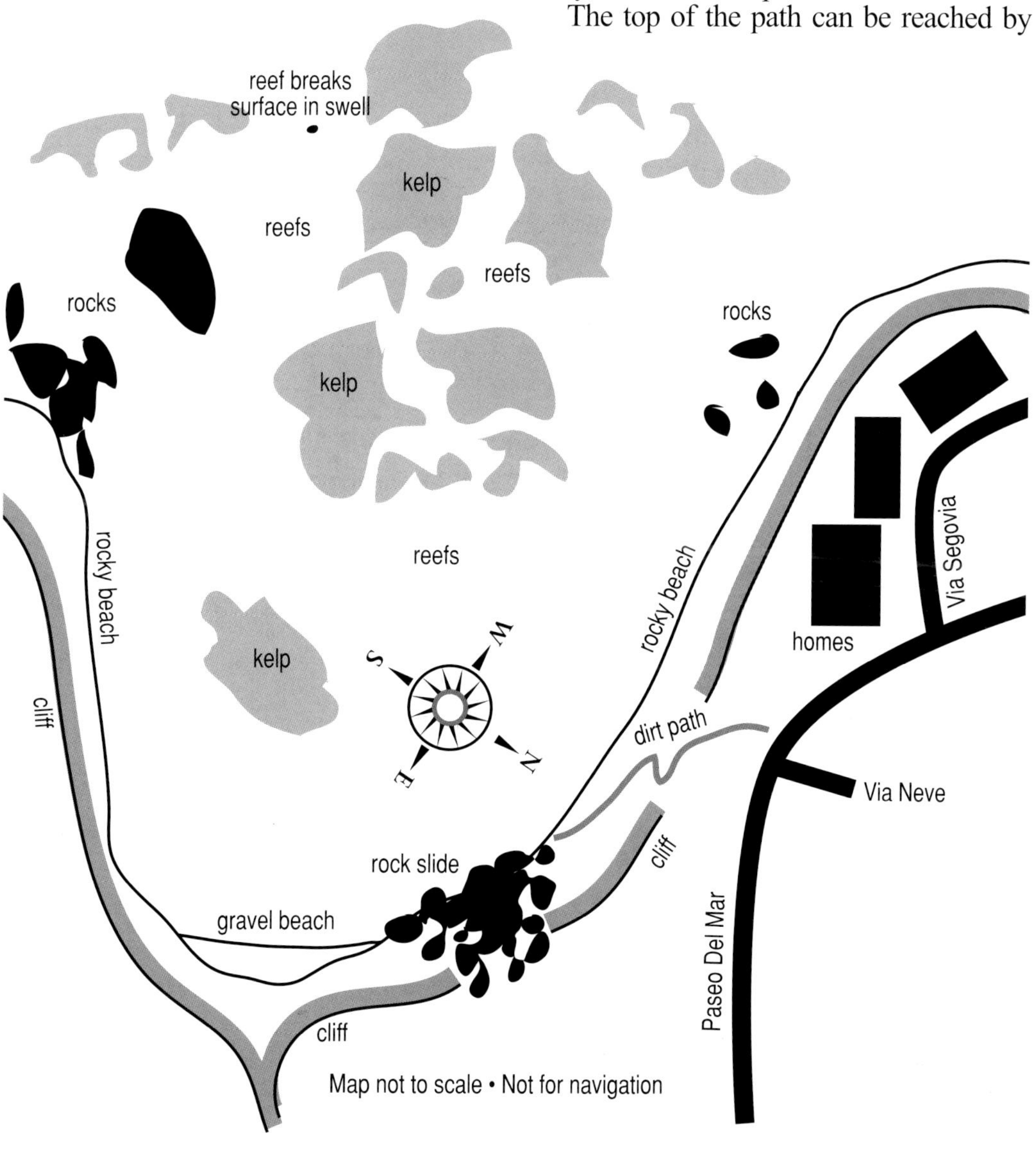

Map not to scale • Not for navigation

proceeding south on Palos Verdes Drive West off Pacific Coast Highway (Highway 1). Drive through the town of Palos Verdes Estates for roughly five miles and turn west on Paseo Lunado. This will turn into Paseo Del Mar as it swings along the coast. The foot of the path is located at the 2800 block of Paseo Del Mar, near the intersection with Via Neve. There is limited but usually ample parking along the street. There are no facilities. Ocean conditions can be easily observed from the top of the bluff.

After proceeding down the steep trail, water entry can be made through the surf at the stone and gravel beach in the center of the cove or, if conditions permit, over the rocks on either side of the cove. It is a long swim through thick kelp to reach the best reefs on the outer edges of the kelp. There are, however, interesting reefs and kelp beds closer to shore. If conditions are poor elsewhere, Christmas Tree Cove usually holds the best possibility for good diving.

Island kelpfish

Point Vicente Fishing Access (a.k.a. "Cardiac Hill")

Diving around Palos Verdes is excellent but shore access can be very poor. Divers take what they can get, and one of these shore access points is the Point Vicente Fishing Access, aptly nicknamed by locals as "Cardiac Hill." Luckily, however, it's not as bad as it sounds.

The steep trail is located just to the west of the Point Vicente lighthouse. There is good parking and restrooms with a drinking fountain at the top of the trail. The trail, or Cardiac Hill, is long and steep but fairly safe. Diving along the shoreline at the bottom of the hill is worth the effort.

The beach between Point Vicente and Long Point is fairly large offering a wide diving area; however, the best location is to the west at the end of the branch trail that heads toward a small rocky point. The west branch trail is a little narrow in spots, but visibility is usually best here and, depending on conditions, entries are usually best here as well.

Entries are over rocks and are sometimes difficult. The beach in the center of the cove offers possible easy entry and exit but requires a longer walk and longer swim to the clearer waters to the west. Before descending the trail, determine the conditions and your diving goals to best choose the areas where you wish to dive and also where to enter and exit the water.

The bottom drops off at a moderate

slope reaching as much as 50 feet within 150 yards of shore where it begins to level out to sand. Most of the reefs consist of boulders of varying sizes; some are very large and extend to within 10 feet of the surface, creating large caves and overhangs that are exciting to explore. These large boulders can sometimes be spotted from the cliff top when water visibility permits.

Visibility here is fair, averaging 10 to 15 feet. Once again, it is usually best on the west side of the cove, which is somewhat protected from northwest swells and weather but open to south swells during the summer. The bottom is covered with much silt that can ruin the water clarity in times of heavy surf. Close to shore, strong currents are usually not a problem, but near Point Vicente, currents have been known to reach two knots. Although there is great diving out there, the very long swim out past Point Vicente is not recommended.

On the rocks, life is not as abundant as in other areas around Palos Verdes, but there is certainly enough to see, photograph, and hunt. Invertebrates calling this area home include giant keyhole limpets, nudibranchs, and, on the ledges and overhangs, corynactis anemones. For color, look for the small but numerous stands of gorgonian in the deeper water. Sea hares and sea cucumbers are also common in the deeper waters. Fish life includes garibaldi, señoritas, and for the hunter, opaleye, and an occasional halibut on the sand. Hunters will also find a few scallops and lobster. Kelp cover on the reefs is hit and miss. If the kelp growth is heavy, you can expect more game moving in the cove. Spearfishing improves as you move toward the point.

Calico bass

Terrenea Resort (a.k.a. "Old Marineland" or Long Point)

Diving the reefs and kelp off Palos Verdes is such a wonderful experience that it is worth the extra effort. It is made that much nicer, however, when access to the shoreline is made at least somewhat easier. Such is the Case at the Terrenea Resort. While at the time of going to press with this book, plans call for 100 public parking spaces and a gently graded pathway to the water. Construction is scheduled for completion in 2009. While construction is underway, temporary access is provided although it is a long walk.

The terminus of the walk is a cove with a cobble beach about 300 yards east of Long Point. Being that the small cove is on the inside of Long Point and facing away from the prevailing northwest weather conditions here are generally calmer that the west side of Palos Verdes.

Water within the cove is generally dirty and the bottom uninteresting but there are several options. There is a small reef directly out, several small kelp forests around the corner to the east, but my favorite is to head westward toward Long Point. The water is clear and reefs abundant with marine life.

From shore, the bottom drops off rapidly to 15 or 20 feet. Kelp is fairly close to shore in 20 to 30 feet of water. The rocky bottom continues to drop away at a moderate rate to between 35 and 50 feet where a gently sloping sand bottom takes over 50 to 75 yards from shore. The bottom tends to drop away quicker and deeper, westward closer to Long Point.

The varied depth, rocky reefs, kelp forest and sand bottom make up an interesting underwater terrain that is rarely boring. In the shallows are patches of eelgrass, ribbon kelp and a lot of urchins. The kelp forest near the point is full of fish. Look for the bright orange garibaldi as they dart in and about the rocks and kelp strands. The garibaldi are less friendly here than at other more popular dive sites as they're probably not yet used to divers that are always willing to give a handout of food. In the kelp you will find small schools of opaleye and perch. Kelpfish move into and out of the kelp blade trying to conceal themselves.

Hunters will be pleased on how easy it is to approach such favored game fish as calico bass, sheephead, and sand bass. Although scallops are common, some being quite large, lobster seem to be rare in spite of the excellent habitat of jumbled boulders.

The rocky reef is highly varied with crevices, large boulders and ridges that rise as much as 15 feet from the bottom. Sand pockets and channels break up the bottom that is rarely the same in any two places.

Out from the kelp is probably the most interesting portion of the dive. As the kelp disappears, gorgonian sea fans take over. In the deeper (40 to 50 feet) portions of the reef, large stands of

Cabezon

golden gorgonian cover the boulders. As the boulders taper off into the sand, tube anemones become abundant and large.

Don't stop at the sand. Frequently buried in the sand near the reef's edge are large Pacific Electric or "torpedo" rays. Sightings of these incredible creatures are common here. A word of warning: Look but don't touch! Torpedo rays have the capacity of electric shock and will deliver a powerful blow if provoked. Also be aware that these creatures are not afraid of human beings. They have been known to aggressively pursue divers.

Other interesting creatures abiding along the edge of the reef include octopus (often quite large); a variety of sea stars in a number of shapes, sizes and colors; and colorful nudibranchs.

In shallower waters, 6 to 30 feet down, you may find what remains of the Civil War era ship known as the *Newbern*. On October 13, 1895, the wood hulled, steam powered vessel ran aground in thick fog and subsequently broke up on the rocks. Although most of the $250,000 cargo of silver bars was recovered, two 25-pound ingots remain missing to this day. For divers, all that remains now are an occasional piece of brass, rotting wood hull, or corroded iron spikes. The remaining debris from the wreck lies just east of the point.

Reaching the temporary parking area is not well marked. In the city of Rancho Palos Verdes turn from Palos Verdes Drive S onto Seawolf Drive. Turn Right on Beachview Drive then left on Nantasket Drive. The parking is at Nantasket and Seacove Drive. There are no facilities. Access to the parking once construction is complete is not as clear but will likely be directly off Palos Verdes Drive S into the Terrenea Resort (6610 Palos Verdes Drive S) and then follow the signs. It is unclear as to what facilities will be available.

Old timers call this site Old Marineland for the theme park that was at this location for 33 years, shut down in 1987.

White Point

Is Palos Verdes really a seething volcano? Hardly, but you'll find evidence of volcanic heat on this placid peninsula. You just need to know where to look. And the best place to look is underwater.

Geologically, the Palos Verdes Peninsula is a fascinating place. It is laced with faults. It was once an island, much as Catalina is today. Hollywood was the distant beach. Look closely and you can still see evidence of ancient sea cliffs on the slopes of these green hills. But perhaps the most curious geological feature of Palos Verdes is the hot springs at White Point.

The dry visitor to White Point will only get a hint of the hot water springs and only by looking in just the right places. Just follow your nose. During low tide, several of the springs are exposed in the tide pools. A rotten-egg, sulfur smell will waft through the air. The vents in the tide pools are relatively small and hard to find, but they leave a distinctive trail of odor in the air. This is not a rotting,

Black perch

polluted beach. What you are smelling is natural sulfur, bubbling up from deep in the bowels of the earth. The largest vents are offshore but easily within diving range.

Japanese immigrants in the early century capitalized on the hot springs, building a small resort at water's edge. Wells were drilled to tap into the main source of the hot pungent waters. It was then plumbed into pools and baths to be enjoyed by individuals seeking healthy relief. Evidence of the resort can still be seen in the form of concrete blocks along the water's edge.

The hot springs resort is only part of this beach's rich history. White Point has a rich diving history as well. At the turn of the century and up till World War II, White Point (also known as Issei Cove) was the area's first abalone fishery. Japanese immigrants (the only people who would eat the snail that was considered by most to be inedible) worked the waters in cumbersome hard-hat gear for the delicacy. The abalone are, however, now long gone.

These days, divers visit the site for other reasons. First, it is the easiest access around the entire peninsula. There are miles of spectacular reefs for diving along the Palos Verdes coastline but only a few access points, most difficult. Another reason to visit is the underwater scenery. While only average by Palos Verdes standards, there is still a great deal to see in the rocky cove and nearby kelp forest. But the main reason to come to this location is the curious underwater hot water vents.

If you watch PBS often, you have probably seen footage of the deep submersible *Alvin* exploring deep hot water vents on the mid-Atlantic ridge. A myriad of fascinat-

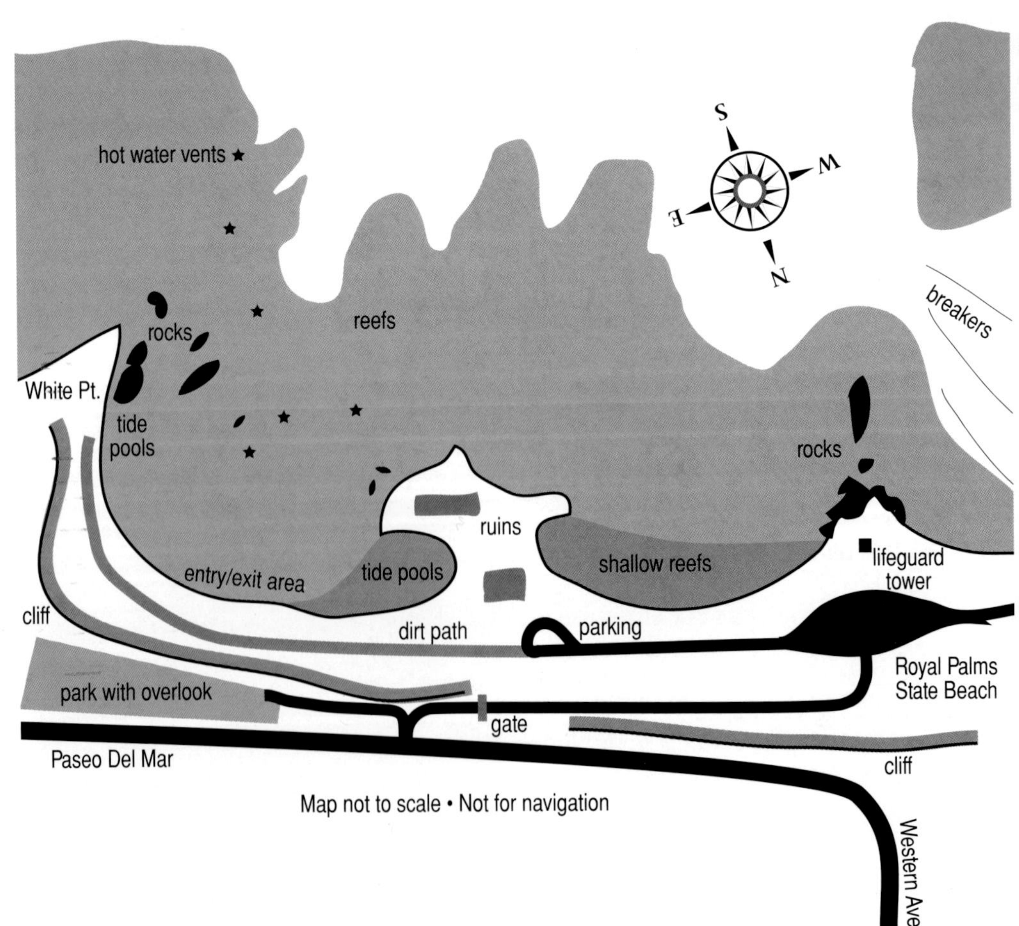

ing creatures live near these vents without the benefit of sunlight and photosynthesis. They grow by metabolizing the hot chemicals spewed from the vents in a process known as chemosynthesis. An entire ecosystem is created. While it is very small and limited by comparison, a very similar biological community exists around the underwater volcanic vents at White Point.

The vents are easily spotted by the white fuzzy growth on the rocks surrounding the vents. The white fuzz is actually a fungus that lives off bacteria that uses chemosynthesis to gather its nourishment from the hot, chemical-laden water. None of the vents are large enough to dramatically affect the surrounding water temperatures, but you can see heat waves from the larger vents. Removing your glove, you'll be able to warm your hands in the balmy liquid.

The geology behind the vents is really very simple. As previously stated, the peninsula is permeated with faults, some quite deep. Sea and ground water trickles deep into the faults until reaching rock heated by magma. The hot water rises until emerging from the springs.

A dive trip to visit the hot springs at White Point is fairly easy. White Point adjoins Royal Palms State Beach. The road leading down the bluff is located at the end of Western Avenue, off Paseo Del Mar in the city of San Pedro. There is a day-use fee. It's a good idea to check out the diving conditions and the lay of the coast from the bluff above before descending.

The gate at the top of the bluff is closed at sunset. There are restrooms and a lifeguard at Royal Palms Beach (to the right at the bottom of the hill) but no facilities other than parking to the left toward White Point. The area most often dived is the cove to the far left. Park as far south the road will take you, then you have to hike a few steps to the water entry point.

Water entry is best across the rocks in the cove. The cove is somewhat protected but shallow. Some divers prefer to enter the water at low tide, but I prefer high tide to avoid the slippery rocks. Somewhere in between may cause problems in swimming over the shallow reefs. If conditions are calm, experienced divers may choose to enter the water off the rocks on either side of the cove. This entails a walk but shortens the swim dramatically.

Once out in the cove, 50 yards or so, the bottom drops away rapidly to 15 feet and then to 25 feet deep. Jumbled boulders, ledges and overhang dominate the bottom topography. Look for the patches of white fungus to locate the hot springs. There are several locations scattered in 15 to 25 feet of water in and around the mouth of the cove.

Painted greenling

In your survey of the bottom, also keep an eye out for random pieces of wreckage. The ferry *Melrose* ran aground in a 50-knot gale in 1932. Only bits remain, the bulk of which can be found off the southern point, in 6 to 20 feet of water.

The bottom off the northern point is more interesting for marine life. There is a small kelp forests with a good amount of fish, stars, snails, nudibranchs, and lobster. 200 yards out are three parallel reefs that host an intermittent growth of kelp. It's a long swim, sometimes plagued with cross currents, but it is here you'll find the best diving. Visibility averages 20 feet. Marine life in and around the reefs, as well as over the sand, is abundant.

What deeply committed California divers have not gotten themselves into hot water for diving too much. On your next dive, try White Point and getting into hot water may take on a whole new meaning.

Point Fermin West

Just to the west of Point Fermin, on the eastern corner of the Palos Verdes Peninsula, lies a kelp bed that stretches westward for a mile to White Point. Although this area does not hold the best diving that the Palos Verdes Peninsula has to offer, it does hold its share of diving experiences

The kelp starts only a few yards from shore, in as little as 10 feet of water, and extends outward as much as 300 yards into 30 feet of water. The bottom consists of rocky reefs interspersed by boulders and patches of sand. The kelp is healthy and grows quite thick in spots.

This area does have more game than the neighboring, and more frequently dived, White Point. Although not available in large numbers or size, lobster and a variety of game fish can be found here.

Although there is some marine life for the photographer and sightseer, the poor visibility may create problems.

The visibility averages 5 to 10 feet on the outer edge of the kelp and deteriorates toward shore. Close to shore, the waters tend to be muddy. The outer edges of the kelp hold the best diving, but it is long swim from shore. Other water conditions such as currents and surge tend to be a limited problem. The area is fairly well protected and only subject to an occasional strong current.

Shore access is available but is a steep long haul to a rocky surf entry. There are two paths that lead to the shore. The best access is across from 980 Paseo Del Mar and Meyler Street. Parking is on the street adjacent to the park. The top of the path is behind the restrooms and is marked with a sign near the street. The paved path is long and steep in spots ending in a steep flight of steps just before the beach.

The second path is four blocks to the west at Barbara Street; this path is also long and steep but is only paved two-thirds of the way down. Water entry at both locations is difficult. Although the area is protected from most large surf, shallow reefs and rocks in the surf can make entry and exit hazardous. Diving here in high tide is best. In addition, water visibility close to shore is often very poor. Good alternate dive spots include White Point.

If you are exploring the shoreline, don't miss the historical lighthouse at Point Fermin.

Cabrillo Beach

The Cabrillo Marine Aquarium, formerly the Cabrillo Marine Museum, has a long time history of educating the public about the Southern California marine environment. Its location at Point Fermin is ideally suited along the coastline. The Aquarium is located in a large park that includes a wonderful stretch of sand beach and rocky shoreline. The beach is a result of the harbor breakwater, debris from the harbor dredging, and the rocks of Point Fermin. Thousands of families flock to the beach every year to enjoy the protected waters, tide pools, and excellent facilities. Unfortunately, few divers visit here.

While there is abundant and colorful marine life on the bottom just off the beach, the not-so-clear water just makes it hard to see. Cabrillo Beach's biggest handicap as a dive site is poor water clarity. The cove created by the breakwater and the point does not work well with cleansing currents, and dirty water gets trapped.

The best part of this dive site for marine life and bottom terrain is toward the point. Patch rock reefs support a small kelp forest made up mostly of feather boa kelp. Crustaceans are abundant with a variety of crabs, including the large sheep crab. This is also a good spot for lobster, with few commercial traps and fewer divers. A large part of the site is part of the Point Fermin Marine Life Refuge, but taking of lobster and halibut is acceptable.

The farther you head toward Point Fermin the more interesting the bottom becomes, with steep rock pinnacles off the point. The pinnacles top out at just below the surface and drop to 50 feet. But this is an unrealistically long swim. Use kayaks from the beach or an inflatable or another private boat launch from—where else?—the Cabrillo boat ramp inside the harbor. Visibility improves somewhat toward the point but is still usually poor, falling in the 10-foot range. I had a dive here years ago, however, with a 70-foot visibility.

Out from the beach is a sand bottom. Water visibility is a more consistent 10 to 15 feet. The bottom slopes gently out to 20 to 25 feet just beyond the jetty. Course sand is home for hermit crabs, small clams, and sand dollars. Beyond the sand dollar beds the clay substrate is tunneled by worms leaving a quicksand-like silting mud on top.

Around the jetty it is interesting but surgy. The sand can swirl in the surge dropping viz to zero. Schools of tiny baitfish provide food for barred sand bass on the bottom and an occasional kelp bass. Urchins and stars occupy the rocks. Like the reefs across the cove, crabs are abundant.

Out across the sand you'll find an occasional rock pile, but the main event will be the sand dollar beds. These interesting animals, kin to the sea urchin, prop themselves vertically in the sand to filter organic debris from the surgy water. With only sand around, small fish, crabs, clams and worms make the slight shelter of the sand dollar beds home.

Cabrillo Beach's best dive is at the aquarium. Extremely knowledgeable staff and a fine collection of specimens with informative displays will teach you volumes about local marine life in only an afternoon. The aquarium is open Tuesday through Friday, 12 p.m. to 5 p.m. and weekends 10 p.m. to 5 p.m. Admission is free, but there is a charge for parking. For more information in the aquarium, visit their web site at www.cabrilloaq.org.

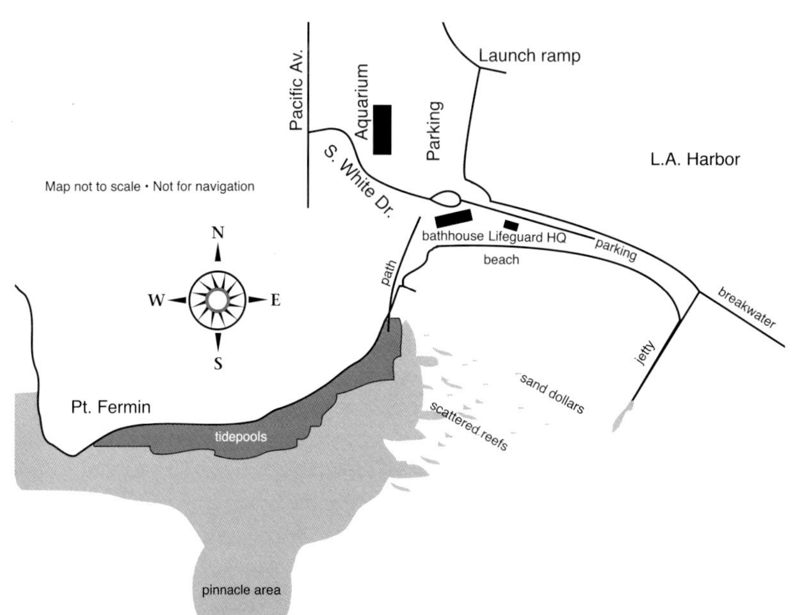

Introduction to Orange County

Perhaps the most concentrated area with excellent beach diving locations is the southern Orange County coastline. From the Los Angeles County line to the southern side of the mouth of Newport Harbor, diving is generally limited to sandy bottoms or under piers, where permitted. When the surf is down, diving under the **Newport Pier** can be very interesting as the pier reaches to the lip of the Newport Submarine Canyon.

Just south of the mouth of the Newport Harbor is the beach at Corona Del Mar. At Corona Del Mar State Beach there are two diving areas. The **Corona Breakwater** can only be dived early in the morning and at night, but is a great dive with some lobster. To the south at the same beach are the reefs off **Inspiration Point**. The next small beach down the coast is known as **Little Corona**. The small cove at Little Corona is flanked on both sides by rocky reefs that make for interesting underwater exploration.

Past the town of Corona Del Mar is Crystal Cove State Beach. Having undergone extensive renovation, the facilities here are now excellent. There are several good shore access points in the park but the one that leads to the best diving is at **Reef Point** (a.k.a. Scotchman's Cove).

Heading southward into the town of Laguna Beach, one finds the largest concentration of beach diving spots. Starting with Crescent Bay, most divers head for a frolic with the pinnipeds at **Seal Rocks**. Also at Crescent Bay is the long swim out to **Deadman's Reef**.

The next cove over is the famous **Shaw's Cove**. Although generally crowded with divers, this beach dive spot is not to be missed.

Equally spectacular and much less crowded is the diving off the small **Fisherman's Cove**. One hundred yards to the south and within the ecological preserve is **Diver's Cove**. From Diver's Cove, the coastline stretches out into a small sandy beach known as **Picnic Beach**. Picnic Beach offers excellent facilities and good

Conditions:
Newport (949) 673-3371, Laguna (949) 494-6573
http://cdip.ucsd.edu/models/spc.gif
www.ocregister.com/weather/ocean.shtml
www.lagunaseasports.com/conditions/conditions.asp

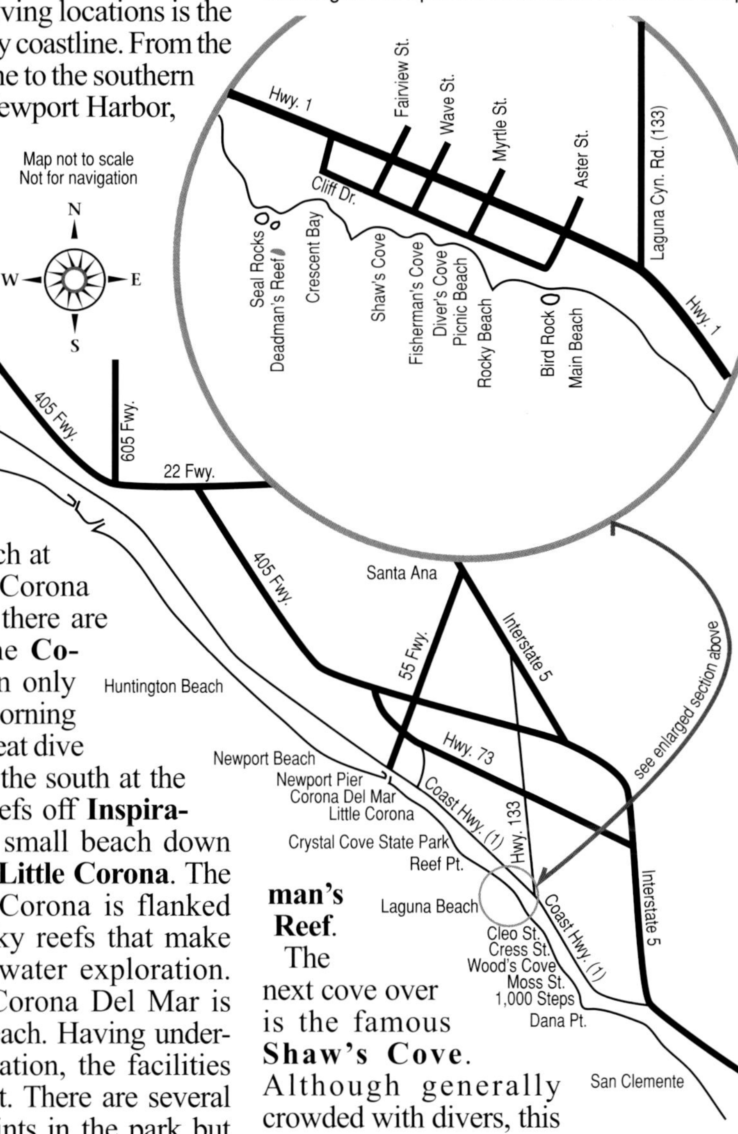

Green anemone

easy diving. **Rocky Beach** uses the same facilities, but entries are slightly more difficult over the rocks. Diving is, however, just as good if not better. The excellent reefs off the point at Rocky Beach can also be accessed from **Main Beach** near the center of town.

Reefs thin out and hang farther offshore directly in front of Main Beach. Heading southward, there is occasional patches of kelp that comes and goes and there are many good access points and dive sites. There is a barge wreck off **Cleo Street** but it is a long swim. The access at **Cress Street** leads to exceptional diving over a rocky bottom. Small coves such as **Woods Cove** or at **Moss Street** are more protected from the weather and offer excellent reef formations close to shore.

Excellent facilities and easy access can be found at the newly opened **Montage** Resort (a.k.a. Treasure Island). There are also good facilities and easy access at **Aliso Beach** and diving is sometimes very good but the area is open to the swells. Visibility is also variable. An exciting dive can be made in the underwater arch at a point known as **1,000 Steps**. Salt Creek near Dana Point has excellent diving for game but visibility is poor. At **Dana Point**, behind the Ocean Institute, is access to some good diving over reef both close and far from shore.

Newport Pier

Divers love the vertical environment underwater. Underwater "walls" are discussed with gasps of excitement. Kelp forests intrigue divers because they provide a vertical environment for a huge entourage of marine life. In the kelp forest, life fills all three dimensions, especially "UP." A vertical environment often ignored by divers, however, is under piers. Pier pilings provide a solid base for marine life to cling and grow. Competition for the space is intense and the biomass on these solid man-made intrusions into the marine environment is huge. Piers become an abundant oasis on sparsely populated planes of sand.

For the underwater explorer, however, diving under piers offers challenges. It is prohibited under many municipal piers, dangerous under others. And finally, many piers extend only over gently sloping sand bottom to only 18 feet of water or less. Surge can be difficult and visibility poor. There are exceptional pier dives, however. One of them is under the Newport Pier.

A big plus for the Newport Pier is that it extends to the edge of the Newport Submarine Canyon. While this submarine canyon is not noted for its spectacular drop-offs like its brothers at La Jolla to the south or Redondo to the north, the pier's proximity to the moderate slope enhances the underwater environment greatly. Depths at the end of the pier are from 30 to 35 feet, saving divers from a great deal of surge.

Effects of the nearby submarine canyon are particularly pronounced during the late fall through early winter when offshore winds are common. Known as "Santa Ana" winds, these winds move from the land out to sea, laying down the surf and creating a

Under the Newport Pier

condition known as "upwelling." Upwelling brings the cool water from the depths close to shore. A bonus for divers is this water is usually very clear. Furthermore, this effect is most pronounced near submarine canyons and off the Orange County coastline. The Newport Pier fits both of these criteria. When the Santa Ana winds blow strong for a day or two, and the surf is low, this is an outstanding beach dive site. Visibility can run upwards of 40 feet. Wandering through the columns covered with life becomes an incredible experience.

The predominant life form on the pilings is mussels. With an abundant food supply, sea stars are abundant and very large. The majority of the stars are of the pisaster family including ochre stars, in a variety of colors, the blue-gray giant-spined star, and the pink short-spined stars. Some of these starfish are three feet across!

Dotting the pilings are iridescent green anemones. When conditions are calm this is an excellent place to photograph these simple but colorful creatures. Look under the tentacles for tiny shrimp that take refuge there.

On my last dive at the pier, there was an explosion of navanax sea slugs. These colorful mollusks feed on nudibranchs. While we did see some nudibranchs here, there were only a few, perhaps because of the large number of navanax. When food is in short supply, navanax will sometimes turn cannibal, feeding on each other!

Food supply is always an issue in the sea. The pier provides food for a host of animals, not just with the life that grows on the pilings but also the debris from fishermen above. Scavenging from both sources is a variety of crabs with the most common being the quick blue swimming crabs and large cumbersome sheep crab. Averaging two feet across, sheep crabs can provide hours of entertainment for divers with their clumsy movements and seeming ineptness. We spotted one crab that had apparently fallen from a piling weeks before. Still on its back, mussels had grown in around him, making him prisoner upside-down. With food literally falling from the pilings above, he was still quite alive. It was one of the oddest things I'd ever seen underwater.

In spite of the large fishing pressure from above, fish are abundant here, but perhaps not the kind fishermen are after. Huge schools of silvery anchovies wind their way between the pilings. With sunlight dancing through the waves above, this sight alone makes this dive worthwhile. Barracuda are frequently seen schooling here. Small calico bass, perch, rock wrasse, and opaleye are also present in abundance. On the bottom are small halibut, scorpionfish, and turbot. The scorpionfish are particularly tame allowing very close approach. They make excellent macro photo material with their fringe-covered head and often bright colors. Don't get too close, however, as the spines are sharp and venomous. Diving under this pier does have its hazards. Fishing line is common. Bring a sharp knife or clippers and move through the pilings slowly and cautiously. Because of the fishing line, this dive is best avoided in low-visibility situations. Another hazard is the surf and surge. The gently sloping sand bottom (until the canyon) and open beach location make this a popular spot for surfers. Dive this site only on days of exceptionally calm surf. Waves of one to two feet in height should be maximum. You'll be less likely to be slammed into a pier piling, and you'll dodge fewer surfers this way on entry.

Boats can also present a problem. The base of the pier is home of the Newport Dory fishing fleet, an old-fashioned way of harvesting from the sea is still preserved here. The problem is they launch and recover their boats through the surf using modern outboards. To avoid the boats, conduct all of your dives either right under the pier or very close by.

This is a popular public pier, consequently facilities are excellent. There are clean restrooms, showers, and many restaurants nearby. Parking is also abundant but expensive so bring lots of quarters. Parking is located at 2111 West Ocean Front in Newport Beach.

Corona Del Mar Breakwater

Breakwaters are fascinating places to dive. They are artificial reefs created by man usually with huge boulders jumbled in a haphazard fashion on a formerly desolate sandy bottoms. Hard real estate is in much demand by ocean inhabitants. Many breakwaters, however, have limited or no access or are constantly being pounded by surf. The Newport Bay harbor breakwater at Corona Del Mar State Beach is an exception.

This breakwater is located on the southeast entrance of the Newport Bay Harbor and is the northwest boundary of Corona Del Mar State Beach. It is approximately 300 yards long and made up of jumbled rocks and boulders lying on a sand bottom from 15 to 35 feet deep.

Several things make this a very good dive: excellent surface facilities, lobster, protection from prevailing weather, abundant fish, and a good variety of marine life. The down side is the lifeguard's unrealistic restrictions on diving activities.

The restrictions don't seem to be imposed to protect the diver but rather some absurd notion that scuba divers are a hazard to bathers in the surf. Consequently, diving activities here must be limited to when the lifeguards are not present, namely early in the morning (well before 8:30 a.m.), during winter weekdays (and sometimes weekends), and night.

Those divers dodging the lifeguards will be treated to a cornucopia of marine life. The tip of the breakwater is the best with gorgonian being the most predominant biology. While the stands of the sea fans are not particularly large, they are numerous, thick and varied. They are California's own version of soft coral, swaying in the currents filtering out tiny bits of food.

Perhaps the reason these filter feeders are so prolific here is because this is the mouth of the Newport Bay. Newport Bay is a rather large tidal basin that has been largely converted to a pleasure boat harbor. A big portion, however, has been preserved in its original state of tidal marsh. Tidal

California spiny lobster

marshes are the nurseries of the coastal ecosystem. Far too many have been destroyed. The Upper Newport Bay Ecological preserve is a triumph for conservationists.

What does this have to do with diving the breakwater? A lot. During tidal changes, nutrient and life-filled waters flow in and out of the bay. The gorgonian are just one life form that stands ready to catch some of the harvest.

Tidal currents at the mouth of the bay (the very end of the breakwater) can be dramatic. Outgoing tides wash the rocks with life-filled waters (often not very clear) from the inner bay. The incoming tide sweeps clearer ocean waters into the bay. While you can dive the breakwater during an incoming or rising tide, watch out for the strong currents that may draw you into a busy boat channel (It is, by the way, illegal to dive within the channel). The best time to dive here, in term of tides, is right after a rise in tide during "slack tide."

As you can imagine, with all this water movement, gorgonian is not all you will find on and around these rocks. Rock scallops are filter feeders and can be found under dark ledges. Also plankton feeders, schools of blacksmith fish hover near the boulders. Opaleye, rockfish, and garibaldi take advantage of the growth between the gorgonian stands. Sea stars feed on mussel-encrusted rocks in the surge zone and the rock scallops deeper. Dotted here and there between the rocks are green anemones. Urchins are prolific and big. Also adding color are nudibranchs that munch away on the algae and hydroids that are abundant on the rocks.

If you have some time during your dive, head out across the sand. In 12 to 18 feet of water is a wide band of sand dollars. Sand dollars are a relative of the sea urchin. If you look closely, their bodies are covered with tiny purple spines and they have a mouth at the center of the body. They prop themselves up in the sand to catch floating particles, using the tiny spines to move the food into their mouths. Between and around the sand dollars are sea pansies. These relatives of the sea anemone also feed on particles pushed about in the surge.

Near the end of the breakwater, halibut, moon snails and barred sand bass

Tube anemone

inhabit the sandy plains. Water depths here run 25 to 35 feet. Do not venture far from the end of the breakwater, however, as this is a high traffic boat area.

Spearfishing is fair at this location with moderate populations of medium-sized calico bass, barred sand bass, sheephead, rockfish, and perch.

Rather than a speargun, bring a light to search the many fascinating crevices and mini-caves of the breakwater. Under ledges and in the deep crevices of the breakwater you will find scorpionfish, schools of big opaleye, and the yellow and black-stripped treefish. Lobster also scurry about in the crevices and caves created by the huge boulders.

Lobster? Did somebody say lobster? This dive site has always been a favorite beach dive for lobster. The jumbled boulders of the breakwater create a habitat that house a multitude of the tasty crustaceans. Being scavengers, the lobster have a large food supply from debris washing out of the bay, and there are no commercial traps on the breakwater with which to compete.

This is an excellent lobster dive early in the season, but be prepared to deal with the crowds. The population of readily available legal-sized lobster is depleted in a matter of a few weeks. By mid-season, most divers ignore this site for more favorable sites elsewhere. But all those little guys that were not quite legal-sized at the beginning of the season continue to grow. The Corona Breakwater may be just the place for an end-of-the-season lobster dive.

While lobster can be spotted in the daytime, most are backed into crevices that penetrate deep into the breakwater. At night, the smaller lobster scurry about the rocks. The larger, legal-sized bugs venture out from their sanctuary deep from within the rocks. While it is rare to see the bigger bugs out in the open, a lucky and persistent diver will catch one off guard. The easy access, usually calm conditions, and excellent facilities make this site a good choice for a relaxing night dive.

Fire pits scattered around the west end of the beach make for a peaceful post-night dive barbecue. Near the parking area are restrooms, freshwater showers and changing rooms. There is a parking fee but it is often not enforced on winter weekdays. If you are planning a night dive, be aware that the beach closes at 10 p.m.

You may want to consider bringing a second tank and make it a full day of diving. There are some great reefs at the opposite end of the beach off Inspiration Point, and nearby is the popular beach dive of Little Corona. While these sites are not as protected as the breakwater, these reefs offer another interesting dive close by.

Underwater conditions at breakwater are generally good. The angle of the breakwater protects the beach from the prevailing westerly swell. If a south swell is running, however, avoid this dive site. Visibility is fair, depending on a variety of conditions. Offshore or "Santa Ana" winds create good beach diving conditions all up and down the Southern California coast line but are especially important here. The geography of the region creates a wind funnel right over the southern Orange County area, namely, Newport Beach and Corona Del Mar. When the Santa Ana winds are blowing strong, they blow the strongest here. Clear waters and good diving conditions usually follow.

To reach this dive site, head for the southernmost corner of Newport Beach, known locally as Corona Del Mar. Turn south off Coast Highway (1), toward the ocean, on Marguerite. Turn right on Ocean and look for the beach entrance on your left. Proceed down the hill to the gate. There is an entrance fee. Park as close to the breakwater as possible to avoid a long walk in dive gear.

Water entry is usually easy with a gently sloping beach face. In your underwater explorations, don't ignore the shallow sections of the breakwater. This area is excellent for beginning snorkelers when calm, and lobster are often found in shallow waters as well as deep.

Inspiration Point

When I was told I couldn't dive where I wanted because as a scuba diver I was "a hazard to swimmers," I was angry. The lifeguard pointed 300 yards down the beach to some rocks in the distance. "Dive there," he said coldly. While I'm still angry about what I consider unrealistic restrictions, I have to thank the pompous bronze kid for some excellent advice. It was a fantastic dive! There are still great beach dives with easy access and Inspiration Point is one of them.

Corona Del Mar State Beach lies just south of the mouth of Newport Bay. Its south breakwater is the border of the beach. The breakwater is a great dive, but with a "safe swim area" along nearly the entire stretch of the beach the lifeguards will not allow you to access the water with scuba gear anytime they're present (the beach opens at 6 a.m., but lifeguards usually are not there until about 8:30 a.m. and usually only on weekends).

From the south end of the parking lot it is about a 200-yard walk to where the sand meets the rocks and the safe swim area ends. There is also access to this location down a steep paved path at Inspiration Point Park on Ocean Blvd. I recommend using the parking lot access. You'll have showers and restrooms at your disposal and more parking to choose from. There is, however, a fee but it can be avoided if you arrive early as the toll gate is usually not staffed early in the morning.

The five-m.p.h. buoy marker placed to keep personal watercraft (a.k.a. jet skis) at bay is almost perfectly placed to guide you to the reefs. The inner buoy indicates the end of the safe swim zone. The outer buoy is to the south a bit and out about 150 yards out. There is a great reef just inshore and another to the east.

The sand bottom surrounding these reefs varies in depth from 20 to 30 feet. The reef closest to the buoy has a very large overhang—big enough to easily swim under in full scuba gear. There are

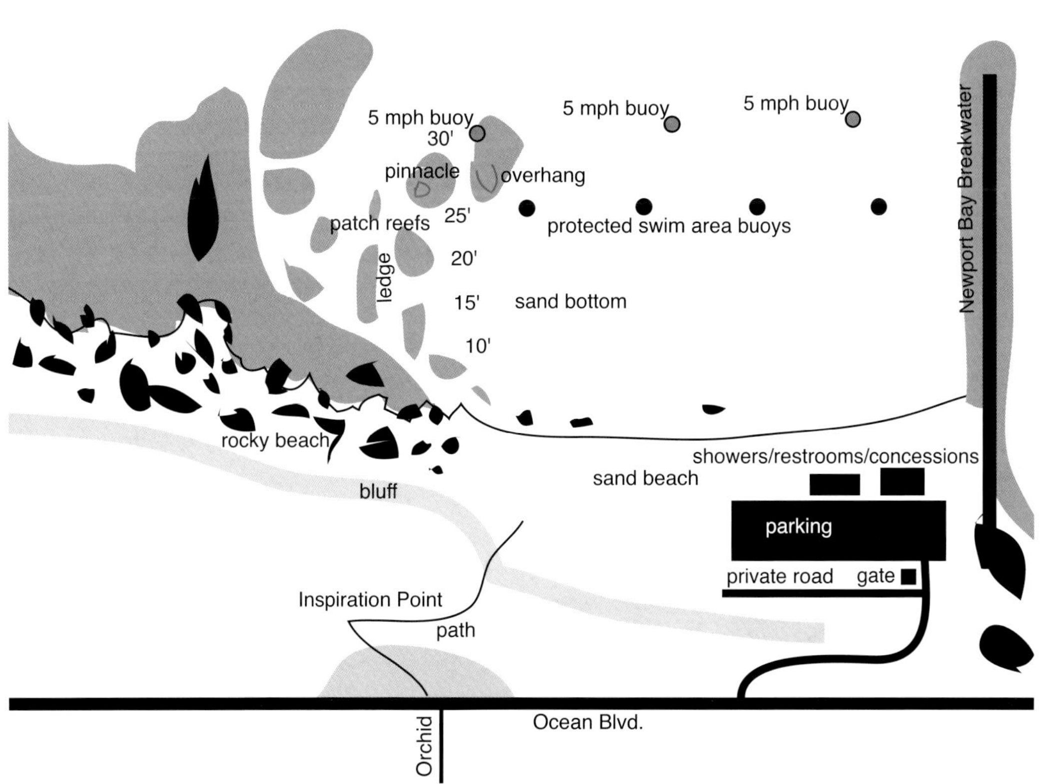

Moray eel

This is a good fish dive. There are calico and barred sand bass, some large. Blacksmith and mackerel school over and around the rocks. Reef fish included opaleye, sheephead, halfmoon, and painted greenling. This is not just a fish here and there but good-sized and in abundance. The nearby sand habitat also presents other fish, including rays, halibut, and leopard sharks.

Invertebrate life is good here as well. Small stands of gold gorgonian dot the reef like trees on a steep mountain side. Stars included the giant spined, bat and in the sand the (what else?) sand star. Spanish shawl nudibranchs dot the reef and you'll see their slug cousin predator, the navanax, in hot pursuit (for slugs, you've got to be patient). You'll also see sea hares, colorful encrusting sponges, wavy turban snails and an over-abundance of urchins. The urchins could be why the kelp is thin. There is kelp, but only in sparse clumps. Looking for lobster? They are here, way back in crevices, but not in large numbers, and not very big.

Save the last third of your tank for the swim back in. There are shallow reefs with octopus, eelgrass and more garibaldi. One section has a mini-wall rising from 20 to 8 feet. Some of these inshore reefs are boring and surgy, others interesting. If you're lucky, you'll see shy leopard sharks that lounge in the shallows over the sand bottom just outside the surf zone.

moon sponges, scallops and other filter feeders benefiting from the surge that course through this location. Garibaldi dance under the ledge with the light playing from above. It is a beautiful spot. A bit farther out, the reef climbs rapidly to a small mountain with tiny arches like windows where the fish swim in and out.

But you ain't seen nothin' yet. Inshore and to the east is another reef that reaches from the bottom at 28 feet straight up to within 8 feet of the surface. This mini-pinnacle is easy to spot from the surface, even in poor visibility.

Little Corona

Experienced divers often shy away from the more crowded dive spots thinking that great diving must lie in some remote location below sheer cliffs. In some cases this is simply not true. One of these fine, yet often crowded, dive spots is Little Corona.

Located in the southern corner of Newport Beach, less than a mile south of the mouth of Newport Harbor, Little Corona gets its fair share of summertime crowds, but divers keep coming back.

Perhaps the biggest reason for this dive spot's popularity is that it rarely fails to surprise. At any given time, large halibut can be found in the sand or a four-foot horn shark can be seen cruising these reefs. Although the area has been worked over by divers for many years, lobster, kelp bass, and rockfish are still in residence.

While the reefs to the south, off Laguna Beach, tend to be more colorful and livelier, Little Corona has a good supply of sightseeing and photo subject matter. On the reefs, in water 20 feet and deeper, small gorgonian sea fans, starfish, feather-worms and different varieties of other invertebrates can be found.

Visibility here is generally good. Water clarity on the outer reefs can reach 30 feet, but the visibility usually averages 15 feet. Nearer to shore, the visibility can drop due to water turbulence over the sand, but is usually good enough over the shallow reefs for snorkeling in calm weather.

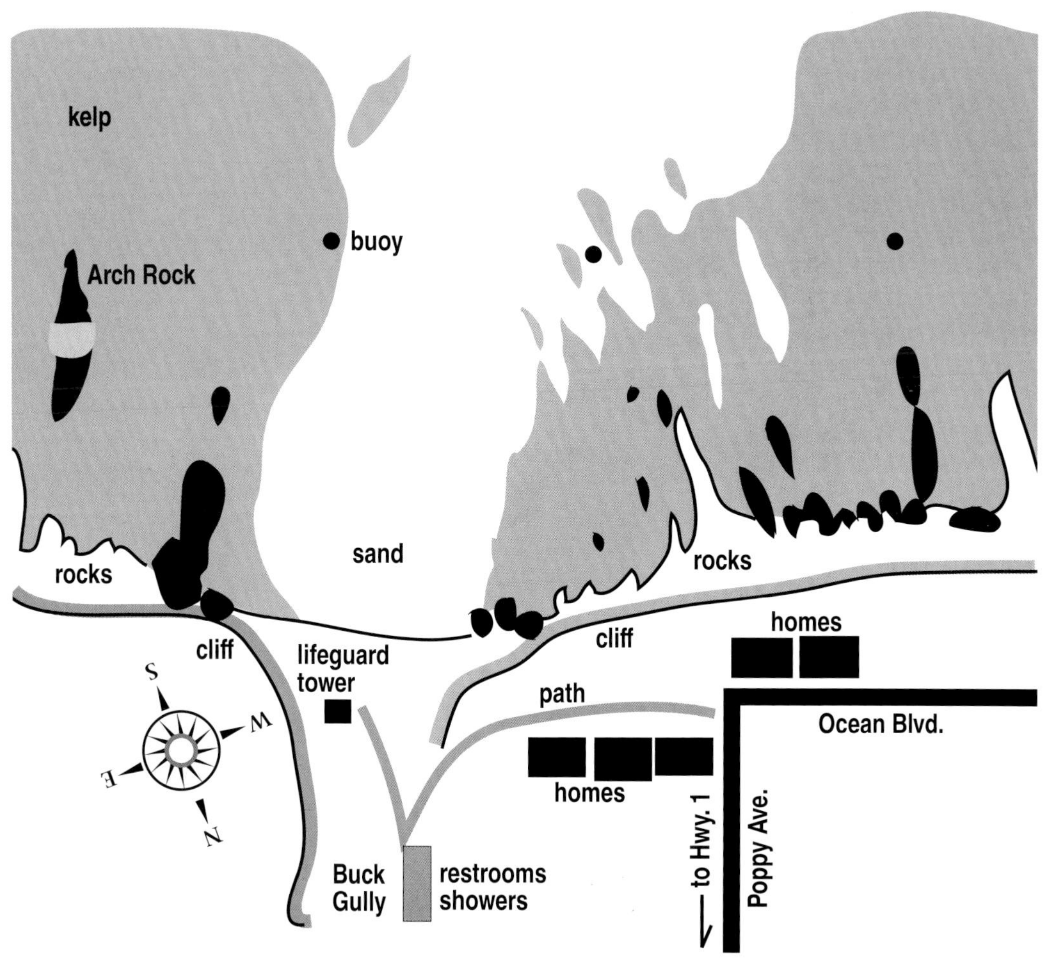

Treefish

The reefs start shallow and, near shore, drop on a moderate slope to 30 feet deep 150 yards out. The shallow reefs are often covered by a thick growth of eelgrass. The middle of the cove is mostly sand, but there are numerous small rocks in the surf line that can trip you up in entry and exit. The reefs lie on either side of the sandy cove with the most interesting ones to the south and out about 100 yards. Note that there is a buoy in this area that directs boats to stay clear. Several interesting reefs lie just outward and to the south of this buoy. Farther down the coast is the interesting Arch Rock that rises from the water and is usually inhabited by several birds.

Keep in mind that this is a part of the Newport Beach Marine Life refuge. It is illegal to take any marine life other than normal game. Check the specific regulation posted along the path that leads to the beach.

Little Corona can be easily reached by turning south on to narrow Poppy Street off East Coast Highway (Highway 1) in Newport Beach. Poppy Street will end overlooking the sea and turn sharply on to Ocean Boulevard. There is very limited free parking on Ocean Blvd; the path to Little Corona is just to the left of this intersection. A paved, moderately steep path winds down to the beach. From the top of the path, sea conditions can be easily observed. Halfway down the path, tucked in a corner to the left, are restrooms and showers.

On the beach is a lifeguard tower that is manned on busy summer days. The lifeguards do discourage spearfishing because of the crowds. If you would like to spearfish, dive during a less crowded time. As with Corona Del Mar State Beach, you may be prohibited from scuba diving to "prevent you from endangering swimmers." If there is a lifeguard on duty, check with them to see if he or she will be enforcing this so-called rule before you haul your gear down the path.

Giant kelpfish

Reef Point

In the short history of sport diving, this dive site looms large for game hunting. Old-time divers know this site as Scotchman's Cove, but renovations in the '80s to this section of Crystal Cove State Park has brought a new name to the dive site—Reef Point—as indicated by the sign posted on Highway 1. This location has produced many world records, as well as personal records for white sea bass and other game.

Although Reef Point does not produce the game it has in the past, many beach divers still find it a reliable spot for the hunting of all types of species. Lobster can still be found in water 30 feet or deeper and sometimes in the shallows among the eelgrass. Scallops are also available but usually in outer waters. The best quarry seems to be the game fish. The most common are calico or kelp bass and sheephead. Other varieties are available, but most are very cautious due to the heavy spearfishing activity in the area.

Reef Point is also a delight for the underwater photographer and sightseer. There are large-reef structures that rise from the bottom as much as 20 feet in some locations. These create walls of rock on which gorgonian, sea stars and anemones attach themselves. With the crevices, cracks, and overhangs, in addition to the patches of sand between the reefs, the varied bottom makes for interesting exploration. Kelp comes and goes in patches further enhancing the underwater scenery.

Anisodoris nobilis nudibranch

Visibility is good. It averages between 10 and 15 feet but can reach 20 to 30 feet in the winter. The area is open to heavy surf and as a consequence, visibility can suffer during times of large swells.

Perhaps what makes Reef Point even more attractive are the excellent facilities recently installed on the bluff overlooking the beach. Reef Point lies in the southern end of Crystal Cove State Park. There is plenty of parking, clean restrooms as well as freshwater showers and sinks. All of this does not come without cost, however. A day-use fee charged at the gate.

To reach the gate at Reef Point, proceed along the Coast Highway (Highway 1) until just north of the town of Laguna Beach. The gate is indicated by the sign "Reef Point."

The path and stairs to the beach are just beyond the restrooms on the bluff. The path is moderately steep but safe. Observation of the diving area is excellent from the bluff. A large reef extending from the point is located just up the coast to the right. Diving is good on both sides of the reef but weather, surf and currents will determine the best area in which to dive. Entry on the sand beach is through the surf.

The bottom drops off quickly to 10 to 20 feet. Several shallow reefs with much eelgrass make this an excellent area for snorkeling during calm weather. The deeper and more interesting reefs lie 100 to 200 yards out. Try closer to the exposed offshore reef for best sightseeing and game.

Crystal Cove State Park is a large section of coastline with other access points and adjacent reefs to the north. There is good diving here as well, but the walk is much farther to the water's edge.

Seal Rocks/ Crescent Bay

Diving with sea lions is just about as much fun underwater as anybody can have. They are enormously entertaining with their underwater acrobatics and antics. They will loop, spin, and rocket through the water column. And they will interact with divers. Juveniles are the most curious. They love to dive, zoom right at your face, and then pull up at the last second, mouth open, blowing bubbles. It is all at once terrifying, thrilling, yet humorous.

Although sea lions are common to our shores, there are only a handful of places along the coast and out at the islands where you are guaranteed an underwater visit. A "rookery" is your best bet. Hundreds of animals congregate at rookeries to mate, and bear and nurse their young. Only two rookeries exist in the southern portion of the state, both at island locations (Santa Barbara Island and San Miguel Island). The next best is at a popular "haul-out." This is where sea lions in small to moderate-sized groups "haul-out" for extended periods to rest and sun themselves. There are several popular haul-out areas around the islands, as well as a few along the coast. One of these is at Seal Rocks out from Crescent Bay in Laguna Beach.

While the best bet for enjoying the underwater antics of sea lions is still the islands, Seal Rocks offers the only opportunity for Southern California beach divers to experience a sea lion haul-out first hand.

Before ever heading to the water entry point at Crescent Bay, first take a side trip to a small bluff park known as Crescent Bay Point Park. The park, perched on the cliff overlooking Seal Rocks, gives you the perfect vantage point to observe conditions, study the reefs, make a dive plan, and see if the sea lions are "in." (Sometimes they are not, in which case you may want to plan a dive elsewhere.) There is no shore access at this vantage point and no direct way to reach the shore access.

Sea lion

The overlook is reached at the Crescent Bay Drive off Pacific Coast Highway.

There are two shore access points at Crescent Bay. Turn off Pacific Coast Highway on Cliff Drive and turn right at Circle Way. The closest to the north point, and Seal Rocks, is a few steps to the beach. The other entry, 200 feet to the south, is a paved ramp to restrooms and showers on the beach. While the ramp and showers make the south access more desirable, you'll have to walk (or swim) farther. Parking is very

The Laughter of the Sea Lions

There were a lot of seals on the rocks and in the water that day. This could be an excellent opportunity to get some good seal shots, I thought. My wife, Kim, joined me as buddy and off we went, camera in hand.

Dropping to the 20-foot bottom was a little disappointing. A sand storm raged in the surge and visibility was only about 10 to 15 feet. Looking for photo subject material on the bottom was fruitless. Then a seal appeared.

Quick as a rocket, the torpedo-like animal dived at us, paused at the bottom looking up and darted out of sight as quickly as he came. More seals showed up. They, too, looked us over pulling sharp curves, dives and ascents that made us appear to be moving in ultra-slow motion. They were difficult to track with their speed in the poor visibility. I popped off a few shots, but the seals lost interest, and with only half a tank gone, we chose to start heading back.

Rounding the corner, the visibility improved some. We ascended to determine exactly where we were before heading in. About 10 feet from the surface I recoiled from the dark, brown blur that had passed inches from my face only a moment before. I stopped, looked around and I saw the young seal then take a pass at Kim. Her body also jerked and twisted trying to follow the apparition that had startled her. I quickly signaled to drop back down to the bottom.

On the bottom, Kim and I spied the surface like soldiers looking for an enemy plane. The seal came in low, out of my field of vision and then burst into view inches from my right shoulder. I raised my camera and he was gone. Did I hear laughter?

It was a young seal, only about four feet in length. Its speed and agility in the water was amazing. I had seen seals before but none that moved as this one. It darted about like a child, with grace, freedom and energy. I was sure it was enjoying itself.

The young seal returned again and again. At one point he decided to taste me. He nipped at my fins, camera strobe and BC straps. In attempting to taste my wife, he bit her underwater light and tried to nip her fingers, though it was nothing more than a playful nip you'd get from the family dog.

After a time our air was beginning to run low but not the seal's energy. I watched him rise to the surface, dive to the bottom and, in an arch, rise to my face blowing bubbles like some horrible monster. I reacted with appropriate terror. Laughter. There it was again. Perhaps Kim was laughing in her regulator. The seal grinned.

He rose and dived again coming in very close across my shoulder. I froze as he brushed against my neck and slid behind me. I frankly didn't know what he might do back there. Chuckle, chuckle. The sound passed through my head. Was that seal laughing at me?

He darted between my wife's legs, behind her and then was gone again. By this time our air was low and we decided to surface. Back on shore, I asked Kim if she was laughing in her regulator and she said yes. But I know my wife's laugh from years of marriage, and it just wasn't the same.

As we swam in I looked offshore and saw the seal's head break the surface. He grinned, and then quietly departed.

limited at Circle Way. If you find yourself shut out of parking here you can head to the "upper" parking area along Crescent Bay Drive. There is a small set of stairs between the small spur road off Crescent Bay Drive that leads to the shore access at Circle Way.

Seal Rocks are a pair of rocky spires off the point on the northwest side of Crescent Bay. The Bay is a large cove with a sandy beach. The rocky points to the north and south give the cove a limited degree of protection for water entry and exit. The rocks may look to be a moderate swim, but shallow reefs block a straight line path to the rocks. Passage through the reef is possible, but only when the surf is calm. It's a little over a 100-yard swim through the reefs, farther if you go around them.

The reefs themselves are not spectacular but they are fun. Fish life includes opaleye, garibaldi, and surfperch. Fish populations are thinner here, probably due to the presence of the sea lions. Depths around Seal Rock are from 10 to 25 feet. Visibility is good, averaging 15 to 20 feet, but there is almost always a surge, especially on the far side of the rocks.

The options are many at Crescent Bay. To the south are reefs with huge crevices, one of which leads over to Shaw's Cove (beware of the strong surge in these channels). Beyond Seal Rocks is Deadman's Reef (see next chapter). It is a spectacular offshore reef that, lying 1/4 mile offshore, is only for the strongest swimmers. Don't try to do two areas in one dive. The sea lions at Seal Rocks are enough entertainment for one dive. Swim on over, plunk yourself down on the bottom, and enjoy the ballet.

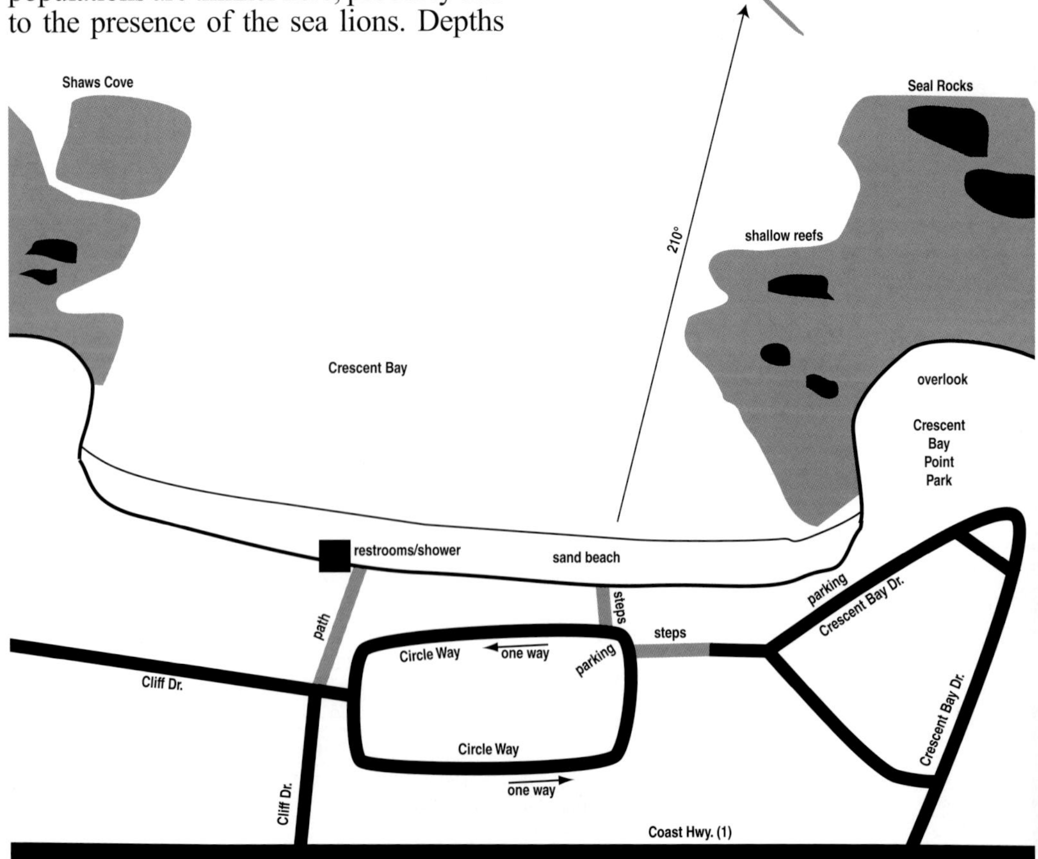

Deadman's Reef

Not a very attractive name, is it? I heard it said that it comes from a body that was once found out there. Another story is that an early diving visitor to the spot came so close to being run over by a boat that he surely thought he was a "deadman." Probably the most plausible story, however, is that nearly everybody that takes the time to swim the approximately quarter plus mile out to find the reef is so tired that they feel, well, dead.

The swim out to Deadman's Reef is indeed a long one, but well worth the effort. The reef structure is remarkable, starting at a sand bottom of about 47 feet and rising to as little as 15 feet from the surface. There are small pinnacles, mini-walls, and many cracks and crevices, some quite large. The far side of the reef reaches 60 feet deep — not bad for a shore dive.

The amount and variety of marine life you will find is equally remarkable. There is no kelp but encrusted on the rocks are a variety of colorful algae, bryozonan, and blotches of lavender and pink corynactis anemones. In the cracks and under overhangs are rock scallops (look but do not touch as they are protected here). Toward the tops of the reef the growth of mussels and barnacles are thick. With the mussels come their primary predator, large colorful ochre and giant-spined stars. This is an excellent spot to find nudibranchs. Keep an eye out for numerous Spanish shawls, as well as an occasional dorid or Hilton's aeolid. Other invertebrates to be found on this reef include octopus, sea hares, a few small lobster, and green anemones.

Juvenile garibaldi

Perhaps the best reason to visit this reef, however, is the fish life. This is possibly the fishiest reef off Laguna Beach. Small giant black sea bass have been seen here. In the sand you will spot guitarfish and huge bat rays. Across the reef it gets even better. Large sargo cruise the rocks. Perch of a number of varieties dart here and there. Calico and sand bass are abundant but most are small, so spearfishers should not get their hopes up. Also adding color are numerous small sheephead and a huge amount of garibaldi.

Conditions at Deadman's are generally good, better than nearby close-to-shore sites. Visibility averages 15 to 20 feet. A gentle current sometimes sweeps the location with clean, clear water. Watch out for the surge in the shallow portions of the reef.

Another reason to dive this site is to avoid the crowds. Laguna Beach is a very popular beach diving locale —the most popular in the L.A. metropolitan area, if not all of Southern California. But most of the activity here concentrates around three dive sites: Picnic Beach (Heisler Park), Diver's Cove, and Shaw's Cove. While these are great dives, the heavy weekend diver traffic at times can be a bit daunting. Another popular dive is Crescent Bay. But most divers here stick to the nearshore point to the southeast and Seal Rock on the northwest. Sea lion encounters are great, but the best diving is further out at Deadman's Reef.

Surf entry at Crescent Bay is frankly not as easy as the other nearby spots at Laguna Beach (Shaw's, Fisherman's and Diver's Coves). The beach is more open to the surf and the shore break can be a bit more intense. Beach diving experience is a must and time your entries and exits. Remember — know your limitations! Surf can come up unexpectedly here.

From the beach it is about a 100-yard swim out to Seal Rock and another couple hundred yards to Deadman's Reef. To shorten the swim a bit, head straight out from the beach 210 degrees, line up the two seal rocks with the big gray-roofed house on the bluff and drop down. Sounds simple, right? It is, however, surprising how many miss a structure like this that is quite large. When you drop down, if you find yourself in 45 feet of water or less, head out angling to the right of the ripples in the sand. If you hit 47-48 feet with no reef in sight, turn right and you should run into the reef. If you run into a small strip of rocks out on the sand, follow this to the reef. This mini-reef was put here years ago by some diver and is affectionately known as "deadhenge" (after "Stonehenge) because of it mystery appearance.

For coming back into the beach, start back with about 1,200 p.s.i. left in your tank so that you can lessen the arduous swim back by exploring the underwater environs across the sand flats.

While reaching the staging area for diving off Crescent Bay is easy to reach, it is parking that can be troublesome — but not if you know where to go. Turn off Pacific Coast Highway onto the north entrance of Cliff Drive. The steps to the beach will be straight ahead. There is another access point down the street to the left but this is further from the beach entry for Deadman's (but it does have the added bonus of restrooms and a shower). Parking is along the street but is extremely limited. If you find yourself shut out of parking here you can head to the "upper" parking area along Crescent Bay Drive. There is a small set of stairs between the small spur road off Crescent Bay Drive that leads to the shore access at Circle Way.

Crescent Bay is a beautiful beach and worthy of a full day of just lounging. And although Deadman's Reef is a long swim, it is definitely worth a full dive.

Spanish shawl nudibranch

Shaw's Cove

Shaw's Cove is one of the most frequented dive spots in Laguna Beach. Every weekend, it is not uncommon to see two or three classes using the cove for checkout dives and several buddy teams entering and exiting the water with smiling faces. Conditions here for beach diving come as close to being ideal as any other place along Laguna Beach. The crowds are perhaps the only drawback, but don't let the crowds stop you from diving this superb location.

The cove is well protected from wave action; consequently, the surf averages only one to two feet. Currents are weak or nonexistent and the visibility is only occasionally below 15 feet and often exceeds 30 feet.

Classes are conducted here for the excellent variety of instructional conditions. Students can be taught surf as well as rock entries and exits under mild conditions. Instructors must keep in mind, however, that no classes can take place on Laguna Beach City Beaches before 7 a.m. or after 10 a.m. from June 15 to September 15.

The "Crevice" from the inside looking out

The bottom terrain is both interesting and varied. On the western side of the cove, the rocks extending from the point drop rapidly to the sand in 20 to 35 feet of water. At the end of the point, there is a large channel 15 feet wide that starts in 20 feet of water and cuts deep into the reef. Divers that frequent the area call this "the crevice." Near the entrance, part of the rock gap has collapsed creating an underwater arch.

To locate the crevice, swim on the bottom along the edge of the rocks toward the sea. The crevice begins as a 15-foot-wide cut into the reef running approximately west. The crevice then narrows to a tunnel or arch that is often filled with garibaldi and is a photographer's dream. The crevice then continues to branch off into smaller channels and tunnels; some of which hold octopus that can be hand fed. Each crack holds something different: yellow sponges, moray eels, lobster.

One large passage leads directly to the cove next door, Crescent Bay. Be aware: surge can affect the area creating currents in the crevice. For the more experienced diver, this can be used to their advantage by allowing the surge to whip the diver in and out of the channels. During low tide, the underwater activities can be observed from the rocks on the surface directly above the crevice. Simply stated, diving the crevice can be just plain fun.

Farther out along this reef, the water deepens and sea life becomes even more abundant. Beginning in about 30 feet of water, large fans of gorgonian adorn the rocks. Garibaldi become more abundant and are just as friendly. Adding to the color are nudibranchs and a variety of anemones.

Shaw's Cove is part of the Laguna Beach Marine Life Refuge, which permits the taking of most game fish and lobster. Disturbing all other forms of aquatic life is prohibited. Game is sparse in Shaw's Cove, probably due to the frequency of divers. On the outer fringes of the reefs, an occasional morsel can be found.

Diving on the eastern side of the cove is less spectacular but far less crowded. A shallow reef covered with blade kelp and eelgrass extends from the eastern point out about 100 yards ending in sand 25 feet down. This reef tops out at 10 to 15 feet and is excellent for snorkeling. At several points along the sand, the reef rises vertically from the bottom as much as eight feet. Colorful gorgonian and anemones inhabit these mini-walls. On the far side of the eastern reef, there is a shallow channel that is inhabited with a variety of fish and has a horizontal crack that extends through the reef some 30 feet and is sometimes inhabited by moray eels.

Shaw's Cove is located between two other favorite Laguna Beach dive spots: Crescent Bay to the northwest and the lesser-known Fisherman's Cove to the southeast. A short walkway and stairs that lead to the cove are located at the end of Fairview at Cliff Drive, a block from North Coast Highway (Highway 1). Parking is on the street and is very limited. It is best to arrive early or go on weekdays. If the nearby parking is full, deposit your gear and buddy at the top of the stairs and park farther away to avoid a long walk with your equipment. The cove is surrounded by private property. Respect their privacy by keeping quiet and not trespassing.

A block south from Fairview at Wave Street and Highway 1 is a dive store if you'd like to fill your tank for a second dive.

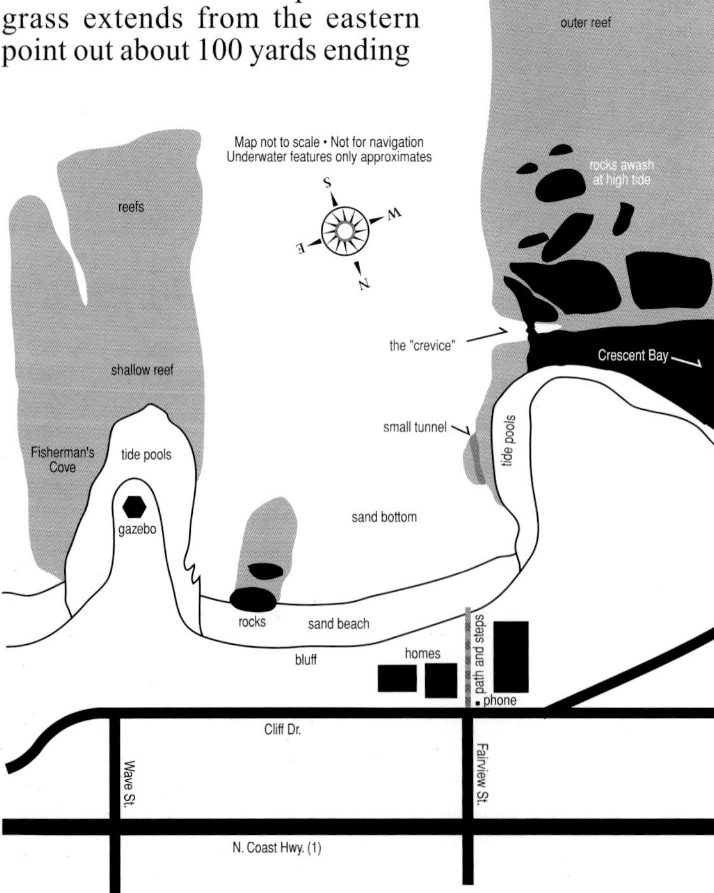

Fisherman's Cove (a.k.a. Boat Canyon)

It's a small spot, not much bigger than a small hotel room, but it's one of my favorite underwater spots off Laguna Beach. Mermaid's Grotto is a hole in the reef off Fisherman's Cove. I'm not sure of the geological forces behind its creation, but it appears to be a large fracture with crevices radiating outward. At the center is a large hole where you can tuck down inside, out of the surge, and watch the waves push about the large stands of golden gorgonian sea fans on the vertical rock faces as the numerous garibaldi come to visit. The play of light on the narrow rock crevice walls adorned with gorgonian is absolutely enchanting.

Fisherman's Cove is also sometimes referred to as Boat Canyon, probably because of the numerous catamaran sailboats stored ashore. It's a small cove with a tiny beach that disappears at high tide. Divers often overlook it as it is wedged between two very popular dive sites: Shaw's Cove to the north and Diver's Cove to the south. Access to Fisherman's Cove is immediately adjacent to the Diver's Cove access and parking. Turn off Pacific Coast Highway at Cliff Drive. The parking at Diver's Cove is at the extreme north end of Heisler Park. There are only a few metered parking spots, so arrive early in the morning and bring plenty of quarters.

This is also the north end of the Vedder Ecological Preserve. Nothing from Diver's Cove and south to Main Beach may be taken or disturbed. Although Fisherman's Cove is just to the north, and out of the preserve, it's suggested you not hunt here as enforcement officers may have trouble differentiating between who just came out of the water at Diver's Cove and who just stepped out of Fisherman's. Besides, short of a few small lobsters, there is little to take at Fisherman's Cove.

Access to the cove is a partially hidden narrow path, just to the north of the apartments on the point. Although scheduling a dive at high tide is usually good planning for best water visibility, you may have to compromise here; otherwise, there won't be any beach to stage your dive. You'll want to enter the water from the northwest side of the cove as there are numerous shallow rocks on the southeast side, near the point. A

Garibaldi in "Mermaid's Grotto"

portion of the reef can be seen breaking the surface offshore. That is your target. Mermaid's Grotto is just to the seaward of that breaking reef. The cove is well protected, and the sand drops off to deep water quickly.

Portions of the reef top can be very shallow, but, in general, it averages 15 to 20 feet. If the surge permits, spend some time in the shallows with the numerous opaleye and zebra perch. Schools of salema and anchovies are also sometimes seen.

Around the base of the reef, in the sand, its water depth is 25 to 30 feet. I like to skirt along the edges until I come to one of the large cracks that leads into the hole. The edges hold small rockfish, gobies, sea stars, urchins, and nudibranchs. Look for barred sand bass that like to patrol the sand bottom near the rocks. You'll see small rockfish in the large cracks.

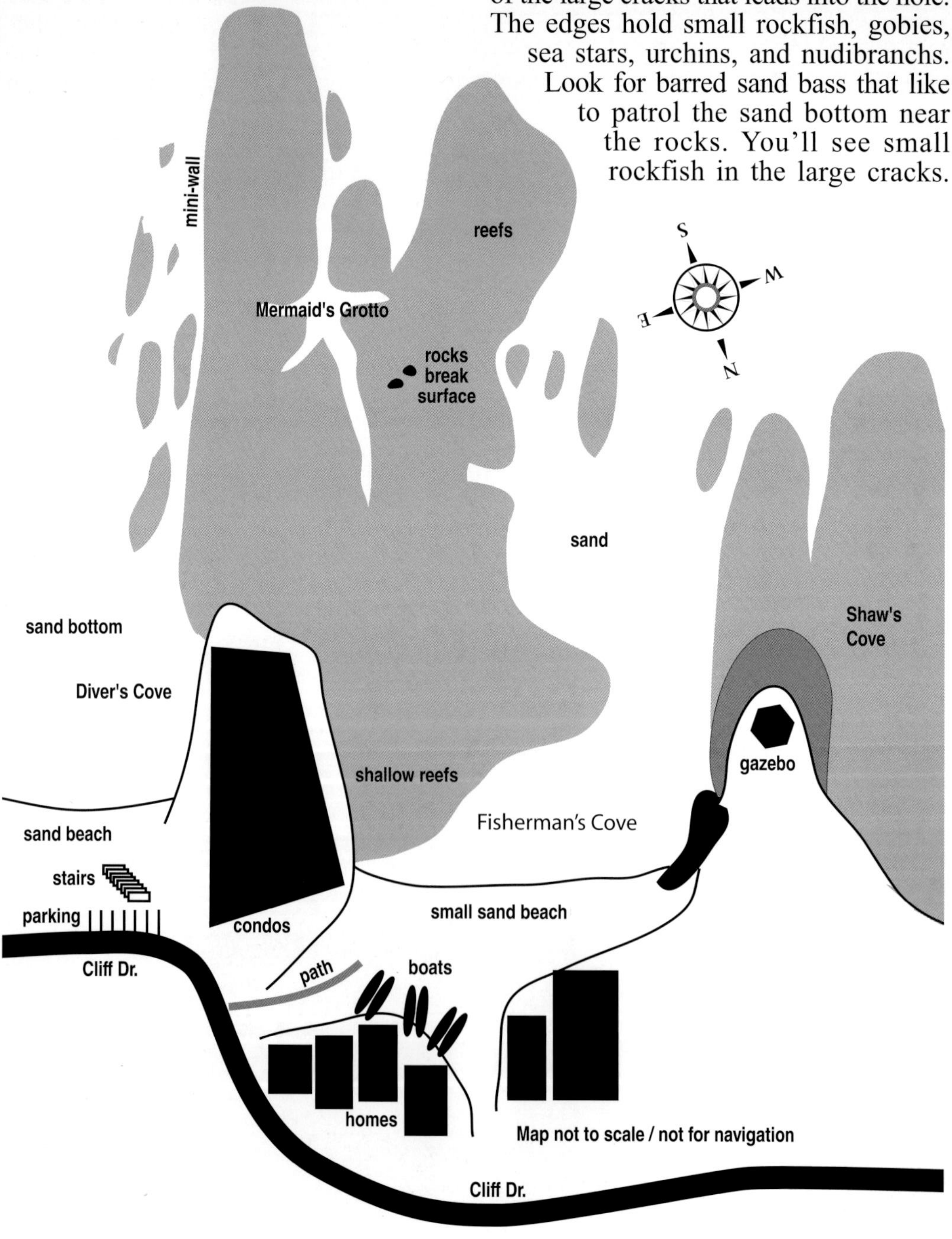

The cracks leading to the grotto are only about three feet wide or just large enough for a diver to pass through. The top of the reef is at about 15 feet deep, where the bottom of the cracks and holes are at 25. It's not a huge vertical drop, but large enough to make it fun. The light here is good, due to better-than-average water clarity. The crevices and holes offer protection from silt stirred by surge. This is a good spot for wide-angle photography with numerous angles on rock faces, crevices, and gorgonian. And the garibaldi seem to be especially cooperative.

The swimming distance between Fisherman's Cove and Diver's Cove is only about 200 to 250 yards around the point . An excellent dive plan for intermediate divers is to enter at Fisherman's, swim around the point underwater using navigational skills, and exit at the beach at Diver's Cove. With this plan, the mini-wall reefs off Diver's Cove can be explored on the same dive as a visit to Mermaid's Grotto.

Then again, you can just tuck into your own corner on the reef, a place reported to be a hiding place for mermaids, and wait for a very special visitor that will probably never show up, at least not in reality, but perhaps in your mind.

Diver's Cove

Diver's Cove is a delightfully easy beach dive with some of the friendliest marine life you'll find anywhere along the coast. Bright orange garibaldi practically mug divers. They come in close, pose, and fight with each other for attention from the bubble-blowing intruder. Other fish follow suit. Señorita fish, blacksmith, calico bass, rock wrasse and others join in gathering around underwater visitors at this site. It seems the most popular underwater creatures at Diver's Cove are the divers themselves!

Diver's Cove sits smack-dab in the middle of the most popular beach diving area of Southern California—Laguna Beach. Oddly enough, however, the cove was not named for underwater explorers but rather after youthful acrobatic platform divers that would use the sharp drop-off at the point for pike, swan, and jack-knife dives in the 1920s and '30s.

The Cove is part of an ecological preserve and has been for many years. The friendliness of the fish is probably owed to their protected status. Nothing may be taken or disturbed from this cove and reefs.

The main event underwater is the reef extending out from the point on the northwest side of the cove. This is

Shovelnose guitarfish

Diver's Cove

actually the eastern edge of a large reef system that extends over to Fisherman's Cove. Many divers choose to enter at Diver's Cove, explore the entire reef, and exit at Fisherman's Cove (or visa versa). A "cross-country" dive of this nature can be very fulfilling, but requires some stamina, navigational skills, and good air consumption. Even so, Diver's Cove is an easy place to attempt your first.

Another long swim option is an isolated reef at bearing 160° on your compass out across the sand. If the kelp growth is good, look for stalks floating on the surface.

Parking overlooking Diver's Cove is located at the 600 block of Cliff Drive. There are only a handful of metered parking spaces, and your best bet for getting one is an early morning arrival. There is additional metered parking on the street near Heisler Park. Bring lots of quarters. Access to the cove is down a path and a few steps to a small sand beach that is sometimes overwhelmed by the sea on extreme high tides. In the surf line the bottom drops away quickly, which makes for a short surf zone but a sharp shore break. The point offers some protection from a northwest swell.

For the best easy diving area, follow the reef that extends straight out from the point. About 100 yards out in 25 feet of water the reef will offer you a mini-wall covered with gorgonia, chestnut cowries, and rock scallops. The rock face is great for photos with the sea fans, stars and urchins providing dashes of color. The mini-wall extends out to 30 feet of water and rises from the bottom 10 feet. Around the tip of this reef are more reefs that extend out even farther. Following along the edges of these reefs will eventually put you in front of Fisherman's Cove. In this section are large, deep cuts in the rocks that are fascinating to explore.

Picnic Beach

You can go crazy trying to decide on a place to dive in Orange County. Narrow it down to Laguna Beach and you can get dizzy. How do you decide with so many beautiful spots to choose from? One of my favorite gauges is the facilities. Add easy access, parking, and a place to park family members for a barbecue and the choice is easy—Picnic Beach.

Located off Pacific Coast Highway at Myrtle and Cliff Drive, there is ample parking (though in the summer months that is true only early in the a.m.) and a paved path that takes you directly from your car to the center of the cove. By now, most divers have their gear on wheels, and you can wheel everything down to the beach via a paved ramp and set up a dive staging area on the wide beach. If you choose to dress-in at your car and walk the path, it is a fairly easy and not too steep a walk.

The protected cove makes for an easy and usually uneventful entry and exit, although you may want to watch for rocks in the center of the cove in the surf zone. Snorkeling out, you'll encounter large patch reefs just past the surf zone in about 10 feet of water. This is an excellent area for a casual day of just snorkeling. There is enough life growing on these little reefs to keep you occupied for a dive, but continue moving to deeper water for even more interesting sights.

Barred sand bass

As you cruise the bottom, you'll encounter three rocky ridges reaching up out of the sand bottom, each holding different encounters. They run approximately parallel to each other and the shore. You'll find tall ridges creating a mini-wall environment, reaching from 35 feet to within 10 feet of the surface. Golden gorgonian sea fans grow abundantly—in some cases completely covering the rocky surface. Pink, giant-spined and brittle stars are everywhere.

Marine life here is abundant and colorful. Garibaldi, of course, are on every ridge and in-between. Other bountiful and colorful varieties of fish on these reefs include señoritas, opaleye, and blue-banded gobies. Attached to the rocks are green aggregating anemones and large gray-colored moon sponges. Crawling about are giant keyhole limpets, Kellet's whelk, wavy turbans, and flashy Spanish shawl nudibranchs.

Barred sand bass are huge and unusually friendly. These are normally a very shy fish. We encountered the sand bass circling one ridge about 60 yards from shore. As we approached they all seemed to swim over to us as if to greet us. As we moved out to the next ridge they followed. They stayed with us for most of the return to shore, too, following just a few feet from our fins. And, no, we did not have any food or game with us, and we did not break up urchins to feed them.

We encountered the final ridge about 100 yards from shore. It had what appeared to be a cave on the seaward side. But if you got down really low and peered into it, you could see all the way through. It was a tunnel passing completely under a reef some 30 feet wide! The bottom here is in 36 feet of water. The openings on both sides are very narrow, but opens up into a bigger space under the reef. Do not enter this little opening; the sand shifting in and out and the surge make it a potentially dangerous place to be.

Lobster was seen everywhere a rocky crevice could be found for them to sleep in. It was interesting to see so many rock scallops under the ledges. The entire area is a marine preserve. Hunting is not welcome and sightseers should take nothing but pictures. Though an interesting point to make is the abundance of lobster traps all over the reefs—No hunting, huh?

Visibility typically ranges from 15 to 25 feet and is known to reach up to 40 feet in the winter months.

The park has excellent picnic facilities (hence the beach's name), and restrooms are located a few steps north of the top of the path to the beach. At the foot of the path is a single freshwater shower.

NOTE: As of going to press with this book, Heisler Park is undergoing major renovations that could temporary affect access to the shoreline. There are, however, many alternate dive sites close by to the northwest. The renovations are to bring major improvements to the park, including even better access, upgraded restrooms, and more.

Garibaldi

Rocky Beach

Shaw's, Fisherman's, and Diver's Coves, along with Picnic Beach, are great spots for diving in Laguna Beach, but if you want to avoid the underwater crowds, try Rocky Beach. Diving here is a little more challenging, but you may find it extra rewarding as well.

Overlooking the diving area from the small bluff makes it apparent why this is a good dive location. Approximately 100 yards offshore is a large reef breaking the surface at mid-to-low tide which in turn is surrounded by numerous smaller reefs; this results in a huge diving area large enough to accommodate many divers in an uncrowded way.

Perhaps another reason fewer divers visit here is that the entry appears more difficult. Neighboring Diver's Cove, Picnic Beach, and Main Beach all have easy sand-beach entry, whereas Rocky Beach is just as its name states—rocky. A diver choosing to dive here should have some rock-surf entry experience. There are, however, several good easy entry points from which to choose, making them fairly simple in small or moderate surf.

Close to shore, the bottom drops off quickly to 10 to 15 feet. There are many small, low-lying reefs covered heavily with eelgrass and interspersed with sand patches and channels. The shallow reefs are excellent for snorkeling with little surf, but scuba here can be difficult in moderate surf because of surge.

If on scuba, there is no reason to linger in the shallows because deeper water lays only a few more fin strokes toward the sea. The larger reefs, particularly the one that breaks the surface at low tide, can be quite spectacular. The rock walls of the reefs drop quickly and often vertically in

Green anemone

20 to 30 feet of water and then slope to 40 or 50 feet. Critters that call these rocks home include crabs of several varieties, large and colorful anemones and broad stands of gorgonian sea fans. Photographers will be delighted with the cooperative garibaldis and señorita fish, as well as being surprised by more unusual visitors such as horn sharks and yellowtail.

There is other game in the area, including lobster, halibut, scallops, and game fish. Look only! The entire area is a marine preserve and taking anything in the marine environment is prohibited. The marine preserve provides an excellent opportunity to observe creatures in the wild not always found elsewhere along the coast.

Reaching Rocky Beach is particularly simple if you are familiar with the popular diving area. It lies just south of Diver's Cove and Picnic Beach. Coast Highway (Highway 1) passes directly through the town of Laguna Beach. Turn on Jasmine St. just north of the center of town. The stairs to the water's edge are just behind the shuffleboard and lawn bowling courts. There are two sets of stairs providing a number of water entry/exit possibilities. There is metered parking along Cliff Drive. Try to arrive early during summer weekends as parking is limited. Bring lots of quarters—buying time on the meter can add up quickly

The beautiful park through which you pass to reach the beach is Heisler Park. This park has excellent facilities, including showers, restrooms, and picnic sites. The walkway along the bluff provides views of the diving area from a number of different angles. Study your dive plan carefully from here for a flawless dive.

NOTE: As of going to press with this book Heisler Park is undergoing major renovations that could temporary effect access to the shoreline. There are, however, many alternate dive sites close by to the northwest. The renovations are to bring major improvements to the park including even better access (although access at Rocky Beach is in question), upgraded restrooms and more.

Main Beach

The most popular beach with tourists and sun seekers at Laguna Beach is Main Beach directly off the center of town. In the summer and at other times of the year as well, this beach is often quite crowded. For this reason, many divers avoid this dive spot for other less crowded spots nearby. What many divers are unaware of are the superb reefs that lie less than 150 yards from shore on the northwest end of the beach.

Marked by a large rounded rock known as Bird Rock, the reef begins in as shallow as 10 feet of water. Bird Rock is only 50 to 100 feet from shore, depending on the tide, and just beyond the rock, somewhat to the southwest, is a large reef that extends over 200 yards offshore, for nearly 1/2 mile to the northwest. Ranging in depths from 20 to nearly 50 feet, the reef is full of crevices, boulders and ledges. All of this creates an excellent environment for a bonanza of marine life.

All of Laguna Beach's dive spots are famous for abundant and friendly

Porter's chromodorid nudibranch

bright orange garibaldi. The reefs off Main Beach are no exception. If you have never spent an entire dive feeding, observing, and playing with these wonderful fish, you are missing a relaxing and delightful experience. If you can pull yourself away from the garibaldi, take time to look around at the colorful collection of invertebrates. Although not as abundant as in other Laguna Beach locations, there is enough variety to keep macro photographers busy.

Resident populations of lobster and game fish will tempt hunters. Taking of game is, however, questionable. The reef here is cut in half by the borders of the Vedder Ecological Preserve in which no marine life is to be taken. Because it is difficult to pick out man-made imaginary borders on the sea floor, it is recommended that you take nothing from this area. If you are interested in game, there are plenty of reefs with more bountiful game to the southeast.

Access to Main Beach is quite good. Sunbathers use the access directly in front of the lifeguard tower. Although this eliminates a short stair climb, the best entry point for diving is a moderately long walk to the north but parking here is very limited. A better access point would be from the small bluffs at Heisler Park. From Coast Highway, turn toward the beach on Cliff Drive and within a block, just beside the restaurant, is the access to the shore. Here, at the extreme south end of Heisler Park, is a large gazebo on the point overlooking the diving area. This is an excellent vantage point to study the lay of the kelp (if present), reef patterns, prevailing conditions, and shore entry and exit points. Metered parking is available along Cliff Drive so bring lots of quarters. The path to the beach is just to the left of the gazebo. Entry can be made in a number of points, but most divers prefer to enter off the sand beach. There are numerous shallow rocks and reefs in the surf zone, but the bottom generally drops off quickly to 10 feet deep.

NOTE: As of going to press with this book Heisler Park is undergoing renovations that could temporary affect access to the shoreline at the gazebo. There are, however, many alternate dive sites to the northwest.

Cleo Street Wreck

Wreck dives are special, but it is not something you normally associate with Southern California beach diving. They are there but not much more than bits and pieces on the bottom, and you really have to know what you are looking for. There is one exception, however, and that is at Cleo Street off Laguna Beach.

The wreck off Cleo Street does not have any spectacular history. Known as Foss 125, it was a barge hauling gravel for a sewer outfall when it floundered and sank in a storm November 17, 1958. Having been down for a half a century, it has largely collapsed in on itself but still is a haven for a myriad of marine life.

The wreck is a popular spot for local lobster hunters. The nooks and crannies in the wreckage hold a fair amount of the tasty crustaceans. Be careful in your grabs, however, as much of the wreckage is deteriorated to the point of sharp rusty edges.

A variety of fish call this spot home. Look for sheephead, schools of señoritas, opaleye, perch, and an occasional kelpfish and, of course, garibaldi. One of the highlights of this dive is the possibility of coming across a giant black sea bass hovering over the wreckage. Three feet is typical size and they generally show up in the late summer through early fall. This is one of the few beach dives off the Orange County coastline where giant black sea bass are commonly seen. Other big fish include bat rays in the nearby sand flats, as well as the occasional halibut.

Little critters also can be found on the wreck. There are small stands of gorgonian, nudibranchs and small fish like the black-eyed goby. You'd think this would be a great beach dive to take your camera but think again. There is a downside to this dive site.

The swim out to the wreck from the beach is around a quarter mile — a long haul even for the strongest swimmer. Finding the wreck can also be difficult. Troubles start with trying to find a place to park at the top of the stairs. Parking is very limited. The stairs to the beach are in great shape and not too steep or long. Watch out, however, for the last step as it is quick and a long drop. There are rocks in the surf zone so either enter here at high tide or move down the beach a bit away from the rocks. Do not dive here when the surf is breaking moderate or larger as entry and exit are difficult due to the rocks and the fatigue f

Navigating your way o may seem simple enough, b a long swim and the wreck havi tively small footprint (about 100 fee it is easy to get off course. The comp heading out from the stairs is 220° (reverse heading 40°). You should be directly out from the brown house with white-framed windows. Align yourself so that the tower on Hotel Laguna is due north and drop down. You will be in approximately 40 feet of water. As you head farther offshore you will cross a few small reefs. The wreck is in 47 to 53 feet of water. If you hit 60 feet, you have gone too far; turn around and head back. You might come across a cement pipe or two and this will tell you that you are close. Because of

California spiny lobster

rom shore, water te good, averaging feet or better on a owever, marks this ssible to see it from ur return trip leave tank so you can get m back underwater. Highly reco... nded to dive this site for the first time is to go with another diver or group that has been here before. The group South Coast Divers dives various locations throughout Laguna Beach every weekend (conditions permitting). The Cleo Street wreck is on their list of dive sites often visited. For more information, visit their website at www.southcoastdivers.com.

Cress Street

Experienced lobster hunters know that when the tasty crustaceans cannot be found in their usual habitat of crevices and caves, a likely place to look is in shallow spots among the eelgrass. Eelgrass is the long stringy green plant that grows in thick bunches and patches in shallow rocky reef areas. Lobsters often love to hide in it.

Eelgrass is particularly prolific in the surf and surge zones along the popular Southern California beach diving areas of Laguna Beach. Laguna Beach is so popular with divers, however, that lobsters have become scarce in the more heavily frequented areas. One of the dive sites that still contains a fair amount of lobster among the eelgrass, not to mention a beautiful reef farther out, is off the beach at Cress Street.

The bottom off the sandy beach drops quickly to 10 or 15 feet deep over a bed of strewn rocks and ridge reefs. Looking out from shore, it is easy to spot the inner and outer reefs breaking the surface in the surge. What is not as easy to spot is a third set of reefs about 300 yards out and 35 to 75 feet down. The inner reef is a short swim of 45 to 60 yards and the outer reef is about 100 to 150 yards out. There is a great deal of rocks, ridges and kelp in between. On the inside, eelgrass and feather boa kelp are the predominant plant species. This is the surgy shallow area where lobsters like to hide under the swaying green mop.

Farther out, the reefs on the bottom begin to take on a more regular pattern of being parallel to shore and 30 feet or so apart. They are fairly low to the bottom, rising only five feet or so, but an occasional rocky spire juts up as much as 10 feet. Some of these rock formations take on rather peculiar shapes.

Spanish shawl nudibranch

Spearfishing enthusiasts like this spot for halibut, calico bass and even yellowtail and white sea bass on the outer reefs.

If you are not the hunter type, the middle set of reefs is where the scenery begins to blossom. Garibaldi are abundant and friendly. If you are carrying a camera, try photographing their stark orange color against the rich green of the eelgrass. Wide-angle photography is usually best as the frequent surge makes close-ups difficult.

Moving further out, large stretches of sand break up the bottom until you reach the outer reef. Photographers and sightseers should stick near the edges of the reef and look for bat rays and angel sharks. There is also an abundance of señorita fish, kelpfish, and opaleye. Seals have also been known to frolic over these reefs.

The middle reef is a large house-size boulder rising from the bottom 25 feet below to just break the surface. Surrounding this monolith are smaller auto-sized boulders, probably broken off from the mother rock. In the crevices one can find moray eels, rockfish, octopus, and, if you're lucky, an occasional lobster. Growing over the rocks are a large variety of algae, a few scallops, and colorful anemones. Eyes should also be kept open for the brightly colored lemon and Spanish shawl nudibranchs and tiny blue-banded gobies.

Surge is a little less prevalent out here but still can be a problem. Just for the thrill of it, take a ride through the surge across the top of the rock. If you can stand the excitement, the power of the ocean will toss you about and exhilarate you.

For the really strong swimmers, the reef continues out into deeper water and becomes even more exciting. Since the outer reefs run in small patches, they can be hard to find. Clues include kelp (if growing) and lobster trap buoys, in season.

Crowds do not frequent Cress Street for one very simple reason: water entry conditions are not usually ideal. The beach is exposed and the beach slope is sharp which leads to a short but powerful surf zone. Experience in surf entries is a must. Dive this spot only on days of two feet or less of surf. To dive it in any greater surf is not necessarily dangerous but frustrating. If you make it out past the pounding surf, the bottom will then be very surgy. The good news is Laguna Beach has generally low surf conditions 60 to 70 percent of the year.

More good news is that if Cress Street is not divable, there are plenty of better protected spots like Shaw's or Diver's Cove only a few miles away. Visibility here is variable. If the rest of Laguna Beach is clear, and the surf is down, it will be good here as well. Surf three feet or larger creates a strong surge lifting the sediment off the bottom.

Access to this dive site is reached by turning on to Cress Street off Pacific Coast Highway to the south of the center of town. Parking is limited to just a few spaces, some with meters, some not. A little less than 70 steps lead to the pleasant sandy beach below. Pause at the top of the steps for a good observation of the near-shore reefs below. You will be able to see where the various reefs break the surface, the borders of the kelp forest, and how the shore break is laying out. There are no facilities.

But not to worry: the small beach is right at the town's doorstep. In Laguna Beach there are a number of fine restaurants, as well as the usual fast food joints. Bring your non-diving loved ones as they can spend the day exploring Laguna's fine shopping districts and art galleries.

Juvenile sheephead

Wood's Cove

I have two visions of the underwater world, different, yet often alike. The vision I have most of the time is that of reality. Wonderful—spectacular— but also includes flat sandy bottoms and dirty water.

My first vision of the underwater world, however, was that of young childhood fantasy. As a young boy, before a mask was ever put to my face, I formed a fanciful expectation of the world beneath the waves. Many of these expectations were formed by Disney's cinematic epic *20,000 Leagues Under the Sea*, and other early Hollywood recreations of the underwater world. In these cellulose representations of a world few had ever seen, the bottom terrain was that of reefs with talon-like fingers jutting for the surface, gnarled with wicked shapes, ready to disembowel any ship or submarine that came just a little too close.

For those of us who often revert back to our childhood fantasies, thank God there are places right off our own coastline where we can indulge our imaginations. The reefs off Laguna Beach seem to have more than their fair share of these fantasy reefs. Whenever I visit Wood's Cove on the south side of Laguna Beach, the feature I enjoy most about the dive is the glide through the amazing underwater terrain.

Wood's Cove is a fairly large cove (by Laguna Beach standards) with enough underwater real estate for two dives. The cove is roughly divided in two by a large rock structure in the surf line. Both sides of the cove offer equally fascinating diving. Many divers, as a matter of fact, choose to enter one side of the cove and exit the other.

On the northwest side of the cove, just offshore about 50 yards out, two rocks break the surface, hinting at ship-gutting reefs below. The mussel-covered rocks are just the tips of huge boulders that extended 20 feet down. Around the base are numerous smaller boulders surrounded by fish and covered with eelgrass, feather boa kelp, and any other marine life that can hold on in this surgy middle ground just beyond the surf zone.

Between here and the beach are numerous boulders and eelgrass fields that get the regular action of the surf. This is a nice area to snorkel over when the ocean is calm, but avoid it in when there is any kind of surf. By the way, with heavy pressure from both commercial and sport lobster hunters, the shallows are often your best bet for lobster hunting at Wood's Cove, as well as up and down Laguna Beach.

Beyond the surface, visible reefs are where things get really interesting. Out from the southern-most reef is a small underwater arch. Really not much more that than a window in a tall reef structure, it makes for an interesting photo opportunity with numerous garibaldi dancing in and out of the round hole. The arch lies in 20 feet of water.

The reefs straight out from the wash rock are the most popular and spectacular. Huge boulders tower from the bottom to just below the surface. Ledges and caves are everywhere. Lobsters are present but early or late in the season is best. Sightseers will enjoy the large moon sponges, garibaldi, and Spanish shawl nudibranchs.

This reef extends quite away offshore, offering more sites to see, including gorgonian, very

Gray moon sponges

large sea stars, and halibut lounging in the nearby sand. On the outer fringes of this reef, in 40 feet of water, is wreckage of a long-ago ditched airplane. These days you need to have a keen eye, however, as not much more than the engine block remains and that looks more like a rock than a piece of machinery. The wreck is to the south and out a bit from the outer reef that just breaks the surface. Still further out (1/4 to 1/2 mile) is Miller's Reef (named for popular diving personality Dr. Sam Miller). Depths here are from 40 to 60 feet, but this is simply too far a swim for most beach divers.

Lobster hunters might do better to head to the reefs on the northwest point. It's surgy and a bit of swim, but most divers don't visit here, so there may be a better chance for lobster. Dive here the opening day or two of the season to do best. Depths average 30 to 40 feet but can reach up to 60 feet a quarter mile out. If you dive the location during lobster season, you can often follow the pattern of the reef by the numerous commercial lobster trap buoys. Kelp sometimes also marks the location of these outer reefs.

Far from the marine reserves to the north, spearfishing is popular at Wood's Cove. Due to the site's easy accessibility, however, game fish are sparse and skittish. Even so, calico bass, sheephead, and halibut are available within the cove. For larger or shyer game fish, try the outer edges of the reefs, off the points, and around the corners, particularly to the north.

The outer reefs have little pattern to them. Interspersed with sand flats, reef after reef can be discovered heading offshore across the bottom. The rocks appear out of the haze, first as a silhouette, then as high-density living quarters for residents of this corner of the ocean. Jutting as much as 15 feet from the bottom, these obtusely shaped rock spires support a large variety of marine life.

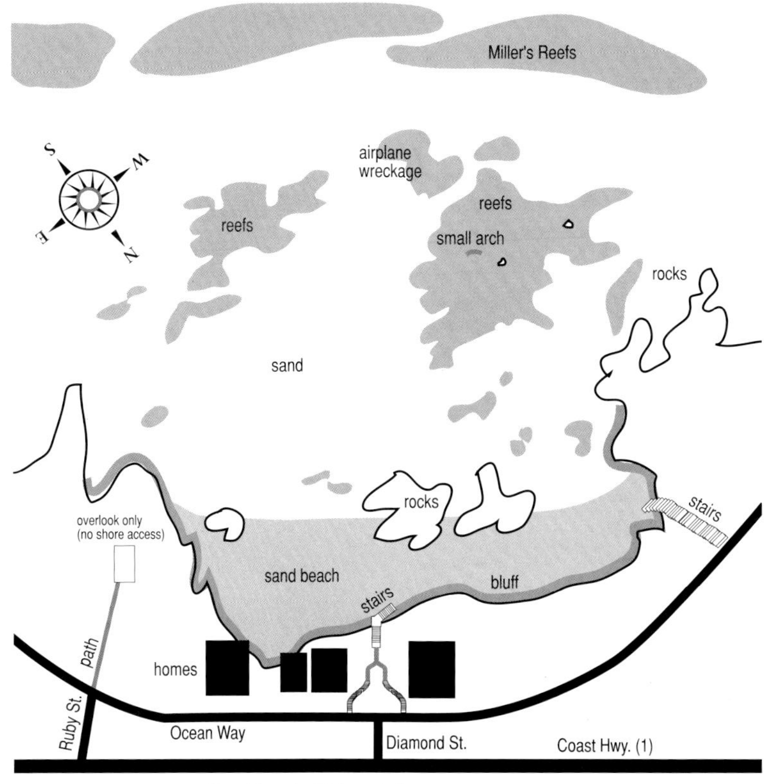

Map not to scale • Not for navigation

Golden gorgonian stands are common. Mini-walls can be covered with these animal colonies, California's version of soft coral. Garibaldi are plentiful and friendly, and, combined with the backdrop of gorgonian fans, make good photo subjects. Put all this in your wide-angle framer along with odd angles of the reef, and you will have photos that will touch the undersea fantasies of the child in all of us.

Macro photographers will have no shortage of material either. Take some time also to look at the variety and textures available in the in the choice of starfish at this site. Mollusks available for observation and photography include nudibranchs, the Norris top shell, wavy turban, and chestnut cowry.

There are two access points to the cove. Access is almost directly off Pacific Coast Highway. Turn toward the beach on Diamond Street. Parking is very limited on Diamond Street or on Ocean Way. Access point #1 is directly off the end of Diamond Street. There is a secondary public access point off the 1900 block of Ocean Street (about a block north of Diamond). Both pathways consist of several steps down to the beach. Halfway down the steps are points at which the entire cove can be viewed. For an additional overall view, try the tiny park just to the south at Ruby Street (there is, however, no beach access here).

Private property surrounds the cove. Please keep your diver etiquette at its best. Do not park illegally and keep noise to a minimum. There are no facilities at Wood's Cove, but businesses offering food and other services are plentiful along Pacific Coast Highway. There is a pay phone at the base of Diamond Street. For your best chance at parking, visit the site on weekdays, early morning, and, if with a group, car pool.

In planning your water entry and exits, plan carefully. The beach slope drops off quickly to 5 to 10 feet onto a slippery loose stone bottom. The wave faces build quickly and the shore break is sharp across the rocks. Water entry is easy during small surf but with any kind of swell, time your entry carefully to take advantage of lull between wave sets.

The next time *20,000 Leagues Under the Sea* is on TV, look for me at Wood's Cove in the days following. I hope you don't catch me playing with my toy submarine.

Moss Street

Another Laguna Beach dive spot that is perhaps less frequented by the crowds is the small cove located at the end of Moss Street. The reefs of Moss Street hold diving pleasures that are as good as any other location in Laguna Beach. There are small walls and ledges and, in spots, the rocks tower as high as 18 feet from the sand bottom. Here and there are deep cracks and crevices that cut into the reef and resemble caves.

The rocks are also thickly covered by a wide variety of marine life. From about 50 yards out to the seaward ends of the reefs, gorgonian sea fans are plentiful. In spots, the rocks seem overgrown with golden-colored gorgonian growth. Feather worms and colorful anemones also make for good subjects for underwater photographers and in the surrounding waters, friendly garibaldi are at every turn of the fin.

The hunter may also fare well here. Although sparse and on the small side, lobster can be taken here when in season; an occasional small scallop can be pried from the rocks, and the spearfisher will find sheephead and kelp bass. The outer reefs are best for the bigger game. A large halibut or two sometimes hides in the sand between the reefs.

Conditions at the Moss Street cove are generally good year round. The cove is well

Señorita

protected and currents rarely affect the area except on the extreme outer reef. Visibility is good, as in most Laguna Beach dive spots. Averaging between 15 and 25 feet, the visibility can reach as much as 35 feet and is seldom below 10 feet. The shallow parts of the reef can have a surge problem, but this can easily be avoided by moving to the deeper (30 to 35 feet) sections of the reef about 100 to 150 yards offshore.

The path that leads to this picturesque cove is easily found by exiting Coast Highway (Highway 1) onto Moss Street, a little over one mile southeast of downtown. After about a block, Moss Street will dead-end. Limited parking is available on Moss Street and nearby Ocean Way. Parking is sometimes filled, in which case it is a simple matter to drop your gear at the top of the stairs and park a few blocks away. Be aware of "no parking" red zones; they are everywhere. Also, the entire area is residential—please respect their quiet and privacy.

There are 62 steps leadi[...] sandy beach from the end of M[...] From the landing at the top of t[...] ocean conditions can be careful[...] served. A gentle rip is common in the m[...]dle of the cove. Note the rocks that brea[...] the surface in the swell at low tide off the point to the southeast and closer in on the northwest side of the cove. The rocks of the southerly point, known as Moss Point, marks the beginning of the reef that is of most interest to divers. There are reefs on the northwest side on the cove, but they tend to be low-lying and sparse of sea life. Farther to the northwest lies Wood's Cove, which is another dive spot worth exploring.

Upon entering, the bottom drops off rapidly five or six feet. Beware of loose stones in the surf as they are common and can hinder entry and exit. This shallow water close to the beach is good for snorkelers on very calm days.

Once again, the best reef is to the southeast, so stay to your left as you face the ocean. If you drop to the bottom, just beyond the rocks breaking the surface, you will avoid the majority of the surge. Beyond these rocks the reef breaks up into a jumble of large boulders that create overhangs, crevices and small caves to explore.

Farther out, the rocks taper off and patch reefs can be found across the sand. On the other side of this reef, to the southeast a few yards, the rocks ascend vertically in spots creating large overhangs; it is here the reef is split in spots forming large crevices.

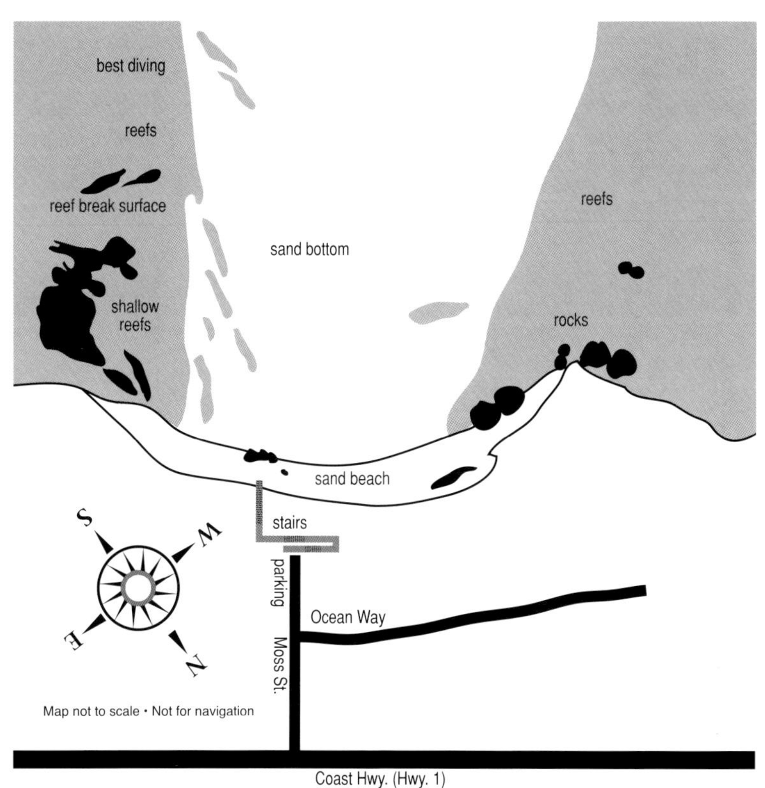

e (a.k.a. Island)

d debate are nothing levelopment along the ie. When developers purchased the Treasure Island property back in 1986, plans were ambitious to create a massive luxury real estate development. But the City of Laguna Beach had a different idea. Eventually, a compromise was formed that benefited all those parties concerned—the city, the resort developers and, most importantly, the public wanting access to this picturesque shoreline. Thus the Montage Resort and Spa complex was born with the public access portion known as Treasure Island Park.

Treasure Island is not an island at all but rather the location gains its name from a mobile home park that used to occupy the area. That park had taken its name from the film "Treasure Island" that was filmed here in 1934. As you could imagine, the beach is here is exceptionally beautiful. Rocky points extend into the sea with an especially long peninsula on the northwest end of the small bay. All this area is excellent for beach diving.

To reach the public access area, turn toward the sea on Wesley Drive off South Coast Highway and swing immediately to your left, which will bring you to the underground parking structure. The kiosk to pay for parking and restrooms are on the south end of the lot. The walkway along the bluff to the north is an excellent way to thoroughly scope out shore access, the dive site and conditions.

There are two main locations to access the shoreline and enter the water. There are the stairs at the north end of the walkway (a bit of a hike) and the ramp that is closest to the parking structure. Most divers choose to enter here. Both spots are reasonably well protected from the prevailing northwest weather and both have excel-

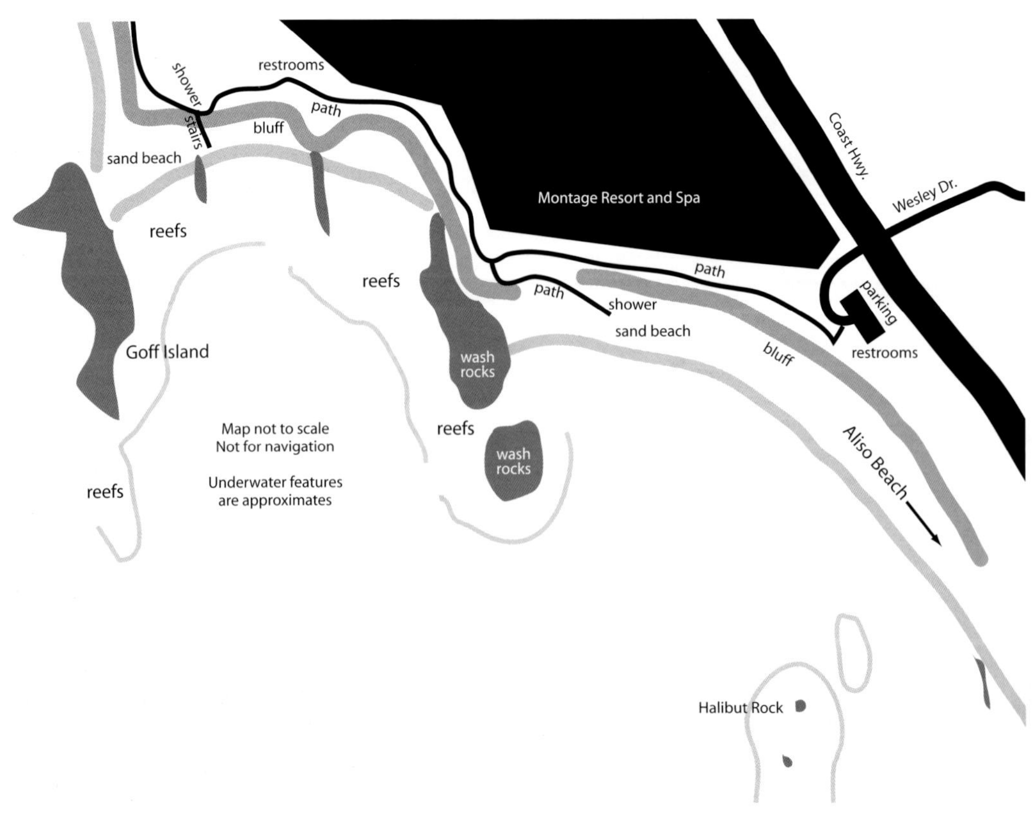

lent diving very close by.

At the bottom of the ramp is a sand beach and reef immediately to the right. During high and low tide this reef breaks the surface in a swirl of white water even when calm. While you do not want to venture across the shallow rocks, don't miss the mini-wall around the edge of the reef. As you follow the reef around to the right, keep your eye on the sand flats as you will almost certainly encounter bat rays, often quite large. Smaller rays and guitarfish also often hug the reef.

Kelp rockfish

As you round the corner heading northwest, the reef will open up into a series of cracks and crevices that are fascinating to explore. Some of the crevices are quite deep and long and will rocket you through in the surge. Look under overhangs for lobster and moray eels. The reefs on the far side are especially noted for their large number of juvenile fish including sheephead, garibaldi, señoritas and blacksmith. Reef structures and boulders in shallow water continue out into the cove. Look for numerous and unusually friendly barred sand bass in this area.

The second section for diving is down the stairs into the cove often referred to as Goff Cove for the rock to the northwest known as Goff Island (again, not an island but a very large rock attached to the mainland by a sand spit.) A reef peninsula extends out from Goff Rock that is quite extraordinary. As you swim outward and around the corner, you will come across mini-walls, overhangs and caves. Lobster and moray eels are prolific. Gardens of gorgonian will greet you as will huge garibaldi. A harbor seal will frequently escort you. Nudibranchs are especially plentiful and in a wide variety. It is not unusual to encounter two or three octopi on one dive.

Moray eel

Reef fish include rockfish, painted greenlings and island kelpfish. In this author's opinion this is one of the top marine biodiversity sites in all of Orange County.

Many divers prefer to enter off the stairs, dive the reefs off Goff Rock then set a compass course for the reef to the southeast and exiting at the ramp. This plan is excellent for a grand tour of the area but best left to those with good underwater navigational skills.

Conditions off the point at Goff Rock, in the cove, and on the reef to the southeast are generally very good, some of the best in Laguna Beach. Visibility averages 15 to 20 feet and days of 30 feet are not unusual. The only area for concern is the surge can be tough off the point and near the shallows of the southeast reef. A light current down the coast has been known to sometimes haunt the area but, generally, is not a cause for concern.

Since its opening in 2003 Treasure Island Park has gained an understandably increased popularity with local divers. Excellent access, great facilities and a fantastic marine habitat make this a place to plan your next shore dive for Laguna Beach.

Aliso Beach

South of the main part of town in Laguna Beach, Coast Highway (Highway 1) dips down to beach level and the view opens up to the sea briefly. If you pass by too quickly you'll miss the parking lot and beach. Unless you're really looking, or pull off into the parking lot, you miss the evidence of offshore reefs and some great diving. Aliso Beach has some of the easiest access in all of Laguna Beach but is not often dived. It is not for the lack of great underwater features and life, but rather that this can be a difficult beach dive. For the experienced diver or intermediate diver, however, who can hit the site on a calm day, this is a treasure of a dive site.

There are a pair of diving areas to explore: the pipelines north of the old pier and the point to the south.

Years ago a fishing pier was removed but the restrooms remain where the foot of the pier once was. Directly out and to the northwest are two outfall pipelines that make for good diving. The pipeline directly off the restrooms is far out and difficult to find, rising above the sand only occasionally at depths of 50 to 75 feet. Easier to find is the pipeline to the north. If diving during lobster season, one needs only look for the string of lobster trap buoys leading off the beach. The pipe is located about halfway between the restrooms and north edge of the parking lot. Depths start at 30 to

Rubberlip surfperch

California scorpionfish

35 feet and out to deeper and farther than you want to go. Viz is again only fair, but hunting is good for calico and sand bass, halibut, and some lobster.

To the southeast is Camel Point. This is fun but sometimes tough diving. The reefs offshore boil and can be dangerous. Waves surge up on the tall flat reefs and then spill off the sides making for confusing currents and rips. Enter off the sand beach and swim to the reefs rather than entering at the point. The outer edges of the reef are quite interesting. There are overhangs, some quite deep, and fractures in the huge rock face creating narrow crevices. This is excellent territory for lobster. Fish are plentiful here. There are sheephead and calico as well as sand bass. The reefs extend for some way to the south, broken intermittently with small sand beaches.

Most of the beach in front of the parking lot has a sharp shore break with waves that build and crash quickly. The surf zone is narrow, but you must time the sets carefully or you'll be driven hard into the sand. Facilities are excclent with a seasonal snack bar, showers, large parking area (bring lots of quarters!) and restrooms.

1,000 Steps

One of the most spectacular dive sights off the Laguna Beach area is largely ignored simply because it takes a bit of effort to reach it. The name of the dive site—1,000 Steps—explains it all. While there are actually "only" 220 steps, all of them are steep and magnified by the weight of scuba gear. And while it may be a tough, long haul after the dive, what lies in the waters just beyond the steps may make the effort very worthwhile.

For starters, there is a spectacular underwater arch in 15 feet of water, less than 100 yards from shore. At 20 feet wide and about 8 feet high at the peak, the arch is large enough for several divers to fit in. The surge whips in the shallow arch making great fun for the diver who wants to play "thread the needle."

The second reason for braving the steep stairs is as compelling as the first: lobster. While certainly not overflowing with the tasty crustacean, this is perhaps one of the most heavily populated locations off Laguna Beach with adequate shore access.

Blood star

The lobsters make their homes in a maze of boulders and reefs that are fascinating to explore. Depths range from a surgy 5 feet to a small kelp bed on the outside that has a sand bottom nearby at 30 feet down.

But it is up among the shallow reefs where the diver is likely to have the most fun. In depths ranging from 15 to 25 feet, there are large crevices, 5 to 10 feet wide, that beg to be explored. At the bottom of the crevices are jumbles of boulders and large rock overhangs where lobster and other creatures love to hide. Look closely and you will find moray eels, kelp bass, and an occasional rock scallop.

On the rock faces are nudibranchs, sea stars, and the tiny, brightly colored, bluebanded goby fish. Darting in and out of the crevices are numerous friendly garibaldi. Also present are large schools of opal-eye and surfperch. The tops of the reefs are blanketed with eel and surf grass, as well as feather boa kelp. Also look under this green blanket as an occasional lobster can be found hiding there.

If surf conditions are low, diving conditions are usually as good here as anywhere else along Laguna. This is an unprotected beach, however, and anytime the surf is three feet or higher, divers should seek alternate

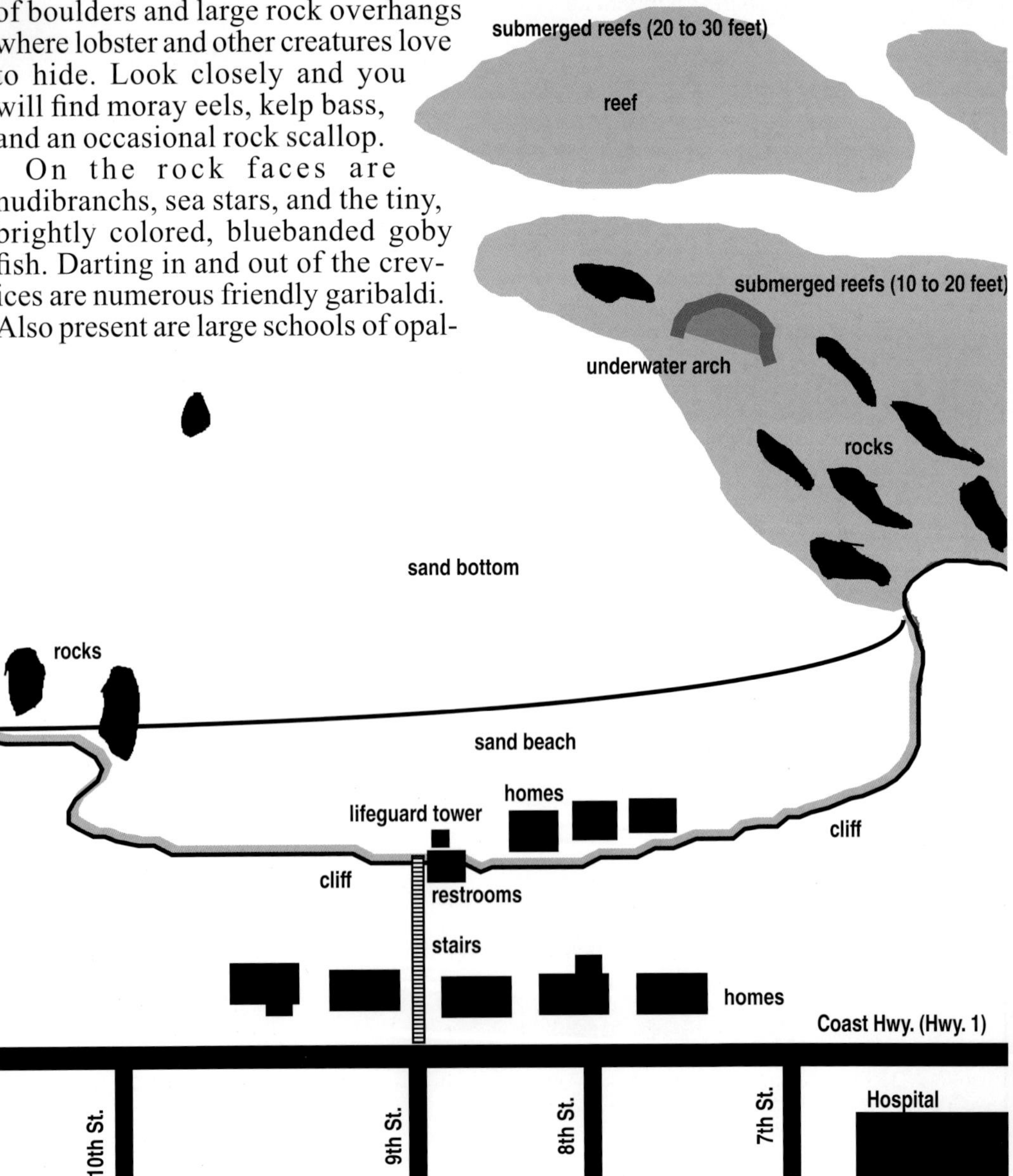

Grabbing Lobster

Congratulations! You just found your first lobster. You now realize that you have a delightful dinner in sight. You're not, however, going to gain the lobster's cooperation easily. You must somehow grab the "bug," measure him for minimum size, and get him into your bag. How you grab that lobster is going to determine whether or not you'll be having fresh lobster with drawn butter—or lima beans instead.

The only time you'll be lucky enough to spot a lobster out in the open will be on a night dive. First, and perhaps the most important point, is do not study the situation for too long. Unlike what you may have heard, lobsters are not particularly bright. They are, however, highly reactive. They will take a few moments to size you up, but if they perceive you as a threat, they will bolt immediately. On night dives, your light will often freeze the crustacean momentarily. This is your chance to move—and move quickly you must.

If you're lucky enough to position yourself from the rear, this is best as lobsters swim backwards. As you go for the grab, aim for the joint between the tail and the body. This will give you a little bit of an edge should the lobster flip its tail and try to swim away at the last moment. If at all possible, avoid grabbing the tail. The large spines on the underside of the tail will pinch around your hand as the tail flaps to swim.

When you go for the lobster in the open, don't go for the grab, go for the pin. The fraction of a second that it takes for you to wrap your fingers around the lobster, it will be gone. Instead, go to pin the lobster to the bottom with the force of the palm of your hand. Once you have the lobster pinned in place, you can close the grip.

More often than not, particularly in the daytime, lobsters will be backed into a crevice. California Fish and Game laws stipulate that lobsters may only be taken by hand. No spears, sticks, hooks, cattle prods or other devices may be used. Hands only!

When a lobster is in a crevice, it is in its best defensive position. You still must move quickly to prevent the lobster from becoming more deeply wedged. If possible, assault from the side. Your target should be the head or the base of the antenna. The antenna itself won't cut it, as they'll just break right off. The legs will also break off. The base of the antenna, also known in lobster hunting circles as the "horns," will not break off.

Once you have the lobster by the horns you all but have him. At this point the lobster will most likely do what's known as "locking-up." The lobster does this by using its legs and pushing its back up against the top of the crevice firmly wedging itself in the crevice. The lobster can be dislodged at this point by a quick shake of the head. This disorients the lobster allowing you to pull it out easily.

Lobster in hand, the struggle is not over. You must now measure for minimum size and get it into the bag without losing it. Whether you have the lobster by the horns or by the body, hold on tight, their swimming kick is quite strong. Lobsters have a predisposition to grasp with their legs; you can use this to your advantage. If you have a particularly large lobster, hold it up against your chest and the lobster will literally grab hold of you. While this may not be a particularly pleasant thought, he's less likely to swim away if he has hold of you. You can grab smaller lobsters from the underside using one hand, and they will wrap their legs around your hand. This sort of switching hands and gripping from underneath also makes it easier for measuring.

If you have a lobster by the horns and you are reasonably confident that it exceeds minimum size, you may want to bag it right away. Since lobsters swim backwards or tail first, that's how you want to put them in the bag. Shove the lobster in tail first and in one swift motion. Don't put them in slowly as that gives them time to grab on to the edge of the bag with their legs.

Congratulations! You just bagged your first lobster! (Oh yeah, don't forget to close the bag.)

dive sites. The beach slope is steep with water depths dropping to 10 to 15 feet only a few yards from shore. This can create a "plunging" wave that can drop a diver quickly.

Surge is generally strong here, but this can be both a problem and an asset. A mild surge in the large crevices can make for a lot of fun—a roller coaster ride if you will. The diver experienced with surge can use it to shoot in, out, and over reefs. If surge riding is not your cup of tea, try the outer reef where the effects of the surge are much weaker.

Visibility is generally good if the surf is down. Over the reefs, it averages 10 to 20 feet with occasional days of 30 feet or more.

To reach the beach access point at the top of the stairs, take Pacific Coast Highway to the town of South Laguna Beach. The access is across Pacific Coast Highway from 9th Street. Parking is limited to the opposite side of the highway and the side streets. Perhaps the most hazardous part of this dive trip is trying to cross busy Pacific Coast Highway! At the top of the stairs take the time to read the signs. They point out that this is a marine preserve and that taking of anything other than what is listed on the sign is prohibited (it is okay to take lobster and most game fish, but not scallops). A second sign points out that the beach closes at 9 p.m., so schedule any night dives carefully.

About two-thirds of the way down the steps you will be able to view the dive area off the point to the right. Broken rocks extend from the point. Several rocks break the surface in the swell. It is between two of these rocks that you will find the underwater arch.

At the bottom of the steps is a lifeguard tower, showers, and restrooms. Water entry is best from the right end of the broad sandy beach, directly in front of the reefs.

If you are into roller coaster rides, this may be just the dive for you.

Dana Point

Dana Point in Southern Orange County has a large area of rocky reefs extending far offshore. Approximately 500 yards out are the prominent San Juan Rocks. While too far to swim for the average beach diver, the reefs extend far inshore. Very close to shore is a natural rock reef structure just off the breakwater that is a haven for a large variety of marine life. The natural reefs extend right up to the base of the breakwater, which offers additional diving opportunities, although it can be quite surgy.

There are two ways to enter the water here. If experienced in rock entries, you can enter off the breakwater rocks. This puts you practically on top of natural reefs. There is also a small sandy beach closer to the point. It has a gently sloping sand bottom with a wide surf zone and sometimes rocks in the surf zone. Use caution here, particularly when the surf is up.

You can literally throw a rock onto the natural reefs near the breakwater, yet the water between the two drops off immediately to eight feet deep. Also, the natural reef provides some protection from the surf for entry off the breakwater rocks.

Jumbled boulders, eelgrass, and feather boa kelp is the prominent bottom scenery on the natural reefs close to shore. There are numerous surge channels that are fun to whip in and out of if you are comfortable with the ocean's raw power. While there is a fair amount of fish, and the overall scene can be described as pretty, this is not an A+ dive for the sightseer and photographer. The rock surf entry (or tough sand beach surf entry, if you choose) and the surge make carrying a camera on this dive an impractical proposition.

Hunters should go elsewhere. Dana Point became a marine preserve for intertidal areas a few years ago. While this does not effect areas below the tide line, the taking of game is heavily frowned upon. There are lobster, halibut, and calico bass. The larger reef structures are laced with crevices and small caves. While it is a far cry from "lobster city," you'll be hard pressed to find an empty crack.

Offshore and to the west toward San Juan Rock and out 200 yards, maximum depth over the reefs is 25 feet. This dive site's proximity to the harbor means boat traffic is common. A flag and float may be a good idea.

Access to the area is quite easy and facilities are good. There is plenty of free parking and the restrooms, while a bit of walk from the dive site, are new and clean. This is the site of the Ocean Institute which takes the form of an informative museum, educational center and research facility. It is open to the public weekends (small fee for admission). A wonderful little gift shop is attached. Park in front of the Institute; the dive site is behind. Restrooms are on the north side of the parking lot.

Blacksmith

Male sheephead

Introduction to San Diego County

Conditions: (619) 221-8824
http://cdip.ucsd.edu/models/san_diego.gif

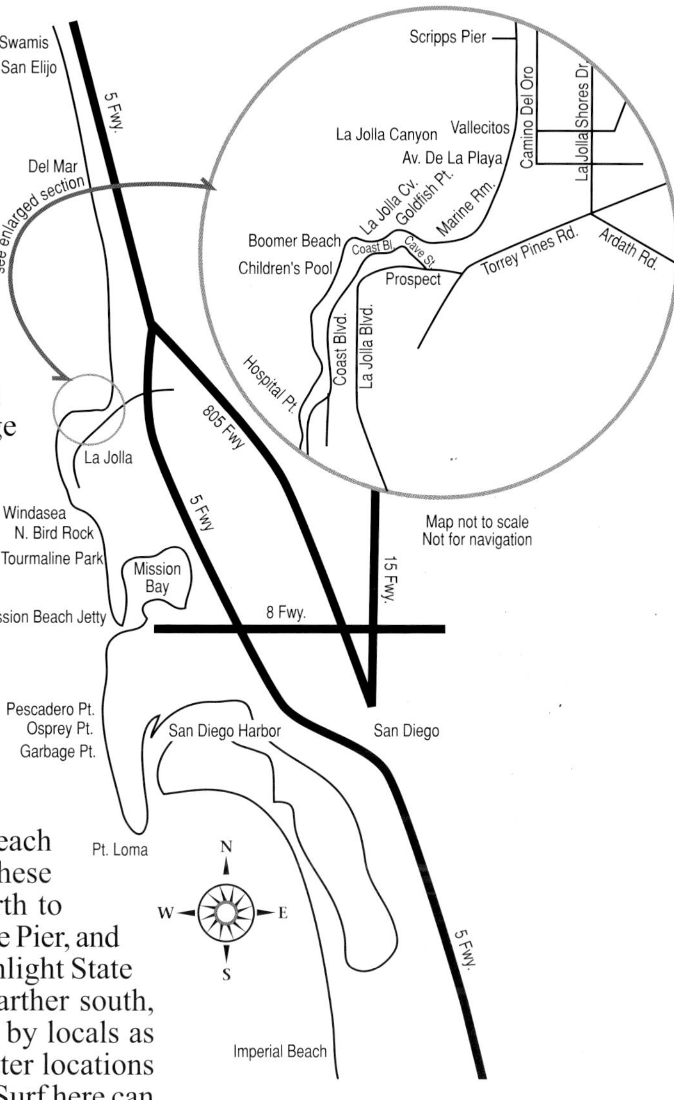

Diving the coastline of San Diego can be rewarding if you are either experienced at diving the area or know specifically where to go for easy, relaxing diving. Much of the shore diving off this county can be difficult, particularly in the northern sections. Large surf, difficult entries, and murky water are the norm along the north San Diego County coastline.

This area is not without its fine reefs and good shore access, however. Reefs with healthy kelp beds are located in several locations, anywhere from 200 yards to 1/4-mile offshore, which mean long swims to reach the best diving. Some of these locations include (from north to south) San Onofre, Oceanside Pier, and Carlsbad State Beach. Moonlight State Beach is good for game. Farther south, Sea Cliff Park (also known by locals as "Swamis") is one of the better locations in north San Diego County. Surf here can still be quite large, but kelp, good diving, and clear water are fairly close to shore.

San Elijo State Park is an excellent beach campground, good diving but you will have to swim a long way. Other access points farther south include Tide County Park, and 13th and 8th Streets in Del Mar.

Just south of Del Mar is the northern border of the San Diego-La Jolla Underwater Park. The park includes many popular dive sites southward to La Jolla Cove. The San Diego-La Jolla Underwater Park is a marine preserve where no invertebrates can be taken except clams, crab, lobster, and sea urchin. In the southern section of the park are several subsections, most of which are preserves in which nothing may be taken or disturbed. The most prominent sub-section is the San Diego-La Jolla Ecological Reserve, which includes such popular dive sites as La Jolla Canyon, Goldfish Point and La Jolla Cove. Nothing—animal, plant or otherwise—may be taken or disturbed.

La Jolla Canyon is a submarine canyon with two branches. The northern branch, known as Scripps Canyon, is the most spectacular with vertical walls. The sharp drop-offs are, however, a long swim out and best dived from a boat by experienced divers. The southern branch of the canyon comes to within 100 to 150 yards of shore near the popular La Jolla Shores Beach. Although not as spectacular as the Scripps Canyon, the La Jolla Branch has several vertical drops of 20 to 30 feet in stair steps to deeper than you'd ever care to go. The water is usually clear and offers one of the most unusual beach dives along the coast of Southern California.

At the far end of La Jolla Shores Beach, just before the sand gives way to rocks, is the hidden access as **Marine Room**. This is a fantastic fish dive. The coast then turns from sandy beach to rocky cliffs along the La Jolla Bay. Access to the rocky shore can be found at **Goldfish Point**; diving the La Jolla Caves and the point are easy from here. **La Jolla Cove** is the most popular beach location in San Diego County. Crowds can be a problem but diving is usually good in clean, life-filled waters.

Around the corner from La Jolla Cove, the beach faces west and is much more open to the effects of the sea. There are access points at Boomer Beach and Shell Beach, but heavy surf and unpredictable rips and currents are a constant problem. **Children's Pool (a.k.a Casa Cove)** is a small cove created by an artificial breakwater. Calm water entries and exits are possible into clear water. Hospital Point is open to the weather, but under the right conditions can offer very good diving between rocky ledges. Diving off the La Jolla peninsula can be very good in an extensive kelp forest, but it is much too long of a swim for beach divers.

Bat ray

Farther south there are access points along the Windansea Beach area. Little Point and Big Rock are diving spots along this beach that can be difficult to dive because of high surf and dirty water. **North Bird Rock** is a semi-protected cove that offers some good lobster diving. South of the Bird Rock, there is good beach access at Sun Gold Point and Tourmaline Park, but swims are long through murky water and high surf. On the far end of Mission Beach, fairly decent diving can sometimes be found on the **North Mission Beach Jetty**.

South of the Mission Bay Channel, there are several points that provide beach access but often difficult entries into murky waters. Some of these locations are Pescadero, Osprey, and Lascomb's Points. Hunting at these locations can sometimes be good but scenery is poor. Visibility improves slightly off spots known as Rock Slide, Rock Pile, and Garbage Points. Diving in the Point Loma kelp beds is excellent, but there is no shore access and a boat is required.

Imperial Beach and Tijuana Sloughs are in the southern portion of the county. There is an old submarine shipwreck off Imperial Beach if you know where to look but the water is quite dirty. Lobster and halibut can also be found at the Sloughs even though water visibility in these areas is very poor and the water is frequently contaminated.

San Elijo State Beach

At San Elijo State Beach in north San Diego County, one can do much more than just lie on the beach. There are camping facilities, some of the best surfing in the state, and of course, diving.

The surfing and diving may seem contradictory and they are. However, San Elijo Beach is very open to both western and southerly swells. The slope of the bottom directly off the beach is very gentle making the surf zone fairly large. The surf here is up more often then it is down, but when conditions are calm, the diving can be good.

Medium-sized healthy kelp beds lie 200 to 300 yards offshore making for a long swim. Closer in, the rocks are covered with eelgrass. Diving on the rocks nearer to shore may be hampered by surge. The bottom in and around the kelp runs between 20 to 30 feet deep, sloping to 60 feet on the outside of the kelp over 1/4 mile offshore.

In the rocks beneath the kelp and to a lesser extent in the shallow water, lobster, and calico bass can be found. The sands in and around the reefs have long been a good spot for halibut.

Visibility at San Elijo is generally poor due to the frequent high surf conditions.

Averaging about 10 feet, the outer kelp is the best and improves slightly to the north.

The photographer and sightseer will be hampered by the poor visibility but the kelp is a good haven for a variety of fish. The reef structure is varied in spots with some deep ledges while on the reef, the usual invertebrates can be found.

San Elijo State Beach is located just south of the beach town of Encinitas. Entry to the park is off Highway S21 which parallels the coastline and Interstate 5.

The park is a joy for the traveler. Facilities include camping, restrooms with showers, a camp store and access stairs to the beach. There is a day use and camping fee. Parking for the day use is on the extreme north end of the park. If you wish, to forego the fee, there is a beach access via a paved path at the north end of the park. There are showers and restrooms. Parking is limited and on the highway. The locals call this spot "Pipes" due to the drainage pipes visible on the hillside. Parking within the park will allow you use of the picnic tables and access to the southern portions of the beach. It is possible to park just inside the main gate for up to 20 minutes to drop off dive gear, use the store, or check out conditions in the vicinity. Near the main gate and throughout the park there are access stairs leading to the beach. Most average 120 steps in length.

Always check the local surf report before going or bring surfing gear as well as diving gear along and you will have a great time at this beach.

La Jolla Submarine Canyon

The largest physical feature on this planet is the Pacific Ocean. To penetrate it and gaze off into its depths is like gazing into the eye of God. One of the best places to do this is on the lip on of the La Jolla Submarine Canyon.

From the lip of the canyon, in 45 feet of water, the bottom drops away to over 200 feet in less than 100 yards in some locations. In less than a mile from shore, the canyon is 700 feet deep. Exploration of the drop-offs is exciting, but nothing compares to the simple act of floating weightless on the edge, peering into the dark blue expanse.

The face of the canyon off La Jolla Shores is large, and there are several sections to explore. Probably the most popular with the best parking, facilities, and shortest swim to the canyon edge is at the south end of Kellogg Park at Vallecitos Street. Just to the north is a large lifeguard tower that is manned year round and posts diving conditions daily. The lifeguards also have at their disposal a rescue boat stationed on the beach. To the north of the main tower is the surfing area; diving here is discouraged. South of Vallecitos Street, at the end of Avenida De La Playa, is a small boat launching area; stay clear of this area also.

Out from Vallecitos Street the sand bottom slopes moderately. Head directly out about 100 yards. This will place you just inshore from the rim of the canyon in about 40 feet of water.

The canyon here drops from 50 feet in a series of ledges that vary in height from 10 to 20 feet. The bottom drops off rapidly to over 200 feet. Visibility averages around 15 to 20 feet but can drop severely with heavy surf or plankton blooms. 30-foot visibility occurs when upwelling from the canyon is present.

Head north along the canyon face and you will find it turning out to sea then back in shore in a peninsula-type formation. Look for deep caves and undercuts on the far side of the peninsula. Climbing the canyon slope to head back in, you'll find an engine block, an old anchor for a buoy, in 50 feet of water.

South along the canyon wall gives you a completely different dive. Here the face is steeper. There is a prominent shelf at 100 feet where, if you travel far enough, you'll find the rotting remains of an old wooden boat.

The structure of the canyon walls is also dynamic. A few winters ago a big storm caused a large section of one of the ledges to collapse into a heap of boulders and another small wreck was moved into deeper waters.

No matter what direction you go, the marine life is a prime attraction here. Upwelling can bring deepwater species near the rim for observation. One of these visitors is squid, found in late fall through early spring. The massive nighttime spawns of these animals are not to be missed. Other large fish are then in turn attracted by the squid for feeding. It is a riot of marine life.

On the clay canyon walls, several varieties of small colorful fish make their home. In the crevices and overhangs are sculpins, gobies, blennies and other small bottom-dwelling fish. Marine life that roam the open sea, known as pelagics, can often be observed here. Schools of fish cruise the walls. Small branches of gorgonian are attached to the ledges below 65 feet, with crab and octopus making their homes in the holes in the clay walls. Some of the deeper

C-O sole

crevices hold large populations of lobster.

Look but don't touch! This entire area is an underwater park and ecological reserve. Nothing is to be taken or disturbed.

Thanks to the offshore deepwater canyon, surf is generally smaller here than at other locations along the San Diego County coastline. The facilities are excellent with restrooms, showers and plenty of parking.

Instructors frequently use this site for student checkout dives. Instructors will take the students to the edge of the canyon but not into it. If you were checked out at this site, it's time to plan for an expedition into the chasm.

In spite of the fact that classes often use the site, it's a dive for both the novice and experienced. It really depends on just how extensively you want to explore this fantastic underwater feature.

Marine Room

The La Jolla Underwater Park and Reserve is an exciting place for divers to visit. Much of the diving activity is centered at either La Jolla Cove or La Jolla Shores, a popular beach access point to the submarine canyon. While these are great dive sites, they can get overcrowded and, if you dive there a lot, a bit old. Halfway between these two popular sites is a little known dive site that offers both the rocky reefs and access to the drop-offs of the canyon. The Marine Room dive site may be the perfect alternative beach dive when the Cove and Shores are jam-packed with people.

Principle attraction at the Marine Room is the fish. To say they are abundant is an understatement. Lying deep within the reserve portion of the park, the fish population over these low-lying reefs has blossomed. Huge schools of silvery black-barred sargo patrol the reef fringes. Opaleye are abundant, large and fat. But the main event here is the calico bass (a.k.a. kelp bass). At no place along our coast will you find larger, and more aggressively curious, calico bass. Normally a shy fish, it can be almost unnerving to have a big-toothed, two-foot long calico stare you down from only a yard away. This site is worth visiting if for no other reason than to see these behemoths.

The reefs are low and rather dull. There is the occasional crab, cucumber, cowry or sea hare, but little else. Much of the rock face is covered with eelgrass. This is a shallow dive with depths of 10 to 20 feet. Surge is common, but being more protected than La Jolla Cove it's

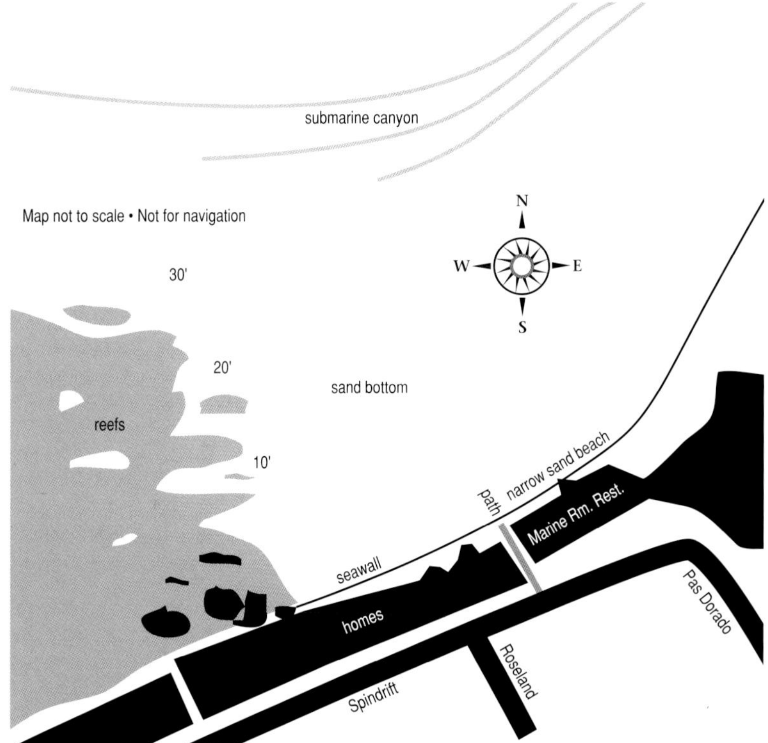

often diveable when the cove is not.

The rock patches are interspersed with stretches of sand. In the summer leopard sharks invade these sand patches. They are harmless and shy but can be approached slowly or by snorkeling. At three to six feet in length with distinctive spots, they are an exciting visitor to observe. Other visitors include bat rays and guitarfish. Summer is a fun time on the shallow reefs of the Marine Room.

To reach the Marine Room, head out Torrey Pines Road toward La Jolla. Before reaching downtown La Jolla, turn toward the sea at Princess, veering right as it splits and turns into Spindrift Dr. The restaurant is on your left just before it swings right and turns into Pas Dorado. Park either on Spindrift or nearby Roseland. The site gains its name from the Marine Room Restaurant on shore (2000 Spindrift Dr., La Jolla). Access to the water's edge is adjacent to this restaurant. Parking is very limited on the street. Do not park in the restaurant parking. The beach here is small and at high tide disappears completely.

The sand bottom slopes away very gently and is only 10 feet or less 100 yards out. The reefs are to the left, off the rocky point toward the La Jolla Caves.

To the right slightly, 300 yards offshore, is the La Jolla Submarine Canyon. It's a long swim, but this section of the canyon is quite interesting. A small cliff begins in 35 feet of water. As you move along the wall, to the north/northeast, the wall becomes larger and more spectacular, dropping vertically hundreds of feet into the abyss. There is another sub-branch of the canyon slightly to the left but, again, a long swim out, 300 yards or so.

Diving at the Marine Room offers an uncrowded yet delightful alternative to other La Jolla beach dive sites. Use it as a choice when the cove is too crowded or as a primary dive site to explore the spectacular La Jolla Underwater Park.

Goldfish Point

Through experience I'd learned that the best time to dive Goldfish Point was early in the morning. La Jolla is a very popular place, not only with divers, but also with sun worshipers and tourists. It gets CROWDED! But the beach diving is excellent, so I'm not about to let a few thousand people come between me and great diving.

This particular day was my earliest dip ever at Goldfish Point. It was barely light when I walked down the easy steps to the water's edge. Using only snorkeling equipment, I entered the water about dawn. A Sunday morning in summer, there was not a soul around. I was the first person in the water that day. The rewards for rising early that day were great.

I've always enjoyed the bountiful life at this place, but I never knew just how much life was really there. I caught most of the local marine life still in bed, fast asleep. The ocean was glass flat. I headed out in front of the La Jolla Caves, moving swiftly. I always enjoy the freedom breath-hold diving affords.

There are large reefs closer to shore. The bottom drops away in shelves, first at 10 feet, then 15, and eventually to 20 or 25 feet. Much of the bottom out from there is, however, relatively flat with low-lying reefs and patches of sand. In the muted light, I could make out outlines in the bottom below. Three large guitarfish where lying on the bottom, their noses touching. A quick breath and silent descent brought me within inches. It was almost a full minute before one of them awoke to my presence, stirring the rest. All three bolted in different directions.

I few minutes later, I did the same with a large halibut. The leopard sharks were less cooperative, but I was able to get close to three. Goldfish Point always holds a lot to see on a dive, but this early morning dip was turning out to be very special indeed.

The night before I had checked the tide tables. They indicated it would be high tide about dawn. My plan was, if it was very calm, to explore the sea cave that

Grandpa Garibaldi

During my certification course, I loved it when my instructor would crack open an urchin in order to have the fish swarm around us. It was fascinating, yet disconcerting. There was too much activity to actually absorb. As the years have gone by, I've learned that I don't need to destroy an urchin or feed the fish in any way to really see them. With many hours underwater staring into the lens of the camera, I have oodles of time to just watch the environment.

On a not too eventful dive, we decided to add some fish/diver photographs to our library. We settled ourselves next to a reef and waited. It didn't take long. The fish will come to you, maybe looking for food, usually to find out what the commotion is all about. As these photographs were being taken, I noticed one particular garibaldi came closer and closer with every pass. Several times he passed between my head and my regulator hose. Feeling a garibaldi rub against your mask, you can feel the strength in its body. You can understand how they swim so fast, sideways and upside down.

I began to study this fellow and wondered how he got his scar on his backside. It looked like a puncture wound healed over. He had other scars on the top of his head and his left fin looked chewed on. He looked older than the others. Maybe I imagined it, but he had lifelines around and under his mouth that reminded me of my grandfather. One eye looked cloudy. Do fish get cataracts? I noticed his color was different, and as I looked at the other garibaldi, I noticed they were all very different. Each had an ever so slightly different shade of orange. Some were downright red.

I began to differentiate the garibaldi by their comfort zone with me. One would come no closer than an arm length. One would zoom in, stare into my mask and leave just as quickly. Of course, grandpa would hover next to my head, leave to swim a couple of circles around me and then hover some more.

After awhile, several señoritas joined in, only they would just stare into the dome port on Dale's camera and ruin the shots he was trying to take. Frustrated by the señoritas, Dale motioned to move farther down the reef. I hated to move, but I was down there for a specific reason.

We settled into a new spot and within a few moments grandpa swam right in front of my mask. I felt that I wasn't the only one who had been studying a species. All the while I was watching him he had been watching me. I just knew he came back for more looks.

We moved to the opposite side of the reef for our next dive. There we concentrated on a large treefish we found perched on the underside of a large rock. Though the angles and backscatter were not the best for photographs, I enjoyed every moment of my newly found activity. I could pose throughout the dive and still study every aspect of a particular fish.

I love renewing my underwater activity. I can always feel like a newly certified diver with each new thing I do or learn. Remember how excited you were when you learned to dive? Try a slightly different activity with each dive. You'll enjoy what you see. You may be surprised by the personality each fish has.

runs completely through Goldfish Point.

With the water glassy and no swell, I entered the cave from the west side of the point. The water was only about 18 inches deep—just enough to still swim. A few years ago I had tried the same thing when a slight swell was running. After a good raking across the rock, I retreated to buy a new wetsuit. Today, however, the Pacific was like a lake, and passage to the center of the large cave was easy.

Inside, the bottom dropped and the ceiling rose. There was room to relax and study the early morning light as it danced through the east passages. The beams penetrating the cave entrance were further shattered underwater. A free dive to the six-foot deep gravel bottom rewarded me with a natural light show. There were several passages, and with such calm conditions I explored them all.

By now other divers were showing up, most with scuba gear. I cruised above to watch the underwater breathers discover lobster and crabs under ledges and make friends with garibaldi. One diver found a pipefish in the eelgrass. Apparently, I had not awakened all the underwater residents, but the roar of regulators was finishing the job.

Goldfish Point lies within the La Jolla Underwater Park, which prohibits the taking or disturbing of any marine life. As a consequence, lobster, octopus and other normally shy creatures can be observed undisturbed. Invertebrates such as sea stars and anemones are also present and create a good backdrop for photographers.

Access to the diving area adjacent to the point can be made in either of two

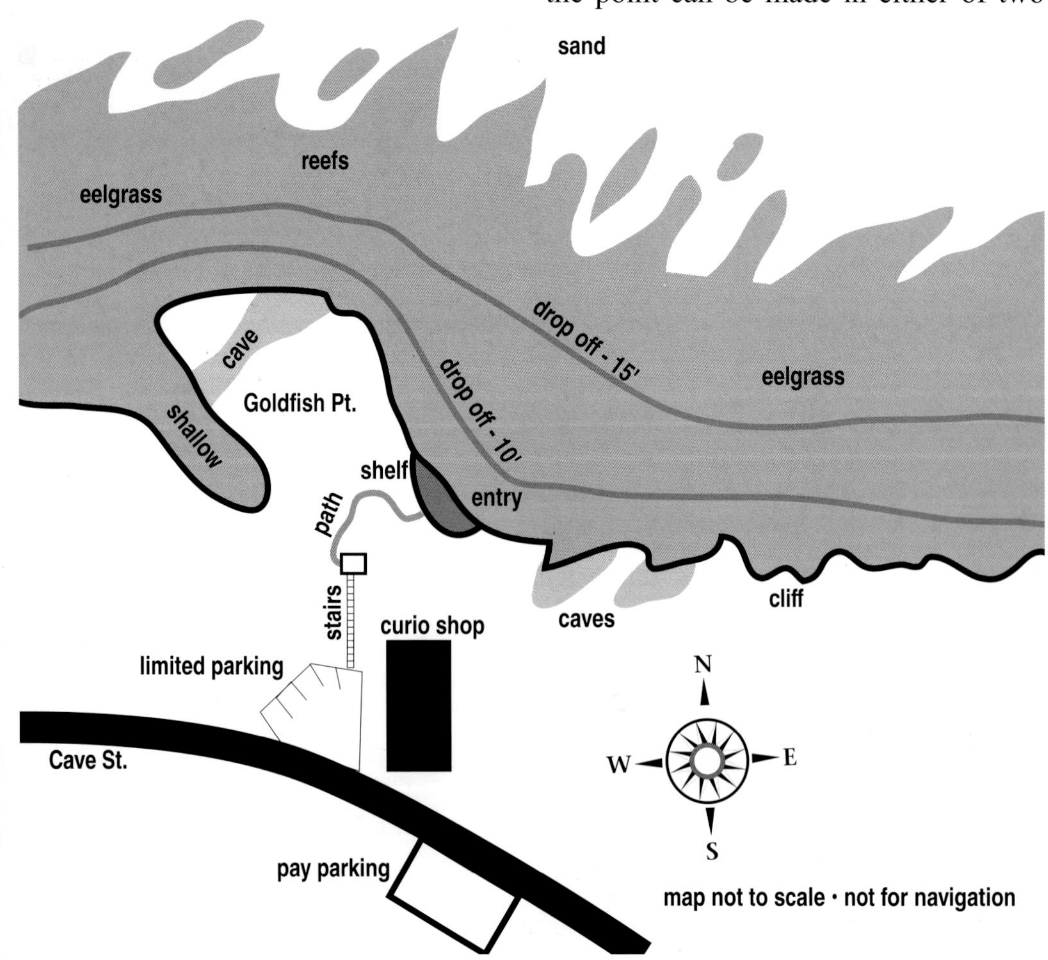

ways. The most direct is via a path down the point located behind the La Jolla Cave Curio Shop. The stairs and short, steep path lead to a small rock shelf at water's edge that is perfect for entries, but only in the calmest weather. The path to the water's edge has become more hazardous in recent years so use caution. The second choice is to enter at La Jolla Cove and swim to the point some 200 yards away.

Goldfish Point is a good alternative during crowded days if you have your heart set on diving the La Jolla area. Across from the Curio Shop is an underground parking area that affords easy access from your car to the top of the path. The cost is not cheap, but it beats driving around for hours looking for a place to park.

La Jolla Cove

Second only to the La Jolla Canyon, La Jolla Cove is perhaps the most popular dive site in San Diego. It is also an extremely popular spot for local beach lovers. As a consequence, if you want to dive La Jolla Cove on the summer weekends, be prepared to battle with the crowds, but don't let them stop you from diving this excellent spot.

La Jolla Cove lies on the northernmost extension of the La Jolla Peninsula. The cove faces north, protecting it from the predominately southerly swell that batters the area during the summer. As a result, the cove is a good dive for the summer months.

Out from the small sandy cove are a variety of rocky ledges, reefs and sand channels. Around the point to the northwest, known by locals as "Alligator Head," the sea life becomes quite abundant. Friendly garibaldi are, of course, everywhere. If you are lucky, you may spot a protected broomtail grouper that is making a slow comeback to the area. Seals are also frequent visitors and are quite used to the divers. On the bottom and in the reefs you will find moray eels, lobster and rockfish that are surprisingly friendly. Their lack of fear is understandable; the diving area lies within the San Diego-La Jolla Underwater Ecological Reserve. Nothing is to be taken or disturbed.

On the other side of the cove, similar conditions exist. The rocky ledges are fairly close to shore all the way to Goldfish Point. Depths on the reefs are a maximum of 30 feet. Farther out, in deeper water, the bottom turns to sand or a flat sandstone bottom with

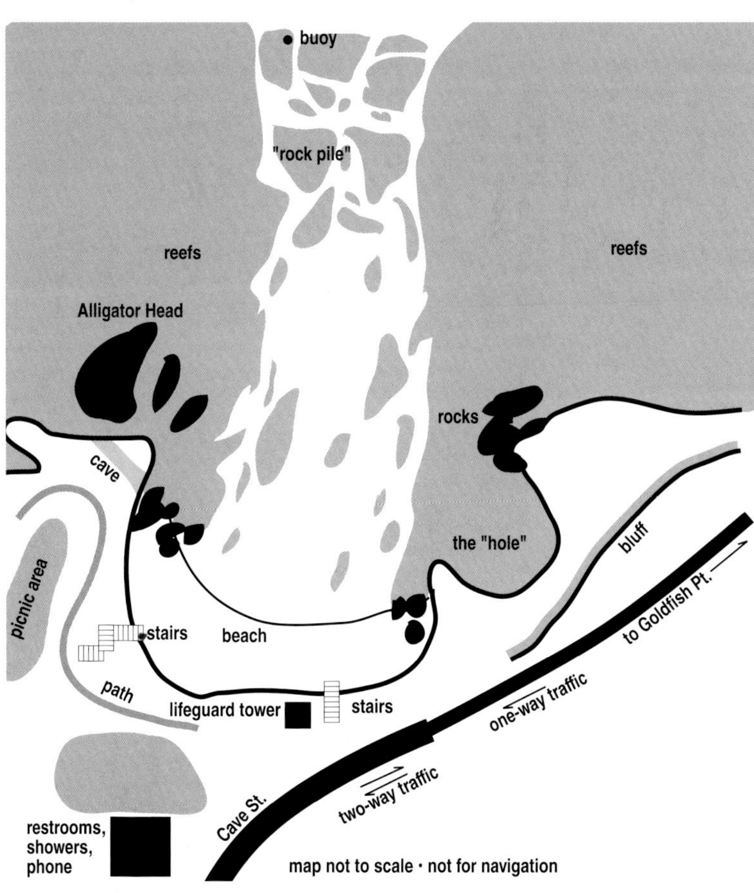

Hilton's aeolid nudibranch

closely but especially so in this reserve. Other rockfish such as the golfer and olive rockfish lounge about in the crevices. A substantial kelp forest usually marks the rock pile or you can head for the buoy offshore.

Perhaps the biggest challenge in diving La Jolla Cove is finding a place to park. You'll have your best luck early in the mornings or on weekdays or both. Parking adjacent to the Ellen Browning Scripps Memorial Park (which overlooks the cove) is very limited. There are no parking meters, but there is a three-hour time limit. The park overlooking the cove has all the facilities you should need: restrooms, showers, telephones, picnic areas, and large grassy areas for suiting up.

There is a lifeguard stand that overlooks the cove. Posted on the stand are daily water and surf conditions. If you are unfamiliar with the area, a quick check with the lifeguard will be helpful. It is always a good idea to call the surf-and-water report before your trip. Although the cove is somewhat protected, large surf and surge are not uncommon.

It is only a few stairs down to the small sandy beach in the middle of the cove; water entry is best here.

A few spots to avoid are "the hole," an indentation in the cliffs on the east side of the cove that seems to generate rips and unpredictable currents, and a dangerous shallow reef farther to the east.

an occasional patch of rocks. Angel sharks and halibut can sometimes be observed.

For those not minding a long swim, there is the "rock pile." At a depth of about 40 feet, about 300 yards out from the beach, the sandstone breaks up to create jumbles of boulders with deep crevices, ledges and small caves. This labyrinth is home to a myriad of sea life, including octopus and its favorite food, lobster. But don't let your mouth water; most of the rock pile lies within the ecological reserve—nothing can be taken, speared, or otherwise disturbed. Even so, most of the lobster seem to be well below legal size. It is nice to see, however, such a large population of the prized crustacean thriving. Sharing the many crevices with the lobster are morays, scallops, and bottom dwelling fish. Photographers will have a large variety of subjects to choose from. The yellow and black striped treefish can always be approached

Children's Pool (a.k.a. Casa Cove)

Kelp rockfish

South of the popular La Jolla Cove is a small artificial cove on a point of land that is protected from the swells by a small sea wall. The small breakwater was erected to create a calm pool of ocean that children could safely play in; hence, the given name of "Children's Pool." The tiny calm bay is an excellent jumping-off point for diving nearby reefs that are a delight to explore. There is just one problem: not only is this location popular with humans, harbor seals have taken a strong liking to the place as well as a "haul-out" beach. Dozens of the pinnipeds can be found on the beach during the fall, winter and spring. Federal law protects these animals and humans are strongly cautioned to stay clear. These are, after all, still very much wild animals. Any disturbance of the seals and sea lions is punishable by a stiff fine.

The issue of the harbor seal and human mix has been further complicated by the animal rights activists who believe that humans have no business being anywhere near the seals. Lawyers and judges and courts actually went to battle and those wanting access to the beach have, at least for now, won. The animal rights activists however still show up at the cove and heckle (often quite intensely) those venturing onto the beach. Steer well clear of the

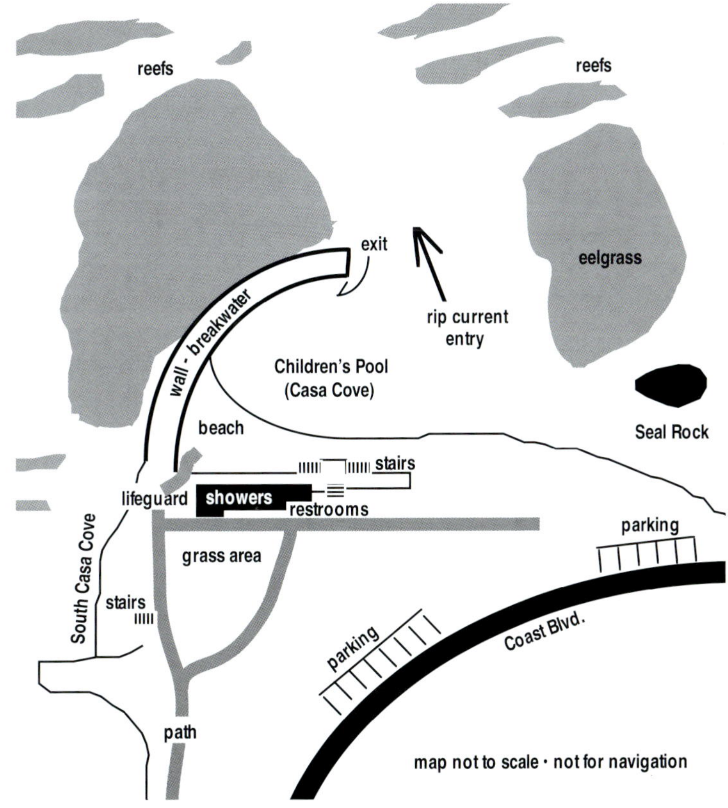

seals and you are well within your legal rights. This issue is, however, far from being decided. Check with the lifeguards first before entering the water. There are other great dive sites up and down the coast that carry much less controversy.

Also, as wild animals, nobody has properly taught the pinnipeds toilet manners. They just go where they lay or in the shallow cove. While it's all very natural, it can still be unhealthy for us humans. Sometimes the cove is closed because of the contamination. There are plans underfoot to open small sluiceways under the breakwater to help keep the small bay clean.

Seals out of the way, the diving on the reefs beyond the cove is quite good. Depths on the reefs average from 10 to 30 feet, most of them running parallel to shore and 20-feet high in some locations. Extreme undercutting on the reefs has created huge ledges that are a delight to explore, with sand and small boulders that also hold a variety of marine life.

In the shallow portions, eelgrass grows prolifically. On the ledges and rocks, it is not unusual to find colorful anemones, sponges, sea stars, nudibranchs, and a number of types of mollusks. The fish surrounding the reef include garibaldi, señoritas, opaleye, and other reef-dwelling fish. Lucky divers sometimes spot groupers that are returning to the area. And, as you can imagine, playful seals are common around these rocks.

Hunting the reefs off Children's Pool is not very productive due to the heavy pressure from divers (and seals). And it is highly recommended you not take a speargun through the surf here (that will really tick-off the animal rights activists!) An occasional lobster can be found on the outer reefs, with lobster also hiding in the eelgrass in shallow water.

Children's Pool is located less than a half-mile south of La Jolla Cove along Coast Boulevard. Parking along Coast Boulevard is limited and allows for a maximum of three hours only. Sightseers wishing to spy on the seals have put parking at an extreme premium. Arrive very early to get a parking space.

There is a good dive-staging area directly behind the lifeguard headquarters. Below these headquarters are restrooms, showers, and a drinking fountain. Behind the lifeguard tower are telephones. The ledge at the lifeguard tower overlooks the small sandy cove. There are reefs outside the wall and directly out from Seal Rock that lies in front of the cove.

Behind the park, to the south, is South Casa Cove; this spot is another good dive location on calm days but is open to southerly swells in the summer.

Entry at Children's Pool is off the small sandy beach. There is a strong prevailing rip that runs out from the end of the wall, which can be an express ticket to the reefs. Returning to the cove is best done by swimming very close to the tip of the wall where there is no rip and the surge will shove you back into the small cove.

Check with the lifeguard tower before entering. Up-to-date conditions, including contamination closures, are posted on the chalkboard outside. If unfamiliar with the area, the lifeguard will be happy to answer any questions.

Calico bass

North Bird Rock

Grabbing a few lobsters on a quicky night beach dive is always a lot of fun. Afterwards, you can either head to your favorite beach campfire or to your home for a late evening snack of lobster tail dipped in drawn butter. But in your underwater endeavors, you want to get away from the crowds. In San Diego, where do you go? North Bird Rock may be just the place.

The La Jolla Peninsula is a treasure-trove of dive spots. La Jolla Cove, within the boundaries of the underwater park, offers spectacular underwater scenery. To the north you have popular dive sites like Children's Pool with easy access and beautiful diving. But as popular as these dive sites are, they are not popular with lobster. In the underwater park it is illegal to take or disturb anything. South, outside of the park, the easily accessed areas are quite picked over. But head a little bit farther south, and you'll come across a series of rocky coves and points that aren't nearly as heavily trafficked by divers. While the underwater scenery is not quite as good, and these rocky points and coves are more exposed to heavy surf, they are still well populated with lobster.

In this area is a prominent rock known as Bird Rock. Just to the north is a cove that offers a limited degree of protection from the surf and deep water for divers seeking to fill their lobster pots. Around the cove there are three access sites. The

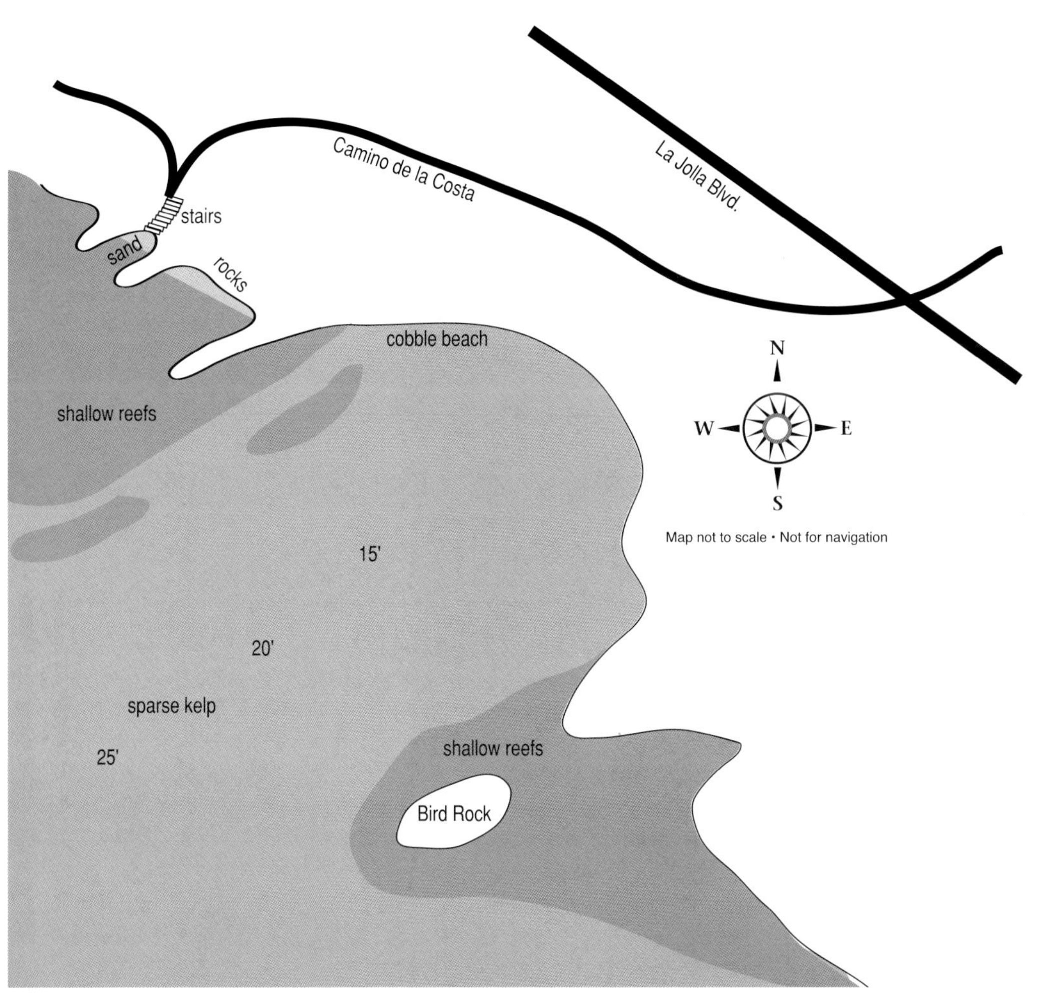

two points to the south lead to a beach strewn with large slippery boulders. Good diving lies beyond, but the trek over the boulders is treacherous at best.

The third access on the north side of the cove from Bird Rock (hence the name) is a relatively easy stairway leading down a scramble down the rocks to small cobble beaches. The rocky fingers and nearby shallow reefs offer a limited degree of protection from the surf. Much of the reefs in the area are very shallow. It is highly recommended that you only dive this site at high tide and during times of low surf, one to two feet or less.

To reach this easy access, turn toward the beach off of La Jolla Blvd. on to Camino de la Costa. Follow this winding street through the residential area until it takes a sharp turn to the right at the 6000 block of Camino de la Costa. To the left, at the dead end, is the stairway leading down to the water's edge. There are no facilities in the area and the only parking is on the street (watch out for the red zones). From the small bluff, you can overlook the entire cove and the ocean conditions below. Assess the conditions carefully and make choices on entry and exits.

The deepest water is in the center of the cove. To the right are a number of interesting shallow reefs, some with deep crevices. Be aware, however, that some of these reefs are just beneath the surface, and any kind of surf or surge could push an unwary diver across a sharp rock. Much of this area is exposed in extreme low tides. Eelgrass is thick in the shallows. While this may not be particularly scenic, it often serves as camouflage for shy lobster.

In the center of the cove, water depths reach 20 to 25 feet, depending on how far out you go. The bottom in the center of the cove consists of small cobble patches of sand, some medium-size boulders and an occasional tall reef. Lobsters can be found in the cracks and crevices created by the medium-size boulders and in the overhangs of the reefs. Fish life is not particularly abundant. There is an occasional garibaldi and calico bass, or, if you get lucky, you might come across a large guitarfish or bat ray.

Water conditions are generally surgy due to the shallow depths, and visibility is only average, running about 15 to 20 feet when the surf is low.

Shovelnose guitarfish

Hidden In the Shallows

When we strap on the scuba gear, many of us have only one thought: how DEEP are we going? We think in terms of double or even triple digit numbers. We think that in order to explore the uncharted ocean floor we must go deep—very deep. The last time you went diving, how many headed for the shallows? Perhaps extreme shallows are the uncharted territory that would be the most fascinating to explore.

Off and on through my diving career I have been a free-diver, using only mask, snorkel, fins, and the power of the breath-hold to explore the underwater world. I mainly used free-diving as a way of moving quietly through the water in pursuit of skittish game fish. Again, depth was an important goal, but I was never very good at diving deep on one breath. The best I could do was 40 feet and I spent most of my time working in less than 25 feet.

It was my children who taught me to appreciate diving in shallow depths. As they began to snorkel, they enjoyed seeing things close up, within just a few feet. Sure it was great for them cruising in 30 feet of water with 60-foot visibility, but even with that clarity, garibaldis on the bottom were little more than orange spots. So I took them into the shallows.

With only a few feet under us you could see small crabs and tiny fish. Then one day, when it was very calm, we moved into only a couple feet of water. Suddenly, tiny fish were right in our faces. The kids loved it. I loved it. I could get within inches of juvenile opaleye and small sculpins. Hermit crabs and miniature octopus scooted across the rocks. The marine environment and life in these shallow waters is quite different and fascinating.

Leopard shark

Years before, I had discovered the value of diving shallow in search of seafood. Lobster can often be found crouching in the thick eelgrass in less than 10 feet of water. In the summer, halibut will move into sandy shallows as little as two feet deep.

Shallow water diving can be done wherever and whenever there is calm water. Visibility is actually not much of a factor. Think about it—seven feet of visibility is plenty adequate if you are diving in only five feet of water.

This kind of diving can be done on scuba but just mask, fins and snorkel is often all you need. Calm water is, of course, a must. Even so, you may find yourself pushed about by the surge. Go with the flow. Gently moving water follows the path of least resistance and will push you with it. If you are going to work around or over rocks, use an old wet suit or add kneepad protection. Sturdy gloves are an absolute must.

Calm waters are easier to find than you might imagine. We often seek out the calm shallow coves to enter the ocean for our deep-water adventures. While those entry waters may not be as chock full of life as the offshore waters, you could probably spend hours hovering over only a few feet of depth, observing hermit crabs, starfish, or small fish. You may even be able to find a calm tide pool large enough to explore.

Shallow water snorkeling is an excellent way to pass your surface interval. Nitrogen flows from your body just as fast while snorkeling as it does sitting on shore. Snorkeling between dives will easily double your in-water time. And if you really want to stretch out your bottom time while on scuba, move into 10 feet of water. There is usually just as much to see, has better light and your tank may last over an hour!

Take your diving in different directions. Explore all the ocean has to offer. The ocean's unique corners are in the shallows. Explore those corners as well.

During the calm summer and fall months there is some sparse growth of kelp in the center of the cove. But the majority of the kelp lies far offshore in the thick La Jolla kelp beds. While there is more interesting diving 200 to 300 yards out for strong swimmers, the kelp beds are at nearly a mile offshore. Diving the kelp beds offshore from Bird Rock is definitely worth it but requires a boat.

Because of the shallow depths, one might want to consider free-diving this area for lobster. There is nothing quite as enjoyable as a late summer evening with glassy conditions at North Bird Rock, skimming across the ocean's surface and diving down looking for dinner.

North Mission Beach Jetty

A trick to successful lobster hunting is looking where the lobster are, but where nobody else is looking—a tough task but not impossible for those hunters willing to try a spot perhaps a bit more difficult than average. But then again, perhaps you just need to time it right.

The North Mission Beach Jetty is just such a site. It's a great surfing spot. As such, big waves, surge, and low visibility are standard. But lobsters love breakwaters, and they love North Mission Beach Jetty. The structure is complex with a lot of large boulders piled atop one another forming many deep mini-caves. The lobsters also love the food-laden waters that flow from the warm Mission Bay every day with the tide.

Again, diving this spot is all in the timing. Fall is best. The surf lies down and on certain choice days you can dive here almost as easily as falling off the back of a boat. Call the surf report number regularly and when the surf goes flat, head for a rewarding lobster dive at the Jetty.

The bottom is very gently sloping sand. You might be better off to hoof it 2/3 to 3/4 the way out along the rocks and enter the water from there. This takes experience and nerve, but in the long run it's much easier than through the sandy surf.

Much of the dive along rocks is shallow—20 feet or less. If a surge is present, the whipped up sand storm can drop visibility to zero in a second. If you're looking up in the shallows (a common practice of experienced lobster hunters) beware of "white-outs" where viz can drop to zero simply from the tiny air bubbles in the water. It can be a wild but fun ride if you are not intimidated by it.

You'll see a lot of lobster, but most will be back far in the holes. Just pass these by for easier pickin's farther down. If conditions are really flat, you might even want to try a night dive here.

Other things to look for along these rocks include some good-size calico bass, cabezon, schools of opaleye, and halibut in the sand. If you are spearfishing, the halibut is your best bet, although there are better places off San Diego for halibut hunting. Seafood seekers can also venture out across the sand for Pismo clams.

Maximum depths at the end of the jetty is 25 feet. Do not dive on the inside as this is illegal. If you are diving near the tip, be aware that strong tidal currents and flows can overpower a diver, sweeping them into the channel mouth.

Facilities on shore are excellent with restrooms, showers, picnic area and firepits. A large parking lot can be found at the end of Mission Blvd.

Index

E

F

G

H

I

J

K

L

M

N

O

P

T

U

V

W

Y

Z

Further Reading

California Diving News
The only publication dedicated to California scuba divers. Available at California, Arizona and Nevada dive stores, on dive boats and with dive clubs. Subscription for 11 issues (1 year) $24. P.O. Box 11231, Torrance, CA 90510. Website: www.cadivingnews.com.

A Diver's Guide to Northern California by Bruce Watkins
Published by Saint Brendan Corp., covers Mendocino, Sonoma and San Francisco Counties as well as the Farallon Islands. Covers 42 dive sites. Available at most western U.S. dive stores. Saint Brendan Corp. P.O. Box 11231, Torrance, CA 90510. (310) 792-2333. Website: www.saintbrendan.com.

A Diver's Guide to Monterey County by Bruce Watkins
Published by Saint Brendan Corp., covers Monterey Bay, Monterey Peninsula, Carmel Bay and Big Sur. Covers over 4 dozen dive sites. Available at most western U.S. dive stores. Saint Brendan Corp. P.O. Box 11231, Torrance, CA 90510. (310) 792-2333. Website: www.saintbrendan.com.